Tarnished

J K Memmi

SOCCIONES

© J K Memmi 2017

All rights reserved

J K Memmi has asserted their right under the Copyright, Designs and Patents Act 1988 to be identified as the author of this book.

No part of this publication may be reproduced, distributed, or transmitted in any form or by any means, without the prior written permission of the author, except in the case of brief quotations embodied in critical reviews and certain other non-commercial uses permitted by copyright law. For permission requests, contact the author.

This is a work of fiction. Names, characters, businesses, places, events and incidents are either the products of the author's imagination or used in a fictitious manner. Any resemblance to actual persons, living or dead, or actual events is purely coincidental.

ISBN-13: 978-1979951906
ISBN-10: 197995190X

Cover design © Socciones

Design & formatting by Socciones Editoria Digitale
www.kindle-publishing-service.co.uk

Prologue

"She's here," Kamal turned round to see Siddharth engaged with his friends. "Okay Siddharth, I'm off. Thanks for the company on the plane."

"Pleasure's all mine. I hope you enjoy your first experience of India Kamal. Kamal, which means lotus flower, do you know the lotus flower is the national flower of India? Welcome home," he held out his hand.

"Yes," Kamal smiled, shaking his hand, "welcome home indeed."

Chapter 1

"Charlene, send the last candidate in please."

"Okay Kamal."

"See if we have any luck with this one," Kamal mumbled under her breath as she put the phone down. Kamal was interviewing for a head barman. Aaron, her business partner, had shortlisted the applicants for her and she'd been interviewing most of the afternoon, but she had neither found the face nor the persona she wanted for her prestigious establishment; apart from the necessary skills, looks and personality were extremely important to her.

"Come in," she said turned around in her leather executive swivel chair to adjust the blinds behind her desk, "come in and take a seat please," she said with her back still turned. She could hear the candidate walking cautiously into the room and approaching the empty seat opposite. She rolled her eyes and let out a small sigh before she turned around. She looked up towards the standing young man with her much practiced smile, which soon faded as her gaze froze. An ice cold sensation ran like a serpent from her head down to her toes, giving rise to flood of goose pimples. Her pulse rate accelerated and she could feel her heart suddenly pounding in her chest.

"Jai," the young man said with his right hand held out. She swallowed the lump in her throat and moistened her lips. Kamal smiled again, as she tried to regain her cool composure. He was still standing with his hand held out.

Kamal shook it casually, "please, take a seat. So…….Jai," she said, clearing her throat, straightening her tailored jacket and beginning to casually look through the application form, rubbing the top of her pen along her brow, trying her best to conceal the fact that she was feeling involuntarily flustered, trying desperately to control her hand from shaking and conceal the quiver in her voice. She eventually moved forward in her seat, straightened her back, crossed her hands on top of the application form, held her chin up high and looked straight at Jai. "So, why have you applied for the job?"

"I am a people person, I like the night life. I like to see people enjoying themselves, letting their hair down, enjoying the weekend, celebrating and I love to be behind the bar, talking and interacting with people, seeing regulars, getting to know them as well as new faces of course….."

Kamal was not registering anything Jai was saying. He could have been speaking an alien language and she wouldn't have noticed. She felt like everything before her was running in slow motion, his speech sluggish, his movements robotic, everything about him, the mannerism, the way he talked with his hands, even his eyebrows, how they curved up at the ends as he spoke, the way his jet black hair was combed back, it was 'him' all over. It was as if an instant rewind button had been pressed. She could feel the room spinning around her, a whirlwind of memories swirling around the room, voices and dialogues of her past echoing about her ears. He stopped talking and looked at her, waiting for her next question. There was a momentary silence between the two.

"Um…..experience…… do you have any?" she said looking through his application again, trying not to look distracted by his face.

"Oh I am still doing some bar work; I started whilst I was studying. But it's nothing like this place."

"You have A' Levels in music, history and art," Kamal said as she continued to look through his application.

"My parents actually wanted me to study further, but I'd rather be sitting where you are now, than slave at uni' for years for a boring dead end job and of course there's the music, which I love. Don't get me wrong, me studying further was my parent's aspiration, you know expectations and all. But I don't particularly want to spend years studying at uni' then struggle finding a job and when I do, lose my life doing a job I don't necessarily enjoy. I would rather have a lucrative business that sells like you have here, and enjoy life at the same time."

"Success didn't come knocking on my door, it made me work for it, ruthlessly," Kamal said raising her right brow and leaning back, rolling her pen between her thumb and forefinger, examining his every move.

"Oh I know you did, I read the article in the Asian Lady Magazine. This place is awesome," he said looking around, admiring the exquisite office, the mahogany desk, behind her a deep burgundy designer wallpaper adorned with copper coloured leaves, black Venetian blinds at the window, a cactus plant, as beautiful as the woman sitting before him and the thorns, just as sharp. The rest of the room painted magnolia, a mahogany bookcase stood behind her its shelves lined neatly with box files and the tropical aquarium was quite a feature. It had a touch of class, pride and quality. Quite a contrast to the office his current boss had, in which a table was parked in the middle of the room, cluttered with invoices, the floor around it surrounded by files bursting with dog eared papers, the bin overflowing with scrunched up junk mail, the wallpaper peeling away, the stench of the staff toilet next to it finding its way through the gap under the door into the office. This in comparison, was in a league of its own.

"Let me see, you do have some experience. Some good references as well. I see you're a DJ as well. Will this job not interfere? You are aware of the days and hours required?"

"I'm just doing the odd parties, you know birthday parties, small weddings, nothing major, though working in your club, with its reputation would be an added bonus for me," Jai smiled. The head barman's job was for regular income, but he was really hoping to get his foot in through this door, by charming this beautiful ice queen, known notoriously by the local bar and club owners as the rival businesswoman and hoping one day, he could ask for a slot to show off his disc jockeying ability.

Kamal smiled, "when would you like to start?"

She genuinely liked Jai; she could see him pulling in the female clients, especially with that effortless smile. His references were excellent and he seemed to have a passion for what he did. Besides, he was the only suitable candidate she had all afternoon.

"Are you offering me the job?"

"Yes, I am, you'll have to come in for a practical first though, my colleague Aaron will arrange that," she said closing the file in front of her.

"Wow. That's fantastic. Thanks!"

Kamal informed the staff she was going home and to tell Aaron the same on his return from the cash and carry. She headed home in her Jaguar; Jai's application form resting on the passenger seat. She glanced at it every now and then, as she stood stationary in traffic, her fingers tapping on the steering wheel, her mind preoccupied. Her eyes glanced fleetingly at the form, as if it were alive and was going to pounce at her at any given opportunity. It had unleashed sleeping ghosts, which were swarming around her in the car, talking to her, reminding her of the past she had long left behind. Her life recapped before her eyes, the mental images projected onto her windscreen, at one point distracting her from the zebra crossing where an elderly woman had just placed her walking stick to make her way over. Kamal slammed her foot down on her brakes and put her hand to her forehead.

"Pull yourself together Kamal," she whispered to herself as the woman started to shuffle over the crossing shaking her head and mumbling under her breath.

She pulled up on the gravelled driveway of her modest detached residence on a quiet suburban cul-de-sac, with her clean cut no nonsense front garden. She stepped into her house, turned off the alarm, threw her keys onto the side cabinet, walked into the kitchen, pulled out a bottle of red from her wine rack, twisted the cap open, fetched a wine glass from the cabinet, poured herself a glass and took a large gulp. It was just after 4pm and not her usual chosen time to indulge in alcohol, but she needed to calm her nerves. She looked through the application form again and again, as she sat on the high stool, leaning on her gleaming, spotless kitchen counter, still unable to believe the irony of the coincidence. Kamal drank and rubbed her forehead, as she continued to think things over; her thoughts were suddenly disturbed by a rumble of thunder. She looked up as she noticed how eerily dark it had become in her otherwise bright white kitchen, as if dark shadows of her past were creeping in on her. She shuddered as she swivelled around on the stool towards the patio window, looking over her back garden. It had turned unusually dark outside for the time of day in August. She stepped down off the stool and walked towards the patio, her heels clicking on the black slate floor tiles. She looked through the blinds towards the sky above. It was full of large, dense, dark clouds. She heard a rumble of thunder again and watched a few drops of rain coming down intermittently, just a few small faint drops at a time, soaking into the decking. The drops then multiplied until they turned into a steady flow of rain, progressively coming down heavier and eventually bouncing off the decking as it came crashing down faster and harder like a tropical monsoon. The heavens had opened just the way they did that night eighteen years ago, when she had left behind a life of deceit and betrayal. She was forty-one years old now and a very successful business woman. She had come a long way from what she was; now owning a prestigious night club, a beauty salon and a string of properties. Her vibrating phone startled her, breaking her trail of thought. She released her head of the haunting memories and walked back over to the kitchen counter to where her mobile phone juddered, the screen and keys lighting with every ring. She picked it up with her perfectly manicured nails.

"Hi Aaron," she sighed.

"Hi. You okay? Charlene said you weren't feeling too well. Is everything okay?" Aaron asked concerned; it was very unusual for Kamal to be torn away from the business.

"Yes, yes, just not feeling too well. Think I could do with some rest actually."

"Like I've been telling you since when? Any success this afternoon?"

"Yes, Jai. He'll be coming in tomorrow night for his practical and if he's all he claims he is, he can start as soon as he works his notice. Can you just call the salon check everything is okay? Have you heard from Michelle?"

"No, too busy enjoying herself in Italy. I'll call the salon; don't worry about that. Are you sure you're okay?" Aaron asked again, he had known Kamal for far too long and he could sense some discomfort in her voice.

"Yes….I'll call you some point later."

"Yes, the party for this evening VIP room two for the ladies hen night wasn't it and the DJ?"

"It's all confirmed. It is VIP room two. There will be about twenty ladies, so all the best. And they requested an 80's theme, it's all sorted, I booked DJ Mark Anthony. VIP room one is for the 30th birthday."

"Okay, great. You take it easy for me okay. See you later. Take care."

"Thanks Aaron."

Kamal headed towards her living room, her phone in one hand and Jai's application in the other. Her feet sank into the thick cream carpet as she entered the room, tastefully designed by one of Aaron's old friends an interior designer, influencing the living room exquisitely with his Italian roots, complete with Italian furniture and art, complemented by large green houseplants, a splash of red and green cushions, vases and wall canvases. She freed her feet of her designer shoes and pulled them up onto the white leather sofa. She looked through the application again, closed her eyes and leant her head back in exhaustion. Her business had all these years kept her so busy it had created a distraction. Although she occasionally had flashbacks, seeing Jai today had reopened healed wounds, some of them, still unhealed.

Chapter 2

Birmingham, July 1986

It was the night before Kamal's wedding and her cousin Kiran was traditionally decorating her hands and feet with henna. Kiran applied the murky, green coloured liquid henna with much, expertise and precision, her hand now aching from trying to keep steady. The henna felt cold as it was applied to the skin and had a very pungent, musty smell. Kamal's right hand and arm was complete and looked like a work of art, the pattern comprising of paisley shapes, fine linear and tiny dots intricately compacted together. As it gradually dried it developed fine cracks, the orange colour it was meant to leave behind now just peeking through. The room was buzzing with her sisters and cousins, each of them decorating each other's hands and nattering away, discussing their outfits and matching accessories for the big day tomorrow. The house was bursting with guests and there was plenty of traditional song and dance continuing downstairs, the sound of which echoed all the way up the stairs into the bedroom. Kamal was being teased by her sisters and cousins, as she was having her hands decorated.

"Oh just imagine, this is your last night of innocence, your last night as a virgin!"

Kamal smiled shyly and lowered her eyes. Her marriage with Raj had been arranged by her extended family. She had only seen Raj once at her cousin's house a couple of months ago when they were briefly left alone, an opportunity for them to get to know each other. She had hardly said a word to him and had with much hesitation managed to lift her gaze ever so slightly. That one moment was imprinted in her mind like a photographic memory; her heart still missed a beat when she recalled the first locking of eyes and his handsome face. He simply asked her if she could cook, what qualifications she had and if she was happy with the alliance, to which she had simply nodded, yes. The family seemed to have made the final decision for her as soon as Raj had given the thumbs up and before she knew it, both families were congratulating each other. Since that day onwards the preparations for the wedding had been continuous. Her knees were pulled up to her chest and her trouser rolled up so that it did not touch the fresh wet henna her cousin was now skilfully applying to her feet. Kamal rested her chin on her knee and hoped, hoped that Raj was a much better man than her father.

She hardly slept that night. The house was still full of guests and the hustle and bustle continued till very late at night. Once everyone had eventually settled down the only audible sound was the snoring from one of the guests in the room next door. She lay in her bed with the dried henna still on her hands, as the longer it was left on the darker it would dye, but it made it very awkward and uncomfortable for her to sleep. Her arms were both above her head resting on an old towel and she was looking up at the ceiling wondering what the future had in store for her, reflecting back on her life so far, which before today was nothing exceptional. She was very limited to what she could do; she had no freedom due to her father's strict and stern upbringing and had led a very reserved life. The only time she was even allowed to wear western clothes was to school and that was because it was compulsory as a uniform. Kamal had never been in any relationship during her schooling and college years, her strict upbringing forbidding her from mingling unnecessarily with the opposite sex. She had been a very simple, shy and quiet girl, unlike her peers who were much more on trend, full of life, confident and sure of what they wanted in life. Her hair had always been combed back and tied into a long tight plait, not one strand coming out of place. Due to her simple looks and shy nature, she largely remained unnoticed at school and blended well into the background. She did not hang around in a group like her peers did up by the shops after school, or sit on the wall talking to the boys, or go to a friend's home to read the latest edition of the Smash Hits magazine, it was straight from home to school and from school to home, to help her mother with the household chores, learning how to cook and sew, continuously being told that she would need these skills for when she would marry and leave her parental home for her marital one. Following school, she attended college to do a secretarial course, but even then her father took her to and from college; her father considered this to be the age when young girls like her could easily go 'astray'. During her college days she was expected to wear traditional Indian dress. She had envied girls in their fashionable leggings, ski paints, tight jeans and batwing jumpers, the bright jewellery and their modern hair styles. She always wished she could dress so and would on occasions experiment with her hair in front of the mirror with her sisters. Kamal was the oldest of three sisters, followed by Narinder, pet-named Nindy and then the youngest, Surinder pet-named Sindy. Due to major complications during labour with Sindy, their mother, Parminder, had to have a total hysterectomy, hence no more children, which was a disappointment to their father Davinder, who'd so wanted a son. Out of the three sisters, Sindy was the rebel. Each morning as soon as she got through the school gates, she would go behind the sports block together with her friends, where she would untie her tight plait and together paint their faces liberally with makeup, which she and they had either picked from their mother's make up bags, or bought on the cheap from the indoor Soho Road market, take off their long hideous socks and replace them with their ankle socks. Kamal would disapprove and warn her of the consequences should their father find out, but Sindy being the rebel she was, ignored her and continued regardless.

As she lay pondering over her life so far, she hoped she would be happier than her mother ever was, she hoped she could have a career after marriage like some married women did, she hoped she would have a good relationship with her mother-in-law, wishing she was nothing like her evil grandmother whose relationship with her mother was despicable. With these hopes and thoughts she finally managed to nod off, but not for long, for it was soon time to wake and get prepared for the day that was going to change her life forever.

Kamal had attended many weddings and watched many brides having their makeover in preparation for the big day and today, it was her turn. The ladies, her mother, aunts and other relatives whom she only ever saw on special occasions, sang the traditional songs as they applied the paste made out of gram flour and turmeric mixed together with mustard oil. It was applied liberally to her upper arms, neck and face. They then rubbed yoghurt into her hair. She wrinkled her nose and frowned in repulse, "this is traditionally believed to be a beauty regime for the bride, so that her skin glowed and her hair shone, especially for her wedding day, do you not want to look beautiful for your wedding day?" her aunt asked her. Kamal lowered her eyes shyly. She was finally left alone to have her much needed shower. She firstly scraped off the dried henna, under the running warm water, revealing the dark blood-orange coloured pattern on the palms of her hands, going halfway up her slim arms; it looked beautiful. She scrubbed herself down with the soap getting rid of the turmeric paste that had been applied earlier. She lathered her hair thoroughly with shampoo twice, and rinsed it until it was squeaky clean ridding her hair of the yoghurt. As she stepped out the shower, patted herself dry, towel dried her long thick jet black hair and wrapped her soft pink robe around her, she could hear her sisters and cousins waiting for her patiently outside.

Kamal's sisters patiently watched their older sister evolve into a breathtakingly beautiful bride. Her skin was flawless, her capped eyelids were covered in a shimmering bronze-gold coloured eye shadow, to match her red wedding dress intricately embroidered and adorned with gold coloured threads, beads and sequences, which shimmered under the light. The tiny bridal *bindi*'s or dots, were painted over and along the eyebrows in the traditional red and white colour. In the middle of her forehead, between her brows a larger round red and white *bindi* was carefully painted on. Her heart shaped lips were coloured in red and the otherwise silent tiny small beauty spot she had above the left side of her lip now seemed to have come alive and accentuated her beauty. The black kohl brought out her sultry almond shaped brown eyes; Kamal herself could not recognise herself, as she stood up to look at her reflection in the mirror. She felt weighed down by her heavily embroidered wedding dress, the red and white bangles going a quarter of a way up her slim arms and her traditional gold jewellery, her ears lobes feeling the weight of the large earrings. Her cousins and sisters gasped as they looked at the beauty that had transpired before their eyes; she looked like an Indian princess. Her mother came up to see her and stood still in her tracks, as she admired her daughter standing before her in all her beauty. She walked over to her and kissed her on the forehead.

"Put a black mark behind her ear Kiran, to protect her from the evil eyes of the world."

The house was now bustling with yet more guests dressed in their colourful fineries. The ladies continued to sing the traditional wedding songs simultaneously followed by rounds of laughter. Kamal could hear her father and uncles shouting out instructions. Her mother was like a headless chicken, looking for this, that and the other; it was a normal chaotic wedding morning household. Kamal was still up in her bedroom, which she had always shared with her sisters. Nindy and Sindy slept on the bunk bed, while Kamal had the one single bed. The bedroom was full of childhood memories, of Kamal playing the teacher her sisters her pupils, playing with their dolls and inviting each other to their imaginative homes, singing songs, dancing, painting and reading. While Kamal sat at the end of the bed, recalling the happier memories relatives came in and out of the bedroom to admire and compliment on how beautiful she looked. Her sisters were both wearing identical pink Punjabi suits, which were stitched for them by their mother especially for the wedding. Their hair was prettily tied up in tight French plaits. Nindy, just like Kamal, had her mother's features, only Nindy had her mother's sharp nose and fair complexion, whereas Kamal's nose was a little smaller and softer, and her complexion not fair like her sisters, but a warm almond. Sindy had inherited their father's much fairer complexion and her nose was just perfectly formed. She had high cheek bones and fuller lips; she had always been regarded as the fairest and prettiest of the three and was nowhere near as passive as her older sisters. Kamal, was never close to her father, nor was Nindy, whereas they both quaked in his presence, Sindy shared a special bond with him.

Kamal's mother came back into the room, breathless and panicky. Parminder looked beautiful in her silk turquoise Punjabi suit, the hem embroidered in gold and the heavily embroidered *dupatta or* scarf, draped around her shoulders. Her dress was accessorised with matching turquoise and gold bangles and a simple gold necklace with matching earrings, which she wore on every special occasion. She had her hair tied up in a tight bun and as always, she wore minimal make-up, to maximum effect.

"Right now time to go. Come," she said holding her hand out, her bangles jingling in her arms. The room now lightly fragranced by her favourite signature *Lace* perfume, which she always purchased from the indoor market. "Come on girls, help her down."

"Is the girl ready yet!" Kamal's father shouted up the stairs.

"Yes *ji*. We are bringing her down. Come dear."

Kamal's heart sank, as her mother held her hand and led her down the stairs. It was all becoming real now. This was her wedding day; after all the planning, it was all really happening now. She stepped slowly down the stairs, holding her mother's and Nindy's hand, Sindy and her cousins following them closely behind, each of them eager to see the groom at the temple. There was an audience watching her coming down the stairs, the murmuring voices turning into a speechless silence, as they watched the beautiful bride stepping softly down the stairs.

Seated in the temple's dining area, her sisters and cousins were reporting back on how handsome Raj was looking in his navy suit and pink turban, as they drank their tea, with samosas, pakoras and Indian sweets. Kamal's sisters and cousins were buzzing around her like busy bees and Raj's friends and relatives were equally as curious and excited.

During the traditional ceremony Raj towered over Kamal; she being a petite five foot three and he standing tall at five foot eleven. They stood side by side in the temple's main prayer hall, in front of the *Guru Granth Sahib*, the Sikh Holy Scripture, sat traditionally on a raised platform under a decorated canopy, its pages open and the *Granthi* sitting in front of it with his legs crossed. He was reciting sacred script, his voice audible to all as he spoke into the microphone. The flames of the oil lamps shone brightly and quivered slightly, as another *Granthi* topped them up with more mustard oil, dressed in his traditional white cotton clothing and turban. The bride and groom kneeled down, said a prayer and sat down with their legs crossed in front of the *Guru Granth Sahib* with their heads bowed, both their families sitting behind them on the soft carpeted floor covered in bleached white cotton sheets, the ladies on the left side of the hall and the men on the right, sat respectively with their heads covered. The photographer continuously clicked away, capturing each moment with his camera, while the prayers were read out and the traditional marital ceremony took place. Kamal's mother watched on with tears welling in her eyes; it seemed like only yesterday Kamal was a baby in her arms and now, she was a bride who would be leaving her home in a matter of a few hours to a new family and a new life.

While Kamal had still hardly looked up at Raj, he had not been able to keep his eyes off her. He had even for a moment doubted whether she was the same simple, timid girl he had seen just a few months ago. Raj had agreed to the marriage because she was the perfect 'wife type ', simple and quiet; "good wife material," is what he'd bragged to his friends and today, she looked breathtakingly beautiful too.

The wedding reception was held at a community hall. The hired live band sang cover songs by Punjabi bands *Alaap, Chirag Pehchan and Heera Group*, quite badly. However, that did not deter the groom's family from their celebrations, drinking and dancing flamboyantly, while the girl's family sat and watched on humbly. Lunch was served in the typical rectangular white, plastic trays which slightly flopped as the separate compartments were filled with the steaming hot daal, meat curry and vegetable curry, along with the cooling yoghurt and salad. These were handed out carefully by Kamal's cousins making sure they did not tip the contents over on any of the respected groom's family. The chapattis were placed in plates in front of the guests for them to help themselves. The men drank the continual flow of alcohol as if there was no tomorrow and as on every occasion, there were the one or two jolly guests who had over indulged, leading them to become a bit rowdy and needing to be escorted out by their not so impressed family members. Kamal's sisters and cousins giggled at the intoxicated dance moves performed by some of the drunkards, totally unaware of their most likely out of character behaviour.

Coming up to just 5pm it was time to vacate the hall and both families headed for the brides's parental home, where she would depart for her new marital world. Kamal was taken back up to her bedroom for the last time by her sisters and cousins and sat numb on her bed, waiting patiently, as the elders prepared for her departure downstairs. Her husband and his immediate family members were welcomed into the home and were seated in the lounge. Today was the start of new beginnings, yet Kamal felt nothing; everything seemed so surreal. She looked around her room and then towards Nindy who was sitting next to her holding her hand, knowing that soon it would be time for her sister to depart. Sindy was too preoccupied talking to her cousins, looking out of the bedroom window down at the boys from the groom's side, who were waiting casually outside on the street, hands in their pockets looking back up at them and smiling. Sindy and her cousins were giggling, enjoying all the attention they were receiving.

"You okay?" Nindy asked Kamal.

"Look after mum."

"I will, I promise," Nindy replied, squeezing her sister's hand.

Kamal was going to miss her sisters and her childhood home, but she was not going to miss the abuse that took place within these walls over the years and still to present day. As she sat on her bed, people coming in and out of the room, memories of her father's physical and verbal abuse towards her mother resonated in her ears, images of him beating her flashed before her eyes and the sound of her helpless shrieks sent a shiver down her spine. Kamal had promised herself that she would not tolerate any kind of abuse, not like her mother had.

The time eventually came for her to depart and she embraced and cried with her sisters, her cousins, her aunts and uncles, her melodramatic grandmother and her plausible crocodile tears, but most of all, she cried with her mother. As she was slowly led out of the house accompanied by her sisters and mother, she saw her dad waiting for her at the front door, as if he could not wait for her to leave. He stretched his right arm out as she approached him hesitantly and to her surprise, she saw his eyes moisten. He hesitantly put his arm around her shoulder, as if not wanting to show her that deep down he actually did have a heart with a beat and some deeply embedded emotions. He led her out the house and to the car where her groom now waited patiently with his family. Sat in the car, with Raj and his sister-in-law, she looked back up at her father and his home, her vision blurred with tears. As she looked up at the world she was leaving behind and her sisters comforting her mother, her father abruptly slammed the door shut – and that was it. She let the tears run for the last time as the regal Royal's Royce pulled away. Suddenly the heavens opened and Kamal watched the rain bounce off the bonnet of the car, bashing the flowers that decorated the car, as she made her way to her new life.

Her marital home in Wolverhampton was situated in a quiet suburban neighbourhood. The streets were lain with huge houses that actually had front gardens, compared to the streets she'd grown up in, which had rows and rows of terraced houses the front doors leading to nothing but the concrete pavement. She looked around observing her new surroundings, as she stepped out the car, being escorted out by Raj's outstretched hand. As unpredictable as the British weather was, the rain had stopped and the evening sun was finding its way through the relieved fluffy white clouds and to her delight - a rainbow had emerged. Kamal looked in awe at the beauty of her new surroundings; the vibrant flowers bowing down, burdened down by the rain drops falling from their delicate petals, the luscious green of the lawns and the rustling tree leaves that lined the suburban neighbourhood was all quite refreshing. She softly inhaled the fresh air and looked at her new home; was this the beginning of a new, brighter and happier life?

There was much fuss as the new bride was welcomed into the home of her new family. She sat patiently in the lounge, surrounded by yet more relatives, as the celebrations continued in the house and her new bedroom was being prepared for her first night with her husband. A little girl stood before her and looked at her curiously, her head tilted to one side and hands on her hips; it was Raj's niece Manpreet. Kamal smiled at her as she continued to look at her curiously, probably wondering what all the commotion was about. She then became distracted by her brother Sukhdeep holding her doll by the hair and scampered up the stairs after him. Kamal smiled and looked around the through lounge, which was huge in contrast to the room at her parent's home. It was brighter too, with the white textured walls, abundant with family portraits, a burgundy carpet and thick burgundy velvet curtains.

Kamal was introduced to many relatives by her mother-in-law, before she was eventually escorted up to her new bedroom. Her parents had given in dowry furniture and bedding for her bedroom, which had already been set up by Raj's friends and cousins, while the song and dance had continued downstairs. She was now sitting alone on her bed, left waiting for Raj. She ran her hands over the burgundy satin throw her mother and aunt had selected. Kamal looked around her new room, as she waited patiently for her husband to join her. The walls were papered in a golden beige colour, the beige velvet curtains were drawn and the burgundy carpet seemed to run throughout the whole house including her new bedroom. It was gone 10.30pm now. She had danced with Raj briefly downstairs, as he held her by her hands; the first physical contact with him had sent an unknown tingling sensation throughout her whole body. She could still hear people downstairs and outside of the room. This was so strange for her; a new house, a new family, a new life, at just eighteen years of age. There was a knock at the door and when she looked up, in walked her husband. He smiled at her and shut the door behind him locking it with the key. She looked up at him properly for the first time as he approached her, her heart beating faster and her pulse beginning to race, anxious, knowing what was going to happen, but not knowing what to say or do. She lowered her gaze as he sat next to her. She could smell alcohol and instantly, unwelcome memories came surging back making her feel slightly uneasy. Raj held her hand. His skin compared to hers was very fair and that horrible insecure feeling came back, like it always did; she'd forever been taunted for her darker complexion, by her grandmother especially.

"It's been a long day hasn't it?"

Kamal smiled and looked up slightly. She noticed for the first time that he actually had hazel brown eyes.

"You look really pretty today."

"Thank you," she said quietly and looked down again.

Raj thought she was perfect; quiet, submissive and shy, not mouthy, know it all and loud, like the girls he had dated, too clever for their own bloody good.

"Are you going to get changed?" he said putting his right arm around her. Kamal felt her body tingle all over again. She could still hear people outside on the landing and it made her feel a little uncomfortable. "Do you want me to help you undress?" he said now bending down, his face was close to hers and the smell of alcohol wafted off his breath.

"No, I'm okay," she said nervously. She knew what happened on wedding nights. Her cousin had told her everything in detail. It's all she ever talked about, sex, and she'd laugh at Kamal when she'd turn away wide eyed and embarrassed. Raj unpinned her *dupatta* (veil) from her hair. Kamal sat numb; a shiver ran down her spine, as he touched her softly. Raj held her hand and could sense she was nervous. He then felt her back and reached for the zip of her top and slowly pulled it down.

"Can we shut the light please?" Kamal blurted out.

"If that makes you feel comfortable, can I leave the lamp on? I would like to see my wife in a little light at least," he whispered softly in her ear.

She nodded her head. He switched the lamp on and got up to switch off the main light. She watched him, as he loosened his tie and undid his top shirt buttons. He pulled her up gently by the hands and put his arms around her. He then tilted her chin up and softly kissed her. Kamal felt like she was suddenly floating in mid-air. Her arms were just flopped to her side, the only thing that was holding her up was Raj's strong embrace. Raj kissed her, his mouth covering all hers, the whiff of alcohol and aftershave combined travelling up her nostrils as he kissed her and pulled her tighter towards him. The only kissing Kamal ever knew was what she had seen on television and the channel used to be promptly changed over by her mother or father, or she and her sisters were instructed to go upstairs to their room, especially when *J.R. Ewing* was up to all sorts in *Dallas*! Raj pulled her arms up and put them round his neck urging her to hold him and she did; her first kiss and it was amazing. He then felt her naked back from when he had earlier unzipped her and slowly removed her top and let it drop to the floor. He slowly removed her trouser as well, stepped back and looked at her in her red underwear and smiled; under all that clothing she had the perfectly formed hourglass figure. She stood nervously almost trying to cover herself with her arms, her bangles clinking as she shifted nervously, her eyes on the ground. He put her arms to one side and kissed her all over. He removed the pins from her hair one by one and let it flow over her shoulders; she was truly beautiful. He gently laid her on the bed and slowly removed her underwear, now totally naked she bashfully pulled the duvet over her while Raj got undressed. He joined her under the duvet and kissed her again all over. Kamal drew her breath in when he touched her all over intimately, a sudden want arising within her. "I promise I will be gentle," he whispered in her ear as he penetrated slowly. Kamal gasped as he did and winced from the pain, as he rocked gently. She put her arms around him; she had never known physically what to expect, it was uncomfortable, but pleasurable as the two bodies met. When Raj finished, he immediately checked the white sheet as soon he pulled away and was pleased with the evident loss of blood. He lay by the side of her panting slightly, his hands behind his head. She was perfect, just the way he wanted.

Chapter 3

Kamal had embraced her new life with open arms, her pre-marital life now buried in the past.

Her relationship with her mother-in-law Joginder was as much as any relationship one had with their mother-in-law. She did like to remind both her daughter-in-laws who was in charge every now and then and would at times, when feeling slightly threatened that her sons were being lured away by their sweet little wives, moan about some overly exaggerated ailment in order to gain their attention. Whilst Kamal was quite unscathed by this typical mother-in-law-type behaviour, Deepa found this quite exasperating and irritating. However, Kamal was well aware that her mother-in-law silently adored both her and Deepa. Whenever they attended any function together - she would stand proud with both of them at her side and gloated at having inherited two so well-mannered and dignified daughter-in-laws for her precious sons.

Her retired father-in-law Balbir spent most of his time on his chair in the lounge quietly reading his newspaper, going for a stroll in the park, catching up with his friendly neighbours as he gardened or watched television with his wife. He was a man of very little words, but a warm, kind hearted and jolly soul. Having worked since the age of sixteen, he was now really enjoying the pleasures of early retirement. He regarded both her and Deepa as his daughters and would step in to defend their corner against his theatrical wife whenever necessary. He had carved himself a special place in her heart.

Her brother-in-law Varinder who worked as a radiographer in the local hospital was the figure of brotherly authority and her sister-in-law Deepa was like the older sister she never had. Their children were like a comical double act and there was never a dull moment in the house. They also brought out the small child in Kamal, whereas Deepa would be exhausted on her return from work, Kamal would never tire in entertaining the kids, taking them to the park, reading to them getting into full character, which had them rolling with laughter.

Kamal herself had changed in appearance. Gone were her days of a fierce tight plait, now she carried a fringe which softened her face and she did her long tresses justice by letting them flow loose freed from any unsightly split ends. Deepa gave her makeup tips, advising her on what colours complemented her complexion. She had also helped her shop for some western outfits and when she learnt of Kamal's father's bigoted views against Western dressing, she did not hesitate in telling her how she felt.

"I'm sorry Kamal, I am going to be quite frank, why is it okay for parents to bring their children up in a Western society and be dead against them adopting Western ways? I mean how confusing is that? I never had that problem with my parents and don't worry, you won't have that problem here, thank God! I mean at the end of the day, your body is still covered, it's not like you are walking around naked, what's the difference? It baffles me to be honest, and at the end of the day, as long as you don't forget family values, everyone is happy whether you are wearing an Indian suit or a pair of jeans."

Her sister-in-law Deepa worked as a manager for the local council and she enjoyed the time away from the house. She could not understand how Kamal was content with staying at home all day. But for Kamal, there was a new found freedom in her marital home. When she was not tied up with the household chores she and Deepa would often go together to the pictures, shopping with the kids, listen to music together and talk for hours on end. When their in-laws were out overnight visiting relatives, they'd make a night of it by popping open a bottle of Babycham, ordering a lazy takeaway and renting a couple of videos. She thought herself to be very fortunate to have inherited a sister-in-law whom she actually got along so well with, as opposed to other girls she knew, who cursed the very existence of their sinister sister-in-laws. Kamal in contrast admired hers for balancing her whole life so well and loved seeing her dressed up in her tailored suits, court shoes, her soft silky hair either sophisticatedly tied up in a bun, looking all trim and proper ready for business, or left flowing half way down her back. Kamal thought Deepa looked the figure of authority each morning, leaving for work with her leather briefcase and subtle hint of exquisite signature perfume; for Kamal, Deepa was an inspiration.

Within a year of Kamal's marriage, as soon as Nindy had turned eighteen, she had also been married off and was happily settled. Her husband and his family were from Southall, London. They owned a grocery store and Nindy was quite content in helping them run the family business. While the two older daughters were settled in their new lives, Sindy in the meantime was breaking every rule in the book. She was dating a boy from college, her parents of course totally oblivious. Kamal and Nindy tried their best to talk some sense into her, but as rebellious as she was, she continued to do as she pleased. She caught the bus with her friends to college, she wore western outfits, she went out to town and to the pictures; something Kamal and Nindy daren't even dream of doing. They discussed how she was able to do all that they were forbidden to and thought maybe it was because she was the youngest or the fact that she was so much like their father, stubborn and adamant to have her own way. Or it could be the fact that she knew how to get round her father and if that proved unsuccessful, she would talk her grandmother round who would in turn talk her son round. Kamal knew it would be only a matter of time before their father found out about Sindy's relationship with a boy; it could not remain a secret forever the way she was carrying on and when he did find out, all hell would break loose, but Kamal was too busy to worry about Sindy; she was perfectly capable of looking after herself.

"Oh Kamal he is so precious," Kamal's mother cradled her just day old grandson in her arms and shed a tear, as she held her first grandchild. For her it was like holding the son she never had. Her father on the other hand was not so emotional and only briefly held the new born, quickly handing the little bundle back to his wife, as if he were handling a freshly baked hot bun! They were waiting for Raj to return; it was gone 10pm and there was still no sign of him. Parminder became concerned, as she saw the anxiety in her daughter's eyes each time her eyes travelled up to the clock.

"Is everything okay between you and Raj?" she whispered.

"Yes mum, he's just out celebrating with his work colleagues, that's all."

"That's okay. He has never mistreated you has he?"

"No mum, never," Kamal smiled.

Her parents had finally left not being able to wait any longer for Raj. Her mother-in-law again suggested keeping the new born with her while Kamal rested and recuperated from the delivery. She was so excited with the new arrival, as he was so much like Raj as a baby and she felt it was like having Raj in her arms all over again. She had even taken to calling him Junior Raj.

Kamal was just nodding off when she heard Raj walk in. She slowly sat up, wincing at the sharp pain from the stitches and switched the bedside lamp on.

"Mum and dad waited for you then left, where have you been?"

"I've been celebrating the birth of my son with my friends," he said, removing his jacket and hanging it on the peg behind the door.

"It would be nice if you could spend some time with him Raj."

"What do you want me to do? Stay home 24/7? You'd like that won't you? I'm only having fun with friends, but you wouldn't understand that. What's your problem anyway? Always bloody moaning lately, don't know why, you have a better life here, so learn to appreciate it."

"Yes, I do, but it would be nice if my husband was a part of it too."

"Do you know what you need to do? You need to get a life!" he said as he sat on the end of the bed removing his socks.

"Well I may well have, had I not got pregnant," Kamal tried to defend herself hopelessly.

"Oh just go to sleep! And you're not the most attractive of sights, have you any idea how much weight you've put on," he said taking his shirt and trousers off and chucking them at the end of the bed, "ruined my whole bloody mood!" he got into bed with his back turned towards her, as it always was nowadays.

Kamal lay in bed and let the tears run down the side of her cheeks, over her ears and creating two damp patches on the pillow. Not everything was perfect in her new world. While she was more than happy and settled with her new family, the initial magic between her and her husband had soon faded away and seemed like a distant memory; he had changed so much. Since her sixth month of pregnancy he was returning home whenever he pleased with the whiff of the local public house wafting off his clothes, churned in with his expensive aftershave. If he did stay at home, it was to watch football with his friends or family who'd come round. Before her very eyes her relationship with her husband was altering and becoming almost similar, to what her mother's was with her father. The only difference was that Raj was not abusive and volatile. When her father would come back home drunk, everyone avoided him, knowing better not to approach him, well aware that drink brought out the animal within him. Kamal would lie in bed, stirring every time she heard any noise indicating unrest and some disturbing memories remained with her. Raj was increasingly becoming distant. She wondered whether it was because she was so busy with the household chores, trying to please everyone, running around the never ending guests, leaving her with hardly any time for him when he returned back from work. His dinner was ready for him when he got in, he'd have his dinner with the rest of the family, watch some TV and then went out normally returning back home late. His father would shout out "stay at home once in a while would you!" But he'd just carry on out. Kamal was always amazed at how he managed to get up for work the next morning, but her dad was also the same; he never missed a days' work, no matter how much he had drunk the previous night.

Things had not always been like this between her and Raj. They would stay up till late at night talking about their families, getting to know each other. They made love many times during the night and sometimes even during the day, when they were alone. But then she got pregnant and it was fine until she was six months, when it got a bit awkward. She had also gained a colossal amount of weight. Deepa had told her that she would lose it being the perfect size ten she was after having two kids, not one stretch mark, perfectly toned body, always managing to look good effortlessly with her flawless fair complexion, perfect height and smile; Varinder was forever buzzing around her like a bee to honey. Kamal sighed and turned her back towards Raj, he was fast asleep already and she too closed her eyes, trying to push away all the negative thoughts.

Raj was up the following morning bang on time, as always, without fail. He had a shave and shower, patted on his favourite aftershave, put on his crisp white ironed shirt and tailored grey suit, neatly hanging in the wardrobe and already polished shoes. Kamal was still sleeping; he looked towards her lying in bed, as he combed his hair back. He wished the arguing would stop, but he could not help it, he had to lash out at someone and she was the easiest target. He looked back briefly at the slick and suave reflection in the mirror and headed off to work after he swigged down the black coffee his mother had prepared for him and kissed his son on the forehead, as he lay in the moses basket in the living room.

After tackling the hindering, notorious morning city traffic, he arrived to his place of work and walked in arrogantly through the revolving glass doors of the corporate accountancy firm, into the reception area with its polished floors, elegant waiting area with black leather suites, and as always – Seema at the reception desk to greet him good morning with her perfectly aligned white teeth, looking as gorgeous as ever in the low cut fitted top. He winked at her as he signed himself in. Seema was his new object of desire and he could not get her out of his mind day or night. The affair started about five months ago. Kamal was a good wife, he could not have wished for a better one, but Seema was exciting, full of life, sexy and very, very good to him in bed and the more he tried to pull away, the more her magnetic force drew him towards her. They lunched and dined together and then he'd take her to a hotel for some enthralling sex. But the guilt would soon kick in when it was time to leave her and head for home. Not being able to face his perfect little wife and parents, he would therefore go to the pub instead for a few drinks, followed by a few more to pluck up the courage to be able to look them in the eye. He needed his wife at home, as she completed his home and family life, but he also needed some excitement and Seema provided that; one woman was never going to be enough for him.

***

Kamal's resentment grew day by day, as Raj continued to distance himself. They hardly made love anymore and when they did, it was convenient sex. It meant nothing, not like it used to. Deepa and Varinder had also moved out, much to her mother-in-law's disappointment and not having Deepa around anymore made life at home even more miserable. Her life had become a boring mundane routine, day in and day out. It was when her son was nine months old and she was reaching the end of her tether she asked her in-laws if she could start looking for a job.

"Well that's fine by us. Have you discussed with Raj?"

"I will, but is it okay with you?"

"We have no problem with you working, we never stood in Deepa's way either, besides it would be good for you to get out," her father-in-law said, "and we'll look after Junior," he smiled looking at his precious grandson who was having a midday snooze.

That same evening, Raj was quite sober and appeared quite down and deflated. Kamal was far too preoccupied with what she wanted right now to spare him a second thought tonight.

"I want to start looking for work, if that's okay? Dad said I should discuss with you," she said as he joined her in bed.

"I think it'll do you good to get out of the house," he sighed.

"So that's a yes then?"

"Yeah, why would I object?" he frowned.

She smiled, wondering indeed why she thought he would. This was of course not the same restrictive household she had left behind. The built up resentment began to melt away and she rested her head on his chest and sighed. Raj closed his eyes in anguish; he felt doubly guilty when she made an effort to get close to him. He placed his arm around her as she touched his chest, feeling absolutely nothing but sympathy for her. Kamal on the other hand, closed her eyes and wished they could rekindle the magic they had between them when they were first married and tenderly began to kiss and caress him.

Following a run of failed interviews due to lack of confidence, nerves getting the better of her, her mind going blank every time a question was fired at her, feeling intimidated by the vultures perched across the interview table, sometimes close to tears for the fear of failing yet again, with some perseverance, interview tips and lessons from Deepa and Varinder, Kamal did eventually manage to bag herself a job as a PA for an engineering company. She was due to start on the Monday and was really looking forward to the challenge.

"That suits you to a T," Deepa said approvingly, as Kamal again tried on her trouser suit with a white striped shirt at home, following their shopping spree.

"Can't believe I'm wearing a size ten again!"

"I told you you'd lose it."

Kamal sighed as she examined her reflection in the mirror. She could not wait to start her new job and work like other women, like Deepa. Monday was going to be a new beginning for her and she could envisage something she had never envisaged before, independence.

Chapter 4

A few months into her new job, Kamal learnt that away from the four walls of home, there was a world that lived and breathed and she felt liberated from her once humdrum life. However, it had not all been plain sailing, from typing a simple letter on her electronic typewriter, which had a mind of its own, speaking confidently on the phone to the alien person on the other end, whom she was convinced was speaking a foreign language, to sending a fax by feeding the paper through correctly on the first attempt and operating the monstrous photocopier without it churning hundreds and hundreds of unwanted copies and then making out to the person waiting patiently behind her that it was exactly the number of copies she required, it took her a few weeks to really find her feet and she did eventually become quite confident in her daily PA tasks. The pursing lips and raising brows from her colleagues soon subsided and transformed into more appreciative smiles. Learning to work with the opposite sex was a challenge in itself. It was the first time she had to really interact with strange men, out of her comfort zone, and she soon overcame her shyness and lack of initial eye contact.

Her life was now busier than ever before. When she got home she still did what needed to be done around the house, as her in-laws were finding it half a job keeping up with their beloved grandson, who was over a year old now and causing absolute mayhem. They spent most of their day chasing him around keeping him out of mischief and when they were not doing that, they took him out to the temple, shopping, to the park and visiting friends and family. He was the apple of their eyes and had injected them with a new lease of life.

Raj's increasing work commitments were his excuse for his lateness each night now and she was usually wiped-out ready for bed by the time he got home. They hardly talked, as they hardly saw each other and their relationship had become like that of two strangers tossed on an island, forced together by circumstances. She was disheartened that Raj hadn't even noticed that she had cut her hair short to just below her shoulders, but then that was hardly surprising, if it was not for his parents, she was sure he would not even bother coming home at night. On the occasions when they were alone in the bedroom and not sleeping the silence was palpable, but it was the only place within the house where they did not have to parade serenity; it was the only place where the pretence was unshackled. While she wished she was not affected by her marital woes, as she heard her colleagues talking to their partners throughout the day, asking each other what they were doing, what they were going to have for dinner, about their plans for the evening or weekend, she did feel the void in her heart.

Kamal shared an office with Danielle and Angela. Danielle, was in her late twenties and Angela in her early twenties. On quieter days, when their engineers were either away or in meetings, they would close their office door and talk for ages, filling each other on the latest gossip, on who was with whom or just talking about soaps, fashion, music, films and general girly chit-chat. Kamal had built a trusting relationship with both and had eventually unburdened her trepidations on her dwindling relationship with her husband. Danielle was convinced Raj was having an affair, but Kamal would not hear anything of it, even though deep down, she had her reservations. Her colleagues could not wait for the clock to strike 5pm, but Kamal's only incentive to return home was to see the smile on her son's face as she walked in through the front door, seeing him waddle towards her excitedly. Her new found freedom and her insight into the liberal life of others aspired for her to want more from her life and she was beginning to yearn for some excitement.

Kamal was having lunch with Danielle in the canteen and her eyes again locked with Rohit Sinha's, as he entered and smiled at her. The first time she had seen him she had almost stood still in her tracks and Danielle, was well clued-up. Compared to the other engineers, stuck in their own engineering world, he was quite apart and very pleasing on the eyes too. Kamal smiled back and continued with her lunch.

"Shall I ask him to join us?" Danielle said noticing the boy meets girl exchange in glances.

"No!"

"Oh you're so boring!" Danielle said in frustration. She liked Kamal. She had doubted that she would have lasted a few days let alone a week when she'd begun. She had never known anyone to be so nervous and lacking in confidence, yet polite, curious and keen to learn. She needed quite a bit of help and support, but she was a quick learner and now, she did the job like she'd done it for years. "I'm going to set you up!" Danielle said.

"Oh don't be silly, he's just being friendly and you're forgetting one small detail, I am married….."

"Oh are you now? Could have fooled me, but do you know what bothers me? He has been working here for four years. I know so many girls here who would drop their knickers at the click of his fingers,.."

"Danielle!"

"Oh well it's true and then you come along."

Kamal smiled looking up towards him and again, as if he had not taken his eyes off her, he smiled back; there was a definite attraction, that, she could not deny.

The smiling soon turned to general banter about how bad the weather was as they waited in the queue at the canteen, how bad the food was at the canteen, thanking God it was Friday as they waited for the lift, briefly discussing weekend plans as they parted ways. He was beginning to play on her mind all the while now. She longed to see him at work and would make any excuse to go up to the fifth floor where he and his team were based, just to catch his attention, making out she had gone up to see his secretary, Christine. Her heart fluttered, as she thought of him on the bus, when she got home, while she was cooking, while she was watching TV and when she was in bed. Mondays could not come soon enough for her now. She was buying more and more outfits for herself and spent ages getting ready in the mornings, making sure her hair looked perfect and her make-up was just right. She felt guilty for thinking of another man and was afraid Raj could hear her thoughts, as she lay in bed next to him, but she couldn't free her head of this growing infatuation.

Meanwhile, Raj had long finished his frolicking with Seema ever since his eyes found his new desire, the breathtaking blonde coming out of the insurance brokers' office block. Ever since Raj had seen Emma, he just knew he had to have her and with his charming smile and morning greetings, deliberately waiting for her in the car park, he soon asked her out. He was not blind to the fact that his wife was looking good these days and it did cross his mind once or twice that she could be making an effort for someone in the office. After all, he knew what was capable of happening within the work environment. He had noticed the change of character too. From the introvert, quiet, shy and unconfident woman he married was emerging not an extravert, but a confident, determined and hard working woman, combining both work and home life harmoniously, not once complaining. Kamal was perfect for his family; but it was Emma that made his pulse race.

Office Christmas party and Kamal was dressed to impress in a long black dress, black suede heels, eyes sultry with black kohl, smoky eye shadow with just a dab of lipstick and her hair sophisticatedly tied up, all with the assistance of her fashion consultant, Deepa. The party was held at the five star City Plaza Hotel and Kamal was taken aback by the splendour; polished flooring, the contrasting dim and bright lighting along the corridors, gleaming bottles with colourful spirits displayed at the bar, smartly dressed bar and hotel staff, finely dressed guests and the impressively laid out reserved tables for Cooper Engineering and Co. While sat, pulling crackers, eating and drinking - some more than others, Kamal was mindful of the watchful eyes on the table to her right and she was lapping up all the attention.

"He can't keep his eyes off you and I don't blame him, you look stunning!" Danielle said as she, Kamal and Angela refreshed in the ladies.

Kamal smiled.

"I think I may put Alex out of his misery tonight, I might just thrill him later when we go out," Angela said, taking her lipstick out her purse.

"Really!" Kamal widened her eyes.

"Well the office Christmas party won't be the office Christmas party if there's no scandal," Angela pouted her lips.

"Yes," Danielle added, "and who can blame Mark for not being able to keep his eyes off this lot," she said juggling her voluptuous assets. Danielle was wearing a daring low cut purple top with a black satin skirt. She had a gorgeous hour glass figure with the tiniest waist and looked absolutely gorgeous, the curls of her glossy brunette hair bouncing about her. Angela was dressed to impress in her perfect size ten little black dress showing off her long pins, her wavy blonde hair trailing half way down her back.

"Oh Kamal come on, come out clubbing with us. We'll have so much fun," Angela pleaded.

"No, I can't, maybe if I was not living with my in-laws, but I am, maybe some other time. Need to get back at a decent time."

"Ooh would that be before the clock strikes 12 Cinderalla! Well we'll hold you to that, but for now, let's go back and break some hearts," Danielle led the way out and Kamal and Angela giggled, as she strutted forward, swaying her hips from side to side.

"Can I talk to you for a moment please?" Kamal stood still in her tracks, as Rohit approached her no sooner had she stepped out the ladies behind her friends.

"Um...," she looked towards the others.

"Somewhere more private perhaps?"

"We'll leave you to it."

Danielle and Angela walked away displaying mischievous grins. Kamal widened her eyes in angst.

"This way," Rohit said, pointing towards the hotel bar. Kamal was still looking at her grinning friends, as they disappeared back into the restaurant and then looked back up at Rohit, "please." After a brief moment of hesitation, she eventually shrugged her shoulders and followed him to a small table tucked away in the corner away from the bar. The lighting was dim and soft instrumental music was just audible over the humming of voices and clanking of glasses at the bar.

"Drink?"

"I'm okay thanks."

"Are you sure, anything, a soft drink?"

Kamal shook her head.

"I'll just grab a beer then."

Kamal watched him, as he stood at the bar. She could not deny he looked absolutely suave tonight in his white striped shirt, a black waistcoat and black trousers. He caught her gaze as he turned round and smiled. She returned the smile and began to fiddle aimlessly in her handbag. What the eyes were saying need not be transcribed and she was afraid he would see in hers some deeply embedded desires.

"So what did you want to talk about?" she asked him, as he sat down trying her best to look cool and unperturbed by his alluring presence.

"Nothing much really, just wanted to be alone with you. Too many people in there, as if we don't see enough of them at work. Are you enjoying yourself?"

"Yeah, it's nice here," she said looking around her.

"We never really get to talk much at work. Would be nice to get to know who you really are," he said looking at her.

"There's not much to know. I am married, my husband's an accountant and I have a son who's two years old now," Kamal felt the need to remind *herself* that she was bound down by matrimony.

"Brothers? Sisters?"

"No brothers, two sisters. And you?"

"Me. I live very far away from home and family. I'm from India, you may have gathered from my accent. I've got my own flat here. You can come to see it sometime if you want," he said smiling. Kamal however did not quite see the humour.

"Are you just married, or happily married?" Rohit asked clearing his throat, realising he should not have perhaps invited her to his flat quite so soon.

"I am happily married," Kamal said raising her eyebrows, now doubly unimpressed.

Rohit smiled, "that's not what Danielle told me."

"Danielle, what has she said?"

"Just that you are not...happily married," he shrugged his shoulders smugly.

"And so you thought you'd get in?" Kamal said getting up grabbing her bag.

Rohit looked up slightly stunned by her reaction. He had been assuming she was waiting for him to make the first move, but her body language was indicating otherwise.

"Sorry, I did not mean to upset you. I was just trying to get to know you better - that's all, please don't leave," Kamal wanted to walk away, "please, I won't ask you anything else about your marriage. Tell me more about.... your son," he said immediately trying to change the subject. She eventually sat back down with her nose tossed in the air, implying reluctance.

"I'm sorry. I guess I misunderstood somewhere along the lines." Kamal remained silent. "Maybe I should talk about myself then."

"If you must."

Rohit smiled inwardly, as she avoided eye contact; she did not have to stay, but she chose to.

"Well as you know my name is Rohit, I moved over to Europe two years ago and over to England four years ago. I am going back to India in the New Year back to visit the family, can't wait."

At this point Kamal took her eyes off the embellished Christmas tree and looked at Rohit, who smiled at her contradicting body language; Kamal could not explain why her heart felt like it had suddenly sunk.

"Are you going back home to visit the family?"

"Yes, my parents, have not seen them for over two years now and my mother's getting quite restless."

"You must miss them awfully. I can't imagine not seeing my mum for over two years."

The conversation was underway. Rohit told Kamal about his studying in India and America, his time spent in Germany, followed by Holland and the move to England. He talked about Bombay, his family and his apparent acquaintance with some Bollywood dignitaries. Kamal was completely mesmerized and listened with much fascination.

"Wow, what a colourful life you have led. I simply have not lived," Kamal smiled, "the furthest I have been away from home is probably London!" Rohit smiled at her innocence. "Oh gosh is that the time!" she said as she saw Danielle and Angela blowing kisses to her from afar and leaving with Tim, Mark, Alex and a tipsy Maria from human resources.

"Oh do you have to? I can drop you off if you want."

"No, no, I'll catch a taxi."

"Oh, I wish you could stay longer," he placed his right hand on hers.

"It is really getting late and I need to get home. Do you mind calling a taxi for me?" she said firmly.

"Okay," Rohit put his hands up as he saw the barriers coming up again.

"Thanks for tonight," she said as they later walked towards the taxi.

"That's okay. Wish we could do this soon again."

Kamal said nothing; the thought of going home had kicked in reality. It was bitterly cold and a film of frost glistened on the parked cars under the moonlit night sky, the taxi motor was running and the exhaust fumes were like smoke chugging out a chimney, as it hit the cold air. Rohit opened the taxi door for her and just as she was about to get in, he held her elbow and turned her gently to face him. She looked up at him questioningly. He bent down to peck her softly on the cheek, and whispered, "Merry Christmas," in her ear.

She looked at him and as if pulled together by a sudden force, their lips were soon locked. He pulled her up towards him and desperately covered her mouth with his, but the moment did not last long. Kamal soon pushed him away and without saying another word she quickly got into the taxi and slammed the door shut.

"43 St. Peters Road please, quickly." Her heart began to pound and she broke out into a cold sweat. The Asian taxi driver was watching her through the rear view mirror. As she saw his eyes, the thought of him knowing the family sent her heart rate accelerating furthermore. She looked away and placed her hand on her forehead. Her head was spinning and she felt sick with revolt.

As the taxi approached home she hoped and hoped that her in-laws were already in bed for she could not bear to look them straight in the face after that absurd moment of weakness. She looked at her watch; it was just after 11pm and they were normally in bed by now. As she placed her hand on her head again she cursed herself; she had not only let herself down, she had let them down too. They had given her so much freedom and trust and she repaid them by betraying them! She avoided any eye contact with the taxi driver as she paid him. Standing in front of the door now, she rummaged in her bag for the house keys with her shaking hand. She closed her eyes in anticipation, took a deep breath before she opened the door as inaudibly as she could; the landing light was on, but thankfully, there was complete silence. She tiptoed up the stairs and into her bedroom and was relieved when she found the bed was empty. Raj had not returned and for once, she was thankful. She slowly shut the door behind her and exhaled. She then removed her coat, chucked it on the bed and sat down with her face buried in her hands. She wrinkled her nose as she sensed the smell of his aftershave faintly about her and immediately went quietly into the bathroom to wash her face several times. She tiptoed back into her bedroom and removed her dress and the pins from her hair; the whole sophisticated look now looked as cheap as she felt within. A voice in her head was taunting her, telling her she had let herself down by proving she had become a shameless loose woman.

She later tossed and turned in bed unable to free her mind of the thought of those nearest and dearest finding out about her despicable act. She sat up in bed to check what time it was; it was gone two thirty and there was still no sign of Raj and then she remembered; he too was at his Christmas works do. She sat up in bed, picked up Raj's pillow and hugged it for a few moments, as she tried to console herself. It was after all just a kiss, which lasted but just a few seconds and she had quite rightly broken it off. But she could still feel his lips over hers and while she knew it was wrong, she wished it wasn't. Lying back down, she eventually slipped off to sleep, waking up to find Raj asleep by her side.

It was 8 o'clock when she pulled herself out of bed and she was determined to blank out the episode from last night. After her shower, she got dressed into a Punjabi suit and prepared a nice cup of tea each for her in-laws, with a generous spoonful of guilt and apologised for being so late.

She embraced her son and silently promised both him and herself that she would never ever again be succumbed to Rohit Sinha's charm and risk losing all the respect and love she had found in this home, her home. She attempted to keep her mind preoccupied by the usual daily chores. She prepared breakfast, washed up, sorted the laundry and made a start on lunch for later. Once she'd done that, she started to clean the oven vigorously. Fortunately she was going to have a busy few days as visitors were expected tomorrow and it was Christmas on Monday, which was going to be a family affair; she hoped she would be feeling more settled by then.

Raj did not come down till gone midday. He played with his son and avoided Kamal; he'd spent all night at Emma's and this time, he knew it was different, she was not a bit on the side like the other women; he was falling desperately in love with her. Unfortunately for him, he had to come home to this dead relationship, for the sake of his parents and for the sake of his son.

Sunday was busy for both Kamal and Deepa. The visitors were their father-in-law's cousin and wife from Leicester and their recently wed son and his wife, who'd had their grand wedding in India a few weeks ago. Kamal looked at the newlywed bride, with her matrimonial bangles and henna still fresh on her hands, so dark and vibrant. She remembered her young bride days. It was so exciting then, but now. She looked towards Raj from the kitchen, sitting in the lounge with the guests. As he spoke to his cousin, he caught her gaze. She was wearing a purple suit, a colour that complemented her beauty, but of course he never vocalised that thought. Kamal smiled slightly and looked away back at the new couple.

"Oh new love," she said turning away and walking towards Deepa, "see how long that lasts."

"Oh they go back a long way. Theirs is actually a love marriage," Deepa said pouring the tea into the cups.

"Whatever that is," Kamal smiled.

"Are you okay?"

"Yeah, yeah, time of the month and all," she wished she could speak to Deepa, but thought better not to. She took the tray of tea to the guests followed closely by Deepa with the tray of sweetmeats.

"You are so lucky to have such good daughter-in-laws, it is so difficult to find the right alliance these days," the aunt said tossing her nose, almost airing the discontent at her son's choice of wife, as Kamal and Deepa walked in.

"Yes we are truly blessed. And they both are so good to each other as if they were real sisters, yes we are very lucky. They never get tired of working. Straight from work, into the kitchen; I will say, rest for a while, but no. I tell you since my daughter-in-laws have come I have not had to lift a finger in this house. They are so good. We have their parents to thank, they have brought their daughters up well, both of them."

Kamal smiled as she handed out the last cup of tea and walked back into the kitchen; if she felt bad before, she wished she could trip into a shallow grave right now.

Kamal called in sick on the Wednesday and did not intend to return to work until the New Year knowing that Rohit would then be in India. After seeking permission from her in-laws and Raj she departed to seek sanctuary for a couple of days at her parents.

Back at her paternal home her mother was overwhelmed to see her daughters together again. Nindy was a picture of glowing health from her pregnancy with twins whom she was expecting in March. The boy Sindy was courting had informed his parents of their relationship and his wish to marry her; they had just this week turned up at the family home unannounced asking for Sindy's hand in marriage for their son Sarbjit. Davinder was stunned to learn the truth, but relieved that the family was of the same caste and pleasantly thrilled that such a noble alliance had fallen straight into his laps for his precious youngest daughter.

Kamal smiled as she watched her mother follow her grandson around with glee; this was the happiest she had ever seen her. Everything was perfect and just the tonic. She laughed with her mother and sisters and at Sindy's overly exaggerated plans for her fairy tale wedding. Even her dad seemed to have mellowed, which made her even more determined, to forget Rohit Sinha.

Chapter 5

"Morning Kamal."

"Morning Jackie."

"Did you have a nice weekend?"

Kamal smiled recalling her weekend in Southall celebrating the birth of Nindy's twins with loads of good food and pumping Bhangra music! It was a joyous occasion, but unfortunately for Kamal she had to cut the celebration short in order to take home a tipsy Raj. Since Kamal had obtained her driving license, attending parties and being able to drink in excess was a plus for Raj now.

"Yes, busy as usual. Had a party and how was yours?" Kamal said rolling her eyes and smiling at Danielle as she walked in, putting her pen to and away from her mouth, as if she were smoking, giving Danielle a clue to whom she was engaged with on the telephone.

"Oh I had a lovely weekend thank you Kamal," Kamal wondered when her manager was going to quit the niceties and get straight to the point.

"Kamal, Christine has called in sick and won't be coming in for the rest of the week. I need someone to cover for her this week and since Craig is not in, I'd like you to go up please."

"Christine's place on fifth floor?" she said now with her back up straight.

"Yes, is that okay?"

"Well actually I was hoping to catch up on filing and things I have not had a chance to get round to…"

"What have I given you a junior for? Get her to do it. This is more important. You know they are amidst a large project. I'm sure Christine would do the same for you."

Kamal frowned in irritation. All this time she had avoided seeing Rohit like a plague, having a packed lunch at her desk, stepping back if she saw him along the corridor, deliberately looking away if they did cross paths and now she had to step in as his PA!

"Okay," she sighed, "I'll make my way up."

"What's up?" Danielle asked, as Kamal slammed down the receiver.

"Christine's off sick, Jackie wants me to go up and step in for her!"

Danielle smirked.

"Well you can wipe that smile off your face Danielle. It's going to be strictly work!" Kamal grabbed her things in frustration and made her way up.

"Morning Angela, see you later Angela!" Kamal charged past her as Danielle laughed out loud.

"What was that all about?" Angela looked from a marching Kamal to a hysterical Danielle.

Kamal walked through the large open plan office on the fifth floor, greeted good morning by engineers, clerks and administration staff sat at their desks with cups of tea and coffee, some already engrossed in their work, other's chatting and some reading the morning paper. As she approached Christine's desk she saw that Rohit had not yet arrived. Christine's desk was extremely tidy, the desk right outside Rohit's office, facing towards the large window with vertical blinds that looked onto the large open office; both desks were practically facing each other.

"Oh this is going to be so awkward," she muttered to herself as she placed her bag under the desk. She slightly pushed back the portrait of Christine's children and looked through her in-tray. There were some reports that needed copying and distributing and some letters that needed typing. There was a folder in Rohit's tray. She looked through it and found that it was an agenda and documents for a meeting this afternoon. She placed the folder back in his tray, answered the ringing phone and took down a message for Rohit. She looked at his diary and saw that he was not due to be in till 10am as he was going straight to a meeting and then when he got back, he had to attend yet another, which meant she'd hardly see him.

"Great," Kamal whispered to herself and looked around her. Unlike herself, Danielle and Angela, Christine worked in an open plan office. The other staff members, predominantly men, were now busy with their heads down at their desks, separated with dividers onto which they had pinned family photos, their fantasies, notes and telephone numbers. They acknowledged her as they went into the photocopying room, located just behind her to the left, some questioned where Christine was and then courteously welcomed her to the fifth floor.

When Kamal later returned with a cup of coffee from the vending machine, she saw Rohit was standing at the desk looking through his diary. After a brief pause, she continued forward.

"Morning Christine, can you get me the number for..,"

"Morning Rohit, Christine's off sick, I'll be helping out for a few days," she said putting her coffee down. Rohit paused. She was wearing a black flowing skirt and mustard coloured top, her hair was layered and shorter, just below the shoulders and it was flicked back. Her eyes were made up with some black kohl and she was wearing a coffee coloured lipstick. He could just smell her subtle perfume, it was not overpowering, just floating about her. She appeared to have lost some weight, but looked beautiful, as always.

"Um, okay. Well, Christine keeps a telephone and address book here somewhere, I need the number for Karl Wilson please," he said walking towards his office. She looked for Christine's telephone book and eventually found it in the bottom of the third desk drawer.

"W, W," she whispered. She wrote the number down on a piece of paper and also picked up the messages she'd taken earlier this morning into him.

"Here's the number and here are some messages, one of them is urgent."

"Oh thanks," he said taking the telephone number off her and picking up the phone receiver, "oh and Kamal, can you shut the door on your way out please? Thanks."

Kamal shut the door and walked back to the desk. Maybe this was not going to be as bad as she thought, if she stuck to her job and he stuck to his, there'd be no problems and after all, he was managing a large Norwegian project hence he would have little time to think about a silly little kiss!

Rohit had soon left for the second meeting and she was not expecting him till after lunch. She later went down to have her lunch with Angela and Danielle in the canteen. They were disappointed to hear no sparks were flying between her and Rohit so they instead caught up on each other's weekend and as always, her friends had a story or two to tell and this Monday, it was Angela's turn.

"I swear he can come back anytime, oh yes please!"

"That good?" Danielle asked wide eyed.

"Danielle, I'm not joking, multiple o's, have you not noticed my glowing face?"

Still grinning from her friend's frolicking stories she made her way back up to fifth floor all be that unwillingly. She continued with some typing followed by photocopying. Rohit was back at 1.30pm and went straight into his office preparing himself for the next meeting, when Kamal received a phone call.

"The meeting's been cancelled Rohit," Kamal called him from her phone, not bothering to get up from the chair.

"Oh that's great, gives me time to catch up. Actually, can you ask Thomas to come into my office and I may need you for some dictation later okay?"

"Yeah just give me a shout when you're ready."

As she typed she could hear the conference call between Rohit, Thomas and Jonathon out on the site in Norway. Rohit was way too busy to even notice she was there and even though she was relieved there was a slight ache within, which she chose to pay no heed to.

"Coffee?" she later called him from her desk when her body itself was crying out for a boost of caffeine.

"I'd love a coffee thank you," he said putting his pen down and rubbing his eyes.

When she returned with his coffee and he asked her to take down some dictation she realised he had circles under his eyes and looked quite exhausted. As she sat down with her shorthand notebook he walked around her with his coffee and dictated the letter, asking her to read it out, chopping and changing it and then asked her to type out as soon as possible to fax over to headquarters.

Kamal was so glad it was time to go home and grabbed her coat and bag ready to dart away. As she put her coat on, she looked into Rohit's office to see him buried head down in paperwork. She popped her head in the office, "I'm off now. Have a nice evening."

"Oh, yes, thanks for all your help Kamal. I'll see you tomorrow."

As she departed, Rohit stood up, put his hands in his pockets and watched her walk away. He had resisted saying anything to her regarding that night. He had to take this nice and slowly, he messed up last time and he did not want to make the same mistake again.

Chapter 6

30th June 1990 - Sindy's wedding day and she looked absolutely stunning; like a model glammed up for a bridal magazine shoot. Unlike her older sisters, she had her big day all planned out; her outfit, her beautician for the day, her jewellery, venue and where she was going to live following marriage, which was not with her in-laws, obviously, that she had made perfectly clear. Sarbjit, her husband, was well wrapped around her little finger. She had made sure he had prepared for them to move out following just two weeks of the marriage and the flat was decorated according to her own taste of course. But there were some things Sindy had no control over.

"Oh why did the weather have to be so crap!" she said in frustration, as she waited in the bedroom with her sisters, friends and cousins to depart for the temple. It was dull and pouring down with rain.

"Well you could always complain to the almighty," Nindy smiled ironically.

"Dad looks happy," Kamal said as she came into the bedroom.

"Yeah, he's finally getting rid of this one!" Nindy laughed.

"Well it's not my fault I know what I want in life," Sindy smiled sarcastically followed by a frown as she looked at her hands, "the *mehndi* has not come out as dark as I wanted it to."

"Don't be silly," their cousin Charanjit said "it's fine. It's as dark as it could get in your case, a reflection of how much your mother-in-law loves you, or not!"

"Well, I am after all taking away her precious son. If she had her way, the marriage would never have happened," she smiled sarcastically.

"Well I wouldn't wish you as a daughter-in-law on anyone," Kamal laughed.

"Well we can't all be as perfect as you Kamal dear," Sindy smiled sarcastically, "and by the way don't expect any melodrama at the end of the day from me. There is no way I am going to have a make-up smudged face for the camera to zoom into, so please, all of you, save your tears."

There was a brief moment of silence as everyone digested the last remark, followed by laughter.

Despite the bad weather and the obvious hostility between the bride and her mother-in-law, the wedding was triumphant and when the time eventually came for Sindy to depart, much to her own disappointment, she had succumbed to overwhelming tears, as the three sisters embraced each other.

"I'll make some tea," Kamal said as her mother put her feet up.

"Oh that would be lovely," Parminder smiled and closed her eyes in exhaustion.

The kitchen looked like a bombsite, but Kamal was too tired to tackle that now, what they all needed now was a nice strong cup of tea. She took two cups to her father and grandmother and then finally sat down with her mother.

"Now I can really rest," her mother said leaning her head back on the sofa. "I hope she is as happy as you and Nindy are. I'm sure she will be. It's been her choice all the way through. You are happy aren't you? Raj has not started to drink too much has he? I do worry sometimes."

"No, no, mum, he just gets a bit carried away at weddings and parties."

"Well that's quite normal, he is a true Punjabi after all," she said sipping her tea and smiling.

Kamal was stopping over a couple of days to help her mother with the post-wedding clear-up. She did not want to burden her mother with the fact that Raj and she hardly spoke to each other, about him coming home late almost every night and over the weekends during the early hours of the morning, that when he was around he was in a world of his own, that she could not remember the last time they made love, that her father-in-law argued with him about not bringing home as much money as he used to, questioning him about where he was spending it; she did not want to tell her how unhappy she really was.

"That's all I ever wanted," Parminder said, snapping Kamal out of her thoughts, "for my daughters to be happy."

"Happier than what you had ever been?" Kamal looked towards her mother. There was silence.

"Promise me one thing Kamal. If your husband ever mistreats you, you will not put up with it?"

"Like you did you mean?"

"I had no choice."

"We all have choices mum."

"No. You girls have choices. I come from a different generation."

"Mum, did you ever consider leaving? I mean walking out?" Kamal asked, almost looking for a solution to her own problem. There was brief silence.

Parminder sighed, "no."

"Never?" Kamal asked her again.

Her mum just shook her head, "I had the three of you to consider."

"And now?"

"Don't be silly! Besides, he's changed."

"Has he, really?"

"Yes, things are nowhere near as bad as they used to be."

"Yeah, probably because he simply hasn't got the energy anymore! I hate him for what he used to do."

"Kamal! That's your father!"

"Yes, but when I think of my father, all I see is an angry man and images of him beating you, dragging you up from your hair, or kicking you relentlessly."

"Yeah well that was a long, long time ago now."

"Why did you never call the police, leave home, seek refuge, anything?"

"It's not the way I was brought up."

Kamal shook her head, "will you promise me one thing now mum? Times are changing. If he touches you now, you just leave him."

"Oh don't be silly, where would I go?"

"Mum there is a world out there, out of this house, just waiting to be explored. You could go anywhere you want. Stop feeling so tied down," Kamal released some of her own anxieties, "promise me, you won't put up with it anymore."

"Okay I promise," Parminder shook her head and smiled at her daughter.

Kamal smiled back; she was sure her mum would not have aged so soon had she have led a happy content life. She had spent almost her entire life within these four walls. Listening to the taunts from her husband and poisonous mother-in-law, yet not once did she retaliate; she had the patience of a saint. Kamal wondered how she herself would be able to keep up the farce of her, having the perfect marriage.

Meanwhile, Davinder and his mother were sat in the dining room.

"Listen son, you are still young, men older than you go to India to remarry all the time, but look at you, no-one can say you are the father of three grown up girls. I know you have desperately wanted a son. Now your responsibility to your daughters is over, you can think about yourself now. I am with you every step of the way. Please also give me the grandson I have wanted all my life."

"Ma, are you going senile? I am a grandfather myself now. My responsibilities have not decreased they have increased. I can't remarry now, it's too late."

Davinder had had this conversation with his mother several times now, while she was adamant he remarried, he thought otherwise. There was a time when he wanted nothing but to walk away from his marriage and following Sindy's birth and Parminder's hysterectomy, he'd thought that the perfect excuse. But pressures from the extended family tied him down and the older he was getting, the more he was coming to terms of not having the son he always wanted or the perfect wife.

"I still think you should think about it son," his mother said as she got up holding her aching knees with her back arched. Davinder watched his mother shuffle out of the room. She had never liked Parminder; he guessed she had her suspicions too, right from the onset, but like him, was too proud to voice the doubt.

Chapter 7

Emma entered the bedroom wearing the plum coloured lingerie Raj had bought for her,

"Wow," he gasped at her perfect size ten figure; long slender legs and hair cascading over her shoulders. She joined him in bed and kissed him on his neck, face, lips and chest.

"Happy belated Valentines," she whispered in his ear and softly chewed at his ear lobe before she caressed his neck again with her soft lips. She did not have to work very hard to arouse him, she did that by just pressing her naked body against his and he in return provided her with complete satisfaction; she loved him and wanted him desperately to be with her the whole time now.

"That was amazing!" she said kissing his chest and then on the lips again as they finished making love for what seemed like forever.

"I just can't get enough of you Em," he said as she looked down at him, he ran his hand through her golden hair and kissed her forehead.

"Well there's nothing stopping you from moving in."

"I will, it is just a matter of time, I promise. You know this is where I want to be. But you know the problem. I wouldn't worry too much though; it's just a matter of time now," Raj pulled her down and kissed her again.

Kamal slung the files onto the floor.

"What's up?" Angela asked, "looks like you're ready to kill Craig."

"Why are men so irritating! I mean just leave the work in the tray and it will get done! Why doesn't he just stay out of my face!"

"He's just finding any excuse to be around you," Danielle winked.

"Oh please!"

"Come on, spill, what's really irritating you?" Angela laughed.

"Just when I thought everything was fine after Valentine's night, he did not bother coming home Friday night."

"He stayed out all night again! What the hell Kamal, why are you not asking him where he is?"

"I do ask. He just says he was at a mate's and I've even called these so-called mates, and they will just confirm that he had been with them and that he stayed with them because he did not want to upset me, because he was drunk. My in-laws have turned blue trying to talk some sense into him, but nothing seems to be getting through. He has to be having an affair, there's no other explanation. We had sex after I've forgotten how long and that was because I made an effort in that tacky underwear I bought, he must've thought I was so bloody desperate. I was just trying to spice things up and then he does not even bother to turn up on the Friday night!"

"He's having an affair, I keep telling you," Angela almost sang out rolling her eyes in frustration.

"But he has even sworn on his son's life, saying he would not even dream of it."

"And you believe him?"

"Well why would he swear on his son's life unnecessarily?"

"I'm not convinced. Why don't you spy on him!" Danielle put her hands together and squinted her eyes.

"Yeah right," Kamal rolled her eyes as the ringing phone disturbed their conversation.

Raj's aloof behaviour towards her was increasing her hidden desires for Rohit. She herself was not sure whether she was frustrated with Raj or with the fact that she had not seen Rohit for two weeks now. He had gone back home for three weeks and she missed him desperately. It's true what people say she thought; absence does make the heart grow fonder and why would she not be fond of Rohit? He was perfect in every way. He was a true gentleman, attractive, humorous, charming, engaging, captivating - he was the complete package and she was falling hopelessly in love with him and she sensed that the feeling was mutual. It was the way his eyes always searched for her in the canteen, or when he found any excuse to see her in her office after seeing Craig, when he'd just sit at the end of her table and talk to her, it was the way he almost seemed to be waiting for her by the lift standing waiting casually with his hands in his pockets, when it was time to go home and then walked out with her and then stand talking in the car park about anything and everything. She missed everything about him, especially the way he made her feel like she was the only person that mattered. She could not wait for him to come back and envisaged to tell him exactly how she felt. Maybe this time apart was exactly what she needed to realise just how much he meant to her.

***

"I don't know why you even bother to come home!"

"I've got no choice," Raj said with his back towards her. Kamal got up and turned the bedside lamp on.

"We need to talk. This cannot go on."

"What?"

"You coming and going as you please."

"Oh I'm sorry," he had said sitting up, "but I don't feel it necessary to seek your permission."

"What, even the fact that I am your wife?"

"Yeah, well wife or no wife, I will come and go as I please. Anyway, what's with the sudden nagging, you're usually fast asleep by the time I come in," he said lying back down again.

"So you are just going to continue doing as you please?"

"Yes. I will, it's my life and I shall live it as I wish. Stop behaving like the nagging wife, it does not suit you. If you have any problems, you know where the door is."

Kamal closed her eyes in anguish and counted to ten.

"Fine. You do what you want, and I will do what I want. Don't say I did not warn you!"

"Yeah, whatever," Raj wished she would do something, anything that would give him that incentive to leave her. It was after all his intention to provoke her, push her away, ignore her, treat her like she was non-existent and irrelevant, giving importance to his friends and family, deliberately forgetting her birthday or their anniversary. He wished so hard that she would just pack up her bags and leave, but following every argument the following day she would behave oblivious to their problems and keep up the bloody false pretence. But he persisted in pushing all her buttons, in the hope that one day she would just snap and walk.

***

Kamal waited all day for Rohit to walk in through the office doors, anticipating that he would be as desperate to see her following his holiday as she was, but there was no sign of him. She knew he was back, as she had heard Craig welcoming him back on the phone.

"You staying for long?" Danielle asked as she got prepared to leave.

"Just finishing this letter off and then I'll be out, you go on ahead. I'll see you tomorrow."

"Okay, don't stay too long. Hope Angela's feeling better tomorrow, she sounded terrible."

"Yeah, I know. See you tomorrow Danielle," Kamal smiled as her friend departed and waited till it was 5.15pm, before she grabbed her coat and bag and made her way up to the fifth floor. She was relieved to see Christine had left. Rohit's office light was still on and she could see him with his head down through the window. A few workers were still engaged in their work, too busy to have noticed her as she walked forward and knocked on the door.

"Come in," he said with his head still down.

"Hi," she said popping her head round.

"Oh Kamal! Hi come on in."

His skin had a healthy glow; kissed by the Indian sun.

"Thought I'd pop in to say hi."

"Oh thanks, first day back and bombarded with work," he said putting his pen down and running his hand through his soft hair.

"Were you going to stop over?"

"Yeah just for a couple of hours."

"How was India?" Kamal said walking in and sitting on the chair opposite him.

"Fine, yeah, stayed mostly with friends and family, three weeks just flew by," he smiled and folded his arms. Kamal silently cursed those three long weeks, which for her were like three weeks of torture.

"So how are you?"

"Fine, fine, same old same old, I missed you," she said softly. Rohit just looked straight at her and for a few seconds or more, they remained static.

"Well I missed you too, as a friend of course," he shrugged his shoulders.

"Yeah, yeah of course," she smiled awkwardly.

"How's your son and Raj?"

"They're fine thanks."

"And your sisters?"

"Oh they're fine, so busy in their married lives, we hardly see each other."

"Good. Listen Kamal, I would love to sit and chat, but I really need to go through all this paperwork. I'll talk to you tomorrow, if that is okay?"

"Yes, yes, sorry, I should know better. I'll see you tomorrow. Don't work too hard will you," she said getting up and going towards the door. She closed her eyes and cringed with discomfort as she walked out. Had she been misreading the signs? He did not seem to be as pleased to see her as she'd thought he would be. His body language and his eye contact seemed so superficial.

"What were you expecting, you stupid fool!" she mumbled to herself as she got into her car, turned on the ignition and put on her belt, "why would he be interested in married with one child pathetic little you! Oh you fool!" she continued to mutter to herself as she started to drive off tormented furthermore by deep feelings she could do nothing with.

Rohit sat back in his chair and smiled smugly. His charm was driving her insane, just as he intended. It was time to turn up the charm and wait for her to be completely and utterly besotted. It was so obvious she was in need of some tender love and care. It was not long now before she would be coming through those doors, straight into his arms and then he could finish off what he started that Christmas.

***

"So come on then, what could you not wait to tell me?" Raj said as he kissed Emma and then sat with her on the sofa.

She held his hand, "you ready?"

"Stop teasing, what is it?"

"Well….I'm pregnant!" Emma said beaming with delight.

"What! But how, when?" Raj asked.

"Well I don't really have to explain how do I?" she rolled her eyes then smiled, "I thought I was just late, but I went to the doctors, gave in a urine sample and it was confirmed this morning!" Emma waited for a reaction.

"But I thought you were on the pill?"

"I must've missed a day, I don't know? Is there something wrong?" she frowned.

"Wrong? We can't have it, you do know that don't you?"

"Can't have it? What do you mean? Are you asking me to have an abortion?" Emma frowned at a totally disorientated Raj; this was not the reaction she had expected.

"Well we can't have it. It's just out of the question."

"And why not?"

"Look, we have plenty of time to have babies, but now, is not the right time."

"Not the right time, well when will it be the right time? That's all I get from you. How long have we been together? No, I refuse to be your bit on the side and I am not getting rid of my baby, whether you like it or not!" Emma was up on her feet now. "How dare you Raj! I thought you loved me!" Emma stormed into the bedroom of her apartment and slammed the door shut. Raj put both his hands through his hair and covered his face.

"Shit! Shit, shit fucking shit!"

***

Kamal desperately needed to clear her head and decided she would meet up with her sister Nindy at her parents' for the weekend; a weekend away with those she loved, where her life was a little less complicated is just what she needed now and the fact their grandmother had gone to India was an added bonus.

Out of all the three sisters it was Sindy who was having the time of her life, as the reins of her life were securely in her hands. She now was the happy owner of a prestigious boutique stocking but only exquisite Indian dresses on the High Street, her architect husband worshipping the ground she walked upon. She was secure both emotionally and financially.

Nindy and Kamal were lying in the new double beds their parents had replaced their old beds with, in preparation for when their daughters came over to stay with their children. The room had been redecorated with a pale pink paper with ditsy flowers and the duvet covers pink with matching curtains, quite a contrast from the drab white woodchip paper they'd had.

"So come on, tell me how you are really? I can tell you have something on your mind."

Kamal covered her son with the duvet, as he lay fast asleep and pecked his chubby cheek softly; he looked so peaceful in his sleep.

"If I tell you something, you promise you won't say anything, to anyone?"

"Yeah okay, I promise," Nindy said curious, propping herself up in the bed, her elbow resting on the pillow and her head resting on her hand eager to hear what Kamal had to say.

"There's someone at work, I fancy, well, like, as in really like," she blurted out.

"You what, you mean as in a man? You fancy a man?"

"Well of course it's a man!"

"Have you lost your mind, you're a married woman!" Nindy was now sitting right up and whispering, patting her twins as they stirred in their sleep.

"Am I?"

"Well of course you are, what do you mean, am I?"

"I mean me and Raj…there's nothing there. You know he enjoyed his drink, stayed out till late and never came home sometimes. Well his drinking has decreased, but he is still coming home late and sometimes not at all. I'll question him, but he squirms his way out each time. We hardly talk and when we do, we argue. The last time we had sex was over Valentines and that was because I bloody made an effort. It's just getting from bad to worse. He treats me like I am non-existent. All I do is work, cook, clean, iron and entertain guests by playing the perfect daughter-in-law. He puts on a fine act in front of friends and family, but when we are alone, we are like strangers. And that is when Rohit comes in,"

"Rohit?"

"Yes, Rohit. He is so lovely Nindy. He is so, charming, intelligent and wonderful to be around. He makes my heart beat."

"You never told me about your problems with Raj before, you always seemed so happy and content."

"Yeah well, that's all been a show. We both know the only people keeping us together are his parents and our son. I needed to speak to someone, it's driving me mad. It's not working between me and Raj. I can't live like this forever. I need to get out of this relationship before it kills me and tempts me to do something I regret!"

Nindy was now sitting with her legs and arms crossed. Kamal looked at her in the dim light; she looked so much like their mother and for a moment, she felt like she was actually talking to her.

"I really think you should try to work things out with Raj. I mean what would people say? I can't even bear to think," she put her hand to her head in disbelief.

"Yeah I know, don't worry, I have no plans on having a full-fledged affair with Rohit! Besides, I'm not even sure how he really feels about me.

He's just a distraction from the problems at home. But I really cannot live on with Raj. Believe me Nindy I have tried. I have tried so hard."

"Have you spoken to his parents?"

"Oh they nag him for coming home late and all that, but I don't think they realise how bad things are between us."

"Maybe that is what you need to do, talk to them."

"I would, if it is what I wanted, but it's not. I simply do not love him Nindy."

"And this Rohit?"

Kamal waited before she answered, "all I know is that I think of him when he is not around, I think of him when I go to sleep, I think of him when I get up in the morning, I like to be around him, I miss him when I do not see him at work...which I guess means, I love him, doesn't it?"

"You are playing a very dangerous game Kamal, a very dangerous game indeed!"

"Yes, but I haven't done anything yet!"

"Yet? If you want to take my advice, don't even go down that road. You're not only going to let yourself down, you are going to let your in-laws down, as well as your own family. You have too much to lose. I mean how much do you actually know about this guy?"

Kamal just shrugged her shoulders. Nindy was younger than her, but right now she felt like an elder.

"Exactly. Make sure it does not go beyond friendship. Like I said, you have too much to lose. Think before you act. How do you know that it's not this - infatuation that you have with this Rohit that is getting between you and Raj? No Kamal. If you don't want to think about anyone else, at least think about your son, you aren't a teenager. You're a mother, a daughter a wife and daughter-in-law. Get your act together and if things don't improve, then you need to sit and talk with all your elders and try to work out a solution, including mum and dad. I mean come on, does he hit you? Your life cannot be as bad as what mum's was and did she ever once let us down? No. So at least think of her before you go dragging her name through the dirt as well! I'm going to sleep now, if you have any sense at all, you will stay away from this Rohan, or whatever his name is, or better still quit the job!" Nindy lay down in bed; she had never spoken to Kamal in this tone before, but she could not believe what Kamal had just disclosed, she'd never have expected such shenanigans from Kamal, Sindy maybe, but not Kamal. How could she be so stupid!

Kamal stayed sitting up in bed and let a tear run down her cheek. She knew Nindy was right, but how was she to explain this to her aching heart? Nindy's wise words played around in her head as she tried to sleep. Maybe she was right; maybe she was not trying hard enough to keep her husband at home. Maybe it was her that was pushing him away, by not giving him the time and the attention he was probably wanting. Danielle once said that men want their woman to mother them during the day and behave like a whore during the night; maybe she was the problem?

A knock on the door at 6.35am woke both Kamal and Nindy. It was their mother; their grandmother had died in India.

***

"Why do they have to bloody howl while crying?" Sindy frowned standing in the kitchen with her sisters, as friends and family came round to pay their condolences, all the sisters dressed in white in respect of the deceased.

"Oh shut up Sindy!" Nindy snapped.

"Well, it's not like any of the women crying liked her. I mean look at *chachi* (aunty) she could not stand her, so why is she crying? And aunty Palo, she did not have one nice word to say about her!" Sindy said, hurt and annoyed.

"I'm glad she's dead," Kamal said under her breath as she washed the tea cups.

"Kamal, she was our grandmother!" Nindy exclaimed.

"Yeah, and the main reason behind mum's misery, the stirring that woman did," Kamal said bitterly.

"Well mum should have just stood up for herself!" Sindy felt the need to defend her deceased grandmother.

"Can you both just stop it and save your opinions for another time and concentrate on the mourners please?" Nindy had her hands on her hips and looked disappointedly at Kamal further still.

Kamal was not going to miss her grandmother; she had always been partial to her sisters, especially Sindy, just like her father. Her words still echoed in her ears, "who will ask for her hand in marriage? Her complexion is so dark, don't know who she has taken on after, it certainly isn't anyone in our family." She had felt excluded from the care and affection she poured out for her sisters, but her mother had always compensated for what she was not receiving from her grandmother, or father.

Being a Sunday, the extended family had gone to the airport to arrange urgent flight tickets to India for Davinder, his older brother Satwinder and Parminder, no expense was spared. The cremation had been postponed until they reached India themselves, which under normal circumstances would have taken place the same day, but Davinder was adamant to carry out all the rituals with his older brother. Parminder had never been back to India since she first came to England in 1967. Since she'd been in England, her father had passed away, her mother had passed away and even her only brother, but not once was she allowed to go back home to mourn their death with her immediate family. Davinder's exact words were, "what's the point of going now? What has happened has happened. You can't bring them back." And what was he doing now? Kamal looked towards her dad as she took the tea round for the male mourners; she could not help but feel bitter. Why did her mum have to go anyway she thought? Why could he not just go on his own and leave her here in peace to celebrate the death of her satanic mother-in-law!

Kamal requested compassionate leave from work, an excuse to have a few more days away. Her parents were on their way to India, Nindy and Sindy had returned to their respective homes and she was alone in the house, having offered to clean and lock-up. She looked out of the window towards the Methodist Church right opposite the house, as she dusted the window sill. She smiled, recalling playing with her sisters around the Church during the long summer holidays. They'd play hide and seek, share the one bike they had and play hopscotch from dawn up to when it was time for their dad to return from work. Nearing that time, they would get back in the house and make sure their bedroom was neat and tidy, for the fear of being reprimanded. Their mother would be busy getting dinner ready, while their grandmother updated their dad on the day's events; even something as trivial as their mum letting the milk boil over got reported back. Kamal was not going to miss her at all; she despised her. As she wandered around, dusting and putting things back in their place, beginning to get engulfed in upsetting memories of years gone by, the empty house suddenly began to feel quite eerie. She looked round at the lounge. The settee was covered in a horrible beige coloured floral cover her grandmother had bought from the Bullring Market, the floor was covered in a brown carpet and the walls were covered in the same old woodchip paper painted beige. Years ago, the room had a black leather sofa with yellow cushions, a loud orange and brown wallpaper and brown carpets. It was a lot trendier then, very retro, but now the room just looked so lacklustre and dated. She felt sadness, in every room she walked through. But, amongst the gloomy sullen memories, much fonder memories broke through, those she spent in solace with her mother or with her sisters. They were like rays of sunshine forcing their way through dense dull clouds. When she thought of those memories, she felt warmth, but when she thought of those of her father and his mother, she felt a chill and a shiver ran down her spine as she now found herself stood in her grandmother's room. The single bed was made up, untouched from the day she had departed three weeks ago; who was to know that she was never to return? She could just see her pink slippers from under the bed never to be worn again. The ticking of the clock seemed to be echoing louder and louder, as she felt unable to move. The room suddenly felt cold. Was she watching her? Was she telling her to get out of her room, like she used to? She stepped backwards slowly out of the room and swallowed the lump in her throat as she closed the door and walked down the dark narrow landing of the old Victorian terraced home and down the stairs, not daring to look back.

Now feeling the need to leave the house she checked all the doors and windows were securely locked and exhaled at the thought of going back to the home where she belonged. That brief period of time on her own, being able to weigh out her past with her present, put everything in perspective. Nindy was right, Rohit was an infatuation a mere distraction; it was Raj she should be concentrating on. She had to win her husband back and make him want to come home to her every night.

As she pulled up the drive of her marital home, she momentarily just sat and stared at the modest detached house and her dear father-in-law's immaculate front garden. She adored him for being the person he was. She shared little dialogue with him, but he was a good man; much more of a man than her dad. She loved the sweet relationship between her in-laws. Her mother-in-law would cluck around him, making him cups of tea, tidying his tie when they were going out and he would in turn admire her, paying her sweet compliments. They both put together had more energy than she did. They loved life and that was a lesson that she needed to learn, to love and respect what she had. Even though times were sometimes testing, she did love this house and it was now up to her to make a perfect house, a happy home.

"Hello," she shouted out as she opened the door and smiled as her son came running towards her, her mother-in-law following closely behind. She hugged her son and then her mother-in-law and walked into the living room to be greeted by her father-in-law. How could she even think of hurting these wonderful people who had taught her how to live?

Chapter 8

Raj put the phone down to his wife, still not being able to process how attentive she had become over the last few weeks. She called him at work asking him what he wanted for dinner, asked him how work was, insisted they shopped together, sat next to him to watch football and her imagination in the bedroom had just soared! He did not know what happened whilst she'd been at her parents', but whatever it was, he couldn't complain. However, keeping two women happy was exhausting. Whereas before he was making the excuses to his wife and family, for coming home late or not at all, he was now making excuses to Emma. He loved Emma, but Kamal was by far a lot less complicated, especially now Emma was pregnant.

"You're on track to breaking your own record, you lucky cow. Can't remember the last time I had one!" Danielle frowned.

"Oh, how sad," Angela was generally devastated for Danielle.

"It was amazing," Kamal smiled and held her head back.

"I still live in hope for that one orgasm never mind bloody multiple! How many again?"

Kamal held out three fingers in the air.

"Three!" Danielle looked on in disbelief.

"And I feel rejuvenated," Kamal closed her eyes in satisfaction.

Rohit looked towards Kamal as she sat in the canteen with her colleagues talking and laughing, oblivious to his presence. She had cut her hair into a short bob now and it suited her, but he preferred it when it was longer. She seemed a lot more happier these days and no longer detected despondency in her eyes; he could not help but feel resentful for the lack of attention he was getting. The tables were turned. He watched her place her dining tray in the trolley, still in deep conversation with her friends and still unaware of his presence. As she walked by, he called out to her.

"Hello Kamal."

"Oh hi Rohit," her colleagues continued forward as she stopped, "how are you? Have not seen you around, busy?" she stood leaning on the empty chair opposite him smiling.

"Seems like you are busier than me, you hardly come up to see me anymore."

"Oh you know what it's like with the new project and all, Craig is so busy and plus, I've been attending a management course."

"Jackie obviously sees the potential. Everything okay at home?"

"Yeah everything is just great," her smile widened.

"Good."

"I better go now. Got loads to do," Kamal smiled inwardly as she walked away, proud that she had managed to move on.

In Venice - Piazzo San Marco and Kamal was in total awe of the architectural splendour surrounding her. The sky was a deep turquoise blue, she was in one of the most romantic cities in the world, walking hand in hand with her handsome husband over Venetian bridges, through the backstreets of quiet and quaint Venetian streets oozing character, through enchanting museums and being dined out in the authentic Italian restaurants. Raj had surprised her on the Friday by presenting her with two tickets to Venice for the weekend and she was totally mesmerized, fascinated by the ingenious glass craft ranging from contemporary vases, glasses, goblets, paperweights to even folded glass shirts exhibited in shop windows and further still by the beautiful array of Murano jewellery.

"Thank you," Kamal squeezed Raj's hand as the gondolier propelled his gondola through the Venetian lagoon.

"You can thank me properly later," Raj kissed her hand.

Raj desperately wanted to confess to Kamal, but he just could not find the right time. Every time he looked at her and opened his mouth to start the conversation, he halted and changed the subject. He promised himself he would tell her tomorrow and then tomorrow again, but he just couldn't do it. Things were so perfect between them and this was the happiest he had ever seen her. If Emma had not got herself pregnant, it would have been easier, he'd have just finished with her and it could have been just another mindless fling, but she was pregnant and he wondered how long he could keep this dark secret from his wife and family. All he could think of was to keep both Emma and Kamal sweet. It was hard work and exhausting, but it was the only way.

**

"Do you like it?" Raj said placing the keys to the new house in Emma's hands. The baby was due in November and Emma only yet had just a very small bump, the rest of her body, arms, legs and face, looked just as they had always been slim, toned and gorgeous. Pregnancy suited her, she looked so radiant and her healthy, long, glossy blond hair was befitting for a hair product advert.

"It's wonderful, but when are you going to tell her Raj?" Emma sighed.

"I'm working on it," he said putting his arms around her and kissed her on the nose. "In the meantime, you are going to want for nothing. Our baby is going to have nothing but the best. Come upstairs."

The house was one of the new modern builds, situated on a new estate just on the outskirts of Birmingham, with the typical magnolia walls, thick beige carpets and low ceilings.

"It's brand new, never been lived in before," he said taking her up the stairs by the hand. He showed her the bright and airy white tiled bathroom. The window was open and she could hear tweeting birds and rustling tree leaves. There were two bedrooms, the master with an en-suite and a brand new bed placed in the middle of the room, the mattress still covered in its plastic cover. She walked round the bed towards the window which overlooked the garden. It was nice, clean and adequate. "Now come through here," he said taking her by hand, "close your eyes." Emma smiled and closed her eyes. Raj opened the door to the second bedroom, "okay open them. What do you think?"

"Oh Raj!"

"I told you, my child will want for nothing."

A solid pine cot stood in the middle of the room with a mobile, a matching solid pine chest of drawers, a small wardrobe and a changing unit. On top of the chest of drawers was placed a great big teddy bear and a vase of flowers. The walls were wallpapered a neutral pale yellow.

"Do you like it?"

"I don't know what to say. You did all this on your own?"

"Yes. Look I've even bought some clothes for the baby," he said walking up to the wardrobe and opening the doors. On small hangers were some baby grows and small outfits for a new born baby. She held the clothes in her hands and smiled. He'd even bought a bath, which was on the changing unit along with bottles of shampoo, baby lotion and some towels.

"It's perfect Raj."

"Thank you Emma, for being so patient. This is all temporary of course, one day we will have a place, which we will both choose together, I promise. You can choose how you want this place decorated in the meantime, but I wanted to get this room ready, I wanted this to be the real surprise."

"It's wonderful," she said looking round again, "I have to tell my mother as well now, I can't keep this quiet from her anymore," she said with her hand on her pregnant belly. "I'm going to need her support. I've avoided her for long enough now." She put her arms round Raj. All she wanted was for them to be together. She knew it was difficult for him, but she was willing to wait.

With Emma's arms around him, Raj could not deny the respect he had for Kamal, but it was all he had for her and his mind was made up. There was no more room for compromise; Emma was definitely the woman he wanted to spend the rest of his life with.

Chapter 9

"Raj's mother, let's go to India!"

"Yes, it's like popping down the road isn't it? Where's this come from anyway?" Joginder stopped dusting and looked towards her husband, who sat reading his newspaper, with his glasses resting on the tip of his nose.

"Well, I think we deserve a break," he closed the newspaper and removed his glasses thoughtfully, "we'll take Junior with us, so that the kid's jobs are not disrupted, besides, I could not imagine being anywhere without the little devil. Or we could ask them to come with us of course, Kamal has never been to India."

"Exactly how long have you been planning this for?" she shook her head and picked up his teacup.

"It was in the pub last night," he put his glasses back on and opened up the newspaper shuffling the sheets straight, "Patel has just come back from India and he said it was just the break he needed. It was then I realised that we had not been for six years. So I was thinking….."

"You were thinking let us go gallivanting to India. What about the children?"

"Children? It may have escaped your notice my dear wife, but the children are no longer children. They are perfectly capable of looking after themselves," Balbir closed the paper again and peered at his wife over his glasses.

"Yes well, I suppose it has been a long time since we've seen the family. But we will need to discuss with the children first."

"Yes, yes. We'll talk to them this evening itself."

Later that Sunday evening, Balbir sat at the end of his dining table looking down proudly at his perfect family seated all around him. At times he wanted to scream out his inner happiness from the top of a rooftop, but remained humble. It was so gratifying to hear his friends, neighbours and family speak so highly of his handsome sons, his beautiful, respectful and dignified, docile daughter-in-laws. He would listen sympathetically to the stories of those who were not so fortunate, who dreaded going home, because the family dynamics were so grim. He smiled down at his future generation; his grandchildren each a replica of their fathers, except for his granddaughter Manpreet who was a mini version of her beautiful mother and then of course his wife, as radiant as she was the first day he saw her on his wedding night. He was truly grateful for having been blessed with a life partner who stood by him from when he had nothing to today, when he had everything.

"Baba, do you want more rice?" Manpreet asked noting that her grandfather had finished his rice.

"Ah, see how my granddaughter cares for me. No darling, no more rice," Balbir smiled at his granddaughter and then looked up towards the rest of the family. "Me and your mother were thinking of going to India next month, what do you all think? We could go as a family, if you all want?"

Raj looked up in horror, "no! I mean sorry, no I can't, there is no question of me going. Really busy at work, could not even think of it."

"What about you Kamal?"

"No dad, I have the same problem at work, it would be very difficult."

"And we can't go, what with the kids and school," Deepa looked towards Varinder for support and Kamal smiled, almost giggled, for she knew Deepa had barely got over the culture shock from the first time she'd gone with her son in the month of January, when he was just three months old.

"Is it okay if we go then and take Junior with us?" Balbir looked towards Raj and Kamal and then the older couple.

"Well I suppose you will have to, since we both need to be at work," Raj shrugged his shoulders as Kamal looked towards him.

"How long are you planning to go for dad?" Kamal asked, the thought of her son not being around made her heart skip a beat.

"Oh no more than two or three weeks, what do you think Raj's ma?"

"Two weeks is more than enough."

"Oh let's make it three, it'll take a day or two getting there and settling in."

"Yes I suppose. Is everybody happy with that?"

"Yes that's fine with us," Raj answered for all four looking round for any objections, "fancy going on an aeroplane Junior?" Raj smiled down at his son.

"Yes!" he nodded his head enthusiastically.

"I want to go too," Sukhdeep frowned and folded his arms. Since they had moved into their own home, he did on occasions feel insecure around his cousin getting all the attention from his grandparents.

"Well you can't. Did you not hear what mommy said? You need to be at school," madam Manpreet threw her brother a ticking-off look.

"I hate school!" Sukhdeep continued to sulk.

"Well sulking will get you nowhere," Varinder chuckled at his son.

"Yeah, I'm going to India, I'm going on a big plane!" Kamal cuddled her saving grace lovingly; though the thought of him not being around made her heart flutter nervously.

"I wish I had more time to think about Junior going away, but nevertheless, that's what I like about this family," Kamal said later as she washed up and Deepa dried, "decisions are made together."

"Yes, we are quite fortunate."

"There were no discussions at my mum and dad's. My dad made all the decisions and my mum would not question any of them, she daren't," Kamal said recalling her dad's hold over her mother.

"How is your mum? It had been a few years since she had been to India, must have been emotional for her."

"Yes, twenty-four years since she had last been to India, can you imagine, going home after all those years?"

"What was it like for her?"

"She said things had changed so much. But when she went home, surprised my dad let her, she felt like she had stepped back in time. Her parent's home lay empty. She got her uncle to unlock the doors and when she stepped into the house, she said all the memories came sweeping back. She sounded so emotional. She even managed to meet an old friend after all these year."

"Wow."

"I remember when we were young, she would tell us stories that my grandfather had told her as a child and she would recollect those memories so fondly. She'd tell us tales of her school days at the village, playing with her friends and cousins, picking fruit from trees, being chased by the farmers, chewing on sugar canes, cooking corn on the cob over an open fire, before they moved to Delhi. She loved talking about her childhood. She used to say that she would do anything to have those days back. But still, things are much better now my grandmother has gone. Mum sounds so much more relaxed."

"And your sisters, how are they?"

"Oh they are absolutely fine."

"And how's work?" Deepa asked as she put the plates away.

"Great. Yeah everything is just fine. Thanks Deepa."

"For what?"

"Nothing, just thanks for being you."

"Silly," Deepa smiled.

Kamal had fallen asleep as soon as her head hit the pillow, while Raj lay awake. Emma's delivery date was fast approaching and he was relieved with his parents' timely plans to go away, maybe it would be the ideal time to break the news to Kamal.

***

"Emma! Why on earth did it take you so long to tell me! I understand why you have been avoiding me now!"

"Because I knew how you'd react," Emma said looking at her mum standing before her in utter disbelief.

"Oh Emma, how could you be so stupid, a married man!"

"It just happened mum."

"These things don't just happen. And this place, how could you afford this?"

"He…Raj, bought it for me, us."

"He bought this for you? I don't suppose he has told his wife has he?"

"Oh what do you think mum? He is working on it," Emma looked away in irritation.

"Working on it? You're eight months pregnant and he is still working on it! He has got you well and truly fooled young lady. Just wait till your brother hears of this. Did you say Raj? Is he Asian then?"

Emma nodded.

"Has he got any children from his marriage?"

Emma nodded her head again.

"Oh this just keeps getting better and better; do you really think he intends to leave his wife? He's bought your silence, by buying you this place, can't you see?"

"No he has promised me he will be telling her soon and then he'll be moving in with me."

"He promised did he? Oh stop being so gullible, wake up and smell the coffee Emma!"

"Look mum, I did not invite you here for you to judge me for what I have done. I am having this baby. I love Raj and he will, I know he will, eventually leave his wife to be with me, I have complete faith in him!"

"I'd like to meet this….Raj, or whatever his name is. In fact I should go to his home right now and give him a piece of my mind!"

"You will do no such thing! I will not have you interfering mum. The only reason I called you here today was because you'd find out sooner or later. Now don't you dare do anything behind my back! You want to see Raj that's fine, I can arrange that, but that is all, is that clear? His parents are leaving for India soon, it will give him time alone with his wife, and that's when he plans to tell her."

***

Kamal sniffled as she hugged her son goodbye at the airport.

"Oh it's only three weeks. You know we will take good care of him," even Joginder was close to tears as she saw Kamal embracing her son longingly.

"Oh I know, I know, I have nothing to worry about. Please keep him with you at all times. Don't let him out of your sight. I wish I was coming with you now."

"Well you still can, Raj can arrange for you to join us too," her father-in-law stepped forward.

"I can't. I've got the training at work, which they've paid for," she hugged her son again. He looked at her face and back up at his grandmother wondering why his mother was so upset.

"God you are behaving like you're never going to see him again!" Balbir laughed, putting his hand on her head while tears ran down her face. She herself could not grasp why she was feeling so emotional; like her father-in-law said, it was after all just three weeks, but she felt like her heart was being torn away from her. She kissed her son on the forehead.

"Now you be a good boy for me okay? And stay with your grandmother and grandfather at all times okay?"

"Yes mommy. Can I go on the plane now?" Kamal could not help but laugh at this point.

"Yes, you can," she kissed his hand as he wiped her tears and hugged her again.

"Bye mommy, bye daddy."

"Bye darling. Go on, off you go now, hold your grandfather's hand tightly and don't let go okay."

"Bye son," Raj kissed him on his cheek.

Kamal hugged Joginder and stepped back as they all made their way towards the departure gate. Kamal blew her son a kiss as he turned back to look at her, he blew one back with his free hand, his other hand still holding onto his grandfather's, just as his mother had instructed, "oh, my baby, bye darling," she whispered and waved. Raj was a lot more casual with his goodbye; he was far too preoccupied with other matters of importance and could not wait to leave now.

"Shall we go now?" Kamal stood still looking at the departure gate vacantly, "Kamal?"

"Yes…let's go," she followed Raj looking back one last time.

Back at the house now, Kamal felt as if all life had been sucked out of it, with nothing left but brick walls and a wide open empty space. There were no calls for "mommy", no muttering mother-in-law and no father-in-law seated on his throne. Raj sat engaged in the TV while she cooked some chapatti to accompany the *daal* and *aloo gobhi* she'd made earlier. She was not accustomed to cooking for just the two of them and it felt so strange and in a strange way, extraneous. Her eyes kept wandering up to the kitchen clock, wondering where they'd be now. She opened the cupboard door to fetch out some glasses and her son's plastic cup stood staring down at her. She picked it up and held it close to her chest. Her eyes then fell on his jumper, left on the dining table chair and she walked over to it. She picked it up and put it to her nose inhaling the familiar smell of fabric softener blended in with baby talc. She closed her eyes in anguish and held it to her cheek; how she missed having him around, having everyone around. The house felt empty, barren and futile and she felt like a lost soul floating around with the preoccupied Raj. She sighed and placed the jumper back on the chair and started to plate up aimlessly.

"It's so quiet isn't it?" she said now sitting next to him, breaking the eerie silence and ripping her chapatti, which tasted like cardboard, bland and tasteless; everything was just so lacklustre without those she loved around her.

"Makes a change," Raj said still looking at the TV vacantly as he ate.

"I can't stand it!"

"Well, I'm going to enjoy it while it lasts."

He was in one of his moods again. Just when she thought things were going okay, he'd revert back to his sarcastic, miserable, not-interested self, but it was worse now, as she had nothing or no-one to distract her.

***

"Morning girls. Oh, late night again Angela?" Kamal laughed as she saw Angela at her desk with her sunglasses and cup of black coffee in her hand.

"You could say that," Angela frowned, "can someone turn the radio down please?"

"You're late in today Kamal," Danielle asked deliberately turning the radio up.

"Slept over. Besides, I think I'll be starting late and leaving late, I'll speak to Jackie. Can't stand being at home, the house is just not the same."

"How's your son, is he enjoying himself?" Angela grumbled rubbing her forehead.

"Evidently so, he's being spoilt rotten. He's got the whole family in India running around him. They all say he is Raj through and through."

"How is Raj then?" Danielle asked.

"Oh going through one of his phases again."

"And they say women are unpredictable," Danielle said pulling her face at her tea and looking into the cup.

"Do you think it's possible for men to have mood swings," Angela frowned curiously looking up at the ceiling vacantly.

"No, just miserable sods sometimes," Danielle shook her head and put her cup down, throwing one disappointing look at the junior who needed to learn how to make a decent cup of tea!

"Danielle! Get me file VA232, need to get in touch with the vendor now!"

"What's the magic word Mark?"

"Danielle, can you get me file VA232 – please."

"That's better Mark," she shouted out as he went back into his office, "think it must be something in the air girls."

"Oh don't shout please," Angela pleaded.

"Oh Rohit came in earlier, he was looking for Craig, said he'd come back later," Danielle shouted out deliberately as she got up to fetch the file for her boss.

"Oh, okay," Kamal said trying not to look bothered, even though whenever his name was mentioned she could not help but still feel a pang of excitement.

Kamal later stood singing out loud with *Bryan Adams - Everything I do*, when Rohit walked into the office; she was oblivious to his presence as she stood standing at the photocopier with her back turned towards him. Danielle put her fingers to her lips, requesting he remained quiet. Kamal was really singing to her heart's content now.

"Oh I just love this song," she said grabbing the copies and turning round to find Rohit standing by her desk with his arms folded, evidently quite amused.

"Did not realise you could sing as well Kamal."

"Oh well there are quite a lot of things you don't know about me," she said, turning her nose up and walking back to her chair, trying her best to hide her embarrassment.

"A woman of many talents."

"Yep, that's me!" she started to envelope her letter, "you looking for Craig?"

"Yeah, yeah, has he not come in yet?"

"He has just popped over to see John. He should be back any minute now."

"So how are all you girls?" he looked round towards Danielle, a sobering up Angela and the new junior, Anne, who looked dead keen and interested, as ever.

"We're fine Rohit. I must say Rohit, you are looking mighty fine these days. Have you been working out?" Angela asked smiling.

"I have actually, can you tell?"

"Oh yeah," she said raising her brows.

"Yes, well got to keep trim hey? No point in letting yourself go is there?" Rohit had his back turned towards Kamal and was unaware of her mocking actions, as she pointed her finger into her open mouth.

"You okay Kamal?" Angela asked grinning.

Rohit turned round to look at her. "Yes I am fine," she said sitting up straight.

Danielle giggled and the junior continued to look around vacantly.

"Am I missing something here?" Rohit asked looking towards Kamal as Angela also broke into a giggle.

Kamal shrugged her shoulders, "oh hi Craig, Rohit is here for you," she diverted his attention rolling her eyes at Angela.

"Yes, yes come on through Rohit," Rohit followed Craig into the office and shut the door behind him.

"Oh you're looking mighty fine these days…" Kamal mimicked Angela.

"Well he is. He looks broader doesn't he? And he has got such a firm arse, I was so tempted to just grab it!"

"Can't say I noticed myself," Kamal said getting up to put the sealed envelope in the post tray.

"Yeah right, pull the other one. I know you still fancy him. It's written all over your likkle face," Angela pouted her lips.

"Yeah, yeah. Sure it's not you falling for him?"

"Actually, I would not mind having him on my reserve list. You never know. Have you got his personal number by any chance?"

Danielle and Angela left bang on 5, while Kamal could not see the point of rushing back to an empty home and to a husband, whose mood was as unpredictable as a woman going through menopause. Craig finished his straining conversation with the workers at the German site, banged the receiver down and came rushing out, with his coat and scarf over his left arm, his briefcase in his left hand and a file in his right.

"Oh Kamal great you're still here! Can you do me a big favour please? I really need to shoot off now. Can you take this file up to Rohit please and hand it over to him personally?"

"Okay, I'll take it up on my way out."

"Sooner rather than later Kamal," he said pulling his coat and gloves on, "please."

"Yes boss," she saluted.

"You're a star. I'll see you Tuesday."

"Okay. Have a nice trip Craig."

"Yes, well not sure it's going to be a nice one!" he shouted as he rushed away.

Kamal tidied her desk up, shut the blinds, stroked the picture of her son and kissed the tips of her fingers, "miss you," she whispered. She picked up her scarf, coat, bag and the file, shut the office light and closed the door.

"Night Brenda," she shouted out to the cleaner, "night Steve," she shouted out to one of the engineers still hanging about, as she made her way to the lift to take her up to the fifth floor and just made out Steve's delayed response. As she walked out towards Rohit's office, she saw that Christine was still at her desk.

"Hi, Christine you're still here too I see."

"Oh hi Kamal, yeah, I'm almost done, Rohit wanted me to do this letter urgently before I left. You okay?" she said looking up briefly from the letter she was typing.

"Yes I'm fine. Craig asked me to bring this up to Rohit."

"Oh you can take it straight in thanks," she said continuing to type.

"Has he got someone with him?" she asked noting the blinds were shut.

"No, no, you go on through."

"Okay."

She knocked on the door and popped her head round. Rohit was standing at the window with his hands in his pockets and looking out the window. He looked round and smiled, as if he was half expecting her.

"Come in Kamal," he said and continued looking out, "beautiful isn't it?"

She placed the file on his desk and stood next to him.

"Yes it is," she looked out with him. He had just his desk lamp on, but the city lights illuminated his office.

"You okay?"

"Yeah, I'm fine and you?"

"I'm fine," she shrugged her shoulders and smiled.

"Good," he said looking down at her. A strand of her hair was on her cheek, he lifted his hand to move it away with his fingers, softly stroking her cheek. She stood static, as he moved closer towards her. She closed her eyes as he stroked her cheek gently again and swallowed the lump suddenly formed in her throat. The warmth of his musky aftershave, the soft lighting and the charisma about him had set the scene and she was finding herself being involuntarily drawn towards him. He stepped closer still and cupped her face in both his hands, running his thumbs softly on her cheeks and then her lips. She looked up at him and moved her mouth towards his, inviting him to kiss her. As he touched her lips with his, she dropped her coat and bag on the floor and wrapped her arms around him. The soft lingering kiss intensified, as the denied for too long desire within both increased. As he pulled her tighter towards him the moment was soon interrupted, by a knock at the door. Kamal let go immediately and stood back to face the window, moving her hair away from her face nervously and then folding her arms, unsure of where to place them.

"Can you just quickly check and sign this Rohit," Christine darted into the room and started to tidy things on his desk as if out of habit while he scanned through the letter and signed it,

"That's great Christine, thanks."

"Okay, I'll quickly fax it and then I'm heading straight off!" she took the signed letter and shot out the room like a bullet. Kamal looked back round at the closed door. Rohit walked towards her and wrapped his arms around her waist, "where were we?" he whispered in her ear, moving her hair away and seductively kissing the nape of her neck. He then pulled her back round and kissed her again, stepping back to sit on the end of his desk bringing her to stand before him. She could feel how much he wanted her now. Her hands were running through his hair as their lips remained locked. His hands travelled up her jumper and were now feeling the strap of her bra; he wanted her so much.

"Come back to my place," he whispered kissing her down on her neck.

"What now?" she said pulling away.

"Yes. Come on please," he stood back up and pulled her towards him again.

"But….." Kamal said pulling back again.

"Ssshhh……" he put his finger on her lips, "no buts, I know you want to, as much as I do, let's stop pretending now."

Kamal moved back, "I do want to, but it's not right," she walked back away from him. Rohit walked towards her and cupped her face in his hands again.

"Sorry," he pecked her lips, "I tell you what, how about we go out tomorrow after work, we can go to a nice restaurant, really spend some time with each other, what do you say?"

"But Rohit…"

"I'm sure you can make an excuse, say you're going out with friends or something."

"I guess so. But, I better go now, it's getting late."

"Oh Kamal," he sighed touching his forehead with hers, sending her melting in his arms again.

Kamal sighed in relief as she pulled up on the drive and saw that the house lights were out. She felt excited yet, scared, guilty, yet thrilled, her head felt like it did not belong to her body and she was sure her feet were not touching the ground. Rohit really was something else; not the boring average men she had grown up to know, stuck in their ways, no spontaneity, no stories to tell, straight from home to work and work to home, or to the pub, or to sit and watch a mindless game of grown men kicking a ball about; Rohit was different. He had travelled the world and had a story to tell. She did not know one woman in the company that did not flutter her eyelids unnecessarily in his presence, but he had chosen and wanted her and she desperately wanted to forget who she was, where she was from and be lost in a world where there were no barriers, no restrictions, just love, excitement and, Rohit.

She quickly got changed into her jogging pants and T-shirt, and went into the kitchen. She cooked homemade chips, spiced up some baked beans and grilled some sausages. Raj was due home soon and she silently wished it was going to be one of those evenings where he would not even bother coming home. She put the radio on and smiled as she heard one of her favourite songs being aired, the lyrics of which were quite synonymous to how she was feeling right now *'bas ik Sanam chaahiye aashiqui ke liye'* (all I want is a lover to love).

As she finished fishing the chips out of the oil, she heard the key turn in the front door. Raj went straight up the stairs to get changed, not feeling the need to acknowledge his wife in the absence of his parents. Changed and refreshed, he sat at the dining table and the only sound came from the cutlery and TV. He was still struggling to say anything to her and was saving the momentum for tomorrow, yet again.

"Is it okay if I go out with Danielle and Angela tomorrow night?" she finally plucked up the courage to lie, as much as it unnerved her, she wasn't the world's best liar.

Raj shrugged his shoulders, "yeah, where you going?"

"Oh just some restaurant, we have been meaning to go for a while."

"Yeah that's fine, I was actually going to go out with the boys after work for a drink too," he said quietly relieved. It was getting closer to Emma's delivery and she was understandably demanding he spend more time with her.

"Okay," she got up, turned her back and closed her eyes in relief as she walked with the dishes to the sink. She was overcome with guilt for lying, but what the hell; there was no harm in living dangerously once in a while. Was there?

***

"So restaurant, or shall we order a takeaway at mine?" Rohit asked clicking on his seatbelt in his leather seated BMW.

Kamal paused as she replicated his movement, "maybe yours," thinking it would be best.

"Okay," Rohit smiled.

She tried her best to appear relaxed and comfortable; she was after all only going to the man's flat, whom she had fantasised being with on numerous occasions!

"Don't know about you, but I hardly slept last night and work, I'm surprised I got anything done," Rohit broke the silence looking towards her as they stood stationary in the evening rush hour traffic. Kamal smiled. "You are okay about all this aren't you?" he asked concerned, as she sat quietly looking out the window blankly.

Kamal shrugged her shoulders, "there is nothing okay about this is there?" she looked towards him. Rohit held his hand out, she placed her right hand in his; he squeezed it and brought it to his lips. He then slowly released it to control the steering wheel, as the signal changed and the traffic moved on.

Rohit lived in an apartment just on the outskirts of the city centre. Kamal followed in his shadow, hiding her trepidation, as he opened the door to the lobby and headed forward towards the lifts. Once in the confined lift, he pressed button four and stood silently by her side. A familiar voice in her head was telling her to backtrack, telling her that it wasn't too late, but she felt an inability to physically move and remained hypnotised by his presence. The only thing she was following right now was her heart. She watched him step out and open the door right opposite the lift. As he looked back towards her she stepped forward following a moment of hesitation, the voice in her head taunting her, telling her to turn back right now.

"You coming?" Rohit stood with the door open.

Kamal fought off the voice, smiled and walked forward. Now in through the doors, she stood in an impressive modern open plan apartment, but what was spectacular was the large window looking out to the city and she was instantly drawn towards it.

"Wow, how amazing!"

"It is isn't it? It's the first thing that struck me too," he said removing his coat. He then walked towards her, "here let me take your coat, make yourself comfortable."

She continued looking out as she unfastened her buttons and let him remove her coat. She looked as hot as the fiery red satin shirt she was wearing, he wanted to wrap his hands around the slim belted waist and kiss those tempting devilish red lips.

"Drink?"

"Yes please."

"Wine?"

"Okay."

She looked back round. The lights were turned dim and he'd put some music on. His tie was loosened around his neck and she watched as he got some wine glasses out the cupboard and a bottle of white from the small refrigerator. There were no personal photos, just a large picture of the New York skyline, above the fire place and a couple of large houseplants adding a splash of colour. The apartment was sophistically furnished with a black leather suite and a small black coffee table, a glass dining table, just before the open plan kitchen, with four black high back chairs, the floor carpeted beige with tiny black squares. Next to the kitchenette was a small corridor with a door to the left and one straight ahead.

"Have you been here long?" she asked as she sat taking the glass handed over to her, feeling a little relaxed now.

"No, well, just over a year."

"It's nice," she said looking at flickering flames of the gas fire.

"Yeah, it's nice, just gets a bit lonely sometimes," he said smiling. He was sat opposite her on the single seat, leaning forward, "so what shall we order to eat?" he said getting up again, "don't know about you, but I'm famished."

"Whatever you fancy."

"How about...Chinese?" he said looking though the leaflets he had in the drawer of the black side cabinet.

"Chinese is good."

He chose a meal for two and she watched him as he made the call; Angela was right, he did have a cute arse. He was wearing navy trousers and a white shirt. He'd unfastened his top buttons and his navy tie hung loose around his neck; he was looking extremely desirable. She had not eaten much for lunch due to nerves and the fact that she rarely drank alcohol meant the wine was surging straight to her head. She was trying her best to appear confident and comfortable. He topped up her empty glass, put the bottle down on the coffee table and sat next to her.

"I don't think I have ever asked you this before, but have you been in a relationship with anyone here, I mean since you moved to England?"

"Yeah, I have, but nothing serious or worth remembering."

"And in India?"

"Aah now in India, yes I did have a few serious relationships, one of them was a serious teenage crush, we had planned to elope and everything," he laughed, "but that soon fizzled out, and then I was in another relationship following that, one pretty serious, started out with all good intentions, but then I realised, she was not what I was really looking for. Unfortunately for me, all the good women are taken," he said smiling at her.

"Taken, but, not necessarily happy."

"You're not happy?"

She shrugged her shoulders, "if I was happy, I would not be here today, having lied to my husband, would I?"

"I guess not."

He put his wine glass on the table, took her glass off her and placed it too on the table and then moved over closer. He kissed her forehead, her nose and then her lips. Her head was spinning from the wine and his touch, warmth and gentleness made her head feel lighter still. She let him take control and lay back as he slowly lay on top of her, slowly kissing her lips and then her neck. Her hands were running over his back, his broad shoulders and through his hair. She wished the moment would never end, when he suddenly pulled away and sat up.

"Sorry, I better stop," he said running his hands through his hair. Kamal sat up and looked at him; she wanted to tell him that she had no objections against him losing all control, taking her straight to his bedroom and making love to her right now, but held back. The doorbell rang causing a distraction and he got up to answer the door. She sat up straight and reached out for her wine glass and drank the remaining wine in one gulp.

She closed her eyes and took a deep breath, as she heard the apartment door close.

"Food," he said bringing in the takeaway.

"That was quick," Kamal said.

"Oh the restaurant is not far from here and I order from them regularly. Still hungry?" Kamal looked up towards him and stood up, slightly giddy. She took the bag off him and placed it on the table and looked up at him, hoping that he could read her mind. She wanted him to make the first move and seeing the invitation in her eyes, he led her by the hand towards his bedroom. He opened the door and turned the light on dim. She looked at the immaculately made up bed and up at him. He was looking down at her, as if asking her if she was sure; she turned the light down so that it was dimmer still and moved towards him, putting her arms around him. He lifted her chin, kissed her and then took his tie off, undone his buttons and removed his shirt. She touched his broad, toned chest and kissed it all over softly, unbuttoned her shirt buttons and let him remove it. He wowed at her hourglass figure, ample breasts and narrow waist. She was wearing a black and white laced bra, which complemented her golden wheat coloured skin. She slowly lay on the bed and welcomed him into her arms.

"I love you Rohit Sinha," she whispered with her head on his chest, still spinning from the alcohol, her naked body lying next to his under the thick duvet dressed with a Playboy cover. He wrapped his strong arms around her and kissed her head.

***

Emma was in early labour with an exhausted Raj close by her side at the hospital and her mother waiting patiently outside in the waiting area. She had broken her waters 10.20am and Raj was at the house within minutes, soon after she'd called him. Her mother did not find out till much later, when Raj was able to call her at home. It was 7.20pm and Emma was now finally pushing. "Okay now," said the gynaecologist, "one more push, I can see the head now, one, two three, push!" Emma pushed with all her strength and let out an almighty yell; a baby boy was born. The nurses took the baby straight away and began to clear out the airways.

"Is it okay, is my baby okay?" Emma struggled to say as she lay fatigued, not hearing any cry; all she could see were doctors and nurses rushing around her baby.

"Raj!" she sat up suddenly alert, "my baby, give me my baby, why is he not crying?" Raj was unable to answer as he too looked on nervously and sighed with relief, as he finally heard his son's little cry.

"He is absolutely fine," the doctor said smiling.

Raj helped Emma sit up in bed. A tear ran down her cheek as her beautiful baby boy was placed in her arms. Raj's eyes also moistened; this was by far the most beautiful picture he had ever seen. He put his arms around Emma, kissed her forehead and then his son's.

"Thank you Emma."

She looked up at Raj and smiled; he looked absolutely shattered.

"Anyone would have thought you'd given birth," she laughed and kissed him. All her worries, fears and anxieties seemed to have suddenly disappeared, while she held her baby close to her bosom. Soft peach coloured skin, hair golden brown, deep blue eyes and lips rose petal pink; he was beautiful.

"Oh. Isn't he the most beautiful little creature," her mum said as she now stood by her side and kissed her forehead. She could not help but feel annoyed with the married man sitting on the other side of the bed with his arm around her daughter, but when she looked at her grandchild, all her fears were diminished. This was the first time Raj had come face to face with Emma's mother. He had avoided all opportunities to meet up with her afraid of the third degree. "Oh Emma, he has your eyes, but he does have his father's face doesn't he?" she said looking up at Raj who smiled proudly. Emma rested her head on his shoulder. "You have big decisions to make now young man, you do realise don't you?"

"Yes, I do and I promise, I won't let you down."

***

Kamal was struggling to call out her son's name. She was trying to scream out 'STOP!' But couldn't, as she was unable to find her voice, as he ran further and further away from her. She was trying to reach out for him, but she was unable to move as her feet felt shackled down. She reached out and painfully tried to scream out again, but to no avail. Her mother-in-law's face flashed before her eyes and she saw Raj just standing by, laughing down at her mockingly as she tried to run and reach out for her son again, who was disappearing fast out of sight and then all of a sudden, he was gone and there was nothing but darkness. She then heard her mum's weeping and a sudden piercing scream awoke her from the nightmare.

She opened her eyes and scanned her surroundings nervously, recalling where she was. She sat up in the bed, sweating and slightly out of breath. She looked down at her naked breasts and covered them instantly with the duvet cover and held her head. She looked round at Rohit, who lay fast asleep. It was 7.50pm on his digital clock. "Oh my God!" she looked at her clothes scattered all over the floor. She shot up out of the bed, scrambled to get them together and went straight into the bathroom. She closed the door and leant her bare back against the cold door. She closed her eyes tormented by the recollection of her sluttish behaviour.

"What have you done!" she gasped and covered her mouth as she looked at her naked image in the large mirror opposite her. She frowned as she noticed a reddish, brown mark on the right side of her neck and went over to study it closer in the mirror, "oh my God," she said looking at it and touching it with her hand; a shameless mark was blatantly staring her in the face, evidence of a lustful moment. Her smudged lipstick, her panda eyes and messy hair added to how cheap she felt within. She turned on the shower, as she felt the urgent need to clean her tarnished self. She washed herself vigorously with the soap and stood still allowing for the hot water to run over her head and down her body; she closed her eyes aware that she could cleanse her body however much she wanted, but how was she going to purify how she felt now within? Realising that it was getting late she turned the water off and stepped out the shower, quickly towel dried her hair and body and got dressed, her shirt sticking onto her still damp back from the panic to leave. She walked back into the bedroom for her shoes.

Rohit was sitting up in bed. Kamal's hair was damp and her face make-up free. This au naturel look made her look even more desirable and a feeling of want arose within him; she really was beautiful.

"Hey, come back into bed."

"I have to go!" she said frantically looking for her shoe and then sitting down on the bed.

"But you said yourself Raj was not going to come back till late, so why are you panicking?" he asked getting up out of bed with just his boxers on.

"I have to go home. I want to be at home when he gets back."

"But.."

"I'm sorry Rohit, this should never have happened," she said getting up, shaking her head and heading out to grab her coat.

"Kamal wait. I'll take you back."

"No it's okay, I'll catch the bus."

"Oh don't be silly. Just wait while I get changed."

"No, really, I want to be on my own right now. Please just leave me alone. It was a mistake, this should never have happened!"

"Well it's not the feeling I got earlier," he said standing before her wanting to hold her, but feeling unable to approach her.

"Well everything is clear to me now," she said looking up at him, "I was not thinking straight, and the wine did not help," she said opening her bag and looking for her purse frantically to check for change, her hands shaking. She checked that she had enough and then put the purse back in her bag and slung it over her shoulder.

"Will you please let me take you back? You'll be waiting ages for a bus. Please, I'll take you back to your car and then you can drive back home."

"Okay, but can you hurry up please."

Kamal paced up and down the room as Rohit got changed. The nightmare that she had earlier came back vividly; she churned over its significance and the repulse of her adultery. She had let everyone that mattered to her down, but above all she had let herself down. How had she allowed this to happen?

Rohit grabbed the keys from the kitchen counter and pulled on his jacket. He was dressed more casually in his jeans and black polo neck jumper now. He did not say anything; he appeared upset and Kamal felt a slight twinge of remorse for being so sharp, but she remained distant. He opened the apartment door for her and she headed straight towards the lift ahead, making it evident that she could not wait to get out. She had stepped into the lift just as he finished locking up, he joined her and pressed button 'G' and stood at a distance, unlike a few hours before. Kamal watched the numbers impatiently going down from four to 'G'. She walked out as soon as the doors slid open. Rohit raced forward to open the front door for her and then the door to his car. There was much less traffic now and Rohit was at the work car park in no time. There was total silence throughout the journey. He could not get to the door soon enough, as she was already standing outside, her car keys already in her hand and she was already walking towards her car.

"Kamal, I don't understand. Why are you being like this?" he asked her as she opened the door to her blue Ford Escort. "Did I do something wrong? Did I say something?" he said holding her elbow desperately. She paused for a moment.

"No, you did not say or do anything wrong. I just forgot for a moment who I was, that's all and now reality has kicked in, it's back to planet earth and the real world. I don't want to see you again Rohit. I'm sorry."

"No wait, wait," he said holding her back, "you cannot leave like this. I don't think what happened tonight was wrong. If anything it was the one of the most beautiful moments in my life."

"One of?" Kamal said looking up, "so you have had many others? I should have known better, after all, it did not take you long to get me into bed!"

"Now wait just a minute, you wanted that just as much as me, you can't accuse me of making you sleep with me, you were ready and willing."

"Yes well, it's done with now, you've had your fun, no sorry, we've had our fun, fulfilled our suppressed desires. I have really let myself down," she said shaking her head, tears welling in her eyes, "how am I going to look anyone in the eye?"

"But Kamal, I love you….."

"Love? How can you love me? There was no love it was just lust and now if you would let go of my arm, I want to go home to my husband!"

Kamal pulled her arm away, got into the car, shut the door, started the ignition, put her seat belt on and screeched off, while Rohit stood by and watched.

"Lust," he whispered to himself. Yes he had wanted her, he had wanted her ever since the first day he laid his eyes on her and he had waited a long time for tonight and it had been well worth the wait, but it was not lust. He walked back to his BMW, started the ignition and drove back slowly to his empty lonely home.

As Kamal followed her usual route home she approached the temple as per usual and slowed down to a halt. She looked up at the temple, the dome of which was lit up with outdoor lightings, making it visible from a far, far distance. She bent her head down in shame and let a tear run down her cheek.

As she approached home, she was relieved to see Raj's car was not parked up, he was not yet back. Once in her bedroom, she changed straight into her nightwear. She looked at her image in the mirror; the love bite was shamelessly staring at her. She applied as much concealer onto it as possible and brought her hair forward; she wished now it was not so short and how she would have to wear her polo neck jumpers every day until it faded away. She went straight into bed, but was unable to sleep for the sick feeling in her stomach.

It was 12.20am when Raj came back home. He had left Emma just after visiting hours at the hospital, the nurses had allowed for him to stay longer and then he went to a bar, to collect his thoughts, later to be distracted by some friends. Kamal made out she was asleep and he too attempted to get into bed as quietly as possible, not wanting to stir her. Both lay with their backs towards each other; both unable to sleep, both wondering where they were to go from here.

Chapter 10

"Oh, you're not ready?" Deepa said coming straight into the house, "and gosh you do look tired, have you not slept? Is everything okay?"

"Yeah, yeah," Kamal said, closing the front door and walking back in behind Deepa into the living room.

"But you don't look well at all," Deepa said, placing the back of her hand on Kamal's forehead, "you do feel a bit hot. I guess shopping and pictures are cancelled then," she said slumping onto the sofa.

"Sorry, I don't think I'm up to it today," Kamal said sitting opposite her, "how are the kids?" Kamal was averting eye contact; even if Deepa would not have suspected any underlying reason to Kamal's withdrawn look, she was not helping herself.

"Fine, at my mum and dad's. Are you really okay?" Deepa looked at Kamal with concern, "is Raj playing up again? Where is he actually?"

"Oh he went out early this morning, while I was still in bed. He did not come in till late."

"Up to his old tricks again? Do you want me to have a word?"

"No, no. He's the last thing on my mind at the moment," Kamal said waving her hand slightly in the air.

"You missing Junior?"

"Yeah, yeah, that's what it is. Two more weeks to go, feel like the house is going to swallow me up sometimes. It'll be a relief when they're back, get some life back into this place."

"I'd make the most of it," Deepa said leaning forward.

"Yeah well, you know how temperamental Raj can be. I don't know whether he is coming or going. He turns hot and cold all the while. Never know where I am standing. It's no wonder I bloody messed up," her voice a mere whisper towards the end.

"Do you want me to ask Varinder to talk to him?"

"No, no. What's the point? He gets a lecture, behaves himself for a couple of weeks and then it's back to square one. I've just got to get on with it, one day at a time, maybe he will settle down with time. Men do eventually, don't they?"

"Yeah, when half your life has been wasted running around them, the children and their families. It's just the way it is, we just carry on for the sake of everyone else. You sure you don't want to go out? It'll take your mind off things. No point wallowing away at home. Come on get ready hey?"

"Okay," Kamal sighed and managed a smile; she definitely needed something to take her mind off things.

***

Raj waited impatiently for Kamal; she had left a note for him simply scribbled *gone out with Deepa, back about 7* and he wondered if that was really, where she was. He sat in the living room irritated further by his surroundings; he had always hated the décor, there was something so typically Indian about it; burgundy carpet, burgundy and cream sofa, the white walls typically overdosed with family portraits. His eyes fell on his wedding portrait placed on the cabinet next to the phone, and he walked towards it. He smirked; she was so simple and plain then, 'good wife material' he had thought. Stay at home, cook and clean type, someone to attend the stupid parties and wedding functions with; someone to keep his parents happy and someone available for the odd shag, whenever it was needed. He held the portrait in his hands. That innocent shy smile appeared so false now. All the time he had wasted reeling over how and when to tell her about Emma, when the whole time...... the rage within him reached boiling point as he hurled the photo across the room, sending it crashing against the wall. He looked down at the shattered glass and the frame lying face down, as he walked over to the window and pulled back the net curtains; there was still no sign of her. He poured himself yet another shot of rum and looked at his watch; it was now 7.25pm. At this point, he decided to call his brother's home.

"Where's Kamal?" he asked when Deepa herself answered.

"Oh hi Raj, I just got in. Kamal should be back soon, she said she was going to grab an Indian movie from the video shop."

"Oh, well she's not back yet."

"I don't think she will be long. I did offer to drop her off, but she said she would be okay."

"Did she now?" Raj said, by now all sorts of thoughts crossing his mind.

"Raj, is everything okay?" Deepa asked sensing a disdained tone.

"Yeah, yeah. Everything is just fine," he hung up, knocked the rum back and ran his fingers through his hair. He then sat and watched the seconds hand tick away around the clock, the ticking echoing around the silent room. It was 7.50pm when he heard the key finally turn in the front door. He could hear the rustling of bags and the placing of keys on the side cabinet in the hall. He rolled the empty glass in his hands, as he waited for her to come in.

"Hi," she said coming into the lounge casually and put a video tape on the dining table. "I'll just take these up," she walked upstairs with her shopping bags.

Raj got up to pour himself another generous shot of rum, added some ice cubes from the freezer and made his way slowly up the stairs. As he walked into the bedroom, he saw she was holding up a cobalt coloured shirt against her, looking into the mirror, her head tilted to the left as she looked at her image.

"Nice shirt."

Kamal quickly put the shirt down and turned to face him; she had not realised he had walked in behind her. He had a glass in his right hand and his top shirt buttons were undone.

"For work?" She nodded. "Making a bit of an effort these days aren't we?" he smirked.

Kamal didn't respond, picked up the rest of the bags and put them into the cupboard.

"Are you not going to show me what else you have bought, some sexy underwear perhaps?" Kamal still said nothing. There was an unusual tone of sarcasm in his voice, nothing like she'd ever heard before. "Well then, you're not going to show me?"

"You never usually want to see what I've bought," she said sitting on the bed nervously and removing her socks.

"Well maybe I want to now."

Kamal swallowed the lump formed in her throat and her heart began to race. Did he know something?

"Where were you yesterday?" he asked sitting on the bed next to her.

"Yesterday?" she repeated.

"Yes, yesterday?"

"I was with Danielle and Amanda, I told you, I was going out with them," she said getting up and walking towards the dressing table and straightened up her bottles of nail varnish. He too got up and walked towards the window. He looked up towards the clear pitch black night sky, lit up by a full moon. He turned round to face her again. Kamal was now placing her watch by the bedside cabinet.

"Are you sure you were with Danielle and Angela?"

"Of course, what sort of a question is that?" Kamal's heart was pounding, as she looked round to face him bravely. His eyes were a blood shot red, similar to her dad's, when he had been drinking excessively.

"I am going to ask you again. Where were you yesterday?"

"I already told you," she said turning her back towards him again and biting her bottom lip unable to face him. Her hands had now started to shake as she removed her earrings. Just then, the glass that he had in his hand went flying past her head and hit the wall.

"I am going to ask you again. Where were you!"

Kamal turned round in fear, as she heard his steps thunder towards her.

"I…I…" he stood towering above her.

"You were having it off with another man, weren't you?" Raj was gritting his teeth.

Kamal covered her mouth with her hand, as her stomach turned. She ran past him towards the bathroom next to their bedroom, and slammed the door shut. With a few large strides, she collapsed down on her knees and heaved her guts out. Holding onto the wall for support, she got back up off her knees and leant on the washbasin with her head bent down, struck by disbelief. She turned the cold water tap and splashed her face. She looked at her reflection in the mirror above and closed her eyes in anguish; wishing this moment was a bad, bad dream. She grabbed the towel and put it to her face, sat down by the hot radiator, too shaken and afraid to leave the bathroom and looked up startled by the knock on the door, still unable to move. Seeing him today like this, brought back unwelcome memories. Her dad would blow up in a fit of rage over the most menial things, such as the one time when her mother had served his dinner lukewarm. She remembered him slapping her in rebuke and flinging the plate across the room, sending the *daal* splattering all over the wall for her to clean up. But Raj, he had every reason to be angry. But how had he found out? Who had told him?

"We need to talk," Raj knocked on the door again. His speech was slurred.

Kamal eventually got up on her shaking legs and wiped her tears. She slowly opened the door and walked timidly into the bedroom, like a child waiting for some severe punishment, her shoulders slouched and her eyes looking down at her feet. He was sitting on the bed with his head bent down, elbows on his knees and his hands held together. She stood by the radiator by the window, her head still bowed down.

"So how long have you been seeing this…… Rohit?"

Kamal looked up, stunned further still; he even knew his name!

"How…how, do you know?" she dared to ask the question.

"Ssshhh. I'm asking the questions," he said putting his finger to his lips, looking at her pathetic state, face withdrawn, shoulders slouched and eyes welling with tears. "How long have you been seeing him?"

"Only the once, I, I only went out with him the once, yesterday."

"Have you slept with him?"

Kamal shook her head vigorously.

"I will ask you again. Have you slept with him?"

A tear dropped from her right eye. She was so translucent, a pathetic liar.

"Well?"

As Raj got up - she crouched down, brought her chin down to her knees and wrapped her arms around them, like a frightened child.

"You have haven't you? You've slept with him. You dirty slag!"

Kamal cringed as he walked forward, closed her eyes and covered her head with her hands, waiting for the first strike.

"Well, well, well, plain, simple, good, innocent little Kamal…… is not so innocent after all is she?" Raj switched on his sarcastic tone again and laughed out loud, "all this time I have been thinking I have the perfect wife at home, but she turns out to be a cheating little whore! Well, well, well, I wonder what my parents will have to say about this, I wonder what YOUR parents will have to say about this!"

"NO!" Kamal was back up on her feet, as if jolted by a vault holding onto the radiator for support, "you can't tell anyone. You can't," she whimpered shaking her head from side to side and then wiping her tears, "you can't tell anyone please, it was only one night, last night. I promise. It was just a big mistake. I got drunk and…."

"Drunk? This just gets better and better. So he got you drunk did he? Well do you remember what he was like? Was he any good? Better than me perhaps? Was I not good enough for you? Is that what it is? Did I not excite you, satisfy you? Is that why you lie there like a dead body most nights?" he pointed at the bed.

"No, no…it's not like that…," Kamal said, her voice breaking.

"Then how is it!" Raj asked raising his voice.

"It just happened. I know it shouldn't have, but it did and I can't change that now. I'm really, really sorry Raj," the tears streamed down her cheeks and neck.

"Well what do you want me to do? Forget it? Like nothing happened? Carry on? Just accept that you made a mistake? How am I supposed to spend the rest of my life looking at you knowing you've slept with another man? Tell me, how am I?"

"I'm sorry."

"Sorry does not make anything better? Just looking at you makes me sick. Last night you said? So come on how was he?"

"Don't, please," she exhaled and turned away in distress.

"Why not? Tell me how he was," he walked up to her, turned her by her shoulders to face him, clasped her face from under her jaw with his right hand and kissed her forcefully. He then grasped her hair with his left hand and moved her face away from him. "If you wanted excitement, I could've given it to you right here. I can give it to you right now if you want," he said undoing his shirt buttons, removing it and chucking it to one side. He started pulling her jumper off.

"No, no, Raj please, not like this," she was pushing him away hopelessly with her hands on his bare chest. He pulled down the straps of her bra strap, unfastened it and flung it to one side.

"Why not? I'm your husband," he grabbed her by the elbows, "I have a right or have you reserved this right for other men like this …..Rohit. Come on I'll show you how exciting I can be."

Kamal felt helpless as he pushed her onto the bed, undoing her jean button and stripping it off and then pulling down her pants. Kamal curled up and covered up her body, now too scared to even cry. He stood in front of her and undid his belt, took down his trousers and boxers and penetrated. Tears again welled and ran down the side of her temples, as he pushed into her with intent to hurt.

"Was he this good? A bit of rough, that's what women like you want," he said breathing his alcoholic breath all over her as he continued to thrust into her, "was he… say something, you slut, bet he was not as good as this."

"Please Raj stop it," she struggled to say.

"Why. This is what it's all about isn't it? Sex?" he continued pushing digging his fingers into her thighs. Kamal lay weak and helpless, hoping this nightmare would end soon. When he finally came, he lay on top of her exhausted. He then propped up the top half of his body, with his hands on either side of her and looked down at her. He then looked closer to the left hand side of her neck and moved her hair away.

"You dirty bitch! You could have at least disguised this!" and it was then he hit her on the left side of her face with a full blow. "Slut!" he said getting up, putting his clothes back on, and stumbling out the room. She could hear him vomiting in the bathroom, the flushing of the toilet and then the tap water running, as she lay naked, stunned and numb, now not even able to cry or move. The left hand side of her face was burning and throbbing. She flinched with fear as she heard him stamp out of the bathroom, afraid he was going to come back in. She closed her eyes in angst when he kicked the bedroom door, before he went down the stairs, stumbling down the last few steps and left the house slamming the front door shut behind him. Kamal lay still in the deathly silence, staring up at the ceiling. She could smell his bodily fluid, her thighs were burning from where he had dug his fingers into her and the left side of her face continued to throb. It was the phone ringing downstairs that eventually made her stir. She dragged herself off the bed and walked into the bathroom. She turned the shower on and let the steam from the hot water slowly fill the room. She stood still momentarily in the darkness, the only light pouring in from the landing and then stepped into the shower and stood still under the running hot water. She put her face up and let the water run over her face, undeterred by the stinging pain from the hot water running over her burning cheek.

With her hair still dripping wet, wrapped in nothing but her dressing gown she lay her head down on her pillow and stared up at the ceiling. The phone rang out again, but she did not get up to answer it. A few moments later, there was knocking at the door, but she remained motionless. The knocking eventually stopped and she curled up on the bed and closed her eyes.

The morning light poured into the bedroom; the curtains left undrawn. She turned onto her side and lay still glaring out the window, wishing the serene, pure and tranquil morning winter sunlight, could wipe out the last couple of days. She closed her eyes and wished they were nothing but a nightmare, but her heart dipped as her conscious told her, the worst was yet to come. She eventually pulled herself out of the bed and tread silently down the stairs. She had heard Raj return last night, but fortunately he had not come upstairs. She had lay in bed still, her heart pounding, fearing the worst and some haunting childhood memories had come back to revisit her. She crept slowly to see he was now splayed out on the sofa, arms stretched out, one leg hanging off the side, still in his shoes and an empty bottle of rum on the coffee table. She swallowed hard and tip-toed back up to get dressed into her jeans and sweatshirt. She then waited patiently for him to sleep his drink off, hoping that then maybe, maybe they could talk properly.

It was the phone ringing at 12.20pm that eventually woke Raj up. Her heart literally jumped up into her mouth as he sat up robotically, running his fingers through his hair and looking down at his feet. "Oh fuck," is all she heard him say, as she stood in the kitchen doorway. She walked forward hesitantly to answer the phone.

"Finally!" Deepa said, "where have you both been? I rang twice yesterday, even came round to see everything was okay. Where were you? Raj sounded quite tense yesterday," Kamal listened quietly as she watched Raj walk out the room and up towards the stairs.

"Oh we went out to eat."

"You sure you're both okay?"

"Yeah, yeah, fine. He's just having a shower now and we're planning to go out again today, when he's ready," Kamal said just in case Deepa was planning to come with her husband and kids.

"Oh that's okay then. I'm going over to my mum's. It's my niece's birthday, so I'll catch up with you later. Any phone calls from India?"

"No, no. Not yet," Kamal said, "we're going to call later."

"Oh okay. Say hello from us will you. Just two more weeks now! I better go now. You take care."

"Okay. Bye Deepa," Kamal hung up. She then sat and waited. She could hear Raj's footsteps up in the bedroom and the opening and closing of the wardrobe. She began to wring her hands nervously in her laps, when she eventually heard his steps coming down the stairs; he walked in with a small suitcase in his hand. She looked up at him and then down at the suitcase.

"I need to get away for a few days and by the time I'm back, I want you to have gone."

"What?"

"I can't spend the rest of my life with you."

"But where am I going to go?" she asked.

He shrugged his shoulders, "go back to your parents."

"But what am I going to tell them?"

"The truth could be helpful."

"I can't."

"Well you should have thought of that before you started to……." he looked away as her bruised cheek stared at him, "look, all I know is that this marriage is over. Things can never be the same again."

"But Raj…"

"Look, I'm sure you've got some money saved from work, mum and dad never asked you for any money and I certainly did not, so you should be okay to just move on away from here," he said waving his hand in the air dismissively.

"Not even one more chance? I will do anything, anything to put things right Raj. I will leave work. I'll just stay here and be as quiet as a mouse. You won't even know I'm here. Please Raj."

"I can't okay! You either walk away quietly. Or I will call a family meeting and shame you in front of everyone, tell everyone the truth, including your parents. Even drag that Rohit in here if I have to. So what will it be?"

"But where am I going to go?"

"Oh for fucks sake, why don't you go to this Rohit! Or were you just a bit on the side, a cheap thrill?"

"But what about our son Raj?" she pleaded, "he needs me, he needs both his parents."

"Mum has been more a mother to him than you have. He will be absolutely fine with me, mum and dad. He won't even know you've gone. What can you give him that he's not already getting from mum and dad hey? All you did, was give birth to him."

Kamal looked at him in disbelief, stumped. But he was right, she had allowed for her mother-in-law to take over the care of her son during the first few days, which turned to weeks, months and then years.

"So what's it going to be? The door or the shame?"

"Walking away would be shameful to both families too, how am I supposed to face anyone then?"

"Walking away would be less shameful than everyone hearing that you spent a night with another man. I'll spare you of that humiliation."

"I need to think about it," she said putting her shaking hand to her head.

"Well you think about it long and hard while I am away yeah?"

"Where are you going?" she asked.

"I don't have to answer any of your questions," and with that he turned. She stood helpless as she watched him walk away. She then walked desperately towards the window and watched him fling the suitcase into the boot of his car, getting in and turning the ignition. He looked up towards the window and looked at her for a few seconds, before he put the car in reverse, released the handbrake, turned out the drive and spun off. She turned round to look at the empty room, wrapped her arms around her body and shuddered in the sudden chill.

Raj ran his fingers through his hair as he waited at the traffic lights feeling slightly remorseful for his despicable act last night; she could have easily reported him for abuse, but she was so damn gullible, just like her pathetic mother! With any luck, he thought, she'd just leave and he wouldn't have to see her pathetic sorry little face again. Besides, she had to leave, it was the only way for him to move on and if she didn't, he would make her. She had actually done him a favour; she had cleared the path for him.

As Raj walked in, he stopped in his tracks. Before him was a heavenly sight; Emma was breast feeding his son, her hair appeared like finely spun threads of gold under the rays of the winter sun, pouring into the lounge. Her fuller naked breasts only added to her desirability and he himself questioned his perverse, sudden urge to make love to her right then and there.

"I've done it. I've left her," he said putting the case down and walking over to kneel before her, "it's finally over…I'm home, home, where I belong.

Chapter 11

"Hello Sarbjit, it's Kamal."

"Oh hello stranger? How are you and the family? They've gone to India haven't they? How's Raj…"

"Everyone is fine Sarbjit, is Sindy around please?" Kamal cut her brother-in-law's formalities short.

"Yeah, I'll just get her for you. Sweetheart," Kamal heard him call out. Raj would always sneer at how pathetic he thought Sarbjit was around his wife, referring to him as a spineless man at his wife's beck and call like a tamed dog. He didn't care much for Sindy either, since she had a tendency to turn her nose up at Kamal running around him and his parents; she was just the sort of 'wife material' he despised.

"Hi Kamal. Where have you been? I have been calling you. Wanted you to come and see the new collection. It's exquisite! The best I have had so far…"

"Sindy…I need to talk. Can you come over?"

"What's up sis?"

"I can't tell you over the phone."

Sindy was at Kamal's within the hour in her new BMW, for which, much to Kamal's amusement, she had thrown a silly little party just a few weeks ago, just like she did after any achievement. But, she had to take her hat off to her, she had it all made; her own little successful business, a nice house decorated tastefully, a doting attentive husband, freedom from in-laws and a complete I don't care attitude.

"Now what's up?" she asked walking in straight past her, making out every minute of her time was invaluable. She was all dressed up in a red sari, draped over her perfect figure and revealing the flesh of a toned waist. Her whole look was accessorised by simple, but elegant fine gold jewellery, her hair tied up high, her lips painted red and her eyes defined with thick black liquid eyeliner; she looked like a movie star. "Sarbjit's just dropped me off, he will be back in half an hour; the venue for the reception is just about twenty minutes from here. Oh all these parties to attend. I told him to give us half an hour. Where's Raj?" she said sitting down and only then noticing Kamal's drained face, sore eyes, uncombed hair dressed in a dull grey sweater, which did her no favours at all; she looked like death warmed over.

"Blimey...are things that bad?" Sindy said raising her brows.

Kamal struggled to find the words to start. She slumped into the single seat opposite Sindy, closed her eyes and let a tear run down her cheek.

"What's the matter sis?" Sindy said walking over to her and crouching down, her bangles jingled in her arms as she placed her hands on her sister's knees, her pungent perfume now engulfing the whole of the lounge and almost choking her.

"I have messed up big time Sindy!" she blurted out.

"You, messed up? Why what have you done? Burnt the rice, left a stone unpicked from the lentils?" Sindy tried to add some humour, not knowing what her sensible sister could possibly have done to have - messed up.

"I had to speak to someone Sindy. I couldn't speak to Deepa and Nindy would just kill me. So I called you."

"Yes and now I'm here, so tell me, what's this all about?"

"I've slept with someone. I slept with someone from work and somehow Raj has found out and now he wants me to leave."

Sindy leant back slightly, wondering momentarily whether her ears were deceiving her.

"You've been having an affair?"

Kamal nodded her head and looked down at her hands, unable to look her perfect little sister in the eye.

"When? Who? Why?"

"Oh I don't know, it just happened and Raj has found out, I don't know how, but he has," Sindy tilted her head to the right and moved Kamal's hair away from her left cheek.

"Did he do this to you?" Kamal nodded. Sindy shook her head in disbelief. "What do I do? He is telling me to leave," Kamal now looked towards her sister still crouched before her.

"What, he wants you to just leave?"

"Yes, he said that the marriage is over, that I should leave or else he will defame me in front of both families."

"And what about you, what do you want?" Sindy got back up on her feet, walked back and sat down opposite her again, looking towards her older sister thoughtfully.

"I don't know. Oh how could I have been so stupid?"

Sindy looked on at her sister as she sobbed and then down towards the pile of scrunched up tissues on the floor.

"Things will never be the same if you stay here, you do realise don't you? He will at every opportunity throw it back at your face. The family won't look at you the same way again, if he told them. Yeah sure it will blow over, but all that respect and trust would all be lost. You'll never get that back."

"Then what do I do?" Kamal searched an answer from her sister.

"Whatever possessed you Kamal? What made you do it?"

Kamal pulled her knees up towards her chest and rested her chin on them. She was looking straight down at her feet now.

"I was foolishly charmed. Rohit, made me feel like no-one has ever made me feel before. I think it was love that made me do it, or the desperate need for something missing in my life. Yeah me and Raj sure had some moments, but they never lasted. He left this afternoon, said he needed to get away and wanted me gone by the time he was back. He was so flippant, not even prepared to talk."

"Could he have even been relieved that you messed up?"

"Relieved?" Kamal frowned.

"Oh come on Kamal you told me how you've been struggling with him."

"So what do I do now?"

"Do you need me to spell things out for you? Does the fact that you went off with this Rohit, despite everything not tell you anything? Why do you want to continue with a marriage, which was over the moment you slept with another man? Why? Look," she got up to walk back towards her sister and put her hand on her shoulder, "I can't say I am happy things have turned out the way they have and yes you should have known better, but life is too short. We grew up watching a sad, unhappy marriage and two people staying together for the sake of society. No one knew what went on within the four walls of that home, and those who did, chose to turn a blind eye and it is because of that reason, I decided I would live my life the way I wanted it and no other way, and if nobody liked it, they could lump it. Take a leaf out of my book sis, maybe it's time you did live for yourself. If this Rohit is as wonderful as you say he is then maybe, it's time you took a chance. On the other hand, if you really want to play it safe, give Raj a couple of days to calm down. He might see things in a different light in a couple of days' time. Hang on in there. See what he says when he returns."

"Yes, I suppose I should wait and try to talk to him again."

"Well there's no harm in trying. Any idea when he will be back or where he is?"

Kamal shook her head. "Well then just wait for him to come back and take it from there. It gives you time to think too, think of what you really want. You never know, you may even surprise yourself."

"Thanks Sindy. Who'd have thought, me asking you for advice."

"Oh well, I always say the quiet ones are the worst!"

***

Rohit had gone straight to Craig's office first thing in the morning in the hope to see Kamal, but gathered she called in sick. She did not come into work the next day either. Rohit sat back in his chair at the end of the

Tuesday with nothing else on his mind but Kamal; hoping she was okay, hoping he was going to see her soon, so he could tell her exactly how he felt. Each night he relived the moment he finally had her in his arms, whilst lying in bed surrounded by the subtle fragrance of her lingering perfume on his pillow. He hoped she was back soon, so he could tell her that the uniting of their bodies was not lust and that he would do anything, anything to prove to her just how much she meant to him.

***

"Hi," Kamal was up on her feet as Raj popped his head round the lounge on the Tuesday evening. He did not find it necessary to acknowledge her and went straight upstairs. She heard the opening and closing of the wardrobe and made her way reluctantly up the stairs. She closed her eyes and took a deep breath before she stepped into the bedroom. He was packing more of his clothes, only now in the larger case.

"I thought you'd have gone by now," he said, aware of her presence whilst he grabbed some shirts with the hangers and dumped them in the suitcase. He then began opening and closing the drawers, grabbing out his undergarments and too throwing them into the case.

"Mum and dad called. They are really enjoying themselves with Junior, even thinking of extending the holiday," she said, but there was no reply, "Raj, can we talk?"

"There's nothing to talk about."

"But….."

"Any talking we do can be in front of the parents. I really do not have the time to chat shit with you, okay?"

"Where have you been staying?" she dared to ask.

"What's it to you?"

"I'm sorry. I was hoping that the time away would have calmed you down."

"Calmed me down? Hardly. Nothing has changed. I still want you out."

Kamal stood still in the doorway. He zipped up the suitcase and sat on the bed.

"Maybe if I had feelings for you, I would have given the marriage a chance. I had respect for you, but now even that has gone. So what's left? So if you thought there was a chance of reviving a non-existent relationship, you can forget it, it's not happening, especially now."

"As simple as that?" she said walking to stand by the window and looking towards him. The time apart had put a few things in perspective for her too and she too had some unanswered questions now.

"As simple as that, now it's up to you, it can be an ugly, unpleasant ending, or you can walk out, leave a note, anything, go back to your parents, say it's not working out, anything, but just go. I have found this relationship suffocating for long enough now and since Friday, well everything is just black and white for me now. I know what I want and this is not it."

"Looks like your mind was made up about our relationship, well before Friday then?"

"No, I had doubts before Friday. What happened, cleared those doubts. I should thank you really, because now I can really stop pretending."

Kamal was finding it difficult to digest his cold and callous words. All these years she had tried so hard to make the marriage work, and he…,"it's no wonder I went searching elsewhere!" she retorted bitterly.

"Oh so it's my fault now?" he said, placing a finger on his broad chest.

"Well I'm not taking all the blame."

"Oh that's just great," he said getting up.

"Well if you'd have paid a little attention, I would not have gone looking elsewhere."

"Okay. Maybe I was not the perfect husband, but you were nowhere near the perfect wife either."

"At least I tried, which is more than what I could say for you. You treated this place like a hotel and we had physical contact when it suited you!"

"Oh don't flatter yourself. You should count yourself lucky I even tried!"

"If I was not good enough for you, why did you ever agree to the marriage?" Kamal felt a hurt deep within now, she already felt tarnished, but now she felt unwanted, discarded; reminiscent of a painful feeling from a time gone by.

"Because I thought it would have worked. You," he pointed his finger in her face, "are a replica of your mother. You both enjoy to be treated like doormats!"

"How dare you!"

"What? Have I said something untrue, or have I hit a nerve? I mean look at you," he stepped back looking down at her in repulse, "if you had any pride at all, you would not be here today, pleading with me. It's so typical. You're pathetic. You love all this don't you, all this melodrama? You strive on it don't you? Well I'm sorry, I can't live like this. I'm out. Leave whichever way you want. This marriage is over. You still have time to sort yourself out before mum and dad come back, if not, well you know the score, I will have great pleasure in telling them what a dirty tart they have for a daughter-in-law. Would you be prepared to sit that through? Would you be prepared for me to shame you in front of your parents? Are you prepared for the hell your mother will go through? Think about it, long and hard, okay?"

Unable to sleep, Kamal later wandered down the stairs aimlessly. As she entered the lounge, her son's portrait sitting in the display cabinet, caught her eye. She stood still and then walked slowly towards it. The lounge was illuminated by the street lights, shining in through the windows, the curtains left undrawn. Her heart sank, as she recalled him waving goodbye to her at the airport. She picked up the photo and ran her fingers over it; she so wished he was here now. She so wanted to see his smile, cuddle him and forget all her woes, but his father's words played around in her head again and again, *"all you did was give birth to him."* He would heartlessly do everything he possibly could, to keep him away from her. She sat on the sofa with the photo close to her chest; the thought of being separated from him suddenly making her feel weak with trepidation. The fear of Raj defaming her in front of those near and dear to her, made her feel physically sick; she just not could bear to think of the shame and disappointment. As her mind wandered, the only sound was the ticking of the clock and for the first time since she had been alone she was scared, really scared, as the realisation of the true depth of her predicament kicked in. Raj had turned the sand timer upside down and the grains were pouring down steadily, the timer was set and she had but a few days to work out what she was going to do.

Daylight could not have come soon enough and she decided she was going into work. She had to at least hold onto her job and she needed to see Rohit; she needed to know how he really, really felt.

***

"Morning," Kamal managed to display a smile for her colleagues.

"Hi, you feeling better?" Danielle asked.

"Much better thanks," she said sitting down after removing her coat and scarf, tonnes of work was piled in her in-tray and her desk was hardly visible through the mail and files.

"Sorry," Danielle said, "we've just had no time. We've been so busy and the junior's not been in either."

"Oh don't worry about it," Kamal said waving her hand, "I need work to keep my mind off things."

"Everything okay?" Danielle frowned.

"Yeah, yeah," she avoided eye contact and started going through the pile of work. Danielle and Angela looked at each other; something was wrong, Kamal was not her usual chirpy self. Danielle shook her head at Angela, her indication to leave it for now and to probe later.

The morning flew by for Kamal; there was so much to do and for a brief moment she did forget all her troubles. She had a working lunch at her desk, despite the girls insisting she came down with them to the canteen, insisting she had a break, but she refused to budge. They had all been very busy, the phone had been ringing endlessly, hence they hardly had time to engage in their usual chatting. Kamal sighed as she looked towards the photo of her son. She picked up the photo of her and Raj, seated in the gondola taken in Venice and put it into her drawer faced down. She returned back to her work as soon as she finished her sandwich, wondering whether Rohit was actually in at all, as she had neither seen nor heard from him.

It was 3pm when Danielle put a cup of tea on her table and sat on the edge of it, "with extra sugar, now come on, spill. Tell us all about it."

Kamal then for the first time looked up properly at her concerned and curious colleagues. Danielle tilted her head, just like Sindy had and pushed Kamal's hair to one side.

"So this is why you've been off. The bastard!"

Angela too got up to look closer, "did you call the police?" she had her hands on her hips.

"No and actually, there's a reason behind it."

"And that makes it alright of course," Angela threw her hands in the air in irritation.

"Want to tell us what the reason is? Looks like a solid right hander to me, would love for you to justify it," Danielle asked shaking her head.

"Not right yet," Kamal said returning to her work. She did not want to disclose the exact reasons, "he wants me to leave him," is all she managed.

"And, let me see, you're thinking about it. Oh come on Kamal, you can do a million times better and you know that better than us."

"Can I?"

"Of course, do I need to spell the name out?" Angela shook her head.

"No, that was just an infatuation," she said continuing to put signed letters into the window envelopes, making sure the address was fully visible. "I really want to continue with my work now. I promise, I will talk about it when I am ready," Kamal swallowed the lump in her throat and held her tears back.

Kamal was in no hurry to go home and stayed over; there was plenty of work and Craig was still in the office. She put up a weak hand to acknowledge Brenda coming out of the lift with her cleaning trolley, as she walked into the large photocopying room; not realising Rohit had also stepped out behind the domestic. She placed the nineteen page document into the photocopier feeder and pressed for thirty copies, to be collated and stapled. She stood and for a moment absently watched the copier chugging away. She then started tidying up the room. She shook her head as she picked up empty boxes, pulled them apart and placed the flat cardboard next to the bin and scrunched up paper wrappings left on the floor and threw them into the bin. She looked up, as the door opened; she was not expecting anyone to come in at this time. It was Rohit. She looked up at him and then away quickly, the episode of Friday night, flashing before her eyes.

"Kamal, you're back."

"Hi," she said turning, to throw more scrunched up paper into the bin.

"Are you okay?"

"Okay?" she turned to look at him.

"What's that?" he said moving towards her. She put her head back down. She had forgotten the bruise; the makeup would have really worn off by now. He moved closer towards her. She could smell his crisp aftershave, as he came closer towards her, despite her reluctance. He put his briefcase down and pushed her hair to one side.

"Was it Raj?" he asked softly.

"Does it matter?"

"Of course it does."

She turned her face away looking back towards the photocopier, which was still chugging away.

"It's no more than what I deserved. He found out."

"Deserve? Found out, but how?"

"Does it matter?" she looked towards him again. "Just leave me alone Rohit, you've had your cheap thrill now please, just leave me alone," she turned her back towards him.

"Cheap thrill? Is that what you think of me?"

She continued watching the photocopier blankly with her arms folded.

"Kamal," he whispered standing close behind her. She could almost feel the energy between them and the concern in his voice weakened her. She leant her head back on his chest in exhaustion and he wrapped his arms around her waist. She turned round and buried her head into his chest for comfort. He rested his chin on her head and held her tight, rubbing her back, "let me look after you Kamal. I promise never to let you down."

She looked up at him. His eyes seemed so honest; they were not empty, cold and full of hate. She saw care, love and warmth. He bent down to kiss the tear running down her cheek and slowly bent down to kiss her on the lips. She put her hand slowly round his neck and kissed him back. Her lips quivering; her emotions and anxieties of the previous four days making her shake like a leaf. He held her tight in an attempt to calm her.

"I love you Kamal," he whispered, as they continued to slowly kiss, "I really, really love you," he said pulling her closer with each kiss.

Chapter 12

"Is everything really okay?" Parminder asked her daughter, running her hand through her hair, as she rested her head on her mother's lap. Kamal had turned up on the Friday night and Parminder had instantly sensed something was amiss. She could see it in her eyes, she appeared exhausted and when they were not talking, she sensed she was preoccupied by some troublesome matter. She could tell the rest of the world that she had bruised her face by walking into a dormant door, but she was talking to a woman who had patched up her wounds with excuses all her life. There was nothing more she wanted than to keep her daughter at home, close to her and protect her from the cruel world and society women like she herself, were drowned in.

"Yes mum, just got a lot on my mind. Mum can I ask you something? I have this friend, her husband has told her that he does not love her and he wants her to leave. What do you think? Should she leave or just stay and keep trying to win him over?"

Parminder sighed and held Kamal's hand, "do I know this friend?"

"No mum, it's a girl at work."

"Does she love her husband?"

There was a momentary silence.

"No, she doesn't want to be with him," Kamal's voice trailed off into a whisper.

"Kamal, our society believes in falling in love after marriage, it can take time, even years. Eventually you get so used to each other's ways and then, you can't imagine life without each other, it comes slowly and gradually, but it does happen. So in my opinion, they should both work on their relationship. Marriage is an institution that one should not give up on so easily."

"Does that mean you love dad?"

"Well, I am still here aren't I? If there is something there, a small spark even, your friend will stay, and if there is nothing, nothing at all, then she will leave. And contrary to what our society expects, she should leave, if she is so unhappy."

Her mother's three words 'she will leave' rang in her ears over and over, like an echo; did she have the bottle to just get up and leave?

"Mum......."

"Hmm."

".....nothing."

Her dad was out and both mother and daughter watched an old classic Hindi movie together. Kamal was lying on the sofa, as an old romantic *Mukesh* song was playing out, the lyrics of which played on her mind, ' *I will talk about only what you want to talk about, if you say it is morning, I will say it is morning, if you say it is night I will say it is night*' , they reminded her of being around Rohit, as whenever she was with him, it was if she was the only person in the room and she was the only person that mattered. Her mother was humming to the lyrics; she loved her old Bollywood music and she'd often listen to it when she was alone. Whenever her father-in-law listened to these old classics on the Asian radio station, they would remind her of her childhood years, of her mother humming away, as if they provided her with escapism from her otherwise constrained life. Now Kamal had learnt the meaning of love, she could not imagine how anyone would not want to experience it. Her heart fluttered as Rohit again played on her mind, body and soul. He was in her thoughts morning, noon and night; he had been so sweet to her over the past few days. Making any excuse to come down to see her, to ensure she was okay, she felt so wanted and cared for and it was on the Thursday when he said the ultimate words....

"Come on, let me take you out for a drink."

"What now?"

"Yes, come on. It's late night shopping. We can find a nice bar, have a drink, maybe grab something to eat and then I'll take you back home. Come on. I promise I won't keep you out long."

Rohit had to wait a good twenty minutes before he was served at the busy bar on Corporation Street, as the bar staff served drink, upon drink. Kamal looked round at friends and couples huddled together at tables, including a group of Asian women cackling away. A couple sitting in a cosy corner were switched off from the rest of the world, the lady who dared to dress in a mini skirt with the cold snap outside was literally gagging a man, her fingers running through his hair, while his right hand rested on the flesh of her bare thighs. A group of men standing at the bar shared a joke as they looked towards the fortunate man. A couple of young men were obviously attracted to a group of girls who were lapping up the attention, laughing spontaneously, as one of the men approached them. Some people sat on their own with just a drink for company, looking through the window, watching the busy Birmingham traffic moving at a snail's pace. The bar was buzzing with life. She imagined how her dad would react if he found out his daughter was sitting in a bar that too with a man, other than her husband, indeed what anyone would think, but she pushed these feelings to one side and tried her best to relax, putting aside her drilled in orthodox upbringing, it was just an innocent drink.

"Any news on Raj?" Rohit asked. Kamal shook her head. "What are you going to do?"

Kamal shrugged her shoulders as she sipped on her coke, "who could have told him Rohit? The only person that I can think of possibly seeing us at all is Christine, but she does not even know Raj."

Rohit shook his head, "no, can't be Christine. What about Danielle, Angela?"

"Oh don't be silly, they'd never do that!"

"Well you said so yourself, they've forever been telling you to leave him, anyway, regardless, personally I think that night was a blessing in disguise. I mean did it not just clarify things for the both of you? I mean, he told you he did not love you, how he cannot, I don't know," he said placing his hand on hers, "I don't regret that night one bit," he said looking into her eyes. Kamal's heart melted, overwhelmed with the thought of anyone able to love her so much. She smiled at him, kissed him on his cheek and rested her head on his shoulder in relief.

"I am here for you always Kamal, you only need to say the word and I will be by your side, whatever your decision is."

"I'm going to mum's tomorrow night, as I don't know when and if I will see her again if I follow through my intentions."

"I know you've been to my place before," he said sitting up straight and getting a pen from his inner jacket pocket, "but here is my address. My doors are always open for you," Rohit jotted his address on the back of the cardboard coaster and handed it over to her, "I mean where else would you go?"

When she got back to the increasingly isolating, lonely and cold home, she took the coaster out of her handbag and smiled. She felt she needed no-one else now. She had Rohit and felt she could survive the wildest storm with him by her side. He was right and so was Raj, there was no point in carrying on.

"You would not want for anything. I will love you, protect you, we can build a whole new world together, travel the world, look forward to the future. I love you." His last words swam round and round in her head. Rohit was literally waiting for her to fully enter his life and the more she thought about it the more defiant she became, with an increasing will to break down the barriers and just live.

Kamal hugged her mum and held onto her.

"Oh dear, you're behaving like you're never going to see me again," a tear ran down Kamal's cheek. "What's the matter? Please tell me Kamal. How can I help you, if you don't tell me?" her mother asked her desperately.

"I'm sorry mum, but I have to go now. Promise me you will look after yourself. You don't have to keep putting up with abuse you do know don't you? I got this leaflet for you," Kamal fetched the leaflet out her bag, "it's got some contact numbers on there, there is help out there," Kamal placed it firmly in her mother's hand. Parminder smiled. "I really need to go now mum," Kamal squeezed her mum's hands before she turned to leave.

Parminder's heart dropped as she watched her daughter leave her, walking towards the car, looking back at her before she got in, fastening her seat belt and wiping her tears. Kamal looked at her mother one more time, blew her a kiss and drove away. Parminder stood watching the car drive down the road and turn right out of sight. She swallowed a lump in her throat and let a tear run down her cheek.

"I know you will make the right decision. May God bless you my darling," she whispered. Parminder was no fool; she had seen the sadness in her daughter's eyes. She knew it was not her friend that wanted to leave. She knew it was Kamal herself.

Raj was waiting for Kamal to return from her parent's home having been informed by Deepa that she was due to return on the Sunday night. He sat in the living room, the TV was on, but his eyes were fixed on the bay window. He had a little to drink, just to calm him down. He stood up as he heard a car coming up the drive the headlights of which further lit up the room.

Kamal noticed that the house lights were switched on and hesitated; she was not in a mood for confrontation and it was a while before she plucked the courage to step out of the car.

"Is she here?" Deepa said coming in from the kitchen with her husband.

"Yep, she's here," Raj confirmed sitting back down.

Kamal opened the front door, walked in and placed the car keys like she always did on the cabinet in the hall. She slowly walked into the living room and to her surprise she saw her judge and jury before her; Raj sitting on the single seat, his dad's and Deepa and Varinder sitting straight ahead on the sofa. Varinder and Raj looked straight up at her, but Deepa's gaze was lowered, as if she was nervous for Kamal.

"Where have you been?" her brother-in-law asked her, in a tone of voice barely recognisable, he was usually soft and gentle in his approach, a trait he had inherited from his father.

"My mum and dad's."

"And how are we supposed to believe that?" Kamal had to lower her eyes at this point. Varinder was ten years her senior and she had always looked up to him as an older brother.

"Whatever possessed you Kamal?" Deepa finally said looking up, disappointment plastered all over her face.

Kamal shrugged her shoulders, "I'm sorry," was all she managed to say.

"Now, how are we going to resolve this?" Varinder asked getting up and pacing the room.

"There is nothing to resolve! I want her out of the house! Do not try to talk me out of it. I want her out of here before mum and dad come back and try to resolve things as well. I cannot even bring myself to look at her, let alone think of trying to make the marriage work! Again a friend of mine saw her in a bar in town just on Thursday, ask her, ask her yourself. If there was any regret, why was she in the bar with that bastard with her tongue half way down his throat!" Kamal looked at Raj in disbelief, as he exaggerated the whole setting with vulgarity, but even more so of him knowing; who on earth was his informer?

"Kamal?" Varinder looked towards her in repulse. Unable to defend herself, Kamal wished the floor below would just cave in. "Well say something?" Varinder raised his voice, "if you were not happy, you should have come to us, we would have tried to sit and talk it through, why did you have to drag the family name through dirt!"

Kamal stood silently, eyes down, her cheeks flushed red with embarrassment. Her coat and scarf around her neck were not helping the situation, she felt like was cooking on fire. She wanted to strip them off, but felt physically unable to move.

"I think we need to talk to your parents," Varinder said.

"No, no please!" Kamal said finally looking up, the tears that were welling in her eyes, now running down her cheeks. "Please, my mum will die of shame."

"And what about us? What were you thinking of?" Varinder asked.

"I don't know okay! I don't know. It just happened. And I'm glad it happened," her defiance finally kicked in, "if I had got the love and attention from my husband at home, then I would not have gone searching for it elsewhere. Besides, he's said so himself, this marriage was nothing but a compromise to him. Ask him yourself. You tell me, how am I supposed to go on after he said those words and truth be told," she said wiping her tears and holding her head up, "I also have no feelings for him either!"

Varinder and Deepa both looked from Kamal to Raj.

"So what do you both want?"

"Divorce!" both voices synchronised as one.

Deepa walked into the bedroom as Kamal packed her suitcase. She held her son's photo to her chest before she put it in the suitcase with tears streaming down her face. She was not even conscious of what she was putting in the case. Anything she could see that belonged to her was dumped in.

"Kamal, please reconsider, come stay with us. Take time out. Wait for tempers to cool down. Please."

"It's too late Deepa. It's all over. There is nothing left. Promise me, promise me you will look out for my son, until I sort things out," she said holding Deepa by her shoulders, "I know he is in good hands and he would want for nothing, but you must watch out for him also. Raj will go off and do his own thing, I know he will, it's what he's been doing over the years. Please promise me?"

"Of course I will, but..."

"There are no buts Deepa. Please let me go," she said zipping up the case. From the top wardrobe shelf, she took the jewellery given to her by her parents and leaving behind what was gifted by her in-laws, she took all her personal documents, her passport, birth certificate, picture of her parents and sisters and dumped them into a rucksack. She picked up the suitcase, swung the rucksack over her back, grabbed her handbag and took one look back at the room. Many emotions flooded back, from the day she first set foot in this room full of hopes and aspirations, to disappointments, lonely nights, sadness, the deathly silences to the arguments and spiteful words and that one volatile, demeaning moment, that still made her stomach turn. She turned away sharply, turning her back to it all. Deepa followed her, continuously trying to talk some sense into her. Meanwhile Varinder was trying to contact her parents, but the phone just irritatingly rung out. Kamal dragged the case down the stairs, swung it in the back of the car, placed her rucksack on top and threw her handbag onto the passenger street ignoring Deepa's continuing pleas, as she sat in the car. Realising he'd have to provide answers to his parents Varinder joined his wife, embarrassed by curious neighbours peering out their windows, pulling back their net curtains, some even opening their front door to look on, but Kamal could hear nor see anyone, she just wanted to leave. She took one last look at the house and at Deepa, who was now being held back by Varinder, as she started the car. While Varinder was frowning with disbelief and disgust, Deepa stood speechless and gutted and as for Raj, he stood at the window with his hands calmly in his pockets, unperturbed by her departure, just waiting for her to leave. Kamal whispered sorry to Deepa and spun off.

Kamal pulled the car up outside the Asian department store where her mother had purchased most of her marital dresses from; taking her back to a time of purity, innocence. The mannequins in the window were dressed in typical bridal wear; a young girl's dream. Their bodies wrapped in saris, *lehngas* (dresses) and Punjabi suits, the heavily embroidered *duppattas* (scarves) draped over the heads and shoulders, their hands posed elegantly in the air. Never had she thought whilst choosing her clothes, with matching accessories that her marriage was destined to be doomed, that she was one day going to be parked right outside the very same department store, agonising over her quandary; any which way she turned she was a loser. If she stayed she lost and now she had left, she had lost; both ways brought shame on to herself and to those she loved. She was tarnished. But, straight ahead, was a glimpse of love and hope. Kamal could see the dome of the temple lit up in the distance. She closed her eyes, put her head back on her seat, took a deep breath and prayed for strength and forgiveness. She reached for her handbag and pulled out the coaster with Rohit's address, followed by the A-Z from her glove compartment. The thought of seeing his loving eyes and being welcomed by his embrace, gave her some comfort. At least *he* would be happy to see her; happy that she had finally done it. But each glimmer of light was overshadowed by a dark looming cloud. The thought of being separated from her son saddened her and she exhaled as she thought of the long custody battle she would have to fight, knowing full well that her in-laws would not give up their grandchild so easily and after all, it was she that was abandoning him and she that had committed adultery.

With the many thoughts churning away in her mind as she drove with her trembling hands and moist eyes, she soon approached Rohit's apartment. She parked up and looked up towards the apartment block. She decided not to take her suitcase out just yet, as she did not want to startle him. She stepped out of her car and looked up towards the heavens, the sky was eerily dark and she shuddered as she made her way forward, looking about her, the only sound was the clicking of her heels on the tarmac below; it was a quiet Sunday night and the whole world seemed to be tucked up safely in their warm homes. It felt as if she was the only one wandering about like a lost soul. She had dreamt of this moment many times, leaving her world as she knew it for Rohit, but in her imagination, she had always portrayed the rise of a new dawn, the beginning of a new era, this night in contrast, was guilt ridden, taunting and she felt nauseous. Her legs were shaking both from the nerves and the events that led to this moment and she suddenly began to feel quite apprehensive. What if he rejected her?

She pressed the button with 'Rohit Shama' printed against it and waited patiently. Her heart was racing and her hands trembling.

"Hello."

Thank God he was at home she thought closing her eyes in anguish and taking a deep breath before she spoke into the intercom. "Hello Rohit, it's me, Kamal, can I speak to you please?"

"Oh, um," there was brief silence, "yeah, come on up," she heard a buzzing noise and pushed the door open. Her clicking heels echoed as she walked through the foyer towards the lift. She pressed the button for the lift and waited patiently, wondering whether she had exaggerated a hesitation in his voice, or whether it was her being paranoid. As she stepped into the lift and pressed button number four, she swallowed the lump in her throat and closed her eyes in anguish again. As the lift doors slid open she saw that Rohit was already standing outside his apartment with just a white bath robe wrapped around him, the door pulled ajar behind him. She walked towards him with her arms outstretched. She wrapped her arms around him and lay her head on his bare chest in exhaustion. Rohit rubbed his hand on her back gently.

"What's the matter?" he whispered.

"I've left him. I've finally done it."

Rohit stood still, his arms around her suddenly fell lax. He then cleared his throat and eventually spoke.

"Listen Kamal. Now is really not a good time, you should have called me," he said softly pulling back. Kamal looked up at him confused.

"What's the matter?" she asked, "you seem on edge."

"Um," he said with his left hand on his forehead, "well I am actually," he smiled nervously.

"Well what is it, maybe I can help?" Kamal asked, now wondering why he had not even invited her in, when she heard a woman's voice call out to him from within the apartment. Kamal's pupils turned towards the door behind him and then back up at him questioningly.

"Who was that?"

"Um…" he said clearing his throat again and folding his arms, not knowing quite what to do with them.

"Rohit, who is in there?" Again Kamal heard the voice and then the door opened. Standing was a woman who looked to be in her mid-twenties, clear fair complexion, small sharp pointy nose, large brown eyes with beautifully groomed, curved eyebrows. She had typical Northern Indian features and her hair was wrapped up in a pink towel, a small wet lock hung over her cheek, the cheek as pink as the towel. She was wearing a pink bathrobe that came to just above her knees, leaving little to the imagination of what she was, or was not wearing underneath. She stood curiously behind Rohit.

"Oh it's just the neighbour Priya. She's just checking if we've got…..problems… with our… electrics."

"Oh," the lady said looking at Kamal from head to toe and smiling with her perfect white teeth. "Well why don't you invite her in. I think I will like to get to know our neighbour."

"Oh no, she was just leaving, weren't you?" he looked at Kamal with a plea in his eyes, begging her not to say anything.

"Kamal? Is that short for anything?" Priya asked her.

"Um..no, it's simply Kamal. And you are?" Kamal tried to smile.

"I'm Priya, Rohit's wife," she smiled, holding onto Rohit's arm. Kamal felt as if she'd been thumped in the stomach by an iron fist, she tried not to look stunned, even though she felt as if her heart had been pierced through with a searing hot iron rod. Rohit stood still, anticipating the worst. "Are you sure you will not come in Kamal?" Priya asked.

"Um…no, no. I really have to go….but, thanks for asking. It must just be the electrics in my house that are not working, yours are obviously perfectly fine," Kamal said looking at Rohit and walking backwards towards the lift.

"Well can Rohit help you?" Priya asked.

"No, no I'll….just…..call the landlord. You don't worry…..thanks," she turned round. The lift had not gone down and the doors were still open. She walked in, pressed the ground floor button and kept her back turned towards them, until she heard the doors slide shut behind her.

"Oh my God!" she gasped placing her hand to her mouth, "what have you done?" her eyes welled up. She placed her right hand on her faint head and held onto the wall of the lift for support. She felt unable to breathe and suddenly felt claustrophobic as she stood enclosed within the small confined space. Waiting desperately for the doors to open, she gasped for air and carried her shaking legs out of the building. Not once looking back, she staggered her way back to the car. She put her shaking hand on the car for support, overcome by a physical sickness. What had she done? She had turned her back on her family for a man who conveniently forgot to mention that he was bloody married! Her keys were in her hand, but she could not see them, her vision was blurred and she saw nothing but darkness. She subconsciously made out the right key and managed to open the door. She collapsed into the seat and placed her head on the steering wheel tormented by the height of Rohit's deceit, when she could hear her name echoing in the distance.

"Kamal!" she looked up to her right and saw Rohit approaching, in just a white shirt and jeans. She reached out for the door and slammed it shut.

"Kamal wait please!" he ran up to the car and opened the door before she could lock it. Kamal was looking straight ahead holding firmly onto the steering wheel. Rohit felt gutted; as he saw she was physically shaking and placed his hand on her shoulder. "Kamal," he whispered.

"Get your hand off me," Kamal said, her voice breaking.

"But...."

"But what!" she said wiping her tears and turning to look at him her eyes now red with fury.

"I...I was meaning to tell you, she just came without warning, I .... I have been wanting to tell you for ages, just....could not find the right time," he said bent down to the car, guilt and shame written all over his face.

"Well Mr Rohit Sinha, you tell me, what the hell am I supposed to do now? I have just turned my back on my whole world! I have just left my home for you! What am I supposed to do? Where do I go from here? Tell me. How could you Rohit? How could you forget to tell me you were married!"

"Oh Kamal, please try to understand."

"Understand? You want me to understand?"

"Um....it was when I went to India that one Christmas," he put his shaking hand to his forehead as he tried to explain, "my parents didn't even ask me. I had no say. You have got to understand. I did it for my parents. I have known Priya since childhood. We as a family owe her parents a lot. They were the only ones that supported us when dad's business went bust and the success dad has today, is due to their help and support. Then Priya discloses that she was in love with me and wanted to marry me, I was stuck. My family owes them so much. I had no say it was a compromise, you must believe me."

Kamal could not help but laugh then, "you're no different to Raj. He says exactly the same," she shook her head at the irony, "a compromise, you play with our lives and turn round to say it was just a compromise. Well, you go home to your dear little compromise and cosy little apartment, while I go and decide, which way I am going to go from here."

"I can help you. Tell me what I can do?"

"You can get out of my sight!" Kamal pulled down her seatbelt and started the ignition.

"Here have some money," he said pulling his wallet out of his pocket, "stay at a hotel, here, have my number, call me."

"Keep your money and number to yourself," she picked up the coaster she'd left on the passenger seat and threw it at him, "as of today I want nothing more to do with you!" Rohit just about managed to save his hand from being crushed, as she pulled the door shut. He banged on the window, asking her to stop, but she didn't. As she drove off, she saw his wife looking down out of the apartment window.

PART 2

Chapter 13

"Oh come on Aaron," Michelle said looking at her watch and stepping back under the bus shelter, as the rain began to pour down. Michelle looked towards the young woman sitting on the bench, appearing switched off from the hustle and bustle that continued around her, as if encapsulated in her own little world, not even deterred by the rain which was crashing down now. The wet ground of Centenary Square now shimmered under the beaming lights of The Rep, Symphony Hall and International Convention Centre. The rain began to bounce off the surface now, as people ran for shelter or sought sanctuary in local bars and restaurants, but the woman sat numb. Michelle looked at her watch again and exhaled. She looked up towards the woman again and searched in her bag for her umbrella. She couldn't find it. She looked up at the heavens as the rain came down relentlessly and frowned. She couldn't ignore her any further and made her way forward.

"Hiya. Are you okay?" she asked looking down at the soaked woman, with her hands placed on her lap. The young woman looked up at her slowly and stared at her vacantly.

"Are you okay?" Michelle asked her again. She barely nodded and looked back down. Michelle frowned, but persisted. "Do you want to wait under the bus shelter?" Michelle asked.

She shook her head. Michelle wanted to run back, but she could not leave her here, she was obviously not in a fit state of mind. She could just make out that her eyes were sore, possibly from crying. Her hair was soaking wet and rain drops rolled down her face. Michelle was just as drenched as her now, but she continued to probe.

"Can I help you at all?"

The lady looked up again.

"I...I...have nowhere to go."

"Oh, are you homeless?" Michelle asked curiously; she did not look like she was homeless; she was dressed well enough.

"Yes, I guess I am," she whimpered.

"Have you been chucked out or something?" Michelle asked. The woman nodded her head slightly. "Well look....um, you can come to mine if you want," she said with some hesitation, as she could not think of anything more comforting to say.

"Yours?" she frowned, confused.

"Umm, well yeah," she smiled and shrugged her shoulders, "I won't be able to sleep at night, if I leave you sitting here. Besides my mother would never forgive me! So come on then and you can tell me all about it. Well come on then." The woman looked at Michele and frowned again. Michelle smiled, encouraging her, "come." The woman got up slowly and Michelle led the way, looking back to make sure she was following her, all be that slowly and cautiously. "My brother should have been here by now," she said looking round, "God knows what's keeping him! If he does not turn up we'll catch the bus okay?"

"I have a car," the woman said flatly.

"Oh," Michelle said looking round, "okay then," Michelle shrugged her shoulders.

"Just left here," Michelle said as they reached Moseley, South of Birmingham, "and as usual there is no parking space. Oh can you squeeze it in here? If your parking is as bad as mine, you'll have no chance," Michelle laughed and rolled her eyes as she got no reaction. She then nodded, pleasantly impressed at the simple manoeuvre.

"Thank you. I'll check into a hotel, bread and breakfast," the woman said.

"I will hear of no such thing! You are coming in with me to dry yourself off, while I prepare you a nice hot drink. Besides you have brought me all the way here, it's the least I can offer you." There had hardly been any dialect between the two and Michelle stopped trying, as she sensed remoteness, each time she had attempted to break the silence. "Come into the warm for a bit, you're soaked."

The lady, looked down at her clothes, as if she had not even realised and then nodded her head slightly.

"Good. Aaron is at home. I saw his car," she said as they walked out into the rain, which had subsided, "and the lights are on," Michelle said smiling at the stranger as she opened the gate to the old Victorian mid terrace. "Aaron," Michelle shouted out as soon as she opened the front door.

"Where were you Michelle?" a tall slim young man, dark hair, who appeared to be in his late twenties, early thirties, walked out into the hall.

"Oh," Aaron stopped as he saw Michelle wasn't alone.

"Um….this is….." Michelle said looking towards the lady realising they had not even exchanged names.

"Kamal."

"Yes, Camel. She…..she gave me a lift home, I'm Michelle by the way and that's my brother Aaron," Michelle smiled, "here give me your coat," she said looking back at Kamal as she put hers on the radiator to dry off. Kamal took her coat off and gave it to Michelle aware that her brother was still curiously looking on at her.

"Right now, the bathroom is upstairs on the right, and there are some fresh towels in the cupboard, it you want to just dry your hair and in the meantime, I will put the kettle on," Michelle said looking at Kamal and smiling. Kamal nodded and walked slowly towards the stairs, past Michelle's brother who was looking towards his sister with an obvious question mark looming above his head. Michelle watched Kamal walk up the stairs slowly then walked towards her brother, taking him into the lounge by his elbow.

"Who is she?" he whispered.

"She was in Centenary Square, just sitting there in the rain for ages and I could not help but go to ask if she was okay and she just appeared so upset. So I asked her to come home with me."

"What, just like that?" Aaron asked hands on hips.

"Yeah just like that."

"Honestly Michelle, you just can't help yourself can you?"

"Oh well," she said waving her hand in the air and walking into the kitchen, through the lounge, to fill and switch on the kettle, "the least I could do was offer her a warm drink. She did drop me off after all. Speaking of which, where were you?"

"Um hello, I did go to pick you up, but when you were not at the bus stop I just assumed that you'd got the bus."

"I suppose I was with her when you got there. She's either left home or has been chucked out," Michelle whispered.

"Oh and I guess there was no-one else that was half bothered."

"No, there wasn't. I don't know what you're worried about. She hardly looks like a mass murderer."

"And of course you know what a mass murderer looks like. Yeah well, one drink and she can go."

Kamal splashed her face with cold water and dried it with a small towel. The towel was soft and smelt of fabric softener; the bathroom was tiled a cool blue and white, but was warm, if not hot. She looked at her reflection in the mirror above the washbasin. Her eyes were puffy and red. She took her comb out of her bag, combed back her wet jet black hair slowly, while she continued to look at her sorry image. As she put the comb back, she saw her purse. She pulled it out, opened it and looked at the photo of her son taken a few minutes following his birth, tucked under the transparent flap. She stood numb, staring down at the photo vacantly; everything seemed so surreal. She frowned, wondering whether she was indeed not dreaming, whether this was all a nightmare and she would soon wake up safely in her bed to the sound of her in-laws up and about and her son knocking on her door calling out, "mommy."

"Are you okay?" Michelle knocked softly on the door with a tone of concern in her voice.

"Yes," Kamal said, now sure she was not dreaming and this was all really happening. She wiped her eyes, took a deep breath and opened the door, managing to curve her lips into a very unconvincing smile.

"Come on," Michelle said, "tea is getting cold. Is tea okay?"

"Yes, thanks."

Kamal walked into a very regal looking lounge. The walls covered in a maroon and beige vertically patterned velvet wallpaper. The furniture was an elegant mahogany and the period fireplace was the stunning centrepiece. But what Kamal noted more than anything was that somehow, the young brother and sister did not quite fit in with the traditional interior.

"Come and sit down," Michelle urged Kamal to step forward.

Kamal hesitantly sat down on the chunky maroon sofa, splayed with large tasselled gold cushions.

Aaron observed the pretty stranger. She looked up towards him and smiled ever so slightly, putting her head back down and her shoulders slouched down. Michelle handed Kamal a cup of tea and sat opposite her, next to her brother Aaron. She looked towards Aaron when Kamal's hand shook, as she held the cup of tea and steadied it with her left hand.

"Thanks," Kamal said quietly. She felt extremely uncomfortable under the inquisitive eyes of her hosts, "I will leave as soon as I finish this."

"Where will you go?" Michelle asked.

"I'll check into a hotel or something, bed or breakfast."

"Well you can stay here for the night, can't she Aaron?" Michelle said to a rather stunned Aaron. Kamal sensed that she was not so welcome by the brother.

"No, no, really, I'll be okay. Thanks for this," Kamal said drinking the hot sweet tea, the only drink she'd had since she left her mother's.

"No I insist. You stay here today, I mean look at the time? Say something Aaron."

Aaron had to agree, she did look desperate and besides, he would not hear the end of it from his inquisitive sister. He knew she was just curious to know what the story was behind this intriguing stranger.

"Yes. That's fine, just the one night."

Kamal felt obliged to accept, "you sure you don't mind? I don't want to be a burden."

"No. Of course we don't. Are you hungry? Do you want something to eat?" Michelle asked.

"No, no, really I do not have much of an appetite."

"Have you left home? Was it your parents? I have an Indian friend, she ran away from home because her parents would not let her marry the boy she was going out with and......"

"Michelle!" Aaron looked towards his sister in utter disbelief.

"Oh sorry, I was just curious," Michelle said.

Kamal thought Michelle looked to be about the same age as herself, but she was as curious as a five year old, "that's okay," Kamal said. The least she could do now was tell them the truth.

"I left home. My marriage broke down and I had nowhere else to go."

"But you people have really big families don't you?" Michelle said and this time Aaron just turned to look at his sister speechless, "I mean, you're usually quite a close-knit community aren't you?"

"Yes we are, but I have just messed up so badly. I need some time to think," Kamal put her shaking hand to her forehead, as it spun.

"Oh," Michelle said wide eyed, still wondering what had caused her to leave home, "do you live locally?"

"North Birmingham, well that was where my parent's home is. My in-laws are actually from Wolverhampton."

"Won't your parents have you?" Michelle asked.

"I can't go there. There of all places," she whispered, "but I promise, I will be out your hair tomorrow. Do you mind awfully if I put my head down. It's just that a lot has happened today and my head is really throbbing."

"Shall I get you a pain killer?" Michelle said getting up, "and are you sure you won't have anything to eat?"

"No, really, I'm fine thanks."

"I'll show you to the spare room then," Aaron said getting up.

"I don't mind sleeping here on the sofa."

"Oh don't worry we have a spare room," Michelle said also getting up.

"My night clothes are in my suitcase. I'll just go out to get it."

"I'll help you," Aaron followed her out.

"I should really leave," Kamal said looking at the brother as he walked her to the car.

Aaron paused thoughtfully. She did look desolate and then smiled, "we are harmless, I promise, though I can't promise my sister won't talk you to death. Look, it's only a matter of the night and you look innocent enough, so come on."

Kamal smiled and nodded.

Kamal looked round the small box room, in which was a single bed with a solid oak bedstead and a small oak wardrobe opposite. The walls were decorated with a pastel yellow coloured paper with tiny, ditsy flowers and the duvet cover yellow, with a border of contrasting yellow roses. Next to the bed was a small solid oak bedside cabinet, with a yellow and gold based table lamp. She walked over the thick navy carpet towards the window, which looked over the street and drew the curtains shut. She felt really awkward, uncomfortable and wanted to leave, but the brother and sister had been so accommodating. She pulled the duvet cover back, which revealed a plump pillow and a clean white sheet; they were obviously very house proud. Ensuring the door was locked, she got changed into her pyjamas, which smelt of home and added to her sadness. She lay her aching head down on the pillow and looked up at the white ceiling in the soft lighting of the bedside lamp. She covered herself with the duvet, which smelt, as if it had just come out the wash. Aaron had brought her suitcase up to the room for her and said to ask if she needed anything else. She could not believe that people like Michelle and Aaron actually existed, amidst this cruel world, filled with selfish, heartless people.

Her mind recapped over the days' events, from waving goodbye to her mum, the look of disappointed upon Deepa's face, the disgust on Varinder's, seeing the pleasure in Raj's eyes as she left and finally, the deceiving bastard Rohit Sinha. If it was not for him, she would never have been here today. If it had not been for her own foolishness, she would not be here now.

"Hmmm," Michelle whispered, "I wonder what she did to break her marriage?"

"No doubt you'll get to the bottom of it tomorrow," Aaron said as he dried the dishes.

"I was wondering Aaron……"

"What now?"

"Why don't we ask her if she wants to stay here? I mean we were thinking of renting out the spare room anyway and besides the extra income wouldn't hurt would it?"

"Suppose there's no harm in asking her," he said putting the dinner plates away. "Anyway, I am going up to bed now. I got to take the kids to school tomorrow morning and then I got to help out at the club. What about you?"

"I'll just make sure Kam-al is okay before I leave for work. I suppose I could always take her to the salon with me couldn't I?"

"Yeah I suppose. Michelle, promise me you won't get too involved please?"

"Okay, okay, I promise. I can't help it you know, it's in my nature, I take on after mum," she said following her brother out of the kitchen, into the living room, switching off the kitchen light and closing door behind her.

"Yeah, I know, but you should know when to stop. And I think we should just agree on a trial of a month, see how it works out yeah? I mean she may not even want to stay here."

"Yeah, okay. What time is Sandra dropping the kids off tomorrow?"

"Just after eight."

"She expects you to do things at the drop of a hat. Why do you allow her to do it?"

Aaron had been divorced for six months now. He had been together with Sandra for just two years before they got married and broke up six years later. His mother Carol had never approved of Sandra. She had always considered Sandra to be selfish and controlling and she was right. Aaron gave her all of life's comforts and was a true provider, but it was never enough and things got to a point when he could hardly bring himself to speak to her and it was Sandra who eventually demanded a divorce, much to his relief, as he knew he no longer loved her, in fact he was not even sure whether he ever did love her. He remembered the doubts he had on their overly extravagant wedding day, which had taken strenuous months and months to organise. So exhausted was he when the big day finally arrived, he was almost not going to turn up at the church, but the thought of the dreaded consequences urged him to put his best foot forward. The only things that Aaron and Sandra now had in common were their five year old twins whom he had regular contact with, on the days Sandra chose of course, but he was willing to compromise any day for his children. His concern though of late was Sandra's new boyfriend Jack who had moved in with her and the affect this would have on his children. They seemed to be warming to Jack quite well, but he wondered how long this one would last; her spontaneous relationships were doing nothing but sending out confusing signals to the children.

As he made his way from the bathroom to his bedroom he paused for a few seconds looking at the closed door of the spare room next to his. He was slightly curious about this beautiful stranger, and the story behind her distress.

Chapter 14

"Morning. Feeling better?" Michelle asked as Kamal walked into the lounge. She certainly looked a lot more refreshed.

"Yes, thank you. Had to look round twice, completely forgot where I was."

"Did you sleep well then?"

"Eventually. Did I hear children this morning?"

"Yes, Courtney and Zach, Aaron's kids."

"Oh. He looks too young to have children."

"Yeah, he was pretty young when he and Sandra had them. Twins, they just started school this year," Michelle said picking up a portrait of the children and showing it to Kamal.

"Oh they're so cute," Kamal's heart sank as she saw the portrait of the children.

"You okay?" Michelle asked.

"Yes. Yes, thanks. Um, I won't take much more of your time. I'll just get my stuff together and leave you in peace."

"Not before you've had some tea and breakfast."

"No really, I'm not hungry."

"Nonsense, most important meal of the day my mum used to say," Michelle said walking into the kitchen.

"Used to say?" Kamal followed her.

"Yeah, she died earlier this year," Michelle's tone dipped as she spoke.

"Oh, I'm sorry."

"It's okay. This is my mum's house. I never really moved out. Well not permanently anyway. I stayed with my boyfriend for a while, ex-boyfriend now, it did not work out and I came back home. Aaron moved in too, to support me after mum passed. Now what do you want to eat?"

"I'm quite happy with a slice of toast Michelle."

"Okay, come, take a seat."

Kamal smiled sitting at the small dining table and looking down the narrow oak wood fitted kitchen with green appliances, the only white being the fridge freezer and washing machine.

"So what do you plan to do from here?" Michelle asked as she filled the kettle.

"Um, not sure really. May have to check into a bed and breakfast, get a paper and start looking for a flat or something."

"Or, how about you become our lodger?" Michelle asked raising her brows and tilting her head sideways.

"Oh," Kamal frowned.

"Well?"

"Um, are you sure?"

"I would not be asking if I was not sure. I spoke to Aaron last night. He said we could try for a month, see how it works out. So shall I take that as a yes?"

"Well, yes," Kamal was quite speechless, "ummm, how much for?"

"Oh sort that out with Aaron. He looks after the financial side of things."

"Thanks Michelle.... I really don't know how to thank you," Kamal lifted her shoulders and frowned, totally lost for words.

"Well.....can you cook?"

"Yes," Kamal nodded and managed a smile.

"Well me and Aaron, we love Indian food! Would you?" she looked at her enthusiastically.

"Yes, of course, chicken curry with pilao rice maybe?"

"Perfect. Oh look at the time, should be leaving soon," Michele said placing a plate with a slice of toast on the table for Kamal and fetching the butter out the fridge.

"For work?"

"Yes, I work in a salon, I'm a hairdresser."

"I should have guessed." Michelle's long, glossy, blond hair was tied in a French plait. She had beautiful soft peachy skin and blue eyes. Her nose, small and pointy and her thin but shapely lips were painted a glossy pink.

"You can walk down with me," she said as she made the tea, "and I'll show you around the neighbourhood, you might as well get to know it and then, you can make a start on dinner. Aaron will be well thrilled. He loves Indian. We've got some spices in the cupboard, Aaron's always trying, but he never gets it quite right. Now let me see," Michelle opened the cupboard doors, "we have turmeric, ground coriander, ground cumin, chilli powder, is that okay?" she said picking out the spice jars and lining them on the kitchen counter.

"Yes, do you have onions, garlic and ginger?"

"No I don't think so," she frowned thinking.

"I'll get them when we're out."

"Great stuff and we don't mind spicy!"

Kamal would have preferred to stay in the house to gather her thoughts, but she felt obliged to follow Michelle. She so wanted to return to familiar surroundings, to normality, but that was hardly an option now. Instead she was feebly following a stranger, she had hardly known a few hours. Her head felt light, her legs carried on aimlessly, carrying a body that had lost its soul. It had stopped raining, but the air was still damp and the day was as dull and gloomy as her outlook on the future. Exhaust fumes created thick white clouds as they stood stationary or drove down the old street lined with Victorian terraced houses. A few elderly ladies greeted "good morning," as they shuffled by with their shopping trolleys. "Morning Michelle," an elderly man waved his newspaper in the air as he walked by on the opposite side of the road.

"Morning Albert," Michelle shouted back. "It's not far from here, only a ten minute-walk."

As they walked out of Vernon Road, they walked onto a main street. The smell of freshly baked bread wafted through the cold air, as they walked past the local bakery, already displaying Christmas cakes and mince pies packed in boxes of half a dozen. The butchers displayed a deadline for ordering turkey and had a few clients already being served. There was a newsagent, a hardware store, a fish and chip shop, which was not yet open and even a pet shop.

"As you can see we have everything literally at our doorstep. Some of these shops have been here years, like the bakers and butchers. There's an Indian corner shop if there is anything you want to buy specifically for dinner, right at the end of the street and there's an indoor market as well, just over there," Michelle pointed across the road, "there's a Woolworths as well, further down. The supermarket is right in the opposite direction. Our GP surgery is just off this road." Kamal tried to keep up with Michelle, who had already decided this was going to be her neighbourhood, while she herself was still trying to process her current situation. It was as if she had swiftly moved on from one part of a novel to another, as if she was in a play, where the stage had revolved from one setting to another. She pinched herself again, not quite being able to grasp what was happening in her life right now.

"And here is the salon, Veronica's Hair and Beauty Salon. Follow me," Michelle pushed the door open and kept it open for Kamal. "Ooh that's better," she said closing the door of the warm brightly lit salon, the air pungent with the smells of hair products. There were a couple of old ladies sitting under the dryers, nattering away, they smiled and waved at Michelle as she walked in, a young girl was having dye applied to her hair reading a glossy magazine, chewing mercilessly on some gum. Another elderly lady was having her hair blow dried and busy talking to the hairdresser. Kamal could hear the *Heart* radio station jingle, which reminded her instantly of work and again, she was overcome by a sickness in the pit of her stomach and a painful longing for familiarity. She held her tears back. She felt like a lost child who couldn't find her way home and she sat down, her legs feeling weak as she yearned for home.

"Morning girls," Michelle shouted out.

"Morning 'chelle," a tall, slim woman, in about her early to mid-forties said with a wide smile, as she looked up from the appointments book at the other side of the reception counter. Her hair thick, red spiral curls, her skin pale, with a sprinkling of freckles. She wore a matt red lipstick, her eyebrows were neatly groomed and she wore a soft green coloured eyeshade, thick brown coloured mascara, which brought out her dazzling greenish eyes. Her nose thin and sharp and she had the perfect cheek bones; she was a strikingly attractive woman.

"This is Kamal Veronica, our new lodger."

"Oh, hello. I didn't know you were taking on lodgers."

"Well we were definitely thinking about it and then Kamal literally fell at our doorstep," Michelle started laughing, as she removed her coat, "right what have I got booked in?" Michelle started looking through the book. "Has Sarah not come in?" Michelle said flicking through the book, standing next to the leggy Veronica.

"No she called in this morning. I don't know, just can't get the staff these days," the phone rang and Michelle answered.

"Morning Veronica's, Michelle speaking. Oh hello Esther. You certainly can. How about Friday at half nine? Is that okay? That's great I've booked you in. Okay darling see you then sweetheart, you take care. Bye."

Kamal looked around the salon; everyone was busy continuing with their normal daily lives, while hers had been torn apart and she so envied them right now. Veronica was now chatting away with one of her clients while carefully removing some foil like paper from the young woman's hair. The two old ladies were still sitting under the dryers while drinking cups of tea nattering away. There was another plump, pretty lady, dark brown hair, layered softly around her face, which was covered with a thick layer of makeup. She showed the lady in the chair a view of the back of her hair, with a mirror as she finished and the lady nodded and smiled approvingly. She helped her client remove the gown.

"You okay Cheryl?" Michelle asked, as she approached the till with her client following close behind.

"Fine thanks 'Chelle," she smiled at Kamal. Kamal felt like a stray dog, if she had half the energy she would have just got up and walked, but she had neither the energy nor the willpower and was quite happy to just sit vacantly and watch the world go by. The phone rang again and Michelle answered. Kamal continued to observe her surroundings, mindful of Cheryl's inquisitive eyes. The salon was quite modern with white and black flooring, white walls and maroon chairs. The work surfaces black, with hairdryer holders and bottles of hairspray, cans of mousse and other bottles of substances any salon would have, along with a couple of parked trolleys holding curlers, combs and brushes and shelves piled with towels, white, black and maroon. The display of shampoos and conditioners, behind the reception desk were priced up with fluorescent price cards. Around the salon were stylish portraits of models with various hairstyles, some of them quite bizarre, others very sophisticated.

"You okay?" Michelle asked. Kamal nodded and managed a weak smile.

"Is there anything I can do?" she asked.

"Well," Michelle looked towards Veronica.

"Would you mind watching the phones just for the morning please? The junior is not coming in till later," Veronica asked.

"Yeah sure, anything to help."

Michelle showed her the appointment book, the leaflet with the charges and jotted down how long they needed for each booking and Kamal was soon preoccupied with the phones, seeking assistance whenever necessary, sweeping the floor and making cups of tea and coffee. The radio station was airing songs reminding her of her old workplace and the fact that she had not even bothered to call anyone.

"Thanks for your help Kamal," Veronica said as she came back in from her break. "I will take over now, Sarah will be here soon. You have been very helpful. Here." she handed over fifteen pounds.

"Oh no, it's quite okay. I didn't mind helping out."

"Oh don't be silly. Here take it. Who knows, we may call upon your services soon again," she said with her dazzling smile. Michelle had her coat on and held Kamal's in her hand.

"Come on let's get something to eat."

Kamal and Michelle were instantly hit by a wall of cold winter air as they stepped out.

"Nice ladies," Kamal said as they walked down the now busy street, bustling with shoppers.

"Yeah, Cheryl can be a bit funny. And oh you just wait till you see Sarah. Total waste of space. I do not know why Veronica just doesn't get rid of her. She's hardly here anyway. There's a café here we can get some warm food, fancy that?"

"Yeah, my treat though," Kamal insisted.

While Michelle tucked into a chicken dinner, Kamal had a few chips with gravy and looked round the cosy green café, not a greasy one, clean with a homely feel about it.

"We always eat here," Michelle said to a vacant looking Kamal, "sometimes I go home, well most of the time, thing is once I get home, I don't want to leave again."

"I'll get the rest of the ingredients for dinner after and will have a walk round."

"Oh you could go to the market and get a key cut for yourself too."

"Do you mind if I say something?" Kamal asked.

"No, go ahead."

"It's just that you don't even know me, you welcomed me into your home, offered for me to stay and now you are just handing me the key. I mean I could be anyone. You should not be so trusting Michelle, the world is full of cruel people."

"I know. Aaron often tells me I am too friendly for my own good. But I can tell a good soul when I see one, quite intuitive," Michelle smiled.

Kamal smiled, "is there a jobcentre round here?"

"There is one, but you will have to catch the bus. Or you can take the car can't you? I'll tell you where it is this evening."

"I did have a job, but I can't go back there," Kamal looked into her plate reminded again of what she had left behind; Michelle did not pry, she trusted Kamal would tell her about herself in good time.

"Curry!" Aaron came into the kitchen, "oh that smells sooo good!" he looked at his sister and Kamal, still in his coat, dragged in by the aroma.

"What did I tell you?" Michelle looked towards Kamal and rolled her eyes.

"I take it you've asked her to stay?" Aaron asked Michelle, while looking into the pan with chicken curry simmering away and watching Kamal chopping fresh coriander.

"Yep. And she's taken up the offer. I said she can talk to you about the rent and stuff."

"Well, I can promise a discount should you cook Indian every night!" Aaron smiled.

"Maybe you should taste it first," Kamal smiled at his glee.

"I'm sure it tastes as good as it smells and looks," he said walking out of the kitchen, "just getting changed!"

"Anything interesting?" Michelle later asked, snapping Kamal out of her thoughts.

"Oh, wasn't really watching."

Aaron switched off the kitchen light, shut the door and sat with Michelle, opposite Kamal. Kamal got up and sat on the floor by the fire with her cup of hot chocolate. Aaron watched, as she made herself at home.

"So Kamal, you're obviously a good cook, tell us more about yourself," Michelle asked, hoping she was now willing to open up a bit.

"What do you want to know?" Kamal asked looking into the fire.

"Anything."

Kamal looked up at the questioning faces, "I am or was, well technically still am married. I left my husband or rather…..he asked me to leave him."

"Why did he ask you to leave?" Michelle frowned.

"Because…because he found out I was cheating on him. It was not until yesterday that I realised that the man I was having an affair with, was married. Just a minor detail he forgot to mention."

"Oh?" Michelle raised her brows.

Kamal shook her head and sighed; her desolate eyes were drained of all tears now and for a few moments no one said anything.

"I think, in time I may be able to get over the deceit and my husband's apparent relief of seeing the back of me, but I wish I could get rid of this sick feeling I have inside, this unwanted, betrayed feeling, I feel so humiliated, like my feelings, emotions have been mocked, like they count for nothing. And then, there's my son."

"You have a son?" Aaron asked.

"Yes. He's on holiday with his grandparents and will be returning to find his mother has walked out on him. And soon enough, my parents will come to know, may even already have been told. My mum is so going to bear the brunt of my stupid mistake; you have no idea the hell she will go through. So, that's my story, you sure you still want me as your lodger?"

The brother and sister looked on, silently and then Aaron spoke up, "your personal life has nothing to do with us."

Kamal called Jackie first thing the following morning explaining the reason for her absence and intention not to return, limiting the details she divulged. Jackie had been very sympathetic, despite her frustrations at being one PA down, but nevertheless promised to provide references as and when required. Kamal asked her to inform her friends Danielle and Angela that she will be in contact, when she was ready.

She then called Sindy at her boutique.

"Sindy?"

"Kamal?"

A lump formed in Kamal's throat, as she heard her sister's familiar voice.

"Are you okay Kamal?"

"I had to leave Sindy."

There was a momentary silence before Sindy sighed and broke the awkwardness, "your in-laws are back. They went straight to mum and dad's."

"Did they?" Kamal's heart sunk.

"Yes. Dad was livid. Apparently he did not have much to say while they were there, but when they left."

"He took it out on mum, didn't he?" her eyes welled up.

"Well what do you think Kamal? He keeps accusing her of knowing something. Anyway where are you?"

"I'm staying with some…friends," Kamal wiped her tears, confirming to herself that Michelle and Aaron were now her friends.

"Not with Rohit?"

"Wouldn't you like to know," she shook her head.

Sindy listened on in disbelief at her sister's naivety, gullibility and misfortune, at being found out.

"So what are you going to do now?"

"I don't know."

Kamal heard a bell ring in the background; someone had obviously stepped into Sindy's boutique. "Listen I better go Kamal, got a customer. Call me later yeah?"

***

"I don't understand," Joginder said, "I just cannot get my head round it. She just did not seem that way. What made her change? And what kind of a stone hearted mother is she? How can she be sleeping at night without her child?"

"I warned her to stop mum, but then a friend saw her in a bar, even after I told her to stop. I begged her mum. I asked her to please for the sake of our child stop, but she carried on and on top of that she told me that she could not even think of spending the rest of her life here with us. She said she wanted freedom."

"She did say she did not care anymore," Varinder added, "I asked her what she wanted and she said divorce, just like that."

Deepa listened on quietly as Varinder and Raj filled their parents with the overly exaggerated details.

"Oh my God, what did I do to deserve such a deceiving daughter-in-law?" Joginder started to sob, "the shame she has brought upon us. How am I going to look anyone in the eye now?"

But Balbir was not so fooled. He knew his son was nowhere near perfect. He was in general a good judge of character and instinct told him, that there was a lot more to the story than met the eye.

***

Parminder held onto her tears until her husband fell asleep, only then did she painfully creep out of bed and cry in her daughters' bedroom. She ran her hands over the bed where her daughter slept last on Saturday night and wept silently, hoping she was safe.

***

"So when are you permanently moving in Raj?" Emma asked.

"By the end of this month, I promise," Emma lay naked next to him, her head on his bare chest, her fingers softly running up and down his arm. He pulled her closer towards him and kissed the top of her head. With Kamal now out of his life, discarded like a bad fruit, life with Emma was going to be just perfect. He had even managed somehow to get a promotion at work amidst all his domestic complications. He had really turned on the act for his parents, playing the distraught husband, torn apart with the shame and betrayal of his estranged wife. He was spending more and more time away from home, telling his parents he was staying with a friend, as he could not bear to come home and needed his own space. Whenever he did go home, his mother smothered him in love, concern and affection. On the other hand, his father sat back, silently.

Chapter 15

Christmas came and went like any other day and Kamal avoided being in the company of those who wanted to celebrate. While she managed to keep occupied during the day the best she could, now working at the salon part-time, when it was time to go home, she resorted to isolating herself in her bedroom. The separation from her son as a result of her treachery was tearing her apart. She had tried relentlessly to call her in-laws, but each time they answered she replaced the receiver unable to bring words to her mouth from the shame. Then the one day she called to hear the tone of a dead line, the number must have been changed, upholding that they really wanted her out their lives. Every night she went to sleep, determined to make that journey, but come the morning, the shame came back and she cowered at the thought, Raj's words forever echoing in her ears, *"you only gave birth to him...you only gave birth to him,"* and she indeed had let her son down. There were days when she wanted to call Rohit at work and curse him for ever entering her life, but then felt she had no-one but herself to blame for her foolishness. Michelle often tried to divert her thoughts and there were moments of hope, but Kamal soon relapsed into a solitary silence.

Kamal finally managed to find a part-time job as a data typist for the council via a temping agency. Having now two jobs to occupy her time, she was able to momentarily switch off from the harsh realities, pretend she was like any other average person going about normal everyday life, going to work to earn a living, disguise the fact that she had a child that she had not seen for what seemed like an eternity now, for whom she shamelessly did not have the backbone to fight for, afraid of confrontation and being shown up as a failure within her society.

"Oh come on Kamal, you have to, please, for me, pretty please," Michelle said drooping her bottom lip. It was Michelle's birthday and she was trying to talk Kamal into going out with her and the girls for the night. After much persuasion, Kamal eventually gave in.

"Oh, okay, just for you."

"Great! Right what have you got to wear?"

"All I have is in the wardrobe," Kamal was sat on her bed with her legs crossed and the pillow on her lap.

"Okay let's have a look. Well, it is a bit sad, isn't it?" Michelle said looking back in disapproval, mainly thick jumpers, jeans, chunky cardigans and then her office work clothes.

"Right, we'll have to go shopping. Get some colour in your wardrobe, get some colour back into your life!"

"I am not really in a mood to go shopping Michelle," Kamal said putting the pillow to one side, getting up and walking towards the wardrobe to close the doors.

"Okay, but at least something for tonight. We're going clubbing and that stuff in there is not really ideal, unless you want to pretend to be my granny."

"I could do that," Kamal smiled sarcastically at an unimpressed Michelle, "okay, if you insist," Kamal rolled her eyes, "but I'm just picking up the first thing I see. Who's going to be bothered with what I am wearing anyway?"

"I am. Look Kamal, I know it's been hard for you. But I've been thinking, yeah, yeah, I do that sometimes believe it or not," Michelle rolled her eyes, "and I'm going to be honest, so sorry, but, if anyone was really bothered, would they have not come looking for you? I mean has anyone even tried?" Michelle sat down next to Kamal, as she slumped down onto her bed on hearing a truth she was well aware of, "it's almost three months now. It's not like you're on the other side of the world. If anyone wanted to find you, they would have by now. Do you not feel that it is time to move on? Sometimes things happen for a reason. Your marriage, by the sounds of it had been doomed regardless of your actions. And this, what was his name, Robbie?"

"Rohit."

"Yes Row-hit, whatever, if he was half bothered, he could have come looking for you. You're here wallowing away in pain, while no-one else seems to me, sorry to say….. bothered." Kamal looked towards Michelle, "sorry Kamal, sometimes you have to be cruel to be kind. You cannot turn back time. I'm sure a lot of us would want to, but what's happened has happened. It's time to move forward Kamal," and leaving Kamal with those thoughts, Michelle walked slowly out of the room.

Kamal shivered as she stood in the queue outside the club and her teeth clattered furthermore as she looked on at her rather inappropriately dressed friends. Michelle was wearing a mini skirt and so was Cheryl, what they had on beneath their jackets was yet to be revealed once they got in. Veronica was well wrapped up and puffing away at a cigarette; she stamped her feet in her high heeled boots as they waited patiently to get in. Kamal really would have rather been at home.

They finally made their way through the doors of 'The Trance' past the bouncers and paid the entry fee. The music was pumping so loud, Kamal could hardly hear herself think. She waited for her friends to hand in their jackets. Veronica was wearing a red satin halter neck top and some tight black satin trousers showing off her slim bandy legs with black high heeled boots. Her spiral hair was left loose, her eyes tonight were made up quite heavily and her lips painted in her signature matt red lipstick. Cheryl a voluptuous size fourteen brunette, with her shoulder length hair cut into a soft feather cut around her face, looked absolutely fabulous. Kamal could now see that she was wearing a little black dress, showing off her hourglass figure and ample thighs. Michelle was wearing a black miniskirt with black tights, a strapless red top and her blond hair lay loose over her shoulders. She had minimal eye makeup, her red coloured lipstick doing all the work. Kamal looked the least glamorous, having made little effort, dressed in black trousers with a sleeveless mustard coloured shirt with black lace detail on the back and neck; she may as well have been dressed for another day at the office.

She held tightly onto Michelle's hand as they fought their way through the crowd towards the bar, afraid of losing her. The music was pounding in her ears and the club lights were flashing on and off like thunder lightening, sporadically illuminated the many faces. Finally able to breath Kamal stood next to the girls at the bar as Michelle tried to order in the drinks. She looked round to the dance floor and saw people dancing, rubbing bodies together seductively, some lost in their own little world entranced by the music and others adamant to bizarrely out dance the whole club. There were people standing around shouting in each other's ears in order to be heard. There were groups of cackling young women and boisterous young men stood around the bar and some couples stood snogging in dark corners.

"Come on Kamal," Michelle eventually handed her a small glass.

"What's this?"

"This, my darling, is tequila," she said holding Kamal's hand and putting a tiny heap of salt on the back of it.

"Tequila?" she vaguely remembered Angela mentioning this - tequila and blaming it for not remembering what time she had left a club one Saturday night to find herself the following morning in a hotel room next to a stranger she wouldn't have given the time of day to in the right frame of mind. She had vowed she was not going to get so pathetically "smashed" again, and had even got herself checked out at a clinic; of course that vow was soon to be broken. Kamal looked at the glass questioningly; tequila looked innocent enough.

"Ready? Right on the count of four, you lick the salt, take this in one go and suck on the lemon, okay? Ready?" Kamal stood straight and looked at the other three who stood on their marks. Michelle counted to four and she and the girls licked the salt, took the drink in one swoop and sucked on the lemon, slammed their glasses back down on the counter, pulled a face and then all looked towards Kamal, who was still standing static.

"Kamal!" Michelle exclaimed.

"What? Oh okay."

"One, two, three, four," they all shouted, watched her in anticipation and laughed at her eventual facial reaction.

"Right my round," Veronica bought in the second round, Cheryl the third and wanting to keep up with the trend, Kamal bought the fourth.

As 'tequila' began to work its effect, Kamal took a steady seat by the bar. Michelle made her way to the dance floor with Cheryl, while Veronica chose to remain back with Kamal.

"I'm too old for this," Veronica said smiling as she looked towards Michelle.

"Nonsense, wish I look as good as you when I'm your age, no-one would think you're forty-two."

"If only I felt as young as I looked. How are you feeling now, any better?"

"Right now I'm feeling a little giddy and if my eyes are not deceiving me, is that Aaron behind the bar?" Kamal and Veronica were shouting out over the music.

"Yeah. He works here."

"Oh so this is the club he works in?"

"Yeah," Veronica waved at Aaron, he waved back and winked at Kamal.

"They're good kids."

"Well, I don't know what I would have done without them," Kamal smiled at Aaron.

Michelle walked up to Kamal and Veronica, "come on you two," and pulled them both away from the bar.

Kamal shuffled her feet to *Dr Alban's, It's My Life* and waved her hand in the air half-heartedly, all she wanted to do was sit at the bar, as her head felt awfully light and when Michelle was caught up dancing with a young man who'd taken an obvious fancy to her, she went back to the bar for yet another drink, as she felt the intoxication was actually somewhat helping her forget herself. As she was pulled back to the dance floor, by Cheryl this time, an Asian man appearing to be in his late thirties invited himself to dance with her. Standing amidst the dense crowd, she was vacant to his wandering hand travelling up and down her back. He was now pulling her closer towards him, brushing his body against her. Meanwhile Aaron was closely observing from the bar, as he continued to serve.

"Come over to the corner," the man whispered into Kamal's ear and led her off the dance floor. He started to kiss her softly on her neck, Kamal felt like she did not have the energy to pull back and let him continue, her head spinning and the pumping dance music pounding in her ears. He pulled her closer towards him and it was then she tried to pull away, but he now had his lips locked forcefully on hers. Kamal tried to push him away with her drunken arms, which felt like they did not belong to her. Aaron went over to Veronica who was now standing at the bar talking to one of his colleagues and pointed in Kamal's direction; Veronica wasted no time in intervening.

"Okay sunshine, fun's over," she pulled Kamal away from the persistent man. Kamal looked towards Veronica confused. The man grabbed Kamal's hand, saying something inaudible to Veronica at which point Kamal pushed the man away and almost lost her balance. Veronica hoisted her up from her arms and held her up from her waist, "okay time for you to go home darling," she said pulling her away.

"Will you be okay?" Veronica asked Kamal once she'd helped her up to her bedroom.

"Okay?" Kamal looked round her room and slumped down on the bed, "I want to talk to Rohit," she mumbled.

"Who?"

"Rohit."

"Who's Rohit?" Veronica asked as she sat beside Kamal.

"The reason why I am here, away from my family, separated from my son. I want to call him," Kamal said standing up and then collapsing onto the bed again.

"Kamal. It's gone midnight, I don't think now is the right time."

"I have lost my whole family because of him. I'm going down to call him now," she got up again and managed to somehow make her way down the stairs and into the lounge. She picked up the cordless phone, which lay on the coffee table. She stood still for a while unable to remember the number, the number she no longer had. She frowned and put the phone back on the table, confused. Veronica was standing by her side now.

"Do you know the number Veronica?" Kamal frowned.

"Call him tomorrow, when your head is a little clearer."

Kamal sat down on the sofa and put her face in her hands. "What am I going to do?" Kamal started to sob, "I really want to see my son."

"No-one can stop you from seeing your son. Look Michelle has more or less told me what has happened. No-one can stop you from seeing your child. You need to get yourself a good lawyer. Nothing is going to happen if you sit around moping all day. One mistake is all you made and it seems like you're paying a very hefty price, being treated like an outcast. I mean do you still want to get together with your husband?"

"No."

"And this Roy...hit?" Veronica tried to get the name right as she sat next to her.

Kamal shook her head, "all I want is to see my son. Hold his little hands. Put my hands through his hair. Wrap my arms round him. Hold him close to me. Wrap him up in a big soft towel after he's had his bath. Tuck him in bed. Watch him sleeping. Is that too much to ask? But everyone hates me, I've brought shame upon everyone, they'll never forgive me, they'll never take me back." Tears ran down Kamal's cheeks as she spoke and Veronica could do nothing, but put her supporting arm around her.

Chapter 16

"Hello," Deepa answered the phone slightly out of breath, as she came running in from the garden.

"Hello Deepa."

Following a brief silence, Deepa acknowledged the familiar voice.

"Kamal. How are you?" Kamal did not answer. "Where are you?"

"Not far. How's my son Deepa?" Kamal asked in desperation.

"He's okay. He asked for you every day, the first few days especially, when he saw your photos, so then, they took them down, just so that he would not be reminded. He's okay now. I go down with the kids almost every day. Mum and dad are getting there as well, yes they were confined to the home from shame, but things are getting back to normal slowly, if they ever can, of course it will never be the same. What took you so long to call? Oh this is so awkward."

"I know. I'm sorry. Is Varinder home?"

"No, he's just popped out, so you're okay, but he won't be happy if he knows I'm talking to you."

"No, no I understand. They've changed the house telephone number. I thought of calling Raj at work, but then thought why bother, he was quite glad to see the back of me."

"Well, he's almost totally moved out. Said he can't face the humiliation. I think Varinder is back, I can hear his car on the drive. Look Kamal, everyone has just about managed to move on. I think you should too. You made your choice. I did beg and plead with you not to go, didn't I? Your son is just fine. Look I have to go now. Please don't call me unless it's absolutely necessary. Sorry."

Kamal sat still with the phone still to her ear and listened to the tone of the disconnected line.

She then, dialled her parent's number. It was Sunday afternoon, she knew her dad was most likely to be at home, but she dialled the number regardless, she had to get through to someone. She swallowed the lump in her throat as the phone rang out and closed her eyes, hoping and praying her dad did not pick up.

"Hello," Kamal closed her eyes tight in relief and felt her heart in her mouth as she heard her mother's voice.

"Hello," her mum said again. Kamal covered the mouth piece with her hand, as a lump formed in her throat.

"Kamal," her mother whispered.

"Mum," Kamal just managed to say.

"I have just longed to hear your voice," her mum's voice broke as she spoke.

"I'm so sorry mum," Kamal stood up and walked towards the window overlooking the garden.

"Are you okay? Are you safe? Where are you? Why did you not phone Kamal? I have been worried sick!" her mum whispered down the phone.

"I'm okay mum, I promise you I'm okay. I just can't find the face to come back and I just did not have it in me to call you."

"Is it true what they are saying?"

"Is dad at home?" Kamal asked as her mother continued to whisper.

"He's in the shower. Now tell me is it true what they are saying?"

"I messed up mum. I'm so sorry. I thought he loved me mum."

"Are you with him now?"

"No. I was such a fool mum. He was already married. I didn't find that out till it was too late, when I had left home."

"So where are you now?" her mum asked in a whisper.

"I'm with friends mum. I'm okay. I'm working. I was just desperate to hear your voice. They are not going to let me see my son mum and how am I supposed to face them? I have brought both families to shame."

"YES YOU HAVE!" the phone almost dropped from Kamal's hand as she heard her dad's voice blaring down the phone, "you, disgust me!" Kamal's legs turned to jelly, just like they used to whenever he raised his hand or voice and just as she used to as a child, she retreated back into a corner and crouched down, his presence felt physically, as he continued to yell. "The day you walked out on your marriage, you died for us all, for your in-laws and your son you shameless………" he bit his tongue, "now you listen to me carefully okay? I do not even want your shadow anywhere near this neighbourhood. Is that clear? And don't you dare call here again. Do you understand? I SAID DO YOU UNDERSTAND?"

"Y…y…yes…dad!"

"Don't you dare call me dad! I have just two daughters who are living respectful lives, despite the shame you have brought upon them! You wretch! If I see you, I promise I will strangle you with my bare hands and willingly hand myself over to the law. We have no room for you in our lives anymore you parasite!" Kamal's hands shook as she held the phone to her ear, the tone of the disconnected line rang out. Just then, Aaron walked back in from the pub, as she sat on the floor her hands clenched onto the cordless phone.

"What's the matter?" he asked rushing to her side. The colour had drained from her face and she looked at him vacantly. He gently took the phone off her.

Parminder was thrown onto the sofa, as her husband's right hand hit her left cheek with one forceful blow. He then pulled her back up by her plait bringing her face close to his and scowled at her, "how many times has she called?"

"This….this was the first time since….." she struggled to say. He tightened his grasp on her hair.

"Since?" he questioned.

She held his hand as his grasp tightened, "since she left."

"Are you sure of that?"

"I promise."

He pushed her on the floor and kicked her in the stomach, releasing all his frustrations in one blow. Parminder grabbed her tummy in agony and curled up on the floor.

"You listen to me carefully woman. First thing tomorrow I will be getting the phone number changed. Following that, if there is any contact whatsoever, I will track her down and kill her, do you understand? What was I to expect?" he said walking around her, hands on hips, "like mother like daughter hey? I always knew it, do you understand? I ALWAYS FUCKING KNEW!" he kicked her in her back again releasing all his fury. He then stepped over her, grabbed his jacket and walked out the house slamming the door shut behind him. The tears rolled down the side of her face as she lay on the floor. All these years, the guilt had eaten away at her. In penitence, she had never ever defended herself against his vicious ways, always accepting that she was paying the ultimate price for her sin. Even when she had reached her lowest level, she never had it in herself to get up and leave, as she was bound back by her parents back in India; if she was to leave him, they would die in shame and when they did die, she had the girls' futures to consider. No respectful family would have stepped forward and asked for their hand in marriage; their futures would have been tarnished. Today, for the first time since she came to England in 1967, he finally brought the words to his lips. Deep down, she always knew that her husband had doubts that Kamal was his, as well as his calculating mother, though they had never brought their thoughts to their lips, not directly and now, after all these years, he finally said it.

***

Aaron made Kamal a sweet cup of tea while she talked to Michelle. He had become very fond of Kamal. She was a kind and caring person, she worked hard around the house, she could also be quite witty, when she wanted to be and he wished he could learn to know what the real Kamal was like. He liked the way she tilted her head as they watched any TV program together, or the way she'd sit on the floor in front of the fire with her cup of tea reading a magazine; then putting it down and looking blankly out the windows, as if she had remembered something, a memory from her past.

He liked the way she walked around the house with her dressing gown after she'd had a shower, her still wet black hair left loose to dry naturally. He liked to help her cook in the kitchen or dry up while she washed. He liked having her around. There were times when she would be lost in a world of her own; her eyes would be full of pain and today, seeing her sitting like a frightened little child made him feel extremely sad. He wanted to get close to her, but the protective wall she had built around her prevented him from getting in. His growing feelings for her were transparent to his sister, but Kamal was totally oblivious.

"Who could that be?" Michelle asked, as Aaron brought the tea in.

Aaron went to answer, it was Veronica.

"Just come to check on Kamal, she was very upset last night, everything okay?" she asked.

Michelle shook her head slightly.

"I'm sorry guys," Kamal finally said, "I'm spoiling your Sunday afternoon. I'll get out your way."

"Don't be silly and stay put," Michelle said quite firmly.

"Thanks Chelle," Kamal sighed, "I think it's time for closure now. All routes back to my old life are closed. Everyone seems to have moved on. It's time for me to move on too."

"Look Kamal, life's full of knock downs, but it does not mean you give up. You get up again and carry on, learning from your lessons. Yes you made a mistake, you're only human. Learn from it; don't let anyone fool you again. I've been married twice. The second time, when I found love, finally found true love, he left me, he died. He was only 48, died two years ago from a massive heart attack. God knows I felt I could never get over it. The one man who I finally felt settled and content with. I'm never going to find another John and do you know what caused his heart attack? Me. I cheated on him, that too with my waste of space ex-husband. You cannot start to imagine how it feels, when I relive the moment, the moment he found out. I can never forget seeing the look on his face, he was distraught. He gave me everything; I wanted for nothing and I had to give in to that waste of space bastard. Just think, at least you don't have blood on your hands. Not like me. If things are bad today, they will be better tomorrow. If your family are not talking to you today, they will come round tomorrow. As for your son, well I advise you to get yourself a good lawyer. You should be able to come to some sort of arrangement to see him regularly."

"I'm sorry, I had no idea, I'm so wrapped up in myself."

"Well you weren't to know."

"Right," Kamal tried to lift her spirits for the benefit of the others, "here's to a new start," Kamal took a deep breath.

"That's more like it," Michelle smiled.

"How often do you see your kids Aaron?" Kamal asked, in an attempt to divert the attention from herself.

"Not enough. Sandra's in control, always has been, but she's a good mum."

"Hey, hey," Veronica said, "not like you to speak well of Sandra."

"Yeah, but praise where praise is due. She is good with the kids, just wish I could spend more time with them. I will be having them for Easter. Sandra and Jack are going away. I've booked some time off."

"That'll be nice for you," Kamal said hoping she could also eventually come to some sort of amicable arrangement, the thought giving her some comfort.

"You're too soft Aaron," Michelle added, "he just lets Sandra pick and choose when he can have the kids. It's not fair."

"Yeah, well we are finally on good talking terms now. I don't want to jeopardise that, so any time is good time."

"I still think you should demand to see them more."

"This is when separation and divorce gets really tricky, doesn't it, when it comes to the kids?" Kamal thought out loud.

Aaron looked at her, "it's not easy. But, nobody plans a bad marriage."

"I can never understand how you ever got together with her," Veronica shook her head.

"No, nor could mum," Michelle laughed, "she used to call her The Dragon, apart from other things, when she was not minding her manners. Anyway it's over now. So kids are coming over for Easter, that'll be fun!"

"Yes for a week. Oh and I've got them next weekend."

"So, Michelle what about you, any luck last night?" Veronica smiled.

"Actually," Michelle grinned, "I met a pretty nice chap yesterday. Jamie. Got his number. Did you see him? The one I was literally dancing with all night. He was the one with dark hair, with the *Tom Cruise* smile."

"Yes I did as a matter of fact," Veronica teased with her smile.

"He's an accountant and he was quite flash," Michelle said raising her eyebrows.

"Was he now?" Aaron said.

"Don't do the older brother thing," Michelle said rolling her eyes.

"Oh, which reminds me, now that you have Kamal and I am convinced she is not a total nutcase, just kidding Kamal," he smiled, "I will start flat hunting again, I need my own space as well you know."

"You'll be moving out?" Kamal asked.

"Yeah it was always temporary. Lost the house to Sandra and I was staying with a mate, but then I moved in here with Michelle after mum passed away. I think it's time to move on now, considering you're staying of course."

"Yes, I won't be going anywhere for a while," Kamal smiled. "Thanks guys. Don't know what I would have done without your support."

Kamal lay in bed considering the weekend job at the club Aaron had mentioned and as she turned in bed, her eyes fell on the portrait of her son. She picked it up and lay it next to her on the pillow in an attempt to feel close to him. She had put on a brave face for her friends, who were trying so hard to make her feel better and felt it was time to show them that she was willing to try, forget and move on. But while in her bedroom, it was her loneliness and her sadness that surrounded her, she did not have to pretend; here, she could openly mourn her colossal loss.

Chapter 17

"I am absolutely shattered, my feet are killing me and my ears are still buzzing!" Kamal said followed closely by Aaron.

"Yeah, it was quite a night. The R&B nights usually pull in a larger crowd."

Kamal had just finished her Saturday night shift at the club, as a cloakroom attendant. Quite alien to the night life and totally out of her comfort zone, she was apprehensive at first, but was rest assured knowing that Aaron was in the immediate vicinity. She could not help but gawp at some of girls in their inappropriate skimpy clothing. Aaron found her expressions comical and her cloakroom colleague, Patricia, had often discreetly asked her to close her mouth. Aaron had managed to secure the Friday and Saturday nights for her. She was a changed woman from the first time he saw her, soaking wet, cold, lost with no will to live. She laughed now, all be it not wholeheartedly and seemed a lot more relaxed around him. She still had her moments, when she drifted off into her own world, as any event, object or quote had reminded her of a past episode, but she would soon snap back to the present time and brave a smile, but she did not fool him, he could tell she was trying her best to cover her wounds. She was a part of his life now. He could not understand why her husband treated her so badly, but he could definitely understand Rohit falling in love with her.

"That creep David was in again. I was so glad when Bobby came over telling him Mike needed a word," Kamal said as Aaron drove.

"Yeah, I had noticed him lurking around you."

"He makes me feel so uncomfortable," Kamal shuddered as she spoke of a good friend of the club owner Mike, mid-forties, dark complexion, lustful eyes, parading the arrogance of wealth as he walked about his friend's club, as if it were his own.

"I wouldn't worry too much, he'll soon back off, if not, you know where me and Bobby are, and the others will watch your back too."

"I know," Kamal smiled.

"Can't wait to hit the bed," Aaron yawned.

"Me too, you got the kids this week haven't you?"

"Yep. They'll be over Monday morning. So I'll see you then," he said pulling over.

"Thanks, and goodnight, or should I say good morning!" Kamal smiled as she stepped out. As always, Aaron did not pull away to leave for his apartment, until she had opened and closed the door behind her.

Kamal got into the house as quietly as she could. She took off her jacket and hung it on the peg and seeing Jamie's jacket, she gathered he'd stayed the night. She grabbed her towel and made her way to the bathroom for a quick wash. It was 4.30am now. She was planning to have a lazy Sunday in. Along with her weekend job at the club, Kamal managed to secure a permanent job with the council, where they'd increased her hours. If Veronica ever needed a hand at the salon, Kamal was always willing to help, managing to fit it round her job at the council. Michelle could not understand why Kamal wanted the job at the club as well, but for Kamal, any time that caused a distraction was welcomed to help her forget. Besides, everyone was good to her; Mike the owner, Bobby and the other security guards, Nick and Owen. Then there was Patricia whom she absolutely adored, as she could make her laugh with but a single quotation or facial expression. And then, there was Aaron; he made her feel safe and secure and he was fast becoming a very dear friend.

Back in her bedroom, changed into her nightwear, she looked at the framed photo of her son on the side cabinet, ran her fingers over the portrait, like she always did last thing at night, first thing in the morning. No sooner had she put her head down on the pillow, she was fast asleep.

***

Kamal was trying to run, but she could not lift her feet; she felt like they were shackled and weighed down with heavy chains. She tried to scream out, but she couldn't find her voice. She felt unable to move, as she tried again to run, as the figure of her son became smaller and smaller, going further and further in the distance. She tried again to call out his name, but she couldn't. She tried to reach out to him, but her hand was grasping onto nothing but thin air. She then gasped for air as she felt some pressure around her neck, like a pair of hands strangling her. Her son was no longer visible, she reached out again, as she struggled to breath, but there was now nothing but complete darkness all around her. She tried again to run, to reach out, to catch up with him, but felt helpless and then, she saw Raj suddenly appear before her, looking down at her, laughing down at her, taking on a devilish form. He then suddenly pulled out a knife from behind his back, its blade flashing before her eyes, as he went to stab her in the back! Kamal screamed out with all her might! It was then, she realised, she was in her bed. She put her hand to her head, which was wet from perspiration. She sat up, out of breath and looked round at the clock on the bedside cabinet, it was 12.20pm. She lay her head back down on the pillow, picked up her son's photo and put it against her chest, her heart pounding. She had strange dreams like this before, but this time, it was more intense, it was more vivid and for the first time in a long time, she was afraid, very afraid. There was a feeling deep within her that was eating away at her, creating an unexplainable pain, an unfamiliar pain, as if something had happened, or was going to happen, as if her gut was trying to tell her something. She lay still in bed and closed her eyes, catching her breath again. Eventually, she dragged herself out of the bed and made for the shower. The house was empty. Michelle had most probably gone to the local with Jamie for some Sunday lunch. In the bathroom, Kamal looked at her reflection in the mirror. She ran her fingers through her hair and looked back at her drained, ghastly image, dark circles around her eyes. A reflection she managed to cover up when she got ready to go out to work each day, but when the mask was taken off the mirror exposed her true self. She slipped off her nightshirt, stepped into the shower and let the warm water run over her head. The dream was still fresh in her mind, as well as the emotions of angst and fear. She stood still for a while, wishing the water could wash away her sins. She then washed herself down vigorously, like she always did, since that incident with Raj; she never seemed to be able to clean that horrible smell of his bodily fluids away from her.

As Kamal applied body lotion, she continued to ponder over her past and her mind again wandered off to her family. She'd spoken to Sindy a few weeks ago and she was true to her usual form boasting about her business, Sarbjit's promotion and her pregnancy. She had updated her on Nindy buying her own place with her husband away from her in-laws, who liked to subtly bring up the topic of her shameful eloped sister every now and then, but fortunately for Nindy, she had a good supportive husband, who decided it was time for him and his wife to move away. They were both happy now with their twins and their own little grocery store. Her mum and dad apparently never spoke of her, she had become a taboo. Everyone had moved on.

She wrapped her body with her soft pink gown and went down, her hair loose and combed through, but still damp. The house was so quiet and reminded her of the time she had spent alone, before she had left home. The atmosphere became unusually eerie, as Raj's evil face flashed before her eyes yet again. She went into the kitchen, switched on the kettle and stood still, listening to the water simmer to a rapid boil. When the kettle switched itself off, she picked her cup up from the shelf and opened the drawer to get a teaspoon. As she opened it, she saw the kitchen knife and the vision of Raj raising his hand ready to stab her in the back flashed before her again. She stepped back in fright, as the doorbell rang at that precise moment. Kamal shrieked and put her hand to her mouth, her heart suddenly thumping in her chest. The doorbell rang again.

"Oh this is stupid!" she said, slamming the drawer shut and stamped towards the front door.

"God you look like you've seen a ghost. You okay?" Aaron asked walking in as she stepped back.

"Yes, yes," she said pulling her gown tighter around her.

"You sure?"

"Yeah, I'm fine," she said closing the door and walking back towards the kitchen. "I was just going to make some tea for myself, do you want some?"

"Yes please," he said following her.

"Of course you do, I should know you by now. I'd have thought you'd have still been in bed."

"Couldn't sleep."

"You neither?" Kamal said, putting a tea bag into Aaron's Aston Villa mug kept in the cupboard and one in hers with two spoons of sugar.

"Why? Couldn't you sleep either?"

"Horrible dream," she said shaking her head and pouring hot water into the mugs.

"Dream?"

"Yeah."

"Oh well, it was just a dream."

"Yeah, it was just a dream," she smiled as she went to get the milk out the fridge, the smile fading from her face as she turned her back towards him.

Aaron took the two mugs into the living room and Kamal followed him in. She sat down, still in her robe. Aaron watched her as she sat down.

"Are you sure you're okay?"

Kamal looked at Aaron, his eyes full of concern. She had only more recently begun to notice his deep blue eyes, dark brown hair and soft attractive features and when he had not shaven, like today, he looked quite handsome. Many girls flirted with him at the club, but he casually smiled and laughed off their remarks.

"Kamal?"

She looked at him thoughtfully, "would you mind doing something for me?"

"What?"

"Would you come with me to Wolverhampton tomorrow?"

"Wolverhampton?"

163

Kamal nodded.

"I just want to see my son. Just from a distance. Just so I know he is okay, I don't think I can do it on my own."

"Yeah, sure, it's just the kids are over."

"Oh, damn, yes. Zach and Courtney are down aren't they? Yeah we'll go after the holidays. I can ask Michelle if you want, it's just she's got the salon and Veronica relies on her a lot…"

"It's okay. I'll come with you. What's brought this on?"

"Nothing, just want to see him that's all."

"Why don't you start divorce proceedings and have some sort of arrangement put in place. You haven't even seen a solicitor yet."

"If Raj wants a divorce then he can file for it. I'm in no hurry. I've got no immediate plans."

"Yes, but I was thinking of you and your son."

"I don't want to push anyone and start fighting for my rights and all, I've caused enough heartache. I should have thought of those before I went up and left, before I foolishly messed up. I just want to see him that's all. I just don't think I can do it on my own. If you don't want to go…"

"Hey, I said I would okay, relax."

"Thanks Aaron."

"Michelle's out with Jamie I suppose?" Aaron asked.

"Yeah, he's okay isn't he?"

"She's had worse."

"What about you Aaron? Are you not ready for a relationship? I mean Sandra's moved on."

"I'm okay, for the time being. Forget me, what about you?"

"Me? Not a chance!" Kamal laughed at the absurdity of getting involved with someone, anyone ever again, "just going up to get changed, won't be long."

Aaron watched her as she walked away. She was so different to any girl he ever knew. He felt at ease around her, as she felt around him, so relaxed, she was almost horizontal! He could be driving her back home from work and there would be complete silence all the way, neither one of them attempting to break the silence and they'd just listen or hum together to the tune playing on the radio. Other times they would just talk non-stop about work, laugh out loud about an incident at the club. He enjoyed her company and he was glad she'd asked him to go with her. He wanted to attempt to get a step closer to her, but he did not want to jeopardise the trust she had in him and he knew she trusted him. He liked it when she'd do his tie up properly for him at the club, or wipe lipstick off his cheek, printed on by one of the excited clubbers or the way she put her hand on his shoulder when they laughed on their drive back home in the car. These gestures may not have meant anything to her, but with each little gesture she made, he was slowly, falling hopelessly in love with her.

"Hello kids!" Kamal's eyes lit up as she walked back in from the shops with some milk and bread. Kamal loved it when Zach and Courtney were over and the kids had taken to her too.

"Hello Camel," the twins said simultaneously. Kamal loved the way the kids pronounced her name. The first day she introduced herself, Zach screwed his nose up and said, "is that not a name of an animal that lives in the dessert and has a hump?"

"No Kamal, pronounced Kum-ul, is actually the Indian translation for a flower, that is the lotus flower, here, I'll draw it for you, it grows out of the mud and blossoms above the muddy water surface, would you believe it," Kamal had told them.

"How are you two?" she asked, kneeling down with them on the floor. They had their toys scattered all around them. Aaron took the milk and bread from her and went into the kitchen.

"Fine thank you," Courtney said smiling. Courtney and Zach both had their mother's blond hair and their dad's blue eyes and whenever they smiled, deep dimples appeared in their cheeks.

"Oh what have we got here?" Kamal said looking at Courtney's tea set.

"I'm making some tea for daddy."

"Oh can I have some as well? And what are you doing Zach?"

"I'm making a house," he said as he put together some blocks.

"Oh, shall I help you?"

Aaron watched from the kitchen door and smiled as he watched Kamal interacting with his children. She was down on the floor with them on her knees make-believing that she was drinking the imaginary tea that Courtney had just made. Courtney offered her a plastic biscuit with her tea and Kamal's eyes filled with glee.

"Wow, Zach aren't you clever. That looks like a very cosy little home, I could just live in that." Zach stood up and folded his arms, looking very pleased with himself.

"They're just gorgeous kids Aaron. You must miss having them around so much," Kamal said walking into the kitchen.

"Yeah I do. Jack came in to drop them off, while Sandra waited in the car. They both seem quite keen on him."

"Must be difficult, to see another man literally taking over."

"It is."

"Gosh, look at the time! I better be going. Sorry Aaron, didn't mean to cut you off," Kamal said putting her hand on his shoulder, "at least you know he's a good man. I mean would you have rather stayed in a dead relationship for the sake of the children? Both you and Sandra miserable? Sometimes these things happen for a reason. At least you're seeing them on a regular basis and at the end of the day, they will always know who their real dad is."

"Yeah, I know. I'm okay," he said looking at her concerned face, "you get going now, don't want to be late."

"No. I'll catch up with you later," she said walking away, "see you later kids!"

Kamal walked into the boring lacklustre office; she so hated working here, the data entry was so tedious and the people she worked with were a prim and proper, hoity-toity plain faced lot! A far cry from the lively lot she worked with over the weekends at the club and far from her old office colleagues. She missed Danielle and Angela terribly at times and the comfortable, humorous rapport she had shared with Craig.

"I must call them today," she thought out loud as she carried out her mundane daily tasks. Her boss Jonathon Brown seemed to have an inability to smile. His appearance was that of someone refusing to move on from the 60s, with his thick black rimmed glasses, hair combed to the side with Brylcreem and clean shaven pale skin. He always smelt of Old Spice and belted his either brown or beige trousers high up his waist. The ladies she shared the office with were in their fifties and had been working for the council for the best part of their lives. Margaret, with her short mousy coloured hair, pale skin, of a very thin build, always dressed in shades of grey, which did her no favours whatsoever and spoke very nasally. Kamal would often impersonate her when she got back home to Michelle. Diane, the other secretary, whose head looked disproportionate to the rest of her body, Kamal initially found a bit sharp and to the point, but once she settled in, she realised that was just her rigid personality. They came in, did their job and went home bang on five. There were many other workers, who had made little impression on Kamal, if at all; focused on their jobs, in their own little bland offices, pleasant but plain and she missed her old colleagues, who'd have soon livened this place up.

It was when the vultures Margaret and Diane were briefly out the office to attend a meeting, Kamal finally picked up the phone to call her old colleagues. She waited anxiously as the phone rang out, looked round over her shoulder and then back, when she heard Danielle's voice.

"Danielle?"

There was a brief silence.

"Kamal?"

"You haven't forgotten me then?" Kamal smiled as she heard her dear old colleague's voice.

"Oh my God it is. What took you so long!"

"Oh don't ask Danielle. Just don't ask."

"You left that loser then?"

"Yes."

"Well that's a relief. But you could have at least called us! Got a new girl, she's alright, but it's just not the same," Danielle whispered, "she's just gone out the office. Oh my life do we miss you! When are we meeting up? Come on we've got to see you."

"How's Angela?"

"She's fine, literally jumped onto my lap and her head's glued to mine! She's trying to listen."

"Hi Kamal!" Angela shouted.

Kamal laughed, "oh I miss you guys so much. Give me a home number and I'll call you at home."

Kamal hung up and sighed. It was so strange visiting her past and it was good to hear voices that were in contrast happy to hear from her, than not. Margaret and Diane came back in from their 'oh-so-important' meeting.

"Okay Kamal?" Diane cracked a smile as she came in, "any phone calls?"

"Yes there have been a few, I've taken a couple of messages and dealt with the others."

"Thank you kindly," Margaret sat with her nose tossed in the air, back straight and already ticking away at her keyboard.

Kamal read the note left by Michelle, held up with the fridge magnet – *Hey K, out with Jamie, Aaron's taking kids to the pictures and then for a pizza, he'll be back around 6, don't wait up for me! Love you x*

She smiled and then started looking through the cupboards for something to eat. She decided to settle for instant noodles, not in the mood to cook and then, called Danielle.

"Kamal! I've been sat by the bloody phone waiting for your call. Now start right from the beginning."

It was so refreshing to talk to someone who knew who she was and where she was from. To someone who could really connect with the events that led to her departure from the world she once belonged to.

"I'm so sorry things turned out the way they did. What a bastard!"

"You must not mention anything to Rohit or anyone else. Promise me?"

"I'm sorry, but I can't promise I won't hurt him the next time I see him!"

"No Danielle, please, it was my own fault, I should not have been so gullible."

"Gullible? I think vulnerable is more appropriate. He gave you the attention you were not getting at home, and you fell for it. And who would not have? He's an all-out charmer. He's lost the spark in his eyes though. Has looked rough and bothered for a long time now, and I know why now."

"Well, at least he still has his home, family, job and dignity. He has not lost half of what I have. I can't blame him for everything. My marriage was long dead anyway."

"So where are you now?"

"Moseley. I'm staying with a lovely girl called Michelle. Met her the day I walked out. She's been so good to me, a Godsend. You'll have to come down and meet her, you'll love her. She really is something else. I've made some good friends here. Work for the council Monday to Friday and got a weekend job at a night club as a cloakroom assistant. You should come to the club."

"Sounds good to me, looks like you have moved on then?"

"Yeah, I have somehow managed to, but the past is always going to stay with me. I miss my mum so, so much. I called her as well, but soon got cut off by dad. It was horrible. The only person I have been in contact with is Sindy. I've been trying to call her since yesterday, but there's been no answer. Hope all is well. It's unlike her not to answer the phone at the shop."

Aaron came in with the exhausted kids.

"Did you have a good time kids?" Kamal asked bending down, putting her hands on her knees.

"Yes. We had ice-cream after our pizza," Zach said.

"Yes, I had strawberry and vanilla," Courtney added.

"Oh that sounds so yummy. I wish I had come along as well. I've just had boring noodles," Kamal pulled a face, which tickled the children's humour.

"You seem happy," Aaron smiled at her as he removed his jacket and Kamal took Zach and Courtney's. She took Aaron's jacket off him and went to hang them on the stand in the hall.

"Yes I am a bit. Spoke to Danielle, remember I told you about her, she used to work with me?" she shouted out.

"Oh yes. Bet she was surprised to hear from you?"

"Yes she was. It was really nice talking to someone from my past, who wanted to actually genuinely talk to me," Kamal said smiling as she came back in.

"Good. I could kill for a cup of tea," Aaron said collapsing on the sofa.

"One cup of tea coming up."

"Right kids. I'm going to have some tea and then I'll go up, help you brush your teeth, then I'll put you in bed and read you a story. Okay?"

"Yes daddy," they both agreed together.

It was 2.20am when Kamal woke up suddenly and sat up in bed, switched on the table lamp, picked up her son's photo and held it close to her chest. The same recurring dream; something was definitely not right. Her throat was dry and her pulse racing. She got out of bed with the photo still close to her chest, out in the landing she switched on the light for the stairs, tiptoed down and opened the door to the lounge. The light from the hall gave her enough light to find her way to the kitchen through the lounge. She switched the kitchen light on, ran the cold water tap and filled a glass. She drank the water down in one go, placed the glass on the counter, held the photo to her chest with her left arm and placed her right hand on her head.

"You okay?"

Kamal looked up startled, "oh God Aaron! Sorry, you scared the life out of me. I totally forgot you were in there. I'll go back up. Sorry."

"Woh, woh," he held her from the shoulders as she tried to walk by, "what's the matter you look petrified."

"I'm scared Aaron. Something is wrong. I can sense it. Something awful has happened I'm sure of it."

Aaron put his arms around her and held her tight, "gosh you're shaking like a leaf." He rubbed her back in an attempt to calm her down. "Come here," he led her to the sofa, sat her down and put the blanket round her shoulders. "What's the matter?" he said looking at the photo in her hands.

"I had that dream again, only more vivid. I have to call Sindy. I will call her first thing tomorrow morning. If not, I'm going back home. Something has happened Aaron, I can feel it. I really need to go back home."

***

"Proud of yourself are you?" Danielle said as Rohit walked out of Craig's office.

"Sorry?" Rohit frowned. Danielle stood up in front of Rohit and folded her arms. Angela turned her nose up having been updated first thing in the morning. He looked towards both questioningly.

"She told me not to say anything to you, but I just can't sit back and say nothing, I just can't. You couldn't have found a nicer person to deceive!"

"You've spoken to her, haven't you?"

"Oh so you do remember, HER?"

"Where is she? How is she?" he asked frantically.

"Like I'd tell you, don't you think you've caused enough damage?"

"You're all the same," Angela said shaking her head and narrowing her eyes in disgust.

"Danielle," Rohit closed his eyes, "please tell me, is she okay?" Rohit now had both his hands together and looked at her with a plea in his eyes.

"She's as well as she can be," she said turning her back and going back to sit on her chair.

"Have you any contact details for her?"

"Like I'd give you those, some of us have loyalty towards those we care for!"

"It's not the way she told you Danielle. I was meaning to tell her. It's nothing like what she thinks. If she would just give me a chance to explain to her."

"What's to explain? Have you any idea what she has been through?"

"What's going on?" Craig said coming out of his office.

"Nothing," Danielle said looking away.

"Rohit?" Craig searched him for an answer.

"She's spoken to Kamal."

"Oh. How is she?" Craig spoke as if he was well acquainted with the ins and outs.

"Oh yeah, she's doing absolutely fine, no thanks to him," Danielle said folding her arms looking back at Rohit.

"Please Danielle, I need to speak to her," Rohit pleaded.

"Sorry, can't help you," Danielle said leaning forward, looking him straight in the eyes.

***

"Still no answer!" Kamal said in frustration, "I'll have to go down."

"Do you want me to come with you?" Aaron asked.

"No it's okay. Besides you've got the kids," she said looking towards Zach and Courtney who were chuckling as they watched *'Pingu'* on the television, when the doorbell rang.

"Who could that be?" Aaron said getting up.

Kamal smiled, as she watched twins, she could hear a male voice at the door and then footsteps coming towards the lounge.

"Kamal, there are some officers that want to speak to you."

"Officers?" Kamal's heart sank as she saw two police constables walking in behind him.

"Okay kids. Let's go into the kitchen."

"Something's happened, hasn't it?" Kamal swallowed a lump as she looked up.

"Mrs Kamal Kaur?"

"Yes," Kamal said standing up with the cordless phone still in her hand.

"Just a sec, come on kids," Aaron settled the kids down quickly at the kitchen table with a jigsaw puzzle and went back into the lounge, closing the kitchen door behind him and walking over to stand next to Kamal.

"Would you like to take a seat please?" the male officer said to her removing his hat. Kamal looked towards Aaron, her heart rate was increasing and she felt a weakness in her legs, hence did as the officer said holding onto Aaron's hand for support. The two officers sat opposite them. The male officer had a round face and his cheeks and nose were scarlet red. He had a thick ginger moustache. His bold head shone in the sunlight pouring in through the bay windows. He had very warm eyes and discomfort written all over his face. His colleague a female officer had short dark hair, a very sharp nose and big round brown eyes; she reminded Kamal of a famous TV clairvoyant.

"I am PC Richard Cole and this is my colleague PC Sarah Dixon. Mrs Kaur, I'm afraid it's bad news," Kamal's eyes fleeted from one officer to the other. Something was not right, that she had been feeling for a few days now, but what, what had happened? Her heart was thumping in her chest now, her mouth dry and the palms of her hands were sweating, was it her mum, she thought, had something happened to her mum? Aaron held her hand firmly. PC Cole cleared his voice.

"Your sister Surinder Kaur approached us. She had no contact details for you nor address, so she sought our help," PC Cole lowered his voice as he spoke, "Mrs Kaur, there's no easy way of telling you this, but I'm afraid to say, your son, Jaydeep, died from a severe head injury Saturday night."

"What?" Aaron looked towards the officers in horror. Kamal's hand stopped shaking in his; her gaze, transfixed on PC Cole. Her gaze then lowered and she was now looking down blankly at the PC's shiny boots. Aaron was speaking, but his voice was muffled.

"Kamal," Aaron called out to her, but she did not respond.

"Mrs Kaur, are you okay?" the female officer was sitting next to her now. Kamal looked towards her. The colour had drained from her face and she just looked straight through the officer. "I'll get some water."

PC Dixon went into the kitchen. She hated this part of her job and it never got any easier. This lady had not seen her son for months and to receive news that he had died, was understandably devastating. She smiled at the girl and boy who were sitting at the kitchen table with a jigsaw. The boy smiled at her.

"Morning Miss Police Officer," PC Sarah Dixon smiled at the boy, as she took a deep breath, before she went back into the room. She handed the glass over to Kamal; Kamal looked up at the officer blankly; her eyes, glazed.

"Have some water Kamal," Aaron said softly. Kamal looked towards Aaron and then back at the officer, she raised her hand to reach out for the glass, but as she did, it began to shake. Aaron held her hand in his firmly and with the other took the glass and held the glass to her lips. As she took a sip of the water he hoped she would cry soon, she had to cry, but instead she sat speechless. There was a brief moment of silence and then the front door opened and Michelle came rushing in.

"What's happened. Agnes said the police had come in. Are the kids okay?" Michelle stopped in her tracks as she looked at Kamal. "Kamal?" it was obvious she had received some bad news. "Aaron?" she searched Aaron for an answer.

"This is?" PC Cole asked Aaron.

"This is my sister, Michelle. Michelle and Kamal both live here, I was just visiting this week."

"Okay," PC Cole smiled at Michelle. PC Dixon went towards Michelle.

"I'm afraid Mrs Kaur has just had some bad news," she said under her breath, "her son died from a fatal accident on Saturday night. He was with his grandmother at the park. He'd run out into the car park, when a driver hit him. A sad case of hit and run; he died later in hospital from a severe head injury."

Michelle put her hand to her mouth in disbelief. She got on her knees in front of Kamal and held her hands tight. "Kamal, I am so, so sorry," Michelle said her eyes welling up for her friend. Kamal looked into Michelle's eyes and it was then when she spoke, "Michelle," she whispered her voice breaking with emotion. Aaron put his arm round her and Michelle also sat beside her. Both brother and sister comforted Kamal, as she let the first tears run free.

The officers spoke to both Michelle and Aaron before they left, as Kamal had retreated to her bedroom, saying that she needed a moment to herself. She held her son's portrait close to her chest curled up on the bed and looked blankly at the wall, silent tears running relentlessly, while his voice echoed in her head.

"Kamal," Michelle whispered knocking on the door, but there was no reply. Michelle opened the door, "Kamal can I come in?" there was still no answer. Michelle opened the door and sat on the end of her bed, "I can't imagine what you're going through. Losing a dear one is difficult, I know that, but your own child and in such circumstances, I cannot comprehend. The officer said that the funeral is on Monday; apparently the police have very little to go by on tracking down the perpetrator. It has been confirmed however that the death was due to the head injury, nothing else," Kamal closed her eyes, as if feeling her son's pain, "the family don't want to put off the funeral. Sindy wanted to make sure you knew, so that you could be there. I'll come with you for support. It's going to be hard, but you have to say goodbye properly, don't you Kamal?" There was no answer. Kamal lay still, lifeless. "I'll leave you alone for a bit longer. I'm downstairs whenever you need me," Michelle kissed her forehead.

Kamal looked blankly up at the ceiling. She recalled the last time she saw Jaydeep, waving goodbye to her as he walked through the departure gates, the other hand holding firmly onto his grandfather's and now, he had departed forever, never to return. She did not even get a chance to say sorry to him.

She later stirred in her sleep; she could hear Michelle and Aaron's inaudible voices downstairs. She looked towards the digital clock. It was 8.30pm. She sat up in bed and put her face in her hands, as her head throbbed painfully. Was this another bad dream she wondered? She dragged herself out of the bedroom into the bathroom. She shut the door and looked at her ghastly reflection in the mirror; it was not a dream. Those officers were real, and Jaydeep was no more. She splashed water over her face, like she did that first night she came into this house; that night was painful, but today, was intolerable. Never before had she felt so much pain, she felt as if her heart had been callously torn out of her. She balanced herself, by holding onto the washbasin and looked back up into the mirror, water rolling down her face and neck. She wanted to scream, she wanted to yell, she wanted to lash out, she wanted to break the mirror reflecting her pathetic sorry state! Since the day she had left, she had been beating herself up day in day out, but now, she was feeling a surge of anger and she could feel a burning rage building up within her.

Michelle and Aaron watched Kamal walk in, sit down on the sofa opposite, pull her knees up to her chest and wrap her arms around them.

"Kids asleep?" she asked softly with her chin resting on her knees

"Yeah," Aaron cleared his throat.

"You'll come with me on Monday then?"

"Of course I will," Michelle said.

There was a moment of silence, before Kamal spoke again. "It was a long labour you know. For a moment the doctors were concerned. They said his heartbeat was weakening. But he made it. He was a fighter. I did not relax until I heard him cry. I remember the nurses and doctors crowding over him and their sigh of relief, my relief, when he exercised his lungs for the first time. And then he was placed in my arms; it was the happiest moment of my life," Kamal's voice broke, "he was so beautiful, dark brown hair, pink lips, small button brown eyes," a tear dropped down, "I sat up holding him all night, just staring at the miracle in my arms. It was a very special night, just me and him. He was so light and small," Kamal looked down at her feet, as she spoke, reliving the memory, "and then," she wiped her tear and took a deep breath, "when I was sent home, my mother-in-law said that she'd keep him with her, just so that I could rest and recuperate. I was so shattered and in so much pain from the stitches and all, I did not argue. But one day turned to a week, a week to a month and she totally took over. I remember one night, soon after the birth, I got up and was searching the bed for him, like a mad woman. But he was with her of course. I did not even dispute and say I wanted him with me, that he was my child and he should be with me; I just let her carry on. I feel like I've let him down so badly," Michelle and Aaron listened as Kamal talked like she had never talked before, "I wasn't there for him. I blame myself for that, but I blame those bastards for ruining my life," she lifted her head, "that bastard Raj for treating me like a doormat and that snake Rohit, if he were to appear before me now, i'd.......it's their fault I was not with my son when I should have been. I'm going to the funeral to say goodbye to my baby. He was the only link I had with that family and now that he is gone, I can say good riddance to them all, each and every one of them! Now, now, it's over."

Chapter 18

"So many people," Michelle thought out loud, "why are all the women dressed in white?"

"We wear white on funerals."

"You okay?" Michelle asked as she sat in the driver's seat, Kamal in the passenger. Kamal wiped away the tear from her cheek. Her eyes were fixed on the people gathered outside the house, half way up the cul-de-sac. A stream of mourners flowed into the house, while some chose to stand outside, forming small groups. While their car had secured a place at the bottom of the cul-de-sac, cars now arriving had to do a u-turn and park elsewhere. Kamal could just about make out who some of the mourners were. It seemed like it was years since she'd been here, not months. Everything seemed so surreal. She was waiting like an outsider, plucking up the courage to get out the car and walk up the road, up the drive and into the house, where she was once welcomed as the new daughter-in-law, into the home where she was once respected, the house that she once upon a time called her home, but now, she felt like a fugitive, an outsider at her own son's funeral. She wondered whether her parents and sisters would be attending; of course they would be, she thought, they had every right to be there. She wondered whether her sisters would be there too. The thought of seeing all her family again under these dire circumstances, brought a wave of agonising emotion, so painful so severe, it felt as if her innards were being tampered with mercilessly.

She looked away to her left towards a front garden with her blurred vision on this bright, but sombre morning. There was a time when she'd sit at the window and admire the immaculate gardens, the luscious green lawns, the pruned rose bushes and the hedges trimmed to crisp, sharp perfection. She once stood proud as the daughter-in-law to the much loved family on this cul-de-sac, but now, she felt like an outcast.

"Fate has played such a cruel joke on me," Kamal whispered.

"Kamal," Michelle said softly, "are you ready?" Michelle was looking over her shoulder, as she saw the hearse arriving with the funeral casket. Michelle's own eyes now welling with tears, as she remembered the loss of her dear one, her mum. Kamal watched, as the hearse approached slowly and then drove past them. In it was a small casket, with a white wreath placed on top. The words 'Grandson and Son' made of white and yellow posies placed on either side and on the end, a football, made of flowers. Michelle watched the colour drain out of Kamal's face, as her hands lay lax on her laps; she sat motionless. Her eyes were fixed on the hearse, as it drove by slowly, up the cul-de-sac stopping halfway, right outside the house, the house where the now faraway innocent soul, once danced and played. Neighbours came out of their homes, as they watched the casket being taken out of the hearse. As Kamal watched the casket now carefully being taken up the drive, she opened the door to the car. Michelle watched her step out, robotically and then undid her belt and followed her out, after she'd closed Kamal's door, which she had left wide open. Kamal walked up the cul-de-sac like a lifeless soul, followed closely by Michelle, a little apprehensive about the reception Kamal would receive, but she had promised she would go with her and she intended to stay right by her side throughout. She saw that as Kamal approached the house, the faces lifted, the eyes turned and the nudging and whispering began. Even the neighbours stepped forward to take a closer look, as they watched Kamal walk by. Kamal was wearing a white shirt and jeans, her hair tied back. She had lost so much weight overnight, as if all life had been sucked out of her. She had looked so weak and frail. But now, as Michelle watched her walk up the drive, her focus on that casket, which held the body of her child, it seemed like no force in the world could dare to hold her back. Michelle walked in closely behind Kamal; she could hear women crying and some wailing hysterically. She held onto Kamal's arm as she looked round; she had never been to an Indian funeral. The large room was filled with women and men, each and every head covered in white. The casket was now placed in the middle of the room. The mourners stood around it and Michelle saw a man with a blue turban and a long white beard, stood with his hands together. An elderly lady was held by several other women, as she sobbed. Then, one by one, the heads turned towards Kamal. Some women gasped in astonishment, others nudged, pointed and whispered and then Michelle saw one young woman approach Kamal. She put her arms around her and cried uncontrollably.

Kamal held onto Deepa; Deepa seemed unaffected by the reaction of some of the women, she was more sympathetic towards the mother who had just lost her child. Michelle stood by and watched, the eyes curiously studying her also.

"I'm so sorry Kamal," Deepa said letting go, "so sorry. I promised I'd look after him, but I let you down." Kamal shook her head at Deepa and then turned towards the casket. She walked towards it. The ladies standing around made way for her and she ran her hand over the closed casket and wept. Kamal felt a hand on her shoulder, she looked to her right to see Raj's mother; both ladies wept their loss together.

"Why did you leave and not look back once. Why?"

Kamal felt unable to speak, unable to answer the question. She then saw Raj over Joginder's shoulder and slowly let go of her. He was standing on the other side of the casket, rings under his blood shot eyes and unshaven. Kamal looked at the father of her son, standing before her with resentment still fresh in his eyes, but his mother held onto Kamal's hand, almost reassuring her, that it was okay.

"You're not welcome here," he said moving towards her and a silence swept through the room.

"Well you try taking me away," Kamal looked into his eyes defiantly, sore and brimming with tears. Michelle's back was up straight, as she saw Raj just about to make his way round towards her.

"Just you wait there!" Michelle looked to where the voice was coming from. It was from an elderly man, who looked like an older replica of Raj, "I am still alive here. I decide who stays and who leaves this house."

Michelle watched as the elderly man, put his right hand on Kamal's head and then around her shoulder. She looked up at Raj, supported by his father. His eyes were fiery, but he stepped back as his parents embraced

Kamal, baffled by their reaction. But no-one was as surprised as Kamal was. Kamal requested the casket was uncovered.

Kamal ran her hands over Jaydeep's forehead; it was as if he was lying in a deep sleep. Kamal peered down at his peaceful face, "I'm so sorry darling," she sobbed, "I am so, so sorry my sweet. I have so missed seeing you. I love you so, so much." A hand came over Kamal's shoulder. She looked round to find her mother standing with her arms open wide. It was then when Kamal let go of all her emotions.

Nobody questioned Kamal during the funeral proceedings, her in-laws, mother, sisters, extended family and family friends, as everyone was together for one reason only; the mourning of a dear child and all personal prejudice was put to one side for the day.

"Where now?" Michelle asked, after they came out of the crematorium.

"There will be a service at the temple. Do you want to come in?"

"Of course. You okay?"

"Yes, taken aback by everyone's reaction to be honest."

"Maybe they understand more than you think."

"No, I sensed some hostility between Raj and his father. Something's not right."

Michelle removed her shoes and covered her head with a scarf Kamal gave to her. It had been a while since Kamal had been to the temple. As soon as they entered she could hear the familiar chanting of peaceful prayers and clanking of cutlery, stainless steel trays and glasses from the kitchen. She remained the focus of attention, as she and Michelle entered the prayer hall and made their way towards the *'Guru Granth Sahib'*. Kamal offered her contributions and kneeled down. She bowed her head and asked for forgiveness, for strength to overcome her loss and for the strength to carry on.

Following the service, she went with Michelle, her sisters and mother towards the dining hall; hardly a word was exchanged. The only person whom she could not make eye contact with, was her dad; he made no attempt to offer his condolences either. He chose to remain in the background, as if he were there, against his will.

It was outside the temple, whilst standing in the car park when Nindy really asked her how she was, all be that with a tone of resentment in her voice - her making an effort to talk to her, was but a mere formality. She almost tossed her nose in the air as she spoke. She had changed so much, just as she had been informed by Sindy, now being part of a family that had made a small fortune from a chain of grocery stores nationwide. Sindy was a little more compassionate in her approach; pregnancy really suited her and Sarbjit was fussing over her endlessly, insisting that they now left so she could go home and put up her feet.

Kamal looked towards her dad who glared back. She saw her mother make a movement towards her, but he held her back by her elbow. Parminder looked down at her husband's hand on her elbow and then helplessly towards her daughter. She lowered her gaze and stepped back, obediently. Kamal felt helpless, as she saw the desolate look in her mother's eyes and turned away. Michelle was waiting patiently in the car. Other vehicles were now leaving the temple one by one. She watched Nindy drive off, followed by Sindy and her husband and then eventually her parents. She stood motionless as they all went, one by one, back to their lives; not one of them looking back.

"Just want to say one last goodbye to Raj's parents," she said to Michelle, the car window rolled down.

"Take your time Kamal," Michelle smiled.

Joginder finally emerged from within the temple with a group of other ladies and Kamal walked up to her reluctantly, all eyes again focused on her.

"I've just come to say goodbye, for the last time."

"He was looking for you, when we came back from India," Kamal lowered her eyes, "why Kamal? Why did you not turn back for your son at least?"

"I was scared. And I did try, but…."

"I mean what mother walks out on her child?"

"I had no choice," Kamal's voice was breaking.

"We all have choices."

"And I made the wrong one."

"If you had just waited for us to come back, we could have resolved things," Raj's dad was standing next to his wife now and there was a small crowd of Raj's extended family forming in front of her now.

"Would you have? Would you have forgiven me?" she asked looking from one to the other. "Things would never have been the same again, anyway, the marriage was past saving. I just wanted to say goodbye and sorry for the hurt I have caused," she looked at Raj's parents and stepped back, "thank you for everything. If I could turn back time and change things I would, but I can't."

Everyone watched on, as she made her way back to the car. Just as Kamal was getting in, she heard her name being called out.

"Kamal, wait just a minute are you leaving now? At least leave me with your number."

"No Deepa. This is it now."

"But, I just wanted to say something........," Deepa looked round, as if ensuring nobody was nearby.

"What?" Kamal asked frowning, wondering why Deepa wanted to be so discreet.

"I just wanted to say don't take the blame for everything."

"What do you mean?"

"I mean you must not entirely blame yourself for what happened. I mean Raj was never the perfect husband was he? I'm just saying that if you have decided to move on then that's good, but don't keep beating yourself up about what happened. Trust me, it's not worth it."

Kamal looked at Deepa inquisitively, "are you trying to tell me something?"

"Deepa," Varinder called out, "come on let's go," he acknowledged Kamal with a mere nod of the head. Deepa looked at Kamal and held her hand.

"Will I see you again then?"

"We may run into each other again, who knows."

Deepa put her hand on Kamal's shoulder, "you take care, move on, don't look back."

Kamal took one look back up, as she sat in the car. Raj was stood with his hands in his pocket staring straight at her. A chill ran down her spine, as a not so pleasant memory flashed before her eyes. She shuddered as Michelle drove off; he reminded her so much of her father.

Chapter 19

"How are you feeling?" Danielle embraced Kamal, or what was left of her. Her old colleagues had called by to offer their condolences. They had tried not to gasp, as they saw a shadow of their old friend before them. Her hair dull, her face withdrawn, circled eyes, clothes just hanging off and this, according to Michelle, was Kamal better than a few weeks ago, when she was not even getting up out of bed, when in desperation Michelle had to call out the GP. The prescribed antidepressants had to some extent pulled her out the black hole she was in.

"Have had better days," Kamal tried to smile, "it's so good to see you guys again. This is Michelle. I know you've spoken to her quite a bit on the phone." Kamal introduced Michelle properly to Angela and Danielle. "I don't know what I would have done without her. She's been a rock; an angel in disguise."

Michelle smiled at her friend who at one point had her so worried, when she had become completely unresponsive, sitting or lying with the portrait of her son wrapped in her arms.

"How's work?"

"Oh same old, same old, you know what it's like. If you really want some gossip though, Samantha IS seeing Julie from accounts, we found out today!" Angela was bursting to confirm what they had so often speculated in the canteen.

"See, I told you," Kamal smiled.

"Oh I swear the things that go on!"

"Yeah, the things that go on….." Kamal looked down at her hands.

"He's been asking after you," Danielle broke the sudden silence.

"Has he?"

"Is this that guy, what was his name Robbie?" Michelle asked.

"Rohit, Rohit Sinha," Kamal said and again there was a silence. "The one thing that keeps going over and over in my mind of late is how did Raj ever find out? I mean, it's all I'm left with now, that niggling thought rattling around in my head, who was this friend? Was it someone I know?"

"Craig," Danielle said.

"Craig?" Kamal looked up in confusion.

"He just seemed to know something; it was the interaction between the both, you know - that look."

"But he does not know Raj and why would he tell Raj anyway, what was he to gain from it? No it had to be somebody else."

"Who could it possibly be?" Angela placed her finger on her chin thoughtfully. Kamal could not help but laugh then.

"Oh look who's here, Lieutenant Colombo." They all laughed.

"Well at least you've made her laugh again," Michelle smiled.

"I don't think you've probably had a chance to meet the real Kamal. Oh we used to have such a laugh. The office is not the same without you."

"Well life certainly took an unexpected turn that's for sure. They were good days, I did enjoy those days, I enjoyed work. It was my way of escaping and then comes along the perfect Rohit. What a mess."

"I do think he is generally sorry," Danielle said trying to convince Kamal.

Kamal shook her head and grinned, "he said all the right things, but forgot to tell me he had a pretty little wife tucked away."

"Was she really pretty?" Angela asked.

"Yeah, very, cow!" Kamal smirked.

"But seriously Kamal, he has been hassling me non-stop. He really wants to talk to you. I haven't told him anything, nothing at all, about Jaydeep."

"No, I can't. Seeing him would just remind me of what I lost; my whole world."

***

Craig's new secretary Rachel had called in sick again and Jackie had requested Christine to help out seeing that Rohit was out most of the day. The girls of course saw this as a perfect opportunity to start digging for information. Angela and Danielle had a plan; they had been trying to get closer to Christine over the past few days, adamant to find out who the informant was and being Rohit's secretary, maybe she could help them work out who could be privy to the short lived affair.

"Oh Angela, I forgot to tell you. I called Kamal again last night," Danielle winked a play along hint to Angela.

"Oh did you?" Angela gave a gentle nod.

"Yeah she says hello."

"So sad isn't it. I mean to lose a child, and in those circumstances. I wonder whether she will ever get over it?" Angela looked towards Christine, but she was engaged in work.

"Well you just don't do you. Losing a child must be the most painful thing in the world."

"Do you remember Kamal Christine?" Angela asked, trying to get her attention.

"Kamal. Yes, yes of course, Craig's old secretary. What happened?" Christine said ticking away at the keyboard.

"Her son died in a car accident."

"Oh how awful," Christine stopped typing, "the poor woman, how could she possibly be coping with that loss," she shook her head in sympathy.

"Yeah well, just between us, do you know she was seeing your boss Rohit Sinha?" Danielle whispered over the table.

"Was she?" Christine frowned.

"I'm surprised you did not notice? She was up there all the time!" Danielle said raising her eyebrows and then sitting back slowly.

"I can't say I did to be honest."

"Oh come on. We all know who's with who in this place," Angela whispered, nodding in the direction of Michael and Nicola out in the open office, Michael looking quite comfortable perched on the edge of her desk.

"Can't say I noticed and besides, he's a happily married man, so it all just does not ring true at all. You shouldn't speculate," Christine frowned again trying to continue with her work, with no time for idle gossip.

"Okay bye Rachel, see you tomorrow," Danielle put the phone down, as Christine walked back to the desk following her lunch break. "Oh Christine, you'll be glad to know Rachel is back in tomorrow, she just called."

"Oh good, good, I can concentrate on my own work then!"

Christine went into Craig's office with a file and closed the door. Danielle frowned at Angela, as she looked at the closed door curiously.

"How's your grandson Christine?" Danielle asked, as she came back to her temporary seat from Craig's office.

"Oh, absolutely adorable! I've actually got some photos. Do you want to see?" Christine was suddenly overcome with enthusiasm.

"Oh yes please," Angela said, as Christine picked her bag up from under her chair.

"Just had these developed, picked them up during lunchtime," she flicked through some photos, "here he is," she said smiling as she pulled one out.

Angela and Danielle went over to Christine.

"Oh he is so adorable!" Danielle said, "he's got really dark hair hasn't he? Oh look at those great big brown eyes."

"He's gorgeous isn't he?" Christine smiled.

"Oh he certainly is," Angela reiterated, "your daughter's really pretty."

"Yes she is. They're my world. I tell you, your own kids are special but grandchildren bring a whole new kind of happiness into your life," Christine smiled with fulfilment. While she did, Danielle was studying something else in the photo, distracting her, from Christine's excitement. Danielle's phone rang again and she went back to her desk with great irritation.

"Oh I am so not answering that now. It's gone 5.15!" Danielle said. "This phone has driven me insane today!"

"I'm dashing off girls. Rachel's back tomorrow?" Craig asked as he came out his office with his beige mac hung over his left arm and brown, worn out leather briefcase in the other hand.

"Yep, you've got your secretary back tomorrow," Danielle said sitting back in her chair, glad the day was over with.

"Good stuff. Have a nice evening and see you both tomorrow."

"Bye," Danielle waited for Craig to leave. "Angela, did you notice anything in that photo Christine was showing us?"

"What do you mean?" Angela said, sitting on the edge of her desk as she watched Danielle look into her compact mirror, flick her hair with her fingers and then apply her mauve coloured matt lipstick. She pressed her lips together, took one last look in the compact mirror, snapped it shut, and popped both objects back into her bag and pulled the zip to. She sat back thoughtfully.

"There was a photo in the background, a photo over the mantelpiece, did you not notice it?"

"Can't say I did."

"No, it's probably just me then, over thinking things, I just thought, the person in the photo looked awfully similar to Raj. Remember the photo Kamal used to have by her desk, her stood with him in Venice, just looked so much like him."

"But you can't be sure right?"

"No. But the more I think of it," she paused thoughtfully, "Angela, if it is, do you know what that means? Christine's daughter with Raj and a baby….."

"That would be sooo fucked up."

"Yes. I have just been bursting to say something, but she's been here all afternoon, and that bloody phone, I wanted to rip the cable out the socket at one point! I think we should talk to Rohit, see if he can coax anything out of her."

"I think there's no time like the present," Angela stood up ready.

"Angela, just think if it's true, Raj making Kamal suffer for one mistake, while all the while he's been bonking some other woman, and has a child too!" she said as they headed out the office for the lift.

"I can't begin to think," Angela shook her head, "what are we going to say to Rohit?"

"I think we should just say it the way it is," Danielle replied.

They both looked round cautiously, as they walked out the lift, Christine may have decided to go back up to her desk to catch up with Rohit before she left. There were still a couple of heads buried deep in paperwork, they looked up slightly, smiled and then carried on with their work. The cleaner was in the open office space with her trolley emptying bins and chewing mercilessly on her gum.

"All clear and he's there," Danielle whispered, "lights are on. Ready?" Danielle said as she approached the door.

"Yep."

"Come in," Rohit responded to the knock on the door with his head still down.

"Is it okay if we come in?" Rohit looked up with his big brown eyes. His navy tie hung loose around his neck, the top button of his pale blue shirt undone, his sleeves were rolled up and he had a slight stubble; Angela, could understand why Kamal had succumbed to temptation.

"Danielle, Angela," Rohit raised his eyebrows, put his pen down and stood up, "please, come in," he ran his hand through his soft hair as they walked in, "looks ominous," he grinned.

"May we?" Danielle said as she pulled the chair to sit opposite him.

"Please," Rohit said sitting back down, once they were both seated. He leaned on the file in front of him and looked at them both, "what can I do for you ladies?"

"Do you want contact with Kamal?" Danielle asked straight out. Rohit looked from one to the other curiously and then scratched his head.

"Well….yes, I would like to contact her, why, what's happened, what's changed?"

"Well it's like this. We went to see her last week."

"How is she?"

"As well as she can be, considering her son died."

"What, Jaydeep? No," Rohit gasped.

"In an accident, you didn't know?"

"Well, how am I to know?"

"Nobody mentioned anything to you?" Danielle persisted.

"No, nobody. Who else would have told me? Oh no!" Rohit was back up on his feet. He walked towards the window and put both his hands on the back of his head, in disbelief, "she must be devastated."

"That's an understatement," Angela said raising her brows.

"She managed to go to the funeral. But as you can imagine, it was very, very difficult for her to face her family after all that happened." Rohit turned round to look at Danielle as she spoke. "She was given the opportunity to say goodbye properly, considering everyone had cut her out of their lives."

"How does anyone deal with that?" Rohit said shaking his head, still not able to comprehend the agony she'd be going through.

"She said there is just one thing that keeps bothering her now. How did Raj find out? And that's where we want you to help out."

Rohit looked at them both and walked back to his chair. He sat down, evidently gutted by the news.

"How can I help?"

"We really think it was Christine that told Raj, more so now," Angela said.

"Christine?" Rohit frowned.

"Yes. Christine. And worse still," Danielle looked towards Angela, "we think Raj is with her daughter, and furthermore, we think that Christine's grandchild is Raj's baby."

"Christine's grandchild was born......" he stopped.

"Yes, exactly!" Danielle felt her body tingle over with goose bumps, as the realisation of the possible revelation sank in.

"But, how did you come to this conclusion?"

"A photo we saw of her grandchild just this afternoon. I am sure that it was Raj on a photo, within the photo, if you know what I mean."

"But if that is true it means that he had been unfaithful too…."

"And the penny drops. Christine's back here tomorrow. I'm sure you'll think of some way to coax any details from her."

"I'll think of something. I still can't believe Jaydeep's dead. Kamal will never, ever forgive me, never. But if, just if it is true that Raj has another child."

"Then he's going to wish he was never born. Kamal's a scorned woman Rohit and you know what they say hell…"

"…..hath no fury like a woman scorned," Rohit finished off her sentence.

"Yes, the guilt is eating away at her, while all the time, he could have possibly been…..I always told her he must be cheating. It's why it's up to you to find out."

"Leave this with me. It's the least I can do for her."

***

Kamal eventually returned back to work; she was trying her best to pick herself up again for the sake of those around her. A part of her had died with Jaydeep and whilst the pain was forever present, she needed to get some routine back in her life, but she found it very difficult to engage in anything wholeheartedly. She smiled, but there was no spark in her eye. She laughed, but it was not from the heart. She talked, but showed little emotion. She ate, for the sake of eating. She talked for the sake of talking. She breathed for the sake of breathing. Her life was a routine and she lived just for the day. She made no attempt to keep in touch with Sindy. Messages were left for her by Danielle and Angela, but she rarely called them back.

"Is she ready?" Aaron asked Michelle as he came in dressed in his black tailored trousers, white shirt sleeves rolled up showing off his toned arms and black waist coat. It was Friday night and Aaron had come to pick

Kamal up to take her to the club. "Here she is," Michelle looked up and smiled.

"Hi," Kamal smiled, dressed in a white short sleeved shirt and black pencil skirt.

"Hi, ready?"

"Yeah. You all packed Michelle?"

"Yes Jamie will be picking me up, in about, another half an hour," she said looking up at the clock as she finished putting on her mascara, "will you be okay on your own?"

"Yeah, I'll be fine. You have a good time up there in London okay. When will you be back?"

"Sunday evening."

"Well you take care," Kamal hugged and kissed Michelle on the cheek.

"I will and see you on Sunday. Look after her for me Aaron okay?"

"Of course. See you Sunday sis," Aaron kissed his sister goodbye.

It was mid-August and what remained of a beautiful summers' day. Girls were playing hopscotch on the street, some were skipping and a couple of lads were riding their bikes up and down the pavement. Kamal waved at Hilda the neighbour who was standing at her front door with her shopping, as she got into the car. As Aaron turned the key in the ignition the radio turned on. Kamal could not help but grin, as he sang along, he was as usual so out of sync.

"What?" Aaron looked at her.

"Nothing," Kamal looked away smiling.

"Great to see you smile," Aaron said.

"I wonder whether Jamie will be proposing this weekend, he is so obviously in love with her?" Kamal wondered out loud.

"We'll see."

"You know something don't you?" Kamal looked towards a gloating Aaron.

"Maybe."

"Oh come on Aaron, stop teasing. He is going to isn't he? Had he sought your approval?" Aaron was grinning from ear to ear, "he has hasn't he? Oh how sweet. Gosh they've hardly known each other two minutes though."

"I think they'll be okay. I like Jamie. He's a good bloke," Aaron reassured Kamal.

"Yeah he seems nice. And Michelle seems head over heels," Kamal sighed.

"What?" Aaron looked towards her as they waited at some traffic lights.

"Nothing. I'm sure she'll be fine. Not all men are bastards."

"No Kamal, not all men are."

"Hi Pat."

"Alright chick?"

"Yeah, you?" Kamal sat down next to Pat on the crate turned upside down outside the back of the club, as she took one last, satisfying drag from her cigarette.

"Okay. Hi Bobby," Pat looked up as the large bouncer joined them.

"Okay girls?"

"Fine thanks Bobby," Pat said, while Kamal acknowledged him with a smile.

"You're looking better," Bobby said looking down at Kamal as he lit a cigarette.

"So people keep saying. Must be the sun," Kamal smiled looking up at the fading evening sun and the blazing red skyline covering the city with a crimson sheet and then back towards Bobby towering over her. Kamal always thought Bobby was like a big friendly gentle giant. He was tall, had the broadest shoulders she'd ever seen and muscular arms visible through his fitted white shirts. When she saw him the first time she thought his eyes were as cold as ice and he had the ability to intimidate the brawliest of clubbers, but as soon as his face erupted into a smile, his eyes transformed into his much more true to character warm and gentle nature. When she had returned to work a few weeks ago, he said all he needed to say with a warm gentle embrace and told her if she ever needed him, she was to just ask. Kamal had seen Aaron getting rid of unwelcome rowdy customers swiftly and calmly, undeterred by their intimidating stance on a few occasions. She felt safe and protected while working in the club and the energy she was surrounded by, helped her to switch off, all be that momentarily. Mike, the owner, had been quite sympathetic towards Kamal's loss and had allowed her to take as much time off as she needed; of course Aaron being a good friend of Mike's, also helped.

Mike was successful in what he did as a businessman, but was notorious for his weakness for women. While he spent a lot of the time in the office, he made his presence felt as he walked around the club in his polished Italian shoes, designer suits, shining cuff links with matching tie pins, leaving behind a trail of his expensive cologne. Pat had a rotten crush on him and Kamal would giggle every time Pat felt flustered in his presence. Mark was a handsome man, dark brown hair, combed back, naturally greying at the sides, clean shaven and deep dreamy brown eyes, his features as if chiselled to perfection.

"Look at her again," Pat whispered as Natalie flaunted off her 34DD assets, leaning over the bar and whispering in his ear. Bobby had just opened up and was standing at the entrance with Paul the other security guard, equally as big as Bobby, if not as tall.

"He does not seem to be complaining," Kamal raised her eyebrows.

"Yeah, well what do you expect, he's a man. That bulge in his pants does all the thinking for him. Got a drop dead gorgeous wife, but does that prevent him from rubbing his balls on trash like that? I mean look at her. Oh hey-ho, look, he's taking her into his office. Well you can take a wild guess as to what is going to happen in there now."

Kamal looked down to the left from behind the counter of the cloakroom, "oh gosh, he has as well. Where's Aaron?"

"He was stacking the drinks. He knows what's going on. Trust me he is more than aware. She's been hitting on Mike for a while now that Natalie. Looks like there is going to be a lot more pumping than just the music tonight!" Pat said, tickling Kamal into a giggle.

"Oh Pat, you do make me laugh."

"Good," Pat smiled at her. "Let's see just how much of a man he is. See how long she is in there," she winked at Kamal, "no more than five minutes."

"Gosh, you don't expect much of him do you Pat?"

"No. It's just the trash he's taken in. Now if it had been me….." they both giggled again, "oh it's great to see you laughing again. Oh look, here he comes, geriatric David."

"Oh no," Kamal said under her breath as he approached and Pat tended to some excited young ladies.

"Hello ladies. Looking as lovely as ever. Good to have you back Kamal."

"Evening David," Kamal forced a smile.

"So, when are you going to have that drink with me?" he said leaning over the counter. His top shirt buttons were open, revealing the tips of his chest hairs turned silver.

She smiled at David and began to help Pat. She then caught sight of Natalie making her way back to the bar. Completely ignoring David, she whispered to Pat, who was taking a jacket off the obvious birthday girl wearing an 'I'm 21 today' badge.

"Blimey she's already back!" Pat looked up in disappointment and they both broke out into a giggle again.

"Want to share the joke darling?" David was still trying to catch Kamal's attention.

"Oh sorry David, it's a private joke," Kamal tried to ignore him.

"She looks blimmin' devastated! Poor thing, guess he's not all the man I thought he was! Either that or he couldn't get it up!" she whispered into Kamal's ear, tickling her again.

Kamal saw David talking to Mike as he continued to stare at her from the bar later that evening. "Oh he makes my skin crawl," Kamal shuddered.

"Who GD?" Pat said looking round.

"Wonder what he's saying?" Kamal frowned. Mike was looking in her direction, as she handed back a jacket. It was 1.50am now and some clubbers were beginning to leave, some walking as straight as they came in, others as if trying to walk a tight rope. Mike was now talking to Aaron leaning over the bar. Aaron looked towards Kamal; it was so obvious they were talking about her. Aaron frowned, shook his head and laughed, as if in disbelief and Kamal continued to wonder what was being said.

"Is there something you need to tell me?" Kamal said to a slightly agitated Aaron on their drive back home.

"Like?" he blew out the open window, he was unusually smoking this evening, something he only did when he was unduly bothered about something.

"Well I don't know," Kamal said looking out the window, "GD gives me the creeps."

"Who?"

"Geriatric David, that's what Pat calls him, I don't like the way he looks at me Aaron."

"Well you don't have to worry about him. Not as long as I'm around."

David had asked Mike to set Kamal up with him again, this time going as far as offering money. David and Mike went back a long way and they both had the same opinion of women in general, which did not sum up to much. Mike had the nerve to approach Aaron, even after he had openly confessed how he felt about her and knowing what she had been through. He found it half a job holding back from knocking David out. Mike had often set David up with girls he became obsessed with and he'd heard stories of his perverse desires and now, he seemed to have developed an infatuation for Kamal. But she was proving to be a bit of a challenge, which always made the game much more desirable for him. He was excessively drunk today and got to his lowest form by trying to negotiate a sum for one night. Aaron was so agitated and restless; he himself could not believe his inability to keep his emotions under control. Meanwhile, Kamal knew he was reeling over something, she could sense it. He was angry, really angry; she therefore kept quiet for the rest of the silent journey.

"Goodnight Aaron," she said getting out of the car.

"I'll see you in," Aaron said as he undid his belt and stepped out the car. He walked behind her up the drive and looked round as he did; men like

David could not be trusted. Kamal opened the door and switched on the light to the entrance.

"I'll be okay from here."

"I'll see you into the house."

Kamal had never seen Aaron so on edge and she let him walk her in.

"What's the matter Aaron?" she asked as she walked into the lounge switching on the light.

"Nothing."

"What about Natalie and Mike this evening, I mean he's married," Kamal shook her head as she went into the kitchen.

"That doesn't usually stop people," he said without thinking, "oh sorry," he put his hand to his head.

"No, no, don't be. I suppose I should stop talking about people. I'm a fine one to talk aren't I?"

"No. You're different," Aaron was looking down at her, "you are not like other girls." Kamal looked up at Aaron and froze in his intense gaze. It was like dèjá vu, she'd seen this intensity before.

"I think you should leave now," she said looking at him coldly, not moving, or batting an eyelid.

"Kamal," Aaron took one step closer towards her.

"Aaron, please leave," she turned her back towards him and walked over towards the sink. Aaron stood still, as she turned the tap and filled a glass of water for herself. He turned around to walk out and stopped in the doorway. Kamal daren't look up as he halted. He then continued to make his way out and only when she heard the front door open and close, it was then she took a sigh of relief and leant back on the kitchen sink.

"Aaron," she whispered in disbelief.

***

"How's your daughter Christine," Rohit asked his secretary as he sat with her at lunch. Christine had noticed that Rohit seemed to have picked himself up. He was shaving daily, he left his door open as he worked, like he used to, he managed to actually say 'good morning' properly to her every morning, instead of a feeble grunt. She was glad he was getting back on track. She could not help but feel sorry for him looking utterly distraught over the last few months; he had told her that his life's biggest compromise had turned his world upside down and he had nothing to do now but grin and bear.

"You okay?" Rohit asked, "you seem miles away."

"Oh I'm fine. Children, you'd think you worry for them less as they grow older, but no."

"Comes with the territory doesn't it?"

"Yes. How are things with your wife now?"

"Okay," was all he managed to say, but she could see the unhappiness embedded deep in his eyes.

Rohit's wife called the office often. Christine was taken aback by surprise the first time she had the snotty high and mighty Mrs Sinha on the line, especially since she didn't even know Rohit was married. She gathered things were not so rosy in the Sinha residence, what with the tone of voice Mrs Sinha often used whenever she called, demanding to know where he was if he was not at his desk, calling just before his lunch break or just before it was 5pm, wanting to know if he had had his packed lunch or if he was on his way back home. Christine had often put the call through just after 5pm, when she was still clearing her desk, "you still there Christine?" she'd say in her inquisitive, patronising high pitched voice.

"So do you have anything for us?" Danielle called Rohit.

"Well I can't just jump straight in can I? I'm working at it. She speaks to my wife a lot, so I have to be careful and she's very protective when it comes to her family."

"Yeah that's right. Look after number one as always," Danielle shook her head in contempt.

"Have you heard from Kamal?"

"May have, will let you know when you get me my information," Danielle hung up with that.

"Anything?" Angela asked.

"Nothing. Useless. He said he has to be careful because Christine speaks to his wife apparently."

"Why don't we just confront her straight?"

"No. We want to play this nice and easy, for Kamal's sake, we don't want to scare her off. We want something concrete. Besides, after finally speaking to Kamal last night it appears she is just getting back on her feet. Let her build her energy back up and then if our suspicion is proven right, she would have the strength to be able to digest and deal with it."

"That's true. She does sound different though. I mean she's still nice and all, but have you noticed the coldness in her voice?"

"Yes I have. Guess that's what grief does to you. I hope it's not true and my eyes were just deceiving me, for her sake. It could completely break her."

Rohit watched Christine from his office window. She avoided talking about her family, it was as if she was protecting them with a great big wall and they were untouchable. He wanted to get to the bottom of the truth, but at the same time he did not want to jeopardise the peace of his own home, which he had just about restored. If Danielle's and Angela's suspicions were correct and Christine had indeed played a part in tearing Kamal and Raj apart, what was he to do about it? Tell them? She obviously wanted to keep her daughter's relationship guarded and if Kamal was to learn the truth, all hell could break loose and if Christine had no qualms in breaking another woman's marriage for the sake of her daughter's happiness, he could imagine what she would do to his marriage, should he play a part in disclosing the truth to Kamal. He had no doubt she would have great pleasure in calling Priya, telling her the truth he had been denying ever since that night, and that would be catastrophic. He could not risk sabotaging his relationship with his wife, for the sake of his parents and therefore, he could not get involved, he just couldn't, however sorry he was.

Chapter 20

"Oh hi Christine. Our photocopier's on the blink - again!" Danielle said, seeing Christine as she walked into the photocopying room, with a pile of documents that needed to be copied and circulated like yesterday!

"Oh okay, I'm almost done," Christine looked away glumly, as if her mind was preoccupied with matters of more importance.

"What's the matter? You okay?"

"Yeah I'm fine. Actually, no I'm not!" she exhaled and shook her head, "I don't know what to do Danielle," Christine put her hand to her head, her nails as ever pristinely painted in red varnish, her fingers overdosed with rings in all shapes, stones and sizes. Her short blonde hair was as always styled to perfection, held static by a copious amount of hairspray, her lips painted in her signature pink lipstick and her lashes thickly coated in black clumpy mascara.

"What's the matter?" Danielle said, putting her pile of documents down and placing her arm round Christine.

"I guess I am paying the price for what I did."

"No sorry, I'm lost. What is it Christine?"

Christine looked towards Danielle. The only noise between them now was the photocopier, churning out the copied documents. Christine bit her bottom lip anxiously, as she contemplated discussing anything with Danielle. "Oh gosh," she closed her eyes in anguish and sighed, "I need to do something. It's my daughter."

"Yes," Danielle waited patiently. She and Angela were spending as much time as they could with Christine and she wondered now whether their perseverance had finally paid off. Christine took a deep breath and closed her eyes again.

"Raj, Kamal's ex, is with my Emma," she blurted out, "there. I've said it okay, it's what you wanted to know wasn't it!" Danielle raised her brows, but said nothing. "Raj and Emma have been together for quite a while now; while Raj and Kamal were still together actually. Emma had his baby, my grandson is his. I was the one that told Raj his wife was seeing Rohit, a reason he could use to finally leave his family without feeling so damn guilty! Everything was going just fine and then Jaydeep died and Raj has just never been the same since. He is just wallowing away in grief and guilt. It's destroying him and Emma. I need him to speak to Kamal. Nothing can be put right until he speaks to Kamal. He needs to apologise to her, to face her. He keeps saying that he can hear her crying in his sleep. He wakes up in the middle of the night in a panic saying he keeps seeing Jaydeep's corpse and Kamal screaming, he then walks around the house in the middle of the night, unable to sleep, he says he keeps seeing her face pleading with him. He needs to ask for forgiveness Danielle. Can you please contact Kamal for me? Please?" Christine confirmed all Danielle's suspicions just when she least expected and it left her nothing short of speechless. Danielle sat down on the piled up boxes of A4 paper.

"You are in contact with her aren't you?" Christine asked her with a desperate plea in her voice, "will you please call her for me? Please. Maybe I can ask for forgiveness too then. I was a fool to think I could buy happiness for my daughter by destroying another woman's life. I did it to make it easier for Raj; he was finding it so difficult to tell her. The night Emma had the baby, was the night I first saw Raj at the hospital and I kept thinking, I have seen him somewhere before, but I couldn't place where. It was later the following evening, when my mind drifted to Rohit and Kamal, convinced I had seen them kissing in the office and then them leaving the office together the night Emma had the baby, and it finally clicked, her desk, the picture she used to have of her and her husband in Venice. It was then I realised who Raj was and I saw it as the perfect opportunity for Raj to get his wife out his life and get together with my Emma. And it was me that told him of seeing them in the bar, I was out late night shopping when I saw them; all I could think of at the time was that there was no way I was going to have my daughter remain his secret life, she deserved more than that. I brought both my children up without their father around and there was no way I was going to have history repeat itself with my grandchild. But, I never wanted things to turn out like this. Maybe once Raj relieves himself of his guilt, face to face with Kamal, he can move on, then Emma can move on, we all can move on."

"And Kamal, how does she move on? Have you any idea what she has been through? She won't take this lying down, you do realise that, don't you?" Danielle wasn't sure whether she should sympathise with her or despise her.

"I know she won't, but Emma is so stressed. She does not need this. They were so happy together, so perfect and then Jaydeep died, and from then on, Raj is a changed man. Emma's even heard him talking to himself. He's going to drive himself insane. She is so worried for him."

"Death of a child would do that to the coldest of people," Danielle shook her head and looked up at Christine, "would you all have carried on quietly if it had not been for Jaydeep's death? Would you have let Kamal continue to live with her guilt, if it was not for Raj losing his sanity?"

"I guess we are all paying the price now….."

"I guess you are," Danielle got up. The photocopier had stopped. As Christine stood silently, ashamed of her manipulative act, Danielle took her photocopied documents and handed them to Christine.

"I will speak to Kamal. Write down your daughter's contact details here. I will let Kamal deal with this the way she wants to. I think you all owe her that much."

Christine hesitated for a moment, but then quickly jotted down Emma's home address and left. Danielle shook her head in disbelief and fed the documents into the photocopier wishing there was a button which could speed the damn thing up. She had to talk to Angela. As she watched the copier she began to wonder how on earth she was going to break the news to Kamal and how she was going to cope with this blow.

Back in the office Angela was on the phone and Rachel was out. She shut the door and shook her head. Angela frowned wondering why Danielle looked so troubled. She tried to finish off her call, rolling her eyes as the caller frustratingly elongated the conversation.

"What's up?" she asked as she finally slammed the receiver down.

"You are never going to believe what I have got to tell you."

***

Kamal sat still, her head was bent down, her hands were in her hair, her elbows resting on her knees. Michelle had been listening carefully, trying to make sense of the conversation between Kamal and her old friend.

"That bad?" Michelle asked. Kamal had shown little emotions whilst talking on the phone, she had repeated some names obvious to her, but whatever Danielle was telling her seemed to be some sort of revelation. Kamal still said nothing. "Kamal?" Michelle asked again reluctantly. She hoped it was not more bad news, as she was just about getting back on her feet again, any bad news now, could really tip her over the edge. Kamal lifted her head, she appeared furious. Michelle had seen her, sad, devastated, helpless and hopeless, but she had rarely, if ever, seen her this incensed, her knuckles turning pale, as she clasped her fists tight. Kamal was still in her office clothes. She had popped into the local shop to get some groceries and was just putting the shopping away, when Danielle had called asking to speak to her. This was the second time Danielle had called today and she sounded extremely anxious. Kamal looked towards Michelle and said to her in a calm collected tone of voice.

"That bastard Raj is with somebody," Michelle did not react, not quite understanding what the issue was. "The person he is with, is someone he apparently was with, when we were still together," Michelle then sat up straight, "but it gets better than that, he's also got a ten month old son," Kamal stood up and walked across the room and then back again.

"But you've only been separated what eight or nine months."

"The bastard! He stood by and let me beg him! He let me get down on my bloody knees asking for forgiveness, when all the time!"

Michelle stood up, not knowing whether she should approach her, for the fear of being lashed out at. Then Kamal marched back to where she was sitting and picked up a piece of paper she had jotted some details given to her by Danielle.

"I'm going out!"

"Where are you going?"

"To have it out with that snake!"

"No Kamal wait! You are not in a fit state to go out there right now."

"Fit state! How dare he Michelle, how dare he! You saw me. I was a wreck when you found me. You know how I cried myself to sleep every night. You know how every morning was a reminder of what happened. You know everything. I mean what sort of a cold blooded bastard is he, for letting me believe that I was the guilty party, when all the time he was screwing around. Oh but it gets better, he's got a separate home. Oh and guess who told him about my infidelity, Rohit's secretary, Christine, the mother of Emma, the woman he's been leading a secret life with!"

Michelle looked wide eyed in disbelief, "what?"

"You couldn't make it up! Well now, he's going to have a piece of my mind!" Kamal stormed into the kitchen to pick up her handbag and keys left earlier on the kitchen table and looked momentarily towards the kitchen drawer, her impulse interrupted by Michelle.

"I'm coming with you."

"No, I'll be okay," Kamal turned to walk out.

"No, I am coming with you," Michelle said firmly quickly running out behind Kamal.

"Look up the address in the A-Z," Kamal said as she buckled up and handed over the piece of paper.

Kamal was driving fast, turning sharp and braking hard. Michelle held onto her seat, offering to drive, but Kamal declined. Michelle could see Kamal's hands shaking in anger as they waited at traffic lights, her elbow resting on the door, biting her thumb nail.

"Left from here," Michelle directed. She put the A-Z back in the glove compartment, "number 9. This is it."

Kamal looked towards the house on her left. She looked round the quiet cul-de-sac, lined with identical, modern, newly built homes.

"How very lovely," she looked towards the white UPVC front door of house number 9. Double glazed windows, with vertical blinds. There were two cars parked side by side on the drive. One black BMW and the other a blue VW Beetle. Kamal smirked; he always said he wanted a BMW. A middle aged neighbour peered at them through his window, as they sat in the car looking towards the house. Michelle looked towards Kamal.

"You ready?"

"I would have felt better if I had a shotgun," Kamal said coldly, "you stay in the car. I want to do this on my own."

"If you're sure."

"Yes, I'm sure. I'll be okay," Kamal unbuckled her belt and stepped out the car. She looked around the cul-de-sac again and then walked up the drive. She peered into the two cars; the Beetle had a baby seat in the rear seat. She approached the door and rang the bell. Her heart was pounding and her hands shaking from fury; she clenched her jaws as she heard a female voice approaching. The door opened and a young woman, looking no older than 25, tall, slender, long blond hair, peachy skin, making the designer jeans and yellow top look good, stood before her.

"Yes, can I help you?"

Kamal looked straight at her. The woman looked down at her hands as if expecting her to be some sort of a saleswoman, seeing she was dressed for business in a tailored navy two piece suit and crisp white shirt.

"Is Raj in?" Kamal asked.

"Raj?" Emma frowned.

"Yes, Raj, he does live here doesn't he?"

There were a few moments of silence between the two women.

"Yes, he does. Raj!" Emma shouted out, "there's a lady at the door for you," her voice faded and suddenly, as if something had finally clicked, Emma looked at Kamal more closely. Kamal grinned, almost being able to read Emma's mind.

"Who is it?" Raj asked walking out from the kitchen straight ahead. As Raj walked towards the front door and saw Kamal standing, he froze in his tracks. Emma looked round at Raj's look of dismay and then back at Kamal.

"Kamal?" Emma enquired hesitantly.

"Oh. So you do know about me? I'm not a big secret to you then?" Kamal said walking straight in leaving a stunned Emma in the doorway. Emma looked out onto the street and saw Michelle looking at her from a blue Ford Escort; she left the door ajar and walked into the kitchen straight ahead to see to her crying baby. Kamal meanwhile, invited herself into the lounge followed reluctantly by a staggered Raj.

"Well, how cosy is this?" she said looking around the immaculate room. With its beige carpet, black leather sofa suite, with big white cushions. There were large green houseplants either end of the room and a small playpen by the patio window looking over a small garden, in the middle of which stood an old tree. She walked over to the mantelpiece and looked up at the large portrait of a smiling Raj and Emma, with a new born baby cradled in her arms; her heart skipped a beat as she saw the baby and she swallowed the lump in her throat. Regaining her composure, she turned round to face Raj standing with his hands in his pockets, eyes down on the floor. The atmosphere in the room was palpable and he dared to look up slightly. Kamal smirked at the pathetic looking image stood before her.

"So," she said sitting down on the sofa, "how long has this been going on?" Raj chose not to reply, instead buried his head further down into his shoulders. "Am I going to be here all night?"

"I, I, me and Emma….."

"Me and Emma? Nice. How long?" Kamal's tone turned sharper.

"Kamal. I wanted to tell you, but……"

"But?"

"It was hard. And then you…..so I just….."

"You just let me think I had fucked up big time didn't you? So, you still haven't told me. How long?"

"….please?"

"Please? Are you pleading with me? Well that certainly makes a change. You may remember not so long ago, I was pleading with you, do you remember? Or have you conveniently forgotten? I was literally on my knees you cold hearted bastard!" Kamal was back on her feet. She walked slowly towards Raj, "have you any idea what I have been through these last few months? Have you? And then Jaydeep. You even denied me seeing my own son. You cold, callous, deceiving, snake!" Raj winced; her words were like a searing hot rod piercing through his eardrum. "Jaydeep? How often did you actually see him? Did you have time to even see him with all this? I mean, you hardly had time for him when I was there, let alone when I wasn't. So say something you coward. Where's the attitude now? Where're the accusations now?"

"LOOK I'M SORRY OKAY. I'M SORRY!" he blurted out throwing his hands into the air.

"Sorry?" Kamal leaned her head back. "Sorry! Do you think sorry is going to repair everything? Well? Do you!"

"I can't turn back time, but if I could, I would I swear Kamal."

"Yes, you're right you can't. But that does not make me feel any better. You just stood back and let me suffer. You just stood back and let both families believe I was a shameful daughter, daughter-in-law. You just stood back and let me agonise over my son. Does anyone know about this?" Kamal waved her hand in the air, "well, does anyone? Your mum, dad, Varinder, Deepa, anyone?"

"Mum and dad know I am living with someone…."

"No stop! I'll ask you the question again. Do they know the whole truth?" Kamal was gritting her teeth now.

Raj shook his head, "I think Varinder knows."

"Ah, well, that would explain," she remembered Deepa's last words to her.

Kamal stepped back and walked towards the window in repulse. She saw her trusted friend Michelle now standing outside of the car, leaning on the car bonnet with her arms crossed looking towards the door and then window.

"Months, I've suffered for, months."

"I'm sorry."

Kamal turned back around and walked towards Raj who was now standing in the middle of the room, his circled eyes hesitating to meet hers. Without any warning and with all her might, she slapped him. Raj put his hand to his face and looked at her in alarm.

"Sorry! Sorry does not repair my reputation, sorry does not bring back my sleepless nights, sorry does not take back the look of disgust in my dad's eyes when he looked at me at my son's funeral, sorry does not repair the pain and anxiety my mother went through, sorry does not repair the shame my family have endured, sorry does not do anything. SORRY DOES NOT BRING BACK MY SON!" A tear ran down Kamal's face as she painfully poked Raj in the chest, pushing him back with every single point she made. Just then, Emma walked into the room holding her baby followed by her mother. Kamal looked over Raj's shoulder; Emma looked pale with fright and Christine, averted her eyes. But Kamal's gaze was frozen on the baby. Dark hair, big eyes, tiny nose, pink lips, chubby cheeks; he was Jaydeep all over again. He looked at Kamal and smiled, totally innocent and oblivious to the volatile situation. A tear dropped out of Kamal's eye as she looked at the baby, the only difference between her Jaydeep and this baby was the fairer complexion. A shiver ran down Kamal's spine as she stood motionless. Nobody moved. The only sound was from the baby's gurgling, as he looked from his mother to his father. Kamal continued to stare. Christine was bowled over with guilt seeing Kamal standing shell shocked. The tears running out of the eyes said it all, and she was hurting for her. She had seen pictures of Jaydeep and she knew exactly what was going through Kamal's mind at this very moment. Kamal swept her tears away with two swift movements of her tingling right hand.

"Sorry is not going to repair the damage you have done. Yes I messed up, but you, what you did, is unforgivable. Do you remember the night I asked if you were having an affair? You swore on his life you wouldn't even think of it, do you remember? You swore on his life. How do you sleep at night Raj, how?"

Raj closed his eyes tortured by the guilt, "I haven't been sleeping. Every night has been torture."

"Sound's familiar," Kamal sniffed and looked away.

After a moment of silence, Raj looked up, "what now?"

"Now, now I'm going to get the best lawyer money can buy and I am going to screw you for everything you have!" Kamal pointed one finger in Raj's face, "and if you", her finger was now pointing towards Emma, "if you think you can build a home after destroying another, you can think again and you, what goes round, comes round," she said to an equally speechless Christine before she stormed past them and out the house.

Michelle had been waiting patiently, tempted to go into the house, "you okay?" Kamal just nodded her head.

"Just one more stop, and then, I want to go home."

Kamal pulled up just outside her once marital home. Her right hand was still tingling from the slap; months of pain and anxiety released in one solid hit. She was suddenly overcome by goose bumps; the last time she was here was at Jaydeep's funeral and a hurricane of pain and emotions came storming back and she leant her heavy head on the steering wheel.

"Kamal, are you okay?"

Kamal lifted her head, took a deep breath and wiped away the tears, "yes, I won't be long," she swallowed the lump in her throat as memories of painful moments came surging back.

The elderly man that she once loved and respected more than she did her own father opened the door. He seemed to have suddenly aged further. He no longer stood straight, his shoulders were slouched and his face appeared withdrawn, which was understandable, she should not forget that he had also gone through the trauma of losing a grandchild whom he doted over and the once proud man had to live with the shame of an eloped daughter-in-law and now, she was about to shake his world again.

"Kamal," he said as she stood in the doorway. She did not wait to be invited in and walked straight past him, straight into the lounge, as the rage resurfaced. Joginder walked in from the kitchen.

"Who is it?" she said out loud, not realising Kamal was standing in the middle of her lounge. She was wearing the green and white checked apron Kamal used to wear while she did the cooking. The subtle aroma of cooking basmati rice flowed from the kitchen.

A shiver ran down Kamal's spine as she stood in the very spot where the casket had been placed.

"Kamal. Are you okay?" Joginder asked reluctantly. Kamal stood silent.

"Please sit down Kamal," Balbir said coming into the room.

"I have not come to sit down," Kamal closed her eyes, trying to blank out the painful memory of seeing her son's lifeless body. She took in a deep breath, regained her composure and spoke, "did you know your son is with another woman?" Both parents looked from one to the other, "did you?" Kamal turned fully to face both.

"I suspected he was with someone," Balbir looked down at his feet, answering for both.

"Did you know he has a son? Born, while you were in India?"

"What nonsense!" Joginder shook her head in disbelief.

"Don't you believe me? Well here's the address. Go check it out for yourself. I just came here for you to know the whole truth!" with that Kamal stormed out leaving them to work it all out for themselves, to put all the pieces of the jigsaw together. As she opened the front door, she froze in her tracks, distracted from seeing Jaydeep's framed photo placed on a corner table, on the right hand side of the front door. She looked at the wide, innocent, content smile and the twinkle in the eyes; a twinkle she was never going to see again. She could hear his laughter echoing about her and looked back round, as if half expecting him to come running out towards her from the kitchen, like he used to every time she came back home from work and another tear travelled down her cheek.

Balbir picked up the paper from the table. "I could kill him! How many more lies? How many more secrets? I curse the day he was born!"

"Don't say that about your son please!"

"Son! He's made my life a living hell. You go round telling everyone what a disgrace your daughter-in-law turned out to be, now what about your son? What are you going to say about him!"

Joginder started to cry, "I have another grandson."

"AND HE MIGHT EVEN MANAGE TO KILL HIM ASWELL!" Kamal was just about to step out when she paused midway; did she hear correctly? She took one step back.

"Sssshhhh somebody may hear," is all she heard, as she edged back towards the lounge slowly.

"I don't care! It's your fault! You have been covering up his lies. And now this! He should be shot for what he did!" Balbir's voice was broken with pain and anger.

Kamal stood in the doorway and looked towards both parents questioning whether she had heard right or whether her mind was playing games. Joginder looked up in alarm at discovering that Kamal had not left.

"What did he do?" Kamal asked, looking from one to the other, her throat and lips suddenly feeling dry.

Balbir looked back towards her and then towards his wife. Joginder looked at her husband with a plea in her eyes, but Balbir had evidently reached the end of his tether and sat down in exhaustion. Looking down at the paper in his hand, he spoke. "Raj had dropped Jaydeep and her at the park and as usual, he was in a hurry to get away," Balbir put his hand to his forehead, struggling to get the words out, "Jaydeep remembered he left his football on the back seat and ran back towards the car. Raj had not noticed, he just took his eyes away literally for a few seconds as he was pulling out, he did not see that Jaydeep was running back towards the car, wanting to catch his attention. He hit Jaydeep. Jaydeep fell back and banged his head with such force. This woman - told the police it was a hit and run, took full advantage of the fact she could not speak much English, told the police she was too devastated to remember the vehicle. Miraculously, there was nobody to witness what had happened! Now I know why he was always in a hurry to leave, why he was never here for his first born, he was leading a bloody separate life!" He screwed the paper in his hand and threw it across the room.

Kamal looked at Joginder in utter disbelief.

"What was I supposed to do? On the one hand I had my grandson in my arms and on the other, I had a distraught son. It tore my heart apart seeing him, he was devastated, so shocked, he could barely move. It was an accident, a terrible accident. I just did what I thought was right at the time. I told him to leave the scene and called for help. You can't say anything. I beg you," she walked towards Kamal with both hands clasped together, tears running down her eyes. She went to touch Kamal's feet and Kamal stepped back, "please Kamal," she grabbed her hands. I have lost my grandson, I don't want to lose my son as well. Please I beg you. It was an accident, a terrible, terrible accident."

Kamal slowly walked backwards, eyes wide open, back towards the front door, Joginder walking with her every step, pleading with her, sobbing and begging her for her silence, bending her head and touching her feet. Kamal turned round and stepped out the front door. She just about managed to take herself back to the car, she felt like she'd been hit by a force with such ferocity, she could barely feel her feet touch the ground, her legs sure to give way soon, all she could hear were the words, 'he hit Jaydeep,' echoing over and over again. She opened the door and collapsed into the seat and looked back towards the house where Joginder was still standing with her hands together, pleading, her husband now standing by her side. Kamal looked at her and back at her windscreen blankly.

"Do you want me to drive?" Michelle asked, concerned.

Kamal looked at Michelle and nodded.

There was complete silence as Michele drove back. Kamal, told her nothing.

Chapter 21

"She's not available David," Mike said as he joined his friend for another shot of whiskey.

"All women are available, at a price," David's crow feet deepened with his conniving smile, as he looked away from Kamal back to his old mate.

"Face it David. You just don't have the touch anymore," Mike chuckled as he swirled the glass of scotch with ice, "she's more your type. Proper little gold digger," Mike's eyes were on Natalie as he drank back his liquor, acknowledging her with a wink. She looked at him seductively, "look at her, ready and willing," he looked back to his friend grinning.

"Yeah, well I like a bit of a challenge."

"You always have, haven't you? But forget this one Dave. She's a scorned woman and besides, Aaron won't let you touch her."

"Is that right now," David sniggered looking towards Aaron and observed him closely; looks, youth, surrounded by women, whole life in front of him. He too had it all once, women tripped over themselves for him, but the only women interested in him now, were the ones with their eyes on the fat bulge he carried in his back pocket. He liked Kamal, he liked her a lot and he really wanted her.

David's eyes later followed Kamal going towards the staff toilets.

"Back in a sec," David said knocking back his drink; Mike had not noticed where David was heading, too distracted by the signals a young woman was sending to him right now from the dance floor.

The music was thumping and the club jam packed. Kamal much preferred her night job from the day job. The club was a lot more distracting, full of people who wanted to intoxicate themselves into a trance-like-state; just like she wished to be for every second of her life, desperate to forget. She had started helping more around the club, from clearing glasses to helping behind the bar whenever required and had asked for more days and hours at the club to help keep her mind occupied. Michelle warned her from working herself into exhaustion, but Kamal begged to differ, in her view, she was working herself into oblivion. It had been about a month since she'd seen Raj and his parents and she'd chosen to switch off from the revelations; for the time being at least. Nothing was going to bring her son back now and she no longer wanted or indeed needed to go back to the life she once had.

Kamal came out the toilet cubicle and saw David standing outside, by the basin, hands in his tailored trouser pockets, leaning on the wall next to the paper towel holder looking very smug. She stood still in her steps, before she spoke.

"I think you will find the gents toilets are next door David," she proceeded towards the sink, turned on the water, dispensed some hand wash onto the palm of her hand and lathered her hands, the bass from the music, vibrating the door and floor.

"Oh I am well aware of that my sweet," David said looking at her grinning with pleasure. Kamal rinsed her hands, pulled some paper towels and dried her hands. She was used to seeing drunks and being drooled over now, but David, she particularly detested, he had lust protruding through his bones. He stuck his arm out as she tried to walk out. "Kam," he held onto her left arm.

"Let go of my arm," Kamal said looking down at his hand.

"Oh come on, you know why I'm here," he said getting close to whisper in her ear, the smell of alcohol wafting off his breath, bringing back some unpleasant memories, "come on. I can make you the happiest woman in the world," he touched her cheek softly with the back of his fingers.

"Is that right? With what?" Kamal turned to look him straight in the eye, her mouth close to his.

"Now we're talking," he said moistening his lips and then whispered in her ear, "the two things that make this world go round, money and a good fuck."

"And you are going to give me what?" Kamal whispered back.

"I'll give you whatever you want. Just name it," David said raising his arms standing back, this was easier than he thought. Kamal stepped forward towards him.

"How about you get out my face, shove your money up your egotistic arse and take floppy down there to some desperate slut!"

The smile now dropped from David's face. Kamal went back towards the door, but before she reached it, David stepped forward and grabbed her back towards him from both arms, pushed her against the wall and brought his face close up to hers.

"You think you're special don't you?" he said as she tried to break free from his firm clasp, "what was your failed marriage over? A quick shag with one of guys in the office? Let me guess, did he screw you over the desk? Well you're a free woman now, what's stopping you now? Did he not impress you, is that what it was?" Kamal continued to struggle, as he pressed his body against her, pushing her harder against the wall, she could feel his erection rubbing against her now, his face was pressed against her cheek, the stench of alcohol strong and uncomfortable, "do you want me to show you floppy in action, he's got more life than that weasel Aaron out there, you'll be pleasantly surprised my darling. What you need is a nice mature man, who can really show you a good fucking time. Do you want me to show you just how willing floppy is?" Unpleasant memories flashed before her eyes. David let go of her right arm to unzip his trousers and no sooner was her right arm free, she grabbed his hair with her free hand and pulled it with such ferocity, she could feel his hairs pluck loose from its roots in her ruthless grasp. He yelled out in pain, caught quite by surprise letting go of her other arm. She immediately turned round to now fully face him and still holding onto his hair, she brought her right knee slamming up to his crotch, releasing all her fury from a past as well as the current experience. David bent down and yelped out in pain, "oh gaaawd, you bitch!"

She bent down and pulled his hair up again bringing his face up to hers. "I am sick and tired of men like you, who think they can control me! Now you listen carefully you bastard, if you so much as come within an inch of me again I will personally cut off your balls and serve them with some scotch and ice for you! Is that clear?" she whispered in his ear. With no reply she pushed him back and grabbed his testicles, "I said is that clear?"

"Ahh, gaawd! Yes, yes!"

"Good!"

Leaving him bent down in agony, she washed his hairs off her hand, dried them, straightened out her skirt and hair and left him to recover.

The drive home was a quiet one, which had become the norm. Ever since the confrontation with Raj, Kamal was a changed woman to the one Aaron had got to know. He was once able to see vulnerability in her eyes, but now, her eyes showed no emotion, they were ice cold, as if she had stopped caring. There was a time when she would get emotional over anything, like an emotional song, a moving scene on TV, or when she talked of a happy or sad memory, but now, there were no expressions of joy or pain, there was no spontaneous laughter or moist eyes; it was almost as if, she had become heartless.

"Mike wants to sell the club," Aaron attempted to break the silence.

"Really?" all of a sudden, Kamal was alert.

"Yes. He wants to sell up and move to Spain. I would love to buy that place, but I just don't have the kind of money he's asking for," he looked towards Kamal.

Her eyes were looking straight ahead at the empty road, "what if we do it together?" she said turning her head.

"You serious?" he looked at her, quite taken aback.

"Yes, I am."

Aaron pulled over, "you really are serious."

"I want it Aaron. Let's do it together."

"But we can't afford it?"

"Don't worry about the money. I'll sort that out. You just make sure Mike does not talk to anyone else. I want that club. Leave the money to me."

Kamal's mind was preoccupied with nothing but the thought of owning the club. She wanted it so much it hurt. She had often imagined being a figure of authority like Mike, whilst she polished the tables, made the glasses shine till they sparkled and stood behind the bar before opening. She pictured herself sitting in the leather chair in his office, behind the solid mahogany table and being in complete - control. She'd look round the club and often thought how she would prefer the interior, how she would have it changed from the maroon coloured walls, mahogany coloured bar tops, to a more modern touch, like a purple, bright wall lights, lighter bar tables, a more contemporary look. She often wondered how she would have four separate rooms all with separate music, one room with rhythm and blues, one retro, one pop and one for Bollywood and Bhangra music and now, Mike wanted to sell it and all she had on her mind was how to make the club hers.

It was 8.15am and Kamal was waiting at the bottom of Raj's cul-de-sac; her eyes fixed on the rear view mirror. She did not want to see him at his home, not with Emma; she needed to see him alone. She waited patiently, hoping he'd be leaving for work. It was a dull November morning. A few young lads walked by in their school uniforms. Her eyes on the rear view mirror, she watched the bold postman, in his Royal Mail uniform walking up and down the driveways. He'd almost completed the round on the cul-de-sac when she finally saw Raj walk out to his car. He was in his suit so he was sure to be heading to work. She sat up and started the ignition. Raj drove by slowly and as he turned right at the end, she followed him. She had a good idea of where he worked and as he took the route she imagined he would, she concluded that he had not changed jobs.

While he used a staff car park, she parked her car on a pay and display and quickly made her way to the corporate building. She walked through the revolving doors into the entrance of the swanky building. The young Asian lady at reception looked up at her as she looked around for him. Kamal saw Raj just about to step into the lift, with another equally smartly dressed man and a woman dressed in a red pencil skirt suit and white blouse, her heels elongating her legs.

"Raj!" she shouted out. Raj stepped back to look round.

"Kamal," he said, evidently surprised to see her.

"I need a word," she said walking towards him dressed no less smartly in a black pinstripe trouser suit.

"Um okay," he looked back, "you carry on please. I'll be with you as soon as I can," he put his right hand to his red tie and smiled uncomfortably. The lady at reception looked from Raj to Kamal, as they headed back out and sniggered.

"Back to your old tricks Raj," Seema mumbled under her breath, as she filed her nails.

"There's a café just down the road is that okay?"

Kamal nodded and followed him out. The walk towards the café was a silent one, Kamal loathed being around him, but she had to do this and Raj was wondering what this surprise visit was all about. He opened the door for her and she was instantly hit by the smell of brewing tea, frying bacon and sausages, the sound of Radio 1, clanking cutlery and murmuring voices. There were a few builders in their work clothes spread over three tables and some city women and men in their tailored suits, sitting and talking over their breakfast. A man in a grey suit, looked at his watch, took one last swig from his mug, picked up his Financial Times and briefcase and made his way past them towards the door out. Raj walked to the now empty table and moved aside the empty mug, still warm from the tea.

"Coffee?" he asked.

"No," she cut her eyes away, thinking how he did not even know she was a tea drinker, "I'm okay. This won't take long." She wanted to get this meeting over with as quick as she could, being in his presence was sending her on edge, he did nothing but salt her raw wounds.

"I'll just get myself one." Kamal noticed how he seemed to be back to his old form. Dressed in a navy suit, looking well groomed; but he was avoiding eye contact. He came back to the table with a mug of black coffee and seated himself.

"I need some money."

"Okay." Raj hesitated before he moved the mug to one side, picked up his briefcase, placed it on the table, clicked it open and pulled out his cheque book. He pulled out his pen from his inner jacket pocket and looked towards her, "how much?"

Kamal gently took his pen off him and wrote a five figure sum on the white napkin lying on the table and placed it in front of him; Raj widened his eyes.

"How much?" he said with disbelief, "well believe it or not, I don't have that kind of money."

Kamal shrugged her shoulders, "you have two homes, sell one of them, take a loan against one of them."

Raj leant back and put his left arm on the empty chair to his left and then looked at Kamal.

"The divorce proceedings are underway. You will get your share," he sat back up, put his cheque book back in his briefcase and snapped it shut.

"But I need the money now," she looked at him, her eyes as cold as ice.

"Well I'm sorry, I don't have it," Raj was just about to get up.

"Have you washed the blood off your hands?" Kamal said looking down at the table, "I guess, no matter how many times you wash them, the blood's always there, isn't it?" she looked back up towards him and her cold malicious stare penetrated through his soul. Kamal leant forward and whispered, "I know what you did and I know what your mother did, did she not tell you? Well, whyever not?" she leant back and relished the look of fear on his face, "can you imagine seeing your mum standing in court, can you? And what about you? How would you cope? How would your fragile little Emma cope?"

"I think you will find yourself strapped for evidence," Raj loosened his tie, avoiding eye contact, perspiration now visible on his forehead.

"Would I?" Kamal smirked with pleasure. "Look at you. You're a mess. Perspiration above your brow, quiver in your voice, shaking hands. The law would just rip you and your mother apart. How do you sleep at night Raj? That's what I want to know? How do you sleep at night? I could easily bring justice for Jaydeep, but she pleaded with me, your mum, she was literally at my feet. You see, Jaydeep loved his Gran. I know he loved her to bits. I could not punish her for your sins. She just did what any mother would do for her child. But why should you get away with it so lightly? Does Emma know?" Raj swallowed the lump in his throat and shook his head. "Oh, so you have managed to keep one secret from her; living up to your name aren't you? I'll give you one week, till Monday," she leaned forward to whisper, "otherwise, I'll be talking, see how Emma copes with living with a man responsible for the death of his own child." Kamal got up, leaving him stunned. The ground beneath him pulled from under his feet. She looked back at him one more time before she walked out. His eyes remained fixed on the closed door after she left. She asked him how he could sleep at night. She had no idea. He never slept. He couldn't. He was close to insanity. The medication had somewhat pulled him through and he just about managed to put on a front for the world, but he was a shadow of the man he was, underperforming both at work as well as at home. And she was asking him how he slept at night?

***

Kamal was sat in the leather executive swivel chair; the signed paperwork on the mahogany desk and the keys lying on top. She swivelled the chair from left to right her eyes fixed on the paperwork and keys. This was it, a new start, no looking back, just her, her friends and their new business, of which she was seventy percent partner. She leant her head back, inhaled and exhaled.

"Kamal," Aaron popped his head round the door and walked forward. "Michelle called," there was a look of concern, as he approached her, "Sindy called home. Your mum's sick, really sick and she wants to see you."

PART 3

Chapter 22

Kamal observed Jai from her office. He was stood behind the bar serving a group of girls; she smirked, surrounded by girls like bees to honey. He had already requested a weekday slot as a trial for his DJing and Kamal had approved a trial for the Thursday night, following which she said she'd consider weekends.

"He's okay isn't he? Hit with the ladies," Aaron said walking in, seeing Kamal's eyes on the monitor.

"There's a surprise," Kamal mumbled.

"Sorry?"

"Nothing, Michelle back okay?" she looked up towards Aaron and smiled.

"Yeah she's back."

"I'll catch up with her later. Well that's one thing less to worry about now she's back to manage the salon."

"Yeah," Aaron sat opposite Kamal and looked through the invoices in the tray. "Where are you putting him on Thursday?" Aaron saw Kamal observing Jai again.

"Who, Jai? Bollywood most likely."

Aaron wondered what Kamal's fascination with the new boy was. He knew she could never fancy him; she was never the toy-boy type.

"What's the matter?" he asked.

"Oh nothing, he just reminds me of someone," Kamal said twisting her fountain pen in her fingers thoughtfully, as she watched him on the monitor.

Apart from the club, Kamal had also bought the salon from Veronica when she decided to move up North to be closer to her ageing mother. Michelle was assigned manager and it was expanded from just a hair dressing salon to a beauty salon. The upstairs flat was completely refurbished; they had a masseuse, specialists in bridal hair and makeup and a nail bar. She had also over the years bought a string of run down properties, which she took on as ambitious projects, revamping them along with a dedicated team of builders and decorators and then sold off for a profit, or kept to let out. The club was totally refurbished and revamped the third time round over the years since she and Aaron had ownership. The interior was now exquisite attracting a more sophisticated clientele. As they both matured, so did their club; it had changed initially from the original techno club it was, to a club that offered music for all, as she had intended, then to a more sophisticated club, still offering variety of music, but attracting a more classy crowd, by upping the prices, introducing a strict dress code and entry for over twenty-fives only.

Kamal was seated at the Bollywood bar. It was the usual Thursday night crowd, people coming back to life mid-week, warming up for the weekend ahead. The regular businessmen came by as always, flashing their thick wallets to their newly-found easily excitable trophies, their company either deliberately behaving like they had stars in their eyes or seriously believing they were the focus of attention to these men, who most likely had a committed wife or partner tucked away at home, or they could even be playing the game as well as their company for the evening and it was not unusual switched the other way round, mature established women with a younger man at their beck and call. Kamal grinned at the facade surrounding her.

She watched Jai nodding his head to the Bollywood remix tunes and winking at one of the young ladies, who was obviously distracted by the attractive DJ. He was genuinely good; he had a feel for music and had made a good choice for the mid-week crowd. If he understood his Thursday crowd, she wondered how well he would interact with the weekend crowd.

"He's good isn't he?" Aaron sat next to her.

"Yeah he is. A couple more Thursdays and then we'll offer him a weekend slot, what do you say? We need a fresh new face."

"He's hardly been here two minutes."

"Yeah well, I like him."

Aaron looked towards Jai as Kamal walked away; Kamal was getting uncomfortably close to Jai and he could not understand why. He'd only been here a month and she was willing to give him a regular slot for his DJing, as well as increasing his request for more hours at the bar; he could see that Jai was lapping up Kamal's attention and was beginning to sense an air of smugness about him. But Aaron knew Kamal was no fool, he knew she was perfectly capable of looking after herself, but nevertheless, there was something he didn't quite like about Jai.

Aaron could not imagine life without Kamal. They argued, they disagreed, then they talked, discussed, agreed and laughed their differences off. Michelle often referred to them as good as an old married couple. Kamal was as good as family to both him and Michelle. He never once contemplated going his own way. He came in and out of casual relationships over the years, but his love, was reserved for Kamal.

"You like him don't you?" Michelle came by to see her friend and both ladies were seated at the bar.

"What like, like? Don't be silly, I'm old enough to be his mother! Come on let's go into the office."

"How are the kids?" Kamal asked as she opened the door to the office and closed it again, blocking out the music.

"As well as teenagers can be!" Michelle exhaled.

"Jamie okay?"

"Yeah he's okay. Aaron said you're spending quite a lot of time with the new guy."

"Oh honestly it can be like big brother in here sometimes! It's all innocent, trust me."

"You sure?"

"Yes of course. What do you take me for, a cradle snatcher! Please give me some credit," Kamal shook her head in disbelief.

"Well it has been a long time," Michelle laughed at her not so impressed friend, "and I can understand the attraction."

"Oh yeah, sure it's not you who's taken a shine to him? Is the old Jamie charm wearing off?" Kamal teased.

"As if, he is as wonderful as ever, thank you very much."

Kamal smiled at her friend, who like her had maintained her figure and could be a healthy competition to any one of the young women stood now in the club; how could Jamie ever fall out of love with Michelle? She was perfect in every way.

Kamal was still in the office when Jai had packed up. He was in his element at the club, he mesmerised the crowd, charmed his female colleagues and above all, held Kamal's attention; she was sophisticated, beautiful and successful; an enigma, magnetic, a charisma that one could not help but be drawn towards. She was looked up to, respected and admired by her regular customers, her workers and close friends. The younger women vying for his attention, drinking themselves senseless, looking tacky in their little left to the imagination outfits did nothing for him. It was Kamal that left the lasting impression.

***

Kamal stood admiring her refurbished office. She'd changed the dark executive look it had to a more contemporary one. Her desk now a frosted oblong glass table, sitting upon a red and black rug. Her black leather executive swivel chair was replaced with a red one. She now had a small bar to her right on a raised platform, with a frosted glass counter and a few red high stools placed in front. She had a slim line laptop at her desk with minimal clutter. Behind her was a large Kentia palm planted in a large red ceramic pot and opposite the bar, to her left was a large canvas of a red sun at sunset against a blood red sky, just to add that final touch.

"Come in," she called out to the knock on the door and went to collect her bag and coat.

"Looks good," Jai admired the new office.

"Thank you," Kamal said putting on her blazer.

"I probably should not be telling you this, but I've had a few business cards, you know from people who want me to do regular gigs for them."

"Well that's good isn't it? A young kid like you needs to take up any good opportunity," Kamal said looking for her keys in her large designer bag getting ready to leave.

"Less of the kid please," the smile dropped from Jai's face. This was not the response he'd hoped for, he was hoping to see a look of despondency at the thought of losing her new star member of staff, but this was quite the contrary. Her hair shone in the light, her skin flawless, not one single wrinkle. She had such natural beauty, wore minimal make up and her features were just perfect. Jai felt he could admire her all day and night. "Right I better be off now," Kamal raised her brow as he stood in her way.

"Oh, sorry," Jai walked forward to open the door for her.

"Thanks Jai, see you tomorrow then?" she asked questioningly.

"Yes of course, you won't be getting rid of me so easily," he smiled foolishly, who was he kidding, she must have people like him lining up for her.

Kamal did eventually offer Jai a permanent weekend slot and she was surprised he wanted to keep his job at the bar during the week. A young man of his talent could be doing regular gigs anywhere, but he chose to remain at the club. His hard work and dedication, led her further to offer him the post of team leader for the bar staff. Aaron was not overly keen when she had informed him.

"Well why not? He's good at his job, he's dedicated, he's sincere, he's never late, he shows enthusiasm and I know I can leave him unsupervised. Can you suggest anyone else since Matt left?"

"No, but have you ever wondered why he's so keen?"

"What do you mean?"

"I mean have you not noticed the way he looks at you?"

Kamal looked at Aaron confused.

"Oh well. I rest my case. I don't know why I'm surprised you haven't noticed. Sometimes Kamal, I do feel you're totally unaware of other people's emotions."

"What?" Kamal frowned. She had her hair tied up in a high elegant bun today, his personal favourite, bringing out her features.

"Oh forget it. I'll see how long it takes for you to figure it out," Aaron mumbled as he got up, shaking his head and walking out. He looked towards Jai with much apprehension. When he first started he looked like any regular young guy, same as all the young kids they had taken on and let go of over the years, but today he had a look of conceit in his eyes; he was loving every moment of Kamal's undue attention. He must've thought he had hit the jackpot.

Kamal sat in her chair bewildered by Aaron's reaction and smiled as she shook her head; she could not imagine life without him. The years had eventually brought her good fortune. She had no time for a relationship, as she was already married to her businesses. Michelle, Aaron and their families were her family and Aaron was her rock. She could always rely on him to be around for her. Each and every relationship he had was as casual as the last. It was as if like her, he could not fall in love. Unlike him, she did not come in and out of relationships. In fact she had not been in any serious relationship since Rohit. She'd had some casual ones, but feeling unable to commit, as soon as she felt the relationship got too comfortable for her liking, she called it a day. She was aware of the special unique bond she and Aaron shared, but she did not want to complicate their relationship with what people called 'love'; in her view, people confused love with lust. What she had with Aaron was trust, reliability, sincerity and security, so why did she want to compromise these attributes with a physical bonding?

She sighed and went back to studying her new interest and venture on the internet; the restaurant premises not far from the club. She had her heart set on this restaurant; it was in the perfect location and a good investment. After Kamal carefully studied the new venture she got up to, as always, consult Aaron for his opinion. She walked out into the club. It was late Saturday night and the crowds were now dispersing. She looked towards the main bar at the entrance, he wasn't there. She went into the Bollywood room and looked towards the bar; Aaron was serving. She walked towards him in her high heels, black pencil skirt and satin cobalt blue shirt with volume sleeves. Jai's eyes followed her every move as she made her way towards Aaron. She called him over and held him by the arm, got really close to him, cupping his face in her right hand as she brought his ear close to her. Jai watched Aaron nod to her, put his hand on her shoulder and said something back in her ear, the music deafening out their voices. Jai gathered they shared an evidently close relationship, they were either very good friends or extremely good at disguising a possible intimate relationship, but staff had informed him that they were no more than really good friends. An image of the two together was pictured in his head and he could not help but feel a pang of jealously. He clenched his jaw at the thought of the possibility. Kamal walked down the bar, picking up glasses like she often did out of habit. Jai searched his computer for some old Hindi music. It was heading towards closing time and people were winding down. He had in his collection; something he imagined she could relate to, something that would draw her attention towards him. He found the perfect remix of a classical Hindi song by *Asha Bhosle*. Kamal leant over the bar counter and placed the empty glasses behind it smiling at her bar staff, sharing a common joke sending them all laughing. Kamal froze as she heard a familiar tune. She put her elbows on the counter and the palm of her right hand under her chin. The lyrics and music had taken her back. It brought back an old memory, one that she had long forgotten. She looked round to the small crowd equally as absorbed. She smiled at the recollected memory of her mother and for a moment felt her presence. She then looked towards Jai with a twinkle in her eyes; she smiled at him approvingly and he acknowledged her by a gentle nod and wink. He then spontaneously came round to the dance floor and held out his hand.

"Just one dance please," Kamal looked surprised. He gently held her hand and led her to the dance floor. He put one hand round her tiny waist and held her other hand. Kamal smiled and let Jai lead the dance, while she soaked in the nostalgic tune a reminder of better childhood memories, which she had somehow managed to lose amongst the chaos of more painful ones.

"Thanks Jai."

"For what?" he looked down at her.

"This song, it's taken me back, to a good time."

"It's my pleasure," Jai was looking straight into her eyes. His face was quite close to hers, so close, it sent a vivid flashback and she suddenly let go and stepped back.

"I better get back to the office."

"What's the matter?" he asked taking a step towards her.

"Nothing," Kamal walked away back towards her office. Once in the office she poured herself a glass of wine from behind her bar and took one large gulp. The office door opened and she turned round instantly; her heart still beating.

"Oh Aaron, it's you," she sighed and turned back round.

"You wanted to speak to me?"

"Yes…yes. Um, can we do that tomorrow? I've suddenly developed this headache. I just want to go home." Kamal went for her bag and keys and made her way to the door. Aaron held her softly by the elbow.

"Are you okay?"

"Yes, yes. Just need to lay my head down."

Kamal left the club, not once looking back. She could not get into the car soon enough and put her head on the steering wheel. After years of self-control, for the first time in since as far back as she could remember, she felt she had lost her cool, collected composure. Jai had managed to switch an old emotion within her, a feeling that she had felt once years ago, but this was not right.

Aaron watched Jai pack up. Young, handsome, whole life in front of him, could easily pick from a dozen girls in the club, but he had to pick Kamal. He had never felt so insecure before. All these years he was content with the relationship he had with her. They were close, he depended upon her and she upon him, she liaised with him in any decision she was making and he with her, she loved his kids like her own, she loved his sister and her family like her own, she was a part of their lives and he trusted her more than he did himself. Aaron wanted her for as long as he could remember, it hurt him not being able to hold her in his arms, put his fingers through her soft hair, not to be able to kiss her lips, but he had learnt that any advances would only push her away and he did not care how long it took for her to realise that they were meant to be together; he would wait for as long as it took, just remaining in her presence was enough for him, but this special delicate bond they shared was being threatened by this Jai.

Jai could hear a female giggle from Steve's bedroom and smirked, knowing his flat mate had pulled again. He made himself a drink and then picked up the clothes trailing on the floor towards Steve's room and put them over the dining room chair, including a red satin bra. He sat on the sofa and drank his rum with cola; the giggling now turning into pleasurable groans. He rolled the glass in his hands. There was just one person preoccupying his mind; Kamal. He was falling for her and all he had on his mind this evening was the way she looked into his eyes, her sudden reaction suggested to him that he had managed to touch the ice queen deep within and maybe, just maybe, she was melting to his charm. He leant his head back and imagined unclothing her, imagined kissing her soft lips. He closed his eyes with that thought, blocking out the knocking noise from Steve's bedroom, the groans getting louder and louder. Jai never had any problem luring any girl and there was a time when he like Steve, had a different girl back at the flat every weekend, but he did not want any girl now, he wanted a proper woman, he wanted Kamal and he was intent on getting her.

Chapter 23

"I'm going away for a week," Aaron came into the office holding a weekend bag.

"Away? Where? You never said anything," Kamal said getting up from her chair, "I'll call you back Jamie," Kamal put the phone down to Michelle's husband, also her accountant.

"Yes, well it's a last minute thing. I need a break."

"Okay, but where are you going and why so suddenly?"

"I don't have to explain my every move to you Kamal," Aaron said looking down at her, as she now stood before him.

"Is it the kids? Sandra? Have I said something?"

"I'm going."

"Aaron!" Kamal followed him out, "Aaron!"

Aaron walked out ignoring her calls. He slung his case in the boot and got straight into his BMW, but Kamal obstructed him from closing the door.

"At least tell me where you are going!"

Aaron sighed, "I'm just going up to London for a few days. Spending some time at Richard's flat. He's gone to the States."

"Oh, okay. It would've been nice to have had some notice though. We are partners after all, what about the……."

"Look, I'm sure you can cope. Besides you've got Jai at your beck and call now," he turned the key in the ignition and pulled his seatbelt to.

"Sorry?" Kamal frowned.

"Please," Aaron had his hand on the door handle. Kamal, stood still before she eventually stepped back allowing for him to close the door and then the window slid down, "I'll call you."

Kamal shook her head, puzzled by Aaron's sudden plans and placed her hands on her hips as she watched her friend drive off and then, slowly lowered them to her side. She walked back to her office half-heartedly, oblivious to the curious whispering staff, who were preparing to open up. Kamal closed the door to the office and sat down in her chair. She flicked mindlessly through the diary and twisted her fountain pen in her fingers, like she did whenever she was in deep thoughts, now gathering that Aaron may have issues with her relationship with Jai. Yes, she had been spending some time with him, getting to know him and his parents, learning how they'd split up, him being tossed to and fro between the two, getting caught up in their arguments, them expecting him to go to university to study accounting and him choosing music, wanting to be a recognised DJ much to their disappointment, blaming each other for his lack of ambition. Yes, she had spent a lot of time with him and she did enjoy being in his company, but it was never more than that, the thought alone was absurd and she was disappointed with Aaron's reaction.

Aaron was reading much more into Kamal's interest in Jai; hence he had to get away. He had never seen Kamal so entranced with anybody before and he was hurting. But, he was more disappointed in himself for not being able to control his emotions; if she had found someone, then he should be happy for her. But it was so testing for him. Maybe it was time for him to move on. Maybe, he thought, it was time to stop waiting.

***

It had been a week since Aaron had left; his mobile was switched off and even Michelle hadn't heard from him. Every time the phone rang Kamal hurried to answer it, but she was disheartened each time. It was not that he had never gone away before, he always went away, with his kids, away with friends or to visit extended family, but it was always by mutual agreement, but this time, it was different. As each day went by, without hearing from him or seeing him, she realised how much she had taken him for granted.

Each time there was a knock on the door she hoped it was him, only for it to be a member of staff, with one query or other, a query which was usually dealt with by Aaron, her rock; her pillar.

It was a busy Saturday night as always, but for some reason everything was going wrong, from blocked toilets, a drunken brawl to police presence due to suspected drug use. Kamal was exhausted. Even though she had her old reliable security, domestic and bar staff, she did not have Aaron and she was missing having him come in at the end of the day, sitting across the table, sometimes with loads to talk about, other times insisting it was time for her to go home, literally dragging her away from the chair. If she'd had a drink, he'd drive her home and sometimes she'd fall asleep in the car and he would place his hand on her shoulder gently to wake her. Not having him around had created a large void, her day to day life became meaningless and she was at a total loss. She called Aaron's mobile again and left yet another message.

"Aaron. Have had a really bad night. Nothing I could not handle mind," she paused, "I really miss having you around. Please call me Aaron. I'm sorry if I've upset you in any way. I need you Aaron. Please come back home. I…..I.." Kamal stopped, disconnected the phone and placed it on the frosted glass table. There was a knock on the door. She closed her eyes in exasperation; she just wanted to be left alone, wait for the phone to ring and hear Aaron's familiar voice. She frowned and shook her head at the tear that had found its way out and wiped it away, recomposed herself and took a deep breath. "Come in," she said in an almost croaky voice holding her head up high, "oh Jai it's you. You've not left?"

"Was actually hoping to have a drink with you?"

"I don't know. It's been a long night. I really do want to just leave to be honest Jai. Was there something you needed to discuss?"

"Are you okay?"

"Yes. Why?"

"You appear a bit agitated."

"It's nothing," Kamal sighed, "oh okay, just one drink," there was another knock on the door, "oh what now!" Theo the security guard popped his head round.

"Checked all the building Kamal, you going to be long?"

"You be on your way thanks Theo, Jai's here, we'll lock up."

"Are you sure?" Theo looked towards Jai and then Kamal, who was looking unusually drained.

"Yes I'm fine. Thanks Theo."

Kamal knocked back the drink she had on her desk and went over the bar to make herself another, momentarily having to hold her balance, leaning on the glass counter.

"Want to tell me about it?" It was obvious something was bothering her, she had not been her normal motivated self for days and staff had noticed her being unusually distracted and irritated. While the rest of his colleagues drew their own conclusions, he begged to differ. Kamal smiled as she handed Jai his rum and coke and made herself comfortable on the stool next to him, her head light from having started to drink much earlier in the evening.

"Have you got a best friend Jai? Someone who leant you a shoulder to cry on, someone who let you release your anxieties and frustrations on them, not once complaining, someone who you could share your happy times as well as your sad times with, someone who seemed to have all the time in the world to listen to you, have you got someone you are so close to, you almost take them for granted, you expect them to always be there. Have you?"

"Can't say I'm that fortunate."

"I have," Kamal smiled.

"Michelle?"

"Michelle is the best friend any girl would want, but it's Aaron I'm talking about. I feel so lost without him," Kamal was on her feet again and walked towards the window, to open the blinds, looking out at the car park, where Aaron would normally park his car, unaware of Jai's clenching jaws and clenched fist, as he listened to her talk over and over about that – Aaron! "Do you know something Jai?" she paused looking at the empty space, "I think I love him, well I mean I have always loved him as a friend, but I love him as in really, really love him. Gosh, I never thought I'd hear myself say that. But that's what it is. When someone is constantly on your mind, that deep throbbing sweet pain deep within, it's love isn't it?" she placed her hand on her chest, "it's similar to what I felt, or thought I felt years ago, but this feeling I have for Aaron is different, so special. I'm going to tell him when I see him."

Jai got up and walked towards her, as she continued to rant on drunkenly about her sudden emotional discovery and he put his hands slowly around her waist. Kamal looked down as she felt his hands creeping round her waist and stopped talking midway. She then felt Jai's soft breath on her ear. She closed her eyes at the softness of his caress, her head intoxicated. He turned her round to face him slowly and pecked her nose. She stood static as he pulled her slowly towards him. He pecked her all over her face slowly. His softness touched her deep within. She closed her eyes, as he continued to move his mouth softly all over her face and neck. With her eyes closed, imagining Aaron, she wanted him to kiss her, but then she opened her eyes and as before, an old memory flashed before her eyes again. She instantly pushed him away. He looked at her confused and reached out to hold her again.

"Let go of me!"

"But I love you Kamal!"

"Oh don't be so ridiculous!" she shouted making her way to the door, suddenly feeling a little insecure.

"Ridiculous!" he went to grab her.

"Let go of me! You can't love me!"

"Why not? Is it the age? What is it? Tell me please," Jai had her grabbed from both arms firmly now with a desperate plea in his voice.

"Because you're Rohit Sinha's son!"

The office door flung open and Aaron looked from Kamal to Jai.

"Aaron," Kamal gasped in relief.

"How do you know my dad?" Jai shook Kamal by the arms in frustration, as she was suddenly inconveniently distracted by Aaron's untimely return. When she did not answer, her eyes still fixated on her precious Aaron, he asked her again, "how do you know my dad?" his grasp now tightening in irritation, frustrated that he had foolishly misinterpreted all the signs.

Kamal turned back to face him, "maybe you should ask him, yes, maybe you should. It'd be interesting to know whether he still remembers me. Can you leave now? " she looked down towards his hands and pulled her arms free. Jai looked down at Kamal and then up towards Aaron. He grabbed his jacket from where he had placed it on the bar and stormed out.

"So that's what this has all been about?" Aaron asked. "Do you still love him?"

"Who? Rohit? No of course not. Don't be silly?"

"He reminded you of him though, didn't he?"

"He just brought back a lot of memories that's all. Seeing him, took me back. I knew he was Rohit's son, as soon as I saw him. He even has his personality."

"And he hurt you, remember?"

"Yeah I know, but he's the closest I came to knowing how to feel in love. But...." Kamal sighed and walked slowly towards Aaron, "he is also the reason why I have been scared to fall in love again, scared of getting close to someone again, for the fear of getting hurt," Kamal was standing in front of Aaron. She looked up at him and held both his hands. "I've really, really missed you Aaron."

Aaron closed his eyes for a few seconds; he had waited to see an emotional response in her eyes and hear an ache for him in her voice since what seemed like a lifetime. He lifted her left hand in his and kissed it and placed it on his cheek. She ran her thumb over his cheek. He then cupped her face in his hands and kissed her on the forehead. With her face still cupped in his hands, he ran his thumbs over her cheeks looking into her eyes. The messages he'd received over the last couple of days, the desperation and anxiety he sensed in her voice and the love he saw in her eyes right now confirmed her feelings for him and he brought his lips close to hers. She wrapped her arms around his neck and brought her lips up to meet his. Kamal was the first to pull back, but Aaron did not want to let go. He had waited too long for this moment. He held her close with his arms wrapped around her, her head resting on his chest; and he wished time would stand still.

"I can feel your heart beating," Kamal whispered and she put her hand on his chest.

"Why now Kamal?"

"You going away," she held him tighter still, "not hearing from you, not seeing you. I missed you so, so much, thought I'd lost you."

"Maybe I should have done this years ago."

"Maybe," Kamal looked up to him. Aaron lifted her chin and kissed her again. Kamal felt a tear on her cheek. She slowly pulled away and wiped his eyes. Aaron held her hand and kissed it.

"Take me home," Kamal whispered.

Aaron pulled the car up in front of Kamal's house with the familiar sound of the gravel scrunching under the tyres. She sat in the car as Aaron undid his seat belt, opened his door and walked round to open the door for her. Keys ready in her hand she opened the front door and looked round at Aaron who stood away from her reluctantly. Kamal walked towards him and kissed him on his lips gently, held him by the hand and led him into her house. She shut the front door, switched on the light to the stairs and took Aaron by the hand upstairs to her bedroom. She walked towards her bed and switched on the bedside lamp, took off her jacket and then slowly removed Aaron's blazer and let it fall to the floor. Her eyes were lowered as she undid the buttons to his white shirt, kissed his hands as she unbuttoned his sleeve cuffs. She softly ran her hands over his broad chest and pushed his shirt off, letting it fall to the floor. As she placed her hands on his chest, Aaron held her hands.

"No," he said softly.

"But I thought this is what you wanted," Kamal looked up at him.

Aaron smiled, "then you don't know me as well as you think you do. I do want you, but not like this."

Kamal looked up at him and swallowed the lump in her throat and smiled. She rested her cheek on his bare chest and embraced him.

"Come on. I think you need to lay your head down, sleep off some of the drink."

Kamal got changed into her nightwear and let Aaron then tuck her into bed.

"Will you lie down with me?"

"Now you're really testing me aren't you?"

"Please," Aaron's heart skipped a beat as she put her hand out towards him. He slid with her under the duvet. She rested her head on his chest and closed her eyes. She felt as if years of loneliness had diminished in this one moment. There was no lust and no compromise, just two souls finally meeting amidst years of apprehensions and trepidations.

Aaron kissed the top of Kamal's head as they lay with their arms wrapped around each other.

"I love you Aaron."

"I love you too," he whispered kissing the top of her head again and pulling her closer towards him. He switched off the lamp allowing for the natural moonlight to flow into the bedroom through the large bay windows. Aaron looked at the moonlit sky, sprinkled over with stars. Could this night get any more beautiful than it already was?

Chapter 24

"What do you think?"

"I like it," Aaron said looking round the empty restaurant.

"I've even got ideas for the menu, discussed it with Sanjay, the cook who worked here. He's working as an assistant at the moment, totally wasted, a fine chef, he's cooked a few samples of fusion food. He's as excited as me and can't wait to start. I was thinking of browns, reds, gold, as a colour theme, what do you think?" Kamal turned round with excitement to face Aaron.

"What do I think? I think you are amazing," he said pulling Kamal towards him and kissed her. "I love you," Kamal kissed the tip of his nose and put her arms around his neck and smiled.

"Oh come on you two," Michelle said walking back in from the kitchen with Jamie. She linked her arms with her best friend and brother, "I think it's going to be great Kamal! And I think you two finally getting together is fantastic!"

"About bloody time is what I say!" Jamie said, "shall we open this now?" Jamie opened a bottle of champagne and poured it equally into four champagne flutes. "Here's to the restaurant and you two, the best love story ever."

The four clinked their glasses and celebrated the new venture and long overdue relationship.

It was Friday evening and Aaron had booked in another DJ, as they had neither seen nor heard from Jai again. Kamal was busy discussing colours and designs for the restaurant with her team of decorators in the office over the phone. A lot of her time and energy was being spent on the new restaurant, which she had decided to call Jay's. She was so excited, as she became with any new venture and so totally in love, her feet were hardly touching the ground. She was going to have some new kitchen appliances delivered and there was the deciding of what cutlery to have. As she put the phone down and looked through catalogues, a figure in the view of the security camera caught her eye. He was talking to a member of the bar staff. Kamal looked closely, trying to establish, whether it was indeed, who she thought it was. She sat still, with her eyes glued to the screen. She then saw Aaron being called over by Jack the barman. Aaron shook hands and the two men exchanged words. Kamal watched Aaron nod and walk away from behind the bar; he was making his way to the office. Aaron knocked on the door, out of habit and walked in.

"There's someone here to see you."

"I know. I saw him."

"He wants to talk to you," Aaron closed the door behind him and walked towards the perplexed Kamal.

"What does he want Aaron?"

"Just to talk. Maybe you need to do this."

"But there's nothing left to say."

"Yeah, well, I'll have great pleasure in getting rid of him, but maybe you need to do this, get some closure. I'll be here with you if you want?"

Kamal paused thoughtfully, "no, I'll be okay. Just can't understand what he wants to see me for now," Kamal frowned, "just send him in Aaron."

"You sure?"

Kamal nodded and managed a weak smile.

Aaron went back out clenching his jaws. Why did he have to come now? What if he complicated things between him and Kamal? He was a fine looking man, well dressed, some streaks of grey running through his hair, well spoken, well dressed and groomed and did not look much older than himself.

"She said she'll see you, follow me."

"Thanks."

Kamal stood in the window, with her back facing the door. There was a knock at the door.

"You know where I am Kamal."

"Thanks Aaron," Kamal heard the door close. She heard him clear his throat.

"Hi Kamal," he said reluctantly. She closed her eyes as the familiar voice tugged a rusty old heartstring.

"What do you want?" she said, still with her back turned towards him.

"Um, just wanted to see you, clear the air perhaps."

"Clear the air?" Kamal turned round. He had a few grey hairs and she could make out a few fine lines around his eyes. She had always wondered what he would have looked like all these years later. For some reason she had imagined a pot belly and sagging skin, like that of the sleazy businessmen that came into the club, with their company for the evening, but he had matured well. Meanwhile, he looked on at the sophisticated, glamorous woman standing before him; she had taken his breath away, years ago and had done the same all over again. Age had treated her well. Her skin was radiant and her hair shiny and silky smooth. She was wearing a long pencil line grey skirt with matching waistcoat over a black shirt, black heels and minimal make up. She appeared far from the devastated woman that one formidable night, which had haunted him for months and months thereafter. She now looked like a figure of authority, a force to be reckoned with and he felt slightly intimidated in her presence, this was not what he was expecting.

"It's a bit late to want to clear the air Rohit Sinha," Kamal said folding her arms.

Rohit took a few steps forward.

"I tried so hard to trace you."

"Did you? Really? They say that if you look hard enough you can even find God, I'm just a human being. You obviously did not try hard enough."

"I'm sorry."

"Ah. The magic word - sorry," Kamal smirked and walked towards the bar, "drink?"

"Um, I'll have a scotch please," Rohit made his way to the bar, "may I?" he asked pointing towards the stool.

"Be my guest. Ice?"

Rohit nodded. Kamal placed the tumbler with whisky and ice in front of Rohit on a frosted glass coaster and then stood towering in front of him, both hands resting on the bar counter.

"You're making me nervous," he looked down into his glass.

"Why are you here Rohit?" Kamal tried to get to the point. Rohit smiled, took a sip of the whisky and put the glass down.

"Jai, told me."

"How is he?"

"He'll be okay. He, he said that he felt he was getting close to you and then you mentioned me."

"Don't go getting any ideas. Jai had taken me back to a time I had managed to forget, that's all."

"Jai talked about you all the time, said he found you intriguing and funnily enough, he took me back to a time when I was intrigued by a woman, years ago," he looked up at her, "I just had to come and see you. You really do look amazing."

"Hmm, I feel I have been here before. Only, I'm not so gullible anymore. How's the wife? Oh sorry, you split up. What happened? Did she finally see sense? Look Rohit what are you really doing here?" Kamal said in frustration.

"I'm sorry. I know you went through hell after......"

"Well that's one way to describe it. I lost everything Rohit, everything. And no sorry can erase the pain and humiliation, so please drink up and take your apology to someone who cares," her face was close to his, as she almost hissed through her teeth in contempt.

"Why did you keep Jai on? Why did you offer him a managerial post, so soon after he started? He reminded you of me, didn't he?"

"Oh please, in case you can't see, I have managed to move on. I've not been sitting back wallowing over the past, over feeble memories."

"No. But you were not the only one affected. My marriage suffered too and eventually broke down. Priya worked out what had happened that very night. She had already had Jai when she came from India and….."

"Yeah well I worked that one out from his date of birth!"

Rohit cleared his throat, "he was still with my parents and came later. We tried to make it work for the sake of Jai, but we were fooling each other and she knew I did not love her. There is only one woman I have ever loved," Rohit was looking down at his drink again. He then looked up at Kamal, the way he did all those years ago, as the eyes locked, Kamal felt like she was in a time warp, she felt a tug in her heart and there was slight, momentary feeling of weakness. "You have always been the one Kamal. Always," he whispered. Kamal looked at him, trying her best not to lose her composure. "I swear," he whispered again. Kamal looked at Rohit and as before, his eyes touched her deep within. Kamal put her chin up and turned her back towards him as she poured herself a drink, no longer being able to look at him, afraid old emotions were going to take over. "Not one day has gone by when I have not thought of you Kamal. I'd do anything to turn back time and put things right, but you know, our society, our values, what parents expect from us. We go along with them, sacrifice our own happiness, put them first and we lie to ourselves for years and years, and then eventually you realise you just cannot go any further. I'm really sorry for hurting you, but I think even you can understand what I am trying to say."

"Yes, well like I said before. Sorry does not repair anything. But if you have bothered to come all this way to apologise, then apology accepted. And now, it's time for closure, cheers," she said raising her glass and walking back towards her desk.

Rohit knew he had struck a chord. She was avoiding eye contact and she appeared slightly on edge. She flicked through a catalogue on her desk and tapped some keys on her laptop, trying her best to distract herself away from him. Rohit got off the stool and walked towards the desk.

"You may have moved on, but no one has been able to replace that empty space in my heart. Call me an old fool, but it's true. That night we had together, was so beautiful."

Kamal winced and closed her eyes painfully, "and the consequences of that night remind me of nothing but destruction and pain so severe, you cannot possibly comprehend," Kamal looked back up to him and this time, her eyes were vengeful.

Rohit looked down. He then pulled a pen out of his inner jacket pocket and scribbled something on her post-it pad, "here's my mobile number. Maybe if you find it in your heart to forgive me."

Kamal was writing in her diary, making out she was too busy to care, but she was soaking in, each and every word he was saying to her gently and sincerely. "I believe fate has brought us back together again and gosh, how, can't you see? Some things are just meant to be Kamal. I will wait for your call," his soft words were again striking the vital chords of her heart. He walked away and something within her, did not want him to go. He closed the door behind him softly. Her eyes were fixed on the post-it note. She felt flushed; how had he managed to make her feel so weak again after all these years? There was a knock at the door. She picked up the post-it pad and put it in her drawer. Aaron walked in.

"You okay?"

Kamal looked up at the trusted Aaron, smiled and sighed with relief.

"Yeah, fine," she got up and walked towards him, put her arms around him and closed her eyes.

"You're shaking , are you okay?" he pulled away and looked down at her.

"Yes, just seeing him after all these years shook me a bit, that's all. I'll be okay."

Kamal went home early that night. The lights were dim in her lounge and she was sitting on her white leather recliner seat, her feet pulled up and the post-it note with Rohit's number in her hand. She looked towards her music collection, lined on a shelf above the CD player and got up. She ran her fingers along the titles with her acrylic nails and pulled out a disc right at the very end. She turned the power of her CD player on, removed the disc and placed it in the tray. The tray slid smoothly back and she heard the player whizzing, as it read the disc and when the soft, melodious music began, she transported herself back in time. She may not have had the perfect childhood and she may not have had the perfect marriage she had always hoped for, but, they were the days of youth, her whole life was in front of her. If her life was yesterday full of woeful events, it was ironically the consequences of those events that led her to the success she had today. But where had all the years gone? She had minimum contact with her family and could not even remember the last time she had spoken to Sindy, let alone Nindy and had absolutely no idea of what her nieces and nephews looked like now. She sat back and thought how she had managed to let her business take over all emotions and how callous and withdrawn she had become. She ignored her family's call out to her, them trying to get into her life, as she was so adamant to forget, she blocked everyone out. Seeing Rohit again today, brought back a vulnerability and an innocence and brought back the person she once was. Rohit was the reason she left home, Rohit was the reason she lost her family and Rohit was the reason she was who she was today. She was also brought back to the revelation her mother had made before she died on her deathbed; the one she had chosen to ignore and now she knew had it not been for Rohit, she would possibly, never, ever have learnt the truth.

Kamal switched on the lights to her immaculate untouched kitchen; a kitchen where she had no time to cook in, a kitchen where she hardly ever entertained, a kitchen where the only thing that was ever touched was the kettle and wine glasses. She went to the fridge, opened the chilled bottle of wine and poured herself a glass. She looked at the post-it note placed on the worktop and picked it up with the glass, her mind still scattered over events past and present. She went up the stairs to her bedroom, her bare feet sinking into the thick soft carpet and switched on the light. She placed her wine glass down along with the post-it note and opened the large mirrored wardrobe doors. On the top shelf, was her pretty paisley print storage box. She tiptoed to reach up and pulled it out, went over to her bed and sat down with her legs crossed. Removing the lid, she began to take out the memorabilia she'd chose to keep, one by one. She smiled at the old photo of her, Danielle and Angela taken that one Christmas, when she had kissed Rohit for the first time that cold winter's night, the start of a new chapter, or, the beginning of the end, or even, beginning. There was an ethnic bangle in colours copper and turquoise, which her mother had brought back from India, Kamal slipped it on and looked at it on her wrist. She smiled and went back to the box. There was small framed photo given to her by Sindy of her and Jaydeep a few days after he was born, Kamal smiled and put the small frame on her bedside cabinet. She picked up Jaydeep's first socks and mittens, wrapped in a tissue paper and held them close to her face, feeling the softness on her cheeks and held them to her nose and inhaled them, imagining his sweet lingering baby scent. She could feel her eyes welling up and her vision blurring, but she held back the tears and wrapped them back up and placed them back in the box. She picked up a small red plastic box, in which was a gold necklace that her parents had given to her on the birth of Jaydeep, she held it before her eyes and remembered how happy her mum was when he was born, as were her in-laws. They did love their grandson to bits. It was because of the love that they showered on him and their high regards for her, when she was with them, that she never told a single soul of the accident. She put the chain back in the red plastic box and placed it down beside her. She then, eventually, picked up the small red velvet pouch. She hesitantly loosened the top and tipped the content onto the palm of her left hand. She looked at the locket and felt the same familiar stabbing pain when her mother had told her a truth, a truth she had managed to hide from everyone, a truth that she herself denied to be true and erased it from her memory, like an episode in her life she wanted edited out, along with many others. She opened the locket. There were two images in the locket. One of her mother and one of a man; the man her mother claimed to be her father, her biological father. Suddenly, the front door bell rang and Kamal was shaken back to the present time. With the locket still clasped in her hand, she went down to answer the door.

"Hi, I just wanted to make sure you were okay," Aaron said walking in comfortably. Kamal closed the door and followed him into the lounge, the locket still firmly in her hand. She turned the volume to the CD player down. Aaron walked up behind her and wrapped his arms round her waist. She leaned her head back in his chest and put one hand over his. He kissed the top of her head. She opened her left hand and revealed the locket. "What's that?" Aaron asked.

"My true identity."

"Sorry?"

"You and Michelle were always concerned that I did not allow myself to grieve when my mum died. Well this is why?" Aaron stood still with his arms tightly around her. "My mum told me before she died, that the man I always thought was my father ….wasn't," she then opened the locket, "this man, is apparently my father."

"What," he gasped, "you never said anything." Aaron recalled the time of her mother's death. It was since then she had preoccupied herself with the business, it had become an obsession, like nothing else mattered anymore.

"It was a truth that even I did not want to believe. My whole life had become a lie. But I think that it is time, it's time for me to find out who I really am. My mother left me with a contact address and name of her best friend in India, apparently her friend knows everything and she also knows my father and his whereabouts. I need to see him, just the once, that is if he is still around, if she's still around."

"Why now?" Aaron asked softly.

"A ghost from the past, reopening old wounds, some of them left unhealed."

"Kamal….do you still love him?" Kamal felt Aaron's hands around her waist soften, at her elongated silence and he slowly started to let go and stepped back; Aaron had expected an instant response, but all he got was a silence. "You do don't you?"

There was still no response from Kamal. Kamal turned round and looked up at him.

"I don't know. I'm not even sure whether I ever stopped loving him," Aaron stepped further back in disbelief. "I'm sorry Aaron. I'm just really confused at the moment. There are a lot of things I need to get clear in my head right now. I need to get away for a bit. I've thought about it and I'm going to arrange to go to India." Aaron looked at her, the hurt in his eyes clearly evident.

"If it's what you need to do," he stepped back again, "I'll, I'll wait to hear from you," he said walking back slowly, "hopefully you will find what you're looking for." He turned, opened the door and left, not once looking back. Aaron spun his car off while a tear involuntarily ran down his left cheek.

Chapter 25

Dear Aaron

I've lost count to how many times I have rewritten this text. I think the simplest thing to say is - sorry. It was never my intention to hurt you. You mean the world to me. There is just one more thing that requires closure in my life, and it is for this reason I am going to India. I will be in touch and just remember one thing - I will always love you with all my heart. I'll be in touch, when I am ready.

Love you.

Kamal

x

Kamal sent her text and departed from home.

It was a blustery October day, but it was still apparently very warm in Delhi, India, so Kamal had packed her case with T-shirts, linen skirts and trousers, a couple of pairs of jeans and leather sandals. Kamal had never been on a long haul international flight before, in fact the only time she had been on board a flight was when she had travelled to Italy with Raj during their marriage and all she'd done for a much earned short break since then was go on a spa weekend with Michelle, or a trip to the coast with Aaron and his family.

She was allocated a window seat as requested and made herself comfortable as fellow passengers continued to board, tucking their hand baggage away and then back out again as they remembered to pull out a book or a jumper. There were families with excited children, crying babies and an already irritated loner asking to be seated elsewhere. An air hostess assisted an elderly Asian lady storing her baggage in the overhead cabin. The lady was saying something to her in Punjabi, but the European air hostess couldn't understand. The elderly lady looked round for support at which point Kamal intervened; all the lady wanted was to make sure she received a vegetarian meal. As Kamal finished interpreting a young man, with his passport and boarding card still in his hand, looked from the card to the seat number above and smiled down at Kamal. He appeared to be in his mid-twenties, was casually dressed in a checked shirt and jeans. His light brown hair had thick curls, he had a stubble and hazel eyes. He shoved his rucksack in the cabin above, moved the seat belts which were crossed over neatly on the chair to one side and slumped down into the seat.

"At last! Thought I'd never make it," he smiled at Kamal. Kamal smiled back and went back to her personal organiser. "Business trip?" the young man asked. Kamal hoped silently she was not going to have someone wanting to chat with her for the entire journey; she wasn't really geared up for friendly banter.

"No," she said switching off the organiser and reaching for her bag, "I should really put this away."

"Been to India before?"

"No, first time."

"Hope you're prepared. It's my third time. Meeting up with some mates in Chandigarh."

Kamal nodded her head and looked out of the window. "The name's Sid."

"Sid?" she looked back at him.

"Short for Siddharth."

"Hello Siddharth, Kamal."

"Kamal, nice name."

"Thanks," she smiled.

"Staying with family in India?"

"Friends."

"No family in India?"

Kamal smiled, "no."

"Okay. You live locally?"

"Look, sorry Sid. I really was hoping for a quiet journey, so if you don't mind," Kamal smiled.

"Oh okay," Siddharth rolled his eyes and looked away.

Kamal pulled out a book Michelle had given to her from her bag, one of many she'd given to her over the years forming part of a colossal collection, for which she never quite found the time. She used to be an avid reader, before marriage, spent ages lying on her bed, escaping into someone else's world, often an adventurous, mystical and magical world, but following marriage, she had no more time for books, other than the ones she had read to Deepa's children and certainly not since she had her business. Kamal had finished reading the first page when the screen attached to the back of the seat in front, displayed the safety video. When the air hostesses finished doing their rounds, checking belts were on, tables were pushed up bags were tucked safely away, the lights of the plane were switched off in preparation for take-off. Kamal clasped the arms of the chair as the plane picked up speed and thundered down the runway. Her heart dropped to the pit of her stomach as the plane took off. Once air bound, Kamal looked out of the window down at the matchbox cars and lorries travelling along the motorways outlined by the lighting. The amber lights slowly turned into small specks as the plane gravitated higher and higher away. When she could no longer see anything, she sat back straight in her chair. Siddharth was going through the touch screen in front of him. He selected a film and unpacked the earphones handed out earlier by the airhostesses, plugged them in and sat back. While Kamal tried to read, Siddharth began to chuckle to himself. Kamal ignored him and continued to read, until he all of a sudden roared into a not so ignorable raucous laughter. Kamal looked at him in dismay, as well as the other not so impressed passengers.

"Oh sorry, this is just hilarious," and he laughed out loud again. Kamal rolled her eyes and returned to her book, but Siddharth's continuous laughter was making it impossible for her to concentrate and she slammed the book shut. She reached in her bag and pulled out her iPod. She plugged in the earphones, selected an old album, reminiscent of old times, closed her eyes and sat back with her thoughts wandering off to why she was on board this plane, heading to the land of her origin.

Kamal recalled the day Sindy broke the news of their mother being diagnosed with a brain tumour; the prognosis was bleak and her last wish was to see her oldest daughter. Kamal remembered dropping everything and rushing to the hospital. She remembered the journey seeming to be never ending, tears welling as she drove, questioning why, why life was being so cruel to her. She remembered walking into the hospital, towards the ward outside of which relatives stood around casually holding plastic cups of tea and coffee. She had ignored the sudden gasps, whispers, nudges and looks of disapproval and made her way forward ignoring the attention she was attracting, as she was there for one reason and one reason only, to see her sick mother. She remembered being escorted by the ward nurse to her mother's bed, right at the end, with the blue curtains pulled round. Behind those drawn curtains, her sick, pale mother lay with her long black hair, a few strands of grey, loose over the white bleached pillow; who'd have thought her beautiful tresses disguised the disease that had infested her vital organ. Kamal's eyes had remained static; she had wanted desperately to see her mother, but never sick on a hospital bed, waiting for death to take her. She remembered seeing her mother's eyes moving towards her and welling up. Nindy was sitting on the chair to the right of her holding her hand and her dad was sitting to her left with Sindy sat next to him. Kamal had thought she had run her eyes dry of tears, but they persisted, for a new pain. Kamal remained motionless at the foot of the bed, when her mother raised her right hand, urging her to step forward.

"Come," she said, her voice barely audible. Kamal walked slowly towards her side and Nindy got up for her. Kamal was aware of her dad's venomous glare, but she avoided looking in his direction. She placed her shaking hand on her mother's slightly raised hand, urging her to hold it. The tears streamed down Kamal's cheeks, but she was unable to bring one single word to her lips.

"Can I have some time alone with Kamal?" Parminder struggled to say. Sindy looked towards her father and then Nindy; Nindy nodded at her younger sister and they both kissed their mum on her forehead, before they left. However, Davinder refused to budge. Parminder turned her head towards him slowly, "please." It was only then Kamal looked towards him. His eyes were ringed with dark circles, he had not shaved, the top buttons of his beige, checked shirt were open and his sleeves were rolled up. He looked at her with eyes full of detest, but this time Kamal felt unscathed by his torment; he could not break her any more than she already was. The fact that he was playing the distraught husband at his wife's deathbed sent her pulse rate soaring. He had given her nothing but hell, so why did he appear so subdued now? He reluctantly got up with his eyes still placed firmly on her and she in return met his gaze defiantly and when he'd finally left, she turned back to face her mother.

"Are you okay?" her mum asked; her voice dry and harsh.

"Do you want some water?" Kamal wiped her tears, noticing that her mother's mouth was dry. Parminder nodded her head ever so slightly, as if every bone in her body was aching. Kamal poured some water from the jug on the bedside cabinet into the glass and helped her mum lift her head. She put the straw to her lips. Parminder only managed to take just a few sips. She dropped her head back on the pillow in exhaustion. Kamal could feel her mother's pain and tried to hold back her tears.

"Kamal."

"Yes mum."

"Get my bag from the cabinet." Kamal got up from the chair, moved it to one side, so she could get to the hospital cabinet and fetched out the familiar black leather bag. "Open it." Kamal did as she was instructed. "Open the inner zip pocket," Kamal opened the zip, to find but nothing. "If you feel inside the pocket, you will see that there is a hole, put your hand though the hole and look for a pouch." Kamal did as her mother said. She searched for a while and eventually felt something, in-between the leather and the satin lining and just about pulled out a small, red velvet pouch.

"This?" Kamal held the pouch in her hand.

"Yes. Open it." Kamal opened the pouch to find a gold locket and a piece of paper. Kamal took out both. The paper had a name, a number and an address in Delhi, India. "That is my friend's contact details. Suman."

"And this?" Kamal held the locket up by the clasp of the gold chain.

Parminder looked at her and sighed, closing her eyes painfully, "open it."

Kamal carefully opened the locket. There was a photo of a young girl on the left side and a young man on the right. Kamal looked at the black and white picture again, tinted with age around the edges. She made out who the girl was on the left, but she did not recognise the young man on the right.

"Who's this mum?" Kamal asked looking at her mum confused.

Parminder swallowed and moistened her lips with her tongue.

"It's your father."

Kamal looked more closely at the photo, "it does not look like dad," she said examining it closer still.

"No, it's a photo of your real father," Kamal's pupils moved from the locket towards her mother, not sure if she had heard her correctly.

"Sorry?" Kamal frowned.

"That is your father."

Kamal slowly sat back into the chair, totally confused. Her mother was very ill and she for a moment, she thought she had her senses, "what do you mean mum?"

"Mohan and I were together, before I married your dad. We were in college together," suddenly, Kamal saw her mother's face slowly transforming before her, there was a look of immense happiness momentarily visible in her eyes, as if she had recollected a dear memory, but then she frowned. "When your grandparents found out, there was uproar from the extended family. He belonged to a lower caste you see. Your father's, well, Nindy and Sindy's father, was the son of a very close family friend. We had been engaged to marry when we were very young. My family in haste arranged for the two of us to get married, but I had already made the mistake of giving my body and soul to Mohan. I was already pregnant when I married Davinder," Kamal had never heard her mum bring her dad's name to her lips before. "He always knew. But he was too proud to tell his family and instead, he chose to punish me at any given opportunity, and he has never, ever forgiven me."

Kamal sat back with the locket still in her hand and her eyes on her mother. Her head felt faint and giddy, her legs as if they'd turned to water and if she was not seated, she was sure to have lost the strength to remain standing.

"Why," she eventually asked, swallowed the lump formed in her throat, "why are you telling me this now?" Kamal asked, not quite sure what she should be feeling - anger, hate or even relief; relief for the answers to her questions, answers to the deferential treatment and the sense of being despised throughout her life.

"I could not take this secret with me. I had to tell you," Parminder turned towards her, "please don't hate me Kamal. You are the only one that kept me going all these years, you, you were a part of my first love, and then, you left and I felt like I had lost him all over again."

There was a silence as Kamal tried to soak in the truth.

"Did you love him?" she eventually asked.

"Mohan? He's always held a special place within my heart."

"What about dad. Did you ever love him?"

"Some relationships are not based on love, they are just meant to be."

Siddharth laughed out loud this time clapping his hands as well. Kamal opened her eyes and looked towards him.

"Oh I'm so sorry," Siddharth said, as he saw Kamal's moist eyes. He removed his earphones and turned towards Kamal. "I'll stop watching it."

Kamal could not help but laugh, "don't be silly," she wiped her tears, "I'm sorry. You must think I'm a right miserable cow. Please watch the rest of your film. Just because I am sad doesn't mean everyone else has to be."

"Oh well, it's time to eat now anyway. Dare I ask why you're so emotional? I can ask to be seated elsewhere."

"No don't be silly," Kamal laughed again, "it's just me remembering my mum. She died."

"Oh I'm sorry. Recently?"

"No, it's been a few years now. But it's still painful."

"Oh of course. I can understand."

Kamal ordered a white wine from the pretty smiley air hostess to accompany her meal, while Siddharth asked for a beer.

"So Siddharth, what do you do for a living?"

"I'm a youth support worker."

"Challenging?"

"Yes, it is, but I really enjoy my work. What about you? What do you do?"

"Oh I've got my own businesses."

"Cool," Siddharth nodded his head in approval.

Kamal noticed when Siddharth smiled he had a dimple on the right side of his cheek, just like Varinder did. Sadness crept in all over again, as she thought of his deceased brother, Raj; the guilt of being responsible for killing his own son and the increasing questions from the suspicious police, had eventually taken its toll. Raj had been seeing a psychiatrist for his deteriorating mental health. His life had become so unbearable, that one day, he chose to end it, by hanging himself. She had never thought that one day he would become so desperate. She did attend the funeral service and sat at the back of the temple, while Emma sat at the front, in a white Indian dress, looking understandably distraught. She had with no intention come face to face with Emma, as she was leaving the temple and when both women looked at each other speechless, she could almost read Emma's thoughts, recalling her last words to her; she after all could not build a happy home, by destroying that of another. Danielle had informed her that Emma had eventually sold up and left the home, moving away to live closer to her mother. The home apparently was full of disturbing memories of Raj's worsening mental health. Raj's mother passed away not long after; the grief of first losing her grandson and then her son had been too much for her fragile heart to bear and she died of a massive heart attack. Raj's dad, spent much of his time in India now and came back for a few months a year, usually during the summer.

Each and every event had killed a part of Kamal and she seemed to have stopped hurting. She remembered her dad's face when she left the service at the temple, following her mum's funeral and that was the last time she saw him. Their exchange of cold glances, said their departing words to each other. She was never to see him again, refusing to attend his funeral. She was the core reason behind her dad's verbal, mental and physical abuse directed towards her mother and this truth chilled and haunted her down to the bone, a pain so unexplainable that she chose to block out the revelation made to her by her mother and dumped the pouch with its locket and paper slip in the box with the other items she held onto. Kamal blocked everything out, her mother's dark secret, the memories of the bitter man that had raised her, the deceitful Raj and the dishonest Rohit, who now years later, triggered off a tornado of memories.

As her mind wandered over the painful past, rays of sunshine appeared from the dark clouds, when she thought of much pleasanter, comforting memories; Michelle and Aaron, her saviours. She recalled that cold, wet, winter's night, looking up at the complete stranger who welcomed her into her home and life with open arms, like an angel in disguise and Aaron, she closed her eyes with the thought of him in her mind and heart and pulled the blanket snugly around her. She felt sadness, as she relived the last moment she saw him; how could she be so heartless? Why did she keep testing him? Over the years she was quite content merely being in his presence, knowing he was in close vicinity, standing close to him, touching his hand or holding his arm, kissing him on the cheek when saying goodnight or when thanking him for inviting her over to his for Christmas, which he celebrated with his children, making her feel every part of his family, or thanking him for just being there by her side. To date Aaron had never forgotten the anniversary of Jaydeep's death and he would always send her some flowers as she spent the day at home, the only day she insisted to have off each year. Kamal could not imagine life without him; it was inconceivable.

The clanking of the trolley awoke her. It was 7am and the air hostess was handing out breakfast. Kamal saw that Siddharth was not in his seat. She rubbed her eyes and looked out the window with delight. The sky was a clear turquoise blue and below was nothing but miles and miles of fluffy snow-white clouds. Kamal reached out for her bag to get out her travel brush, face towel and small tube of toothpaste still in the plastic bag due to security checks. She brushed her hair out and saw that the trolley was still a way to come, so she got up to stand in the queue for the toilet. After refreshing, she finally made her way back to her seat and Siddharth welcomed her back with a big smile.

"Good morning Kamal."

"Morning Sid."

"Not long now. Did you sleep well?"

"Yes thanks. And you?"

"Yes. I got up well before you though. You were sleeping like a baby. You have really pretty eyes, do you know that?" Siddharth said looking at Kamal.

Kamal laughed, "are you always so cheerful in the morning?" Siddharth reminded her so much of Michelle.

"Yes and why not? Every morning is the dawn of a new day. It's never going to come back again. My motto is to live like there is no tomorrow."

Kamal smiled at his optimism.

"Tea or coffee," the hostess asked after handing them their breakfast trays.

"After the lady," Siddharth said looking towards Kamal.

"Tea please."

"A tea for me too please," Siddharth smiled.

"So, Siddharth, do you live alone, have a partner or are you living with your parents, sorry, my turn for the questions," Kamal smiled.

"My life's an open book," he smiled, "my mum died when I was very young from a drugs overdose. As for my dad, well I don't know who he is, whether he is dead or alive. My grandparents have been my parents; they mean everything to me." Kamal thought if Jaydeep was alive today, he would have loved his grandparents just as much as Siddharth seemed to his.

"It must've been devastating for your grandparents, losing their daughter like that."

"No-one knew she was dead, until my grandparents got concerned that they had not heard from her for a while. She was an addict. Police found her body in her flat. Apparently my dad got her started on them, drugs, he was some dealer apparently. Got her pregnant and left her, not once looking back. I can't remember her, only very, very vaguely, seeing her outside my grandparent's home yelling at them. I suppose she was asking them for money. There is a photo of me and her at home, when I was just born. It was one she had at her flat. She was a uni student, studying law, but then she messed up. Total waste of a life."

"Gosh, must have been so difficult for your grandparents."

"Well, does anyone ever get over the death of their child?"

"No, I guess not," Kamal sighed, "but you seemed to have done okay."

"Yes I have. Have had a good upbringing, so did my mum, but she just got mixed up in the wrong crowd I suppose."

"It is all about choices at the end of the day isn't it?" Kamal said thoughtfully, "you choose which path to take."

"Yes, it's all about choices. Look out there." Kamal looked out the window; they were in India and she smiled as she saw a group of boys far below playing cricket barefooted dressed in nothing but shorts and vests. "Hope you are ready for the experience of a lifetime," Siddharth smiled.

Siddharth stayed with Kamal until they eventually, passed through the chaos of immigration. He waved at his friends as they walked out with their cases.

"Can you see your mother's friend?"

"Well I've never met her; she'll be holding my name card up, hopefully," Kamal said fanning her face, trying to cool herself from the stifling heat.

Siddharth's friends approached them both and shook Kamal's hand as Siddharth introduced her. The friends grouped up together as they talked, while Kamal continued to search. She made out a lady, making her way to the front of the crowd. She was wearing a pale blue cotton Punjabi suit. Her hair was combed back and a long plait came over her shoulder down to her hips. The lady now intently pushed her way to the front of the crowd, held up the name card and Kamal acknowledged her arrival by a smile and wave.

"She's here," Kamal turned round to see Siddharth engaged with his friends. "Okay Siddharth, I'm off. Thanks for the company on the plane."

"Pleasure's all mine. I hope you enjoy your first experience of India Kamal. Kamal, which means lotus flower, do you know the lotus flower is the national flower of India? Welcome home," he held out his hand.

"Yes," Kamal smiled, shaking his hand, "welcome home indeed."

Sid winked and departed with his friends and Kamal, turned back round to meet Suman, pulling her case behind her when she was approached by a very thin man, in an off white shirt, brown trousers, slightly turned up and flip flops asking her if she wanted any help with her luggage. As if having caused an attraction, she was approached by another man, followed by yet another all offering to help carry her luggage for a small fee. Kamal looked at them bemused, as they began to argue amongst themselves.

"Hello Kamal," Kamal looked from the three men towards Suman who before she even managed to greet her back, instantly threw her arms around her and then held her at arm's length. While Kamal was still getting over the spontaneous hug, Suman jumped straight into her first impressions of her friend's daughter.

"I don't believe it! You have your mother's eyes, but your dad's nose!" she put her hand to her mouth, "just wait till he sees you. I won't have to say anything. He will know instantly. It's the smile. It's all your mother's. Oh my dear friend, how I wish she was here today," she said in her very Indian accent, she shook her head, denying her eyes tears, "come let's get to the car, away from here. We shall talk some more on the way home. *Ajo bhai uthao*," Suman instructed one of the men to assist and Kamal followed her like a child.

Kamal had felt flustered in the heat within the airport and no sooner had she stepped out, she was hit by a block of yet more intense heat. Kamal looked up, shading her eyes with her hand. It was just after 10am and the sky was a flawless blue, not one single cloud in sight. All curious Indian eyes were following her as she walked out of Delhi Airport, as if she were an alien from another planet and all Kamal could hear now, was the blaring of car horns and beeping scooters as she followed her mother's friend.

Suman was a slim woman and had typical Northern Indian features, big brown eyes, sharp nose and thin shapely lips. Her fair skin showed signs of age, but only slightly, with fine lines around her eyes and lips; Kamal could imagine how many hearts she stole now, let alone in her youth. Her hair was as long as her mother's was and she could see just a few streaks of silver going through her amazingly, snakelike plait, which swayed with her every step. Kamal tried not to trip over the uneven ground below and huge pot holes, as she followed. A little grubby girl with matted hair, and bare feet approached her, with her hand out asking for some money. Kamal sympathetically reached into her bag for her purse.

"No, no!" Suman said turning round just in time, "this is their job, if you give her money a whole army of them will come swarming from nowhere," she shooed the girl away, but the girl persisted making Kamal feel very uncomfortable. They finally approached a small white car, where a young man stood waiting, "this is my son, Anil."

"Hello Anil."

"Hello Kamal, nice to meet you," he held his hand out.

Anil opened the boot for Kamal's baggage, which the deceiving scraggy man carried effortlessly upon his head. Anil paid the man, while the two ladies got seated.

"Your uncle could not be here, Anil managed to take some time off work."

"Oh thank you Anil," Kamal smiled.

"That's quite okay," Anil said looking back, as he fastened his seatbelt.

"Does uncle know everything about me?" Kamal asked.

"Of course. We were all very good friends, me your uncle, your mother and father," she said fastening her seatbelt, "we all went to the same college. Of course we continued with our studies and did not marry till later, but your mum got married and moved abroad. Not through choice of course. Your grandparents got her married off as soon as they found out about Mohan. Mohan, was devastated. He never got married you know. He said that he would not compromise. He was quite happy with his studying and then his job as a professor. He's retired now of course."

"He spent his whole life alone?" Kamal asked as Anil weaved his way out the, what she assumed was a car park and drove onto roads that seemed to be nothing short of chaos, but accustomed to the pandemonium, he drove on undeterred.

"Well, he had his job and his students, his time was fully occupied," Suman said.

"Watch out!" Kamal said as a cow walked across the road, with not a care in the world. "Is that allowed here! Where is its owner?"

Suman laughed, "this is India my dear. There are many things that will alarm you," the car was stood stationary at traffic lights. A little barefooted boy approached the car chanting the price of his freshly cut coconut slices, the flesh as white as fresh snow. Kamal shook her head and Suman waved her hand, gesturing him to move away as the car drove off again. All traffic was chaotically streaming in one direction accompanied by impatient beeping of horns. Kamal had her heart in her mouth throughout the whole journey. There were rickshaws, small three wheeled vehicles, mopeds, motorbikes, jeeps and bikes. Everyone was in such a frenzy. There was no gentle giving way, the attitude they all seemed to have was 'no, me first!' Anil braked hard and beeped his horn, just as restless. Kamal was relieved when Anil started to turn into some quieter streets. Only then the car rattled over uneven ground and bounced in and out of large pot holes, sending her head banging against the window at one point. The ordeal finally came to an end as Anil eventually parked the car outside some large black iron gates. He undid his belt and got out of the car to open them.

"Here's our home," Suman said unfastening her belt.

Kamal walked through the open gates, which enclosed off a vast open space in the middle of which stood their home. The bright sun reflected off the brilliant white marble floor surrounding the home and she had to put her hand over her forehead for shade.

"Come," Suman walked towards the front door followed by Anil carrying the suitcase. He opened the door and placed the case inside the house.

"I'll be going back to work then ma, Kamal, I will see you later."

"Okay thanks Anil," she smiled.

Anil did not look like his mother at all, Suman's skin was fair and his was more a wheat colour, she had large eyes and his were small slanting, a handsome man, dressed in a pale pink half sleeved shirt with grey trousers held up with a black belt and was well groomed with his hair gelled back and a neat French cut beard.

The exterior space around the house was surrounded with great big potted exotic plants adding a splash of colour against the brilliant white. A couple of motorbikes were parked behind the wall facing the street, next to the large iron gates. The window frames of the house itself were a sandalwood colour and there was a sheet of mesh wiring before the windows, which Kamal assumed was to keep out creepy crawlies.

"Come Kamal."

Kamal walked into the large open space, furnished with a brown coloured sofa suite, a coffee table placed on top of a Persian rug, the flooring a marvellous, cool white marble. A large dining table sat at the far end of the room and to the right there were impressive floor to ceiling wall units, laden with books. Various authentic ornaments were placed all about the room and next to doors, presumably leading to the kitchen and bedrooms. The large houseplants placed around the room added a vibrant green and many pieces of art pieces decorated the walls. Kamal walked towards these, instantly drawn. There was a painting of four beautiful Indian young women, sitting round a man selling bangles, his basket full of colourful wares. The women's heads were covered with thin *dupattas* to match their flowing long skirts, in colours red, yellow, blue and green, their feet bare, their ankles adorned with silver anklets. There was another painting of a young, beautiful woman sitting in front of a mirror combing her long, black tresses.

"These are beautiful," Kamal said as Suman walked out of the kitchen with two cold drinks on a tray. Kamal thought how she would love to have something similar in her restaurant.

"Thank you. You'll find many more around the house."

"How many children do you have?" Kamal asked.

"Come sit down. Have a drink. I have two boys, Anil is the youngest and then there is Sunil, he's living and working in Bangalore at the moment. Anil was fortunate enough to get a job nearer home. Sunil visits every other weekend or once a month."

"They are not married?"

"Sunil is engaged to marry next year, and Anil, well, I've had no choice but to turn away alliances, what can we do? We can't force him. I am sure he will find someone soon," Suman walked up to the wall unit, as she was speaking and took down a framed photo. "Now, see if you recognise your mother," she sat next to Kamal. Kamal looked at the black and white school group photo. She looked at all the smiling faces carefully.

"There," she pointed towards her mother, with two plaits, a big smile, standing up straight, nose in the air and hands behind her back, wearing a Punjabi suit and a sleeveless sweater on top. She looked so happy in the photo. "And that's you isn't it?"

"Yes," Suman smiled, "oh those were the days."

"Mum looks so happy."

"She always was. But she changed when she got married. She hardly kept in contact. I'd write to her and it would be ages, before I received a reply. The last time I saw her was at your grandmother's funeral. A friend had informed me that she was over. She was no longer the Parminder I once knew. She seemed to have lost all the spirit she had."

"No. She never was herself when my dad was around."

"Did he mistreat her?"

Kamal smiled and shook her head. It was obvious her mother had not said anything, which did not surprise her; she never talked to anyone about her problems. If her mother had chosen not to tell her best friend, then she was going to keep it that way. "No. It's just the way dad was. He was a very strong character."

"It was the last letter I received from her which revealed everything. I could not believe it. She said that you may choose to contact me some day and here you are today. She asked me never to tell Mohan, unless you chose to make contact."

"He doesn't know?"

"About you? No. I haven't told him yet, have not even told him she's passed. I was waiting to see if you really would come and then, you could meet him and tell him yourself."

"It will be quite a surprise for him, a daughter he never knew of, turning up at his doorstep," Kamal sat back in dismay.

"You do not know your father. He is a very good man. A true gem. His heart is so big and pure. He will welcome you into his life with open arms. I have no doubt of that. Now, first things first, I'll show you to your bedroom and you can then freshen up, you must be tired from all the travelling and I will prepare lunch and then, we shall talk some more."

"Oh I could always check into a hotel, I had looked some up on the internet. I don't want to get in your way."

"I will hear no such thing! Oh, I can't believe I have Pammy's daughter in my house. It's like having her back seeing you sitting here. Oh how I miss the old days. Me, Pammy, your uncle and your dad Mohan, we were inseparable. It was just not the same when your mum left. She was married within days, so hastily married off and left India within days. Of course it was easier back then to enter England. Then we hardly heard from her," a sudden sadness crept over Suman's face, "anyway. We'll talk some more later. Here I'll show you to your room."

Kamal filled the large red bucket with warm water and poured it over her head with the plastic jug. It's just what she needed after the long journey. The bathroom was completely tiled in red and white. It had no bath, just taps for hot and cold water and the large red bucket. There was a sink, next to the toilet in the far corner of the room and above the sink hung a large mirror. Kamal towel dried her short hair and combed it back. She applied some moisturiser to her face and some lip gloss. She wore her white linen trouser, a turquoise tunic top with sequences and slipped on her flat, white sandals. Whilst putting her toiletry bag back in the bedroom, which was a large room, simply furnished with a large bed and wardrobe, she was instantly drawn towards the aroma, reminding her of home and her mother's cooking, taking her back, yet again. She followed the aroma into the kitchen, where Suman had just finished cooking the last chapatti.

"Smells like mother's cooking," Kamal smiled.

Suman looked up towards a much refreshed Kamal. "You are so like your mother," Suman smiled, "such a shame marriage changed her so much. Still, I guess a lot of people change following marriage, priorities change don't they? I married my childhood sweetheart, I do feel I remained much the same, guess I did not have to change for anyone. But oh my goodness, what a fuss they had caused. In those days it was totally unacceptable for a girl to choose who she wanted to marry, but we did it and we have been happy since. Just wait till your uncle sees you. He called when you were in the bathroom. He'll be home just after six with the Delhi traffic, total chaos. Come."

"Let me help." Kamal picked up the bottle of water and glasses that were ready and waiting. Suman carried the tray with two plates, two small bowels, one with *daal* and the other with *palak paneer* and a plate with the chapatti. It smelt divine.

"This is gorgeous," Kamal said as she ate, "just like my mum used to make it."

"Nothing compares to a mother's cooking does it?"

"No," Kamal smiled.

"So tell me about you."

Kamal avoided going into too much detail. Even though Suman was her mother's best friend, she did not feel that she knew her well enough to disclose absolutely everything.

Kamal later stirred in her sleep. She got up to realise that she had been sleeping for four hours. She could hear the television from the living room. "Gosh." she said getting up, not recalling the last time she had slept so well. She stretched and rubbed her eyes, pulled herself away from the bed which was surprisingly quite comfortable despite the thin mattress, ran her fingers through her hair and walked into the living room to find the family seated in front of the TV.

"Ah. Here she is," Suman said.

"I'm so sorry. I did not realise the time."

"Aah, you were so tired, come join us," Suman said as she stood up. Anil smiled at Kamal as he sat with his feet up on the sofa and a mature man with greyed hair and trimmed beard, stood up looking at Kamal, totally startled.

"My, my, my, she really is like our Parminder," he said walking towards Kamal, his brown leather sandals squeaking on the floor below. He put his arm round her affectionately. "Welcome to India my dear. How was the journey?"

"Fine, thank you."

He led her to the sofa with his arm still around her shoulders.

"Who would have thought," Vinod smiled, "just wait till we tell Mohan. I can't imagine how he will react. But he will welcome you with open arms, because that's the way he is. It's so heart-warming to have you here. It feels like our friend's soul is amongst us today, so sad she is no longer with us. Has Suman told you how close we all were?" Kamal smiled and nodded as she was sandwiched between Suman and Vinod.

"I certainly did," Suman smiled placing her hand on Kamal's.

"Oh yes. We could tell you a tale or two," Vinod stopped to think and smiled. "Sumi, do you remember the time when we set up that arrogant new kid, what was his name Sumi?"

"Mohit."

"Yes Mohit. He was buzzing arrogantly around all the girls, particularly Sumi and your mum like a bee over flowers. So we all planned to teach him a lesson. Sumi and Pammy both individually pretended to have fallen hopelessly in love with him. They arranged to meet him, according to him, secretly from each other. He thought he had won the lottery. He was going round telling all the boys that he had them both fooled, little did he know, the joke was on him. Then eventually when we thought the game had gone far enough, the girls arranged to see him the same day, but different times. He walked around the whole morning like the cat that had found the cream, but when they both turned up at the same time, he was not looking so clever. They made out that they were totally unaware of what was happening and then they both got their sandals off and gave him such a beating."

"And oh my word, did we get some satisfaction from beating him. He thought he was so smart," Suman laughed, "he used the same chat up line on both of us. It was as if they were rehearsed. We used to laugh out so much when we re-enacted it all out. It was so funny."

"What about that time when we all went to watch, which *Shammi Kapoor* film was it Sumi? It was the one with that famous song where Helen does that famous cabaret dance, what was it….."

"*Teesri Manzil*?" Suman rolled her eyes.

"Ha, ha. *Teesri Manzil*, remember when we all went to watch it. Oh my, remember the songs. We were singing the songs together for months weren't we? It was not often we went to watch films, but when we did we made a day out of it. Oh those were the days. Remember Sumi.... *deewana mujhsa nahin is ambar ke neeche...*"

"Oh Vinod stop it," Suman said as he started singing to her.

"Mohan used to sing it to Pammy when she was angry with him. She was never angry for long. Oh remember the time when Pammy had a fight with Meena?"

"How can I forget? When she was flirting with Mohan, oh Pammy was so angry. It was at Shaam's party wasn't it? Meena came in with that tight, tight top and tight, tight trousers. She did have an amazing figure," Vinod recalled the image mentally.

"Um that's enough," Suman looked sternly at her husband.

"Not better than yours of course darling. I tell you Kamal your aunty Suman stole a few hearts in her days."

"See, how he is creeping now. This Meena was very beautiful though, she always had her hair up in a beehive with a headband to match her every dress. She always looked immaculate. The professors used to ask her if she came to college for a beauty contest or to study. She lived with her mirror in her hand. Anyway, back to the story, it was Shaam's birthday party and Meena was dancing with Mohan and every time Mohan would grab Pammy for a dance, she would pull him away towards her, he was a very handsome man your dad and had many admirers. But when Meena tried to push in on Pammy's favourite song of the time.... *oh mere sona, re sona*, Pammy eventually got so frustrated she pushed her to the floor in irritation! The poor thing's top tore all down the back! It was quite childish of Pammy, but she must've felt so threatened. Anyway, Mohan scolded her, for pushing Meena and Pammy stormed off in tears. I in turn scolded Mohan off for yelling at my friend. Then when I saw Vinod helping Meena up, who was hurling abuse at Pammy, it was my turn to get aggressive and it was like a reflex reaction, I pulled her great big beehive. Her hair was such a mess when I finished with her," Vinod and Suman were roaring in laughter, as they relived the moment. Kamal was laughing with them, as was their son Anil.

"These stories can go on all night Kamal. Embrace yourself," Anil laughed.

"Oh but they are so wonderful to hear. It's like getting to know another side of my mother. A side I never got to know at all. How sad is that?"

"Mohan went after Pammy that night," Suman's laugh died down, as if she was recapturing the events of that night. She looked at her husband Vinod and Vinod towards her, as if he knew what she was thinking and they then both looked at Kamal. Was that the night she was conceived?

"It was not long after that her parents got her married off. You see Pammy's parents were originally from a small village, in Punjab. Whereas they were quite modern, the rest of the family, had quite traditional values. When word got to them that Pammy wanted to marry a boy of a lower caste, they insisted she was married off straight away. Her grandparents and uncles, who still lived in the village, were very strict, unlike her dad, who came to Delhi to work and escape village life. While he had adapted to modern city life, the family were still strict traditionalists and they threatened to break all ties with him. Your dad, Davinder, was the son of very good family friend and your mum and Davinder's marriage was fixed when they were very, very young. Once they got knowledge of what was happening in Delhi, they wasted no time at all and before we knew it, Pammy was married. She tried talking to her mum, but alas, they were tied down by family values and she left us. Four of us became three. It was never the same again. Mohan was never the same again. And contact from your mother was few and far between." The happy and jolly mood was dampened by a sudden sadness.

Kamal could just hear the distant late night traffic, as she lay in bed under the whirring fan. Today, Kamal learnt who her mother really was; a happy soul, a daughter that had wanted for nothing and a friend who completed a group of friends. A young woman who would never have guessed what fate had in store for her. Vinod had called Mohan that very evening and told him that they will be coming over to visit, bringing with them a guest from England. Kamal could make out that he was asking who this guest was. Kamal had then questioned why they had not told Mohan about her and it was because they were never sure whether she would indeed ever want to trace her biological father, and what Mohan had lived without knowing all these years, he could have lived without knowing for the rest of his years. It would have only hurt him further, to know he had a daughter who he could not reach out to. While Kamal was initially quite apprehensive about meeting her mother's friends and her father, she was now looking forward to meeting the man who had made her mother smile and laugh, the man who her mother had really loved. She wondered whether Suman and Vinod had got it all wrong. What if he was not happy to see her? What if he denied conception? What if he rejected her? These questions whirred round her head, like the fan above the bed, but whatever the doubts, Kamal wanted to see the man who brought a twinkle in her dying mother's eyes, whom when she thought of, alleviated her of all her pain and sorrow.

The clanking of cutlery, Vinod and Suman talking awoke Kamal. She looked at her watch; it was 8.25am. She was usually up at the crack of dawn, but for some reason, she was able to sleep like a baby here. She grabbed her toiletries, towel, change of clothes and headed for the bathroom.

The family were sat around the table tucking into Suman's delicious, hearty *aloo parathas*. Sunil had also turned up in the early hours of the morning, equally as handsome as his brother Anil, though appeared much more extrovert and jolly.

"Do you know, this is one thing I miss, mama's cooking. Just does not compare," Sunil said.

"And I can't remember the last time I had homemade *aloo parathas*," Kamal agreed.

"Really? You wait till you have tasted my *gobi parathas*."

"I'll have to go on a strict diet when I go back. I've not stopped eating since I've come here," Kamal smiled.

"Nonsense. You are perfect. In fact, I think a little bit more weight will suit you. There's nothing wrong with a little bit of fat," Suman said, placing another thick *paratha* on Kamal's plate.

"No, aunty *ji*. Really, I did not want another one."

"Of course you did."

Kamal's eyes were wide open as she looked at the thick *paratha*.

"Don't worry we'll go for a walk later to help burn some calories," Sunil laughed.

"I think we will need to!" Kamal laughed with her jolly company.

"Ooh that looks lovely," Suman said as Kamal walked out, dressed in the pink coloured cotton top she'd bought for her yesterday, as a small gift when they had gone out for a stroll around the shops late in the evening. It was embroidered delicately with pale blue and white coloured flowers around the neckline and hem. Kamal wore it with her jeans and flat white sandals, her pink lip gloss and minimal eye makeup, a delicate blue to complement the small flowers on her top finished off her casual yet sophisticated look.

"Thank you. It's just right for this weather," Kamal said as she closed the zip of her handbag; tucked safely within, the locket.

"Ready?" Suman asked putting her hands on her shoulders. She could sense Kamal's nerves and kissed her on the forehead, "don't worry, me and your uncle are right beside you."

Chapter 26

Vinod had been driving through the congested city for about half an hour now and Kamal's heart was in her mouth praying that they'd make it to their destination in one piece. "Almost there now," Suman said, "you see that shopping complex there, that is where the cinema used to be. It's all changed now. Now there are great big shopping complexes everywhere." They were driving through what appeared a quite opulent region now laden with apartments and high office blocks and wider roads. People walking and men driving by on scooters, peered into the car with much interest. She did not feel that she looked much different from the people around her, but anyone would have thought she had one eye and three noses. A lot of the bike riders had their mouths covered with a handkerchief tied at the back of their head, she gathered to block out the polluted air. Overloaded buses drove by, with people literally hanging off from the back and sides and sitting on the tops. There were lorries loaded with goods, some of them so dangerously that they looked like they could topple over any minute and she wished Vinod would not drive so close to them. Kamal's eyes then followed a group of people running into one direction, as she looked round to where they were charging, she saw they were all chasing a bus, which had stopped for literally just a few seconds, but that did not stop people from running on and grabbing the ladder attached to its back. Kamal widened her eyes and turned round. As they started to turn into smaller roads, she saw small open front shops with bags of crisps hung onto a string, across the front of the shop with small pegs, containers with biscuits and bottles of Coca Cola and what seemed like a popular lemon drink, advertised quite widely and another bright orange coloured drink sitting on shelves or in buckets of ice. There were little shops selling bangles, jewellery and beauty products and larger shops with mannequins dressed in colourful saris. Driving past the line of shops, they turned into some narrow residential streets now, where she saw smaller businesses, a small tailor's shop where she saw a man taking measurements of a young man, from his shoulder to his wrist and a couple of men sat behind sewing machines, stitching away, next to it a sweet shop with Indian sweets, in colours white, orange, green and pink piled on trays behind a glass counter.

Eventually, they stopped. Right outside some double sky-blue painted doors. Vinod came round and opened the car door for Kamal and she stepped out, her heart beat, increasing. She felt all passing eyes turning to stare at her. A lady in a sari walked by, her eyes not leaving Kamal, an old man walking by slowly with his walking stick, literally stopped to look up at her. A man drove by on a scooter and beeped loudly, for no apparent reason.

"Come," Suman said, as she walked towards the blue doors behind her husband. He banged on the door and pushed it open.

"Mohan," Vinod called out. Kamal's heart dropped, as Vinod called out to her father. Was this really happening now? She pinched herself and hesitated in the doorway.

"Come in, come in Vinod," Kamal heard a male voice call out and she swallowed the lump in her throat.

"Come my dear," Suman placed her hand on Kamal's shoulder and squeezed it.

Mohan stood up from his chair. He had a newspaper in his hand and glasses resting on his nose. He took his glasses off and placed them with the newspaper onto the table next to his chair. Kamal saw that the deceiving doors opened to reveal a wide open courtyard. Straight ahead were three concrete arches, evenly spaced out, a leading entry to three doors also painted a sky blue. Next to each door was an equally sized blue framed window, with mesh wiring. There was another door to the left hand side of the courtyard with a much larger window to its right and then further down on the left, near to the entrance they had just passed, another two doors. In the middle of the wide open space, where Mohan stood now, was a wooden table with chairs, which appeared to be the handiwork of a fine carpenter adding to the rustic feel. There were pots and pots of colourful flowers and cactuses placed around the courtyard. The surrounding walls were painted a sandy yellow. Kamal was instantly drawn in by the homeliness, compared to Suman's and Vinod's quite modern home, this in contrast appeared quite quintessential, traditional, charming, warm and inviting. Vinod and Mohan shook hands and Suman brought her hands together, "*Namaste* Mohan."

"Hello my dear," Mohan said to Kamal and started to walk towards her, as she had stopped back at a distance observing the surroundings and the man, who was apparently, her father. Kamal smiled nervously and he stopped suddenly. He hesitated before he smiled again. "Come my dear, come and sit down." Kamal walked towards the table and chairs slowly, like a child and sat next to Vinod. From out of the doors on the left hand side a lady no older than Mohan walked out.

"Suman, Vinod," the lady came over to hug Suman and said hello to Kamal, bringing her hands together, "*Namaste.*"

"*Namaste*," Kamal too brought her hands together.

"This is Mohan's sister. When did you come Pratibha?" Suman asked. Kamal looked up at the short, fair-skinned, plump woman, dressed in yellow, her hair tied up in a large bun.

"Oh just this morning. Mohan had said that you were coming, so I thought I would come and meet you too. It had been such a long time. I'll just go fetch some drinks for you all."

Mohan was still observing Kamal. His sister also looked back and frowned, before she headed back into the kitchen curiously.

"So how are you two?" Mohan asked his eyes still focused on Kamal.

"What's the matter Mohan?" Vinod asked.

"Oh nothing," Mohan looked away from Kamal towards his friend.

"Does she remind you of someone?" Vinod asked him softly. Mohan looked towards Vinod confused and then back towards Kamal. Kamal's heart was thumping against her rib cage and her hands were sweating, both from the heat and nerves. Mohan looked towards Suman, as if searching her, for an answer. She smiled and nodded slightly. He looked towards Kamal again, who was now looking down at her hands, not quite sure what to do with them. "Is it…." he looked towards his friends again for confirmation.

"Yes. She's our Pammy's daughter," Suman's voice broke.

Mohan looked back at Kamal in amazement. Kamal looked up and smiled a nervous smile.

"Oh gosh, an exact replica! Except…" he put his hand towards his nose. Unlike Parminder, who had a sharp pointy nose, Kamal had a small nose, a bit like…..his. Mohan looked back at his friends. Prathibha brought some cold drinks out on a tray and as she placed them on the table, her eyes remained transfixed on Kamal. Suman and Vinod looked at each other and smiled; they could understand why their friends were perplexed, it was as if Parminder was sitting amongst them again after all these years.

"Pratibha," Suman said standing up, "come let's put some tea on." Kamal looked up nervously towards Suman as she got up. Suman placed a reassuring hand on her shoulder and took Prathibha into the kitchen. Kamal looked back at her father. Mohan was still looking from one face to the other. He was wearing a white short sleeved shirt. He had thick grey hair, combed back and was clean shaven. His skin tone was a golden wheat colour and his eyes hazel brown.

"How is your mother?" he asked eventually, his eyes now looking down at his hands.

"She," Kamal hesitated, "mom died," Mohan looked up in alarm and then back down.

"I'm so sorry," he said following a spell of silence. "Was she ill?"

"Brain tumour," Kamal said softly. After all these years, it was evident that he still cared for her and she was deeply touched.

"Tumour," he whispered and sighed.

There were a few more moments of silence between them. Kamal watched him; he appeared to have gone into a distant world. The only sound was birds tweeting, beeping horns from the passing scooters and cars and children playing out on the street. Vinod did not say anything; he knew his friend was silently mourning. Kamal opened the zip of her bag and pulled out the pouch. She got up from her seat and walked round to her father. He looked up at her standing before him and she held the pouch out to him. He put his hand out and she placed it gently in his palm. He looked down at it and then up at her. Her eyes were welling up and she went back to her seat. Mohan looked at the pouch and then opened it. He looked up at Vinod perplexed and emptied the content onto the palm of his left hand. He exhaled as he saw the locket. He picked it up from the clasp and held it high before his eyes; it was the same locket. He then opened it and smiled. He looked up at Kamal.

"She gave it to me before she died," a tear ran down her cheek, "she told me that…..that….," Vinod put his hand on her shoulder. She closed her eyes and sniffed, "she told me that you were my father."

Mohan sat speechless and looked towards his friend Vinod, who confirmed the words with a gentle nod. Mohan looked down at the locket in his hand and after a few moments, slowly got up.

"I….I, just need a minute. Please excuse me for just a moment. Sorry," he said, with a croak in his voice. Mohan walked towards the door on the far right hand side, through the arch, into his bedroom, the locket still clasped tight in his hand. He held his tight fist to his mouth in disbelief, trying to soak in the revelation. He looked through the mesh wired window. Was this young lady really his daughter? Was she the result of that one night? He sat on the end of the bed as he recalled the events.

It was at Shaam's party, when Parminder had gone off in a strop and he had run out after her. Shaam's farmhouse was in the middle nowhere and Parminder was walking away without direction.

"Pammy! Pammy! Wait! Where are you going?"

"What's it to you! Go back to Meena!"

Mohan was running after her, despite wearing a pencil tight suit, the fashion back then, she was walking away pretty fast. It was dark outside and raining.

"Pammy! Pammy!" There was a rumble of thunder. Parminder suddenly stood still in her tracks and looked up at the heavens. The rain was coming down heavier now. "Don't be so stubborn, come back to the house."

"No!" Parminder saw a barn and she ran into it chased closely by Mohan. Once inside there was a sudden crack of thunder and she shrieked and clung onto Mohan's arm. It was really dark in the barn, the only light they got was from the lightening. Parminder held onto Mohan's arm even tighter. "Wait," he pulled out a match from his pocket and lit it. He searched round the barn and saw an oil lamp on a shelf. He lit the lamp and put it close to them. "We'll wait for the rain to stop and then we'll go back."

Now being able to see, she stood frowning with her arms crossed, evidently still miffed and Mohan started to chuckle.

"Such jealousy, I never knew you loved me so much."

Parminder turned her back towards him. The rain showed no signs of subsiding. There was a crack of lightening again and this time there was a bang at the back of the barn. Parminder shrieked and covered her face with her hands. Mohan walked towards her and put his arm around her and she involuntarily moved closer towards him. As her head lay on his chest, he pulled her closer towards him and she wrapped her arms tighter around him, as if claiming that he was hers and only hers.

"I have to tell you something Mohan."

"What?" he whispered.

"I was engaged to marry when I was very young, the man I was engaged to marry is going to England. My grandparents contacted my parents; they want the marriage to take place now, so I can emigrate with him."

"What?" Mohan pulled away and looked down at her in disbelief.

Her tearful eyes were doing all the talking. He wrapped his arms around her.

"What am I going to do?"

"You're not going to worry, that's what you're going to do. Do you really think I'm going to give up on you so easily? I will beg for your hand in marriage, get down on my knees to your parents, convince them that no one, no one can love their daughter like me. No-one."

It was then emotions began to charge, as they embraced, the fear of separation giving rise to uncontrollable emotions and both souls, united as one.

The following Monday at college Parminder avoided him throughout the day.

"Parminder, Pammy. Please talk to me," he persisted as she walked away at the end of the day.

"I am so ashamed of myself. It should never have happened."

"I'm sorry Parminder. I should have controlled my emotions, but you should not feel ashamed, my love for you is pure, do you not trust me?"

"With all my heart, but it was wrong, you know it was," Parminder could not even bring herself to look him in the eyes.

"I am going to ask for your hand in marriage, today itself, I promise."

When he had gone to her home, with his parents and sister Pratibha, that very night, as promised, her family had been apprehensive; they said that they'd need to consult with their family back home in the village, as every major family decision was passed through the elders first. But, that was the last time he had ever seen her; standing nervously peeking from her bedroom door. Two days later when he'd neither heard nor seen her, he went to her house again, only to find the door securely locked with a padlock. Suman had later gathered and informed him that Parminder had been taken back to the village to be wedded to the man she was engaged to marry, when she was just seven years old. His heart, was shattered.

Mohan looked through the mesh wiring again and sighed. Vinod was walking towards the room. "Mohan," he said popping his head round the door.

"Vinod."

"She has come all this way my friend to see you. Are you not going to sit with her?"

"She's my daughter. I can't believe it Vinod, she's my daughter. What must Pammy have been going through all these years?" Mohan watched Kamal sitting with her head held down fiddling with the zip to her bag. "I can't believe it. All these years I've had a daughter? I have a daughter," he smiled.

"Yes," Vinod put his hands on his friend's shoulders, "and it's time to meet her properly."

"Yes," Mohan got up and wiped away his tears. He went to his bedside cabinet and pulled out a book, from the drawer and walked back out. He smiled at Kamal and sat back on the chair opposite her with his head bent down, still not quite sure how to react or behave. Suman and Pratibha came out of the kitchen. Pratibha looked as white as a sheet, as she had now also been informed of the truth. She went over to Kamal and kissed her forehead, her moist eyes doing all the talking.

"She was very, very, special to me," Mohan spoke softly, his head still bent down. He opened the book and pulled out an old photo, leaned forward and gave it to Kamal. "Taken in 1967 on her birthday, not long before she left," Kamal looked at the discoloured photo; it was her mother and father sitting in a park; her mother displaying a big wide smile and leaning on his shoulder.

"She looks really happy," Kamal smiled.

"She always was, always smiling. Oh but she carried her temper on her nose, but she came round quickly," he said smiling, recollecting old memories, "she meant everything to me. Everything. We'd known each other since school, grew up together. She did not acknowledge me to be more than just a friend till much later. But I used to think, if anyone is going to be my wife, it will be my Parminder. But, it was not to be. I was so heartbroken when she went. Not once did she look back. Not once, no letter, nothing. No mention of me when she wrote to Suman either. Nothing. I often wondered whether she hated me." It was then he looked up towards her properly.

"She didn't hate you. It was the only time I saw a real happiness in her eyes, when she was on her deathbed and spoke of you. She looked like, just for a few moments, she was cured of her illness. That would not have happened, if she hated you."

"No. And she kept this for all these years," he said looking down at the locket in his hand again, "I guess that also means something. I gave it to her on her eighteenth birthday. I had saved and saved. I even sold a few of my text books, to make up for the deficit. I got a right clip around the ear for that, my dad wanted to know where the money had gone. I told him I spent it on my friends in a restaurant," he smiled and shook his head as he relived the moment, "we were meant to be forever," his voice now a mere whisper. Kamal could see the sadness in his eyes and then he looked at her, with a smile. "But, in all of this. I have gained a daughter and you have my nose! But the rest belongs to your mum. I can't believe it. I have a child. I have a family," he got up and walked towards his daughter and lovingly placed his hand on her head. Kamal closed her eyes, she felt as if she had been purified with a paternal love.

"My daughter," he smiled looking at his friends and sister, and his eyes welled up with happiness, "the living evidence of my love."

Chapter 27

Aaron was seated on his retro designer black leather swivel chair in his studio apartment, with a glass of scotch in his hand. He swirled the whisky around in the tumbler, watching the ice slowly dissolve away. He had neither seen nor heard from Kamal for almost a week now and had read the text she had sent over and over again, as it gave him the glimmer of hope he needed.

He went into the club only to do anything that was really necessary and to the restaurant only to check everything was on schedule. In the office, he would sit in her chair and run his hands along the arms, wanting to feel her presence or he would sit at the bar and imagine her sitting beside him. His ears longed to hear her voice and he played the messages she had left him, when he was in London, over and over again. He tried contacting her on her mobile, but it was switched off and could only hope she was okay. He wondered whether she had found her father and what his reaction was and more so, how Kamal was coping. If she'd given him half a chance, he would have gone with her for moral support. Everything was fine until that Rohit came back. He clenched his jaw as he thought of him. Those last few days before he made a dramatic return, signified their unique bond; she was his soul mate and his life now seemed meaningless and insignificant without her around.

The ringing phone broke his thoughts and he picked it up instantly. "Hi Chelle," he sighed, having seen the caller details.

"Hiya. Anything?"

"Nothing."

"Honestly, sometimes she can really drive me up the wall. She should know that we worry about her!"

"I wonder whether something has happened?"

"I don't know. I really don't know what to think. I'm going to kill her when I see her! I mean not even a text. Anything to say she was okay."

"I know."

"Oh well. How are you?"

"I'm okay."

"You miss her don't you?" Aaron smiled and Michelle acknowledged the silence, "stupid question I guess. She's the biggest fool in the world."

"I'm willing to wait."

"Oh Aaron," Michelle sighed.

Michelle was hurting for her brother; she knew he was hopelessly in love with Kamal and she understood why, Kamal was indeed special. She was an important part of both their lives. But the past had forever haunted her. She had developed a hard, protective exterior, but deep down within, Michelle knew she was still hurting. It was evident in her eyes, as she watched their children unwrap presents in glee, as they jumped up and down in excitement over any achievement. Michelle knew that at every such occasion, she would for a slight moment imagine it was her Jaydeep. While Kamal was forever gracious to her and Aaron, she in turn, was grateful for Kamal. What she and Aaron had today was all due to Kamal's commitment to them. She could have easily have gone her own way, but she continued to shower them with gratitude. She bought the salon and left her solely in charge. She did not watch over her, ask her about the takings or interfere with any change. And the club, even though she was seventy percent owner, Aaron was treated as if he were an equal partner. Kamal was more than able to manage everything on her own, but she kept them both close by her side. She needed them, as much as they needed her. Bringing Kamal home that cold, wet, winter's day was the best decision she had ever made in her life. She had not just gained a good friend, but also the sister she never had. She hoped Kamal would get in touch soon. This was the longest time they had not had any contact from her and she was beginning to get quite anxious.

Meanwhile, Kamal was using all her energy into getting to know her father, who she discovered was a most sincere and humble person. He was a happy soul and greatly respected by all those around. He was a highly regarded professor in psychology and was still invited regularly to give lectures following his retirement. Kamal had attended one of these lectures and watched him from a distant, as students listened to his rich wisdom in awe. After the lecture, the students swarmed around him bombarding him with questions and she sat back and watched in admiration. His study area in his home was surrounded with shelves abundant with words of wisdom. She liked his little antique desk, with its small drawers and little pigeon holes where he stored his letters. Everything about him was so endearing and charming.

The bedroom in which she was staying was huge, and even though the bed's mattress wasn't very thick, for some reason she slept so soundly, not once stirring in her sleep. She liked the ethnic furniture her father had in and around the house and rooms, giving her yet more inspiration for her restaurant. She loved waking up to see a clear blue sky on walking out her bedroom into the courtyard and seeing him either watering the flowers or chatting to the neighbours, listening to the radio, reading his post or paper. She liked waking up to the sound of the chirping birds and to the sound of the busy hustle and bustle of the world outside those blue front doors. His friendly neighbours would come by daily to discuss recent events on the news and cricket with passion. Her aunty Pratibha was so loving and mothering. She had been coming over daily and was making such a fuss over her. Vinod and Suman came over regularly and insisted that she came and stayed with them, but she wanted to spend as much time as possible with her father. She liked their evening walks in the park when he would buy her *kulfi* as if she were a child. She imagined how happy her mother would have been, had she spent the rest of her life with this wonderful man and how different their lives would, or could have been.

In all her excitement she had neglected the world she came from. She knew she should contact Aaron or Michelle, but whenever she was in the presence of her father, she forgot everything. Her return day was in a couple of days' time and Mohan was still waiting for her to tell him everything about herself, but she had withheld, saying that she would in good time and tonight, she planned to tell him everything.

They were sat at an old *dhabha* (open café) where he, her mother, Vinod and Suman used to come to eat *sholay-pathoore* (chick peas and soft fried bread) regularly.

"It's changed so much. It was half this size and then they expanded. Now they are also selling pizza, noodles, burgers and chips, whereas before it was your normal savoury *sholay-pathoore, samosa, pakora* with hot sweet tea! What would you like?" he asked as Kamal sat down opposite him

"*Sholay-pathoore!*" Kamal smiled.

Mohan laughed in delight. "Look at my friend Rakesh looking this way?" Mohan whispered. Kamal looked towards the elderly man, who was sitting next to the counter, on a chair peering over his newspaper. "I bet he thinks he has seen a ghost," Mohan smiled. The man continued to look at Kamal and she smiled at him. As she smiled, he put his newspaper down and looked more closely. "How are you Rakesh?"

"I am fine my friend. But I feel I have seen this young lady somewhere before."

Mohan smiled. The *dhabha* was a family run business. It was started up by Rakesh's father, then run by Rakesh and now his son Mohit.

"Hello Mohan uncle. What can I get you?" Mohit got up especially from behind the counter for his special customers.

"Two *sholay-pathoore* please Mohit."

"Coming up," Mohit looked at Kamal and smiled. A foreigner was so easily recognisable by the Indian folk. Even with their brown skin tone and traditional clothing, it was something about their manner, the way they looked around curiously.

Mohan looked on at his daughter. She was in her early forties, but could easily have ten years taken off her age. Her hair had a healthy shine and her skin had taken on a healthier glow, having now been kissed by the Indian sun. It was obvious she took great care in what she usually ate. Her nails were well manicured and her fingers, long and slender just like Parminder's were. Her outer beauty was as beautiful as her inner. He felt for someone who was brought up in a Western world, she adapted well to her new surroundings. She was polite to all his friends and visitors. She helped her aunt in the kitchen with cooking and cleaning, however much they insisted she did not and when he told her old stories, she was like a captivated child.

That evening, in the courtyard, on their own, the world slowly falling asleep, she sat with her father and talked throughout the whole night. She told her father everything, about her mother and step-father's relationship, the abuse, Raj, her in-laws, Jaydeep, Rohit, Danielle, Angela, Christine, Emma, Michelle and, Aaron. She told him about the accident, about Jaydeep's funeral, the business, her mother dying, her last words, Raj's suicide and then Jai. She told him about Rohit reappearing after all these years and above all, her special relationship with Aaron. She wrapped her arms around herself, as there was a sudden chill in the night air. She looked up at the heavens; it appeared even the bright stars had been listening to her story patiently. Mohan got up from out of his chair as Kamal recovered from reliving her life events. Throughout the whole time, he did not speak once and had felt her pain as she talked. On a few occasions his eyes welled up and he looked away painfully. Kamal felt a warm shawl being placed over her shoulders and she pulled it to, snugly. Mohan sat back in his chair and said nothing for a few moments; both of them needing to collect their thoughts.

"That's quite a journey you've been through," he said softly.

Kamal got up out of her chair to go to her bedroom. Mohan watched her turn the light on and walk towards the wardrobe. She pulled something out of her bag and made her way back. It was a photo of her mother holding Jaydeep, when she'd just come out of the hospital. Mohan looked at the photo and smiled, his eyes again welled up and this time he let a tear drop.

He sighed, "my grandchild."

That night, Mohan did not sleep. He lay in his bed, his eyes fixed upon the ceiling above. He wished he could take his daughter's pain away, but he felt helpless. The morning daylight could not have come soon enough and he was up at the crack of dawn. He had his morning wash and chanted his morning prayers, and made a plea.

"It's not often I ask you for anything, but today, I ask you to bless my daughter with the peace and happiness she deserves, that's all I ask of you."

Kamal slept in till gone nine and Mohan did not disturb her. She needed as much rest as possible. She was due to leave tomorrow. He had insisted she extend her stay, but understood that she had commitments back home and she could not delay going back.

"Um....dad," Kamal was still grasping addressing Mohan as her father, "Rohit coming back in my life stirred a lot of old emotions. He was my first love, I think, and you know all about first love don't you? What do you think? Should I give him another chance?" Mohan looked at his daughter in disbelief, as they had their morning tea.

"And what about Aaron?"

"Aaron.."

"My dear. You love him don't you?"

"That's the problem, I don't know. My heart tells me that I do, but if I really did, I would not have hurt him, I would not have hesitated when he asked me if I still loved Rohit, I would have told him straight that he meant absolutely nothing to me, but I didn't."

Mohan started to laugh, "you have not realised have you? My dear if you talked of anyone last night, with warmness, affection, fondness and trust, it was Aaron. So why on earth would you give that Rohit a second thought? It was evident in your voice. It was evident in your eyes. It was evident in your expression. Aaron, is the one. My dear, a man who has waited patiently all these years, who has been their like a solid rock, who has been with you through sorrow, pain, failure, success and happiness, who has protected you, supported you, who has respected your every need and wish, who has honesty and sincerity written all over him is a pure winner in my heart. My dear, why are you even contemplating that, Rohit Sinha! Aaron is the one my dear. It can be no-one else." Kamal looked on at her father, as he banged every nail on the head. "You are in love with him. You just have not allowed yourself to fully believe it. I guess it is because you have been disappointed in the past, but you are punishing a man who evidently loves you with all his heart. It's time you started to believe and repay him with the love he deserves."

***

Kamal took one last look round her father's home. She had so enjoyed being here. It was a whole new world full of warmth, love and happiness. She was going to miss the morning tea, the walks in the park, helping her aunty cook and the long evening chats. She knew she would be coming here more often and she hoped that the next time she came it would not be alone, it would be with Aaron.

She cried as she hugged Suman, her aunt Prathibha and Vinod at Delhi airport. She embraced her father and then stood back, to look at her new family, unable to believe that these gems had been hidden away from her for all these years, just waiting to be discovered.

"You promise to ring as soon as you get back yes?" Mohan held his daughter's hands, wishing silently he could keep her with him for just a bit longer.

"I promise and I will be back soon," she said as she waved and made her way through the departure gates, a tear of happiness dropping from her eye. Mohan watched her walk out of sight; an angel that had suddenly showered his life with an unexpected happiness he could not contain.

"Happy?" Vinod put his hand on his friend's shoulder.

"Vinod my friend, words alone cannot describe how I feel right at this moment."

Kamal pushed her trolley out of the arrivals gate. Her trip on the plane back was in comparison an elation and she so wanted to scream out with joy; she felt like she had been reborn and could not wait to see Aaron, to hold him and tell him how happy she was and how much she loved him. As expected, he was there stood ready and waiting. She was hardly able to get in a word edgeways when she'd called him, asking him to meet her at the airport and had to apologise profusely as he scolded her for sending him out of his mind with worry. She smiled as she saw him casually dressed in his jeans, a black shirt and brown jacket. He had not shaven, which gave him that very desirable look. His chin was as if it was chiselled to perfection, he looked like a model, just before the shave in a razor advert, simply irresistible.

"Wow. You look great," he went to kiss her cheek and had to hold his balance, as she threw herself into his arms. He put his arms around her in relief and pulled her tight towards him. "I've missed you so much," he whispered in her ear.

"I've missed you too," and she reached up to kiss him, undeterred by watching eyes.

***

The pre-opening advertisement proved successful, as the restaurant was buzzing with diners. There was soft, melodious, Indian music playing in the background, the bar stocked with liquor gleaming under the spot lights. The restaurant had a contemporary, yet authentic look; the colour scheme was as planned a mixture of warm earthy browns, reds and gold. The walls magnolia and above every table was a wall lamp, the table cloth on every table white with red and gold napkins and a brown runner going down the centre. The tables laid out with squeaky clean gleaming wine glasses. As inspired back in India, the walls were covered in Indian, antique gold colour framed art work and pieces of ethnic furniture and ornaments, which Kamal and Aaron had chosen and had exported from India. In front of the bar were some lounging red leather sofas for people who just wanted a drink, or had a drink while they waited for an empty table.

"Congratulations," Aaron said smiling at Kamal sat at the bar, while he stood behind it, "looks like we're onto a winner here."

Kamal thought he looked as handsome as ever in his grey tailored trousers, a grey waist coat over a white shirt, sleeves rolled up to show off his toned arms, "yes. Let's hope every night is like this," she smiled raising her glass and leaning over to kiss him.

Aaron had seen a positive change in Kamal since her return from India. After many years, this was the happiest he had ever seen her. She spoke to her father Mohan daily and he himself had also spoken to him on a few occasions. He was heartened by his warmth and he now knew where Kamal had inherited her caring nature from. Kamal had become so much more affectionate and attentive towards him. He could not forget the look on Rohit's face when he casually dropped by the club, as if he could just easily worm his way back into her life and saw them kissing in the office; the audacity of the man, to walk in not even waiting for a response to the casual knock on the door. They'd neither seen nor heard from him again. His son on the other hand displayed better manners. He had come in especially to apologise to Kamal for his behaviour. Kamal had offered for him to stay on at the club and he took the offer up without hesitation. It must have been Kamal's offer to keep him on that made Rohit think he was still in with a chance. But unfortunately for him, and fortunately for Aaron, she had finally realised who she really wanted.

"Oh at last. I'm shattered," Kamal sat at one of the tables away from the glaring window, as the waiters brought round some food. "That's great guys. You go off now. We'll close up. Thanks you were all great today."

"Thanks Kamal."

The staff left one by one as Aaron and Kamal unwound in their new restaurant. Aaron switched off all the lights and lit a candle. The music was turned down and continued playing softly in the background. He opened a bottle of their best champagne and they toasted to their first successful night.

"May this be one of many," Aaron smiled.

Kamal watched him as he talked the day over while he ate. She did not have much of an appetite, which was killed off by all the excitement. She pushed the rice around in her plate as she looked on at him, evermore mesmerised by his presence.

"Why are you looking at me like that? Is there something on my face?"

"Yes. A nose! A pretty cute one at that," Kamal smiled.

"Haha."

"Aaron."

"Yes Kamal."

"Will you marry me?"

Aaron froze. "Sorry?" Aaron looked on, wondering whether he had heard right.

"Aaron Miller, will you marry me?"

Aaron smiled and looked away. He looked back towards her and shook his head in disbelief. He took his napkin off his laps and placed it on the table, got up from his chair and walked round to Kamal, held her hand and got down on one knee.

"Yes. Yes, of course I will marry you," he smiled ecstatically and kissed her hand. She in turn cupped his face in her hands.

"Thank you," she whispered and softly kissed him once on his forehead, once on both cheeks, the tip of his nose and then his lips.

***

Mohan looked so handsome in his new tailored to fit suit Kamal had bought for him and he stood so proud. Kamal had only invited her closest friends, Suman's family and of course her father. She was wearing a pale pink full length dress, embroidered intricately with silver threading. She accessorised it with elegant diamante jewellery. Her hair was tied up with some loose, curly strands of hair on either side of her face, which bounced softly around as she smiled and laughed; she looked radiant and was surrounded by a long overdue aura of happiness and contentment. Aaron was wearing a navy suit with an ivory waistcoat, white shirt and pale pink cravat. The two looked visually stunning. They'd planned to only have a civil ceremony and held the reception in the suite of a grand hotel. Her father was overjoyed, even more so that they had planned to have their honeymoon in India. He was so looking forward to having his daughter come back home for a few days with her dashing English gentleman husband before they set off to Goa on their own.

He watched her mingle with her friends from afar. He felt like he was finally living his life through his wonderful daughter.

"She's wonderful isn't she?" Vinod said to his friend who was captivated by his new found world.

"She's amazing, just like her mother."

Kamal saw the two men talking and looking in her direction. She excused herself from her good friends Angela and Danielle, who were ecstatic to see their friend in this deservedly elating episode of her life, and walked towards them. Mohan thought she looked angelic as she made her way forward. Equally, not being able to keep his eyes off his wife, Aaron finally managed to tear himself away from his friends and walked towards her. He put his arm around her waist.

"Okay?" he whispered pecking her cheek. She looked up at him, smiled and leant her head on his shoulder. Suman joined them too. The five of them now stood grouped together.

Michelle watched her friend with her new found family from a distance holding onto Jamie's arm and leaning her head on his reliable shoulder. She smiled as she saw the glow on Kamal's face; she looked stunning and her brother looked dashing. She had cried helplessly throughout the whole ceremony; she was so happy for them both and wished that her parents had lived to see this day. Kamal gestured for her to come forward with Jamie. As the most important people in Kamal's life stood around her, Aaron asked for a round of champagne. Mohan raised a toast, "to my angel, who walked into my life and made me the happiest man ever. Here's to the both of you. May you be blessed with eternal love and happiness."

As everyone raised their glasses, Mohan looked up and closed his eyes, silently thanking his only pure love, Parminder.

The End

Note to readers

Hi,

Thank you so much for reading my second novel *Tarnished*. All my characters are purely fictitious and any resemblance to persons living or dead is purely coincidental. However, to me my characters are as real as the air I breathe, having taken birth in my imagination, as I go about my everyday life, juggling a full time job, home and social life, with my passion for writing.

If you enjoyed reading *Tarnished*, if you felt Kamal's fear, anger and pain and were touched by her journey, fell in love with Aaron and wished she'd found Mohan much sooner in her life, then please do leave a review on Amazon. Your reviews are invaluable; I thank you wholeheartedly in advance.

You have now been on a journey with *Kamal*, but have you met *Mindy*, my character from my debut novel *Circle of Betrayal*? If not, you may want to meet her too. Circle of Betrayal is also available to purchase on Amazon.

Next, I will introduce you to *Simran* in my third novel named after the character herself, *Simran*. If you thought *Mindy* and *Kamal* had quite a journey, wait till you travel with *Simran* on hers. *Simran's* story, is one I would say, is the closest to my heart.

My writing may not be of exceptional literary flair, but I do believe I can tell an engaging story and that's all I want to do, share my stories and introduce my endearing characters to lovers of fiction around the world.

Continue to read, travel and escape into another world, whilst sat in the comfort of your most favourite reading space. You never know, the journey may just take you somewhere you'd never imagined…..

With best wishes

J K Memmi

Novelist

Printed in Great Britain
by Amazon